BOOK

The Uprising

David F. Farris

www.erafeen.com

Written by: David F. Farris
Cover illustrated by: Alessandro Brunelli

Sphaira Publishing, 2018

IBN-13 978-1976901362

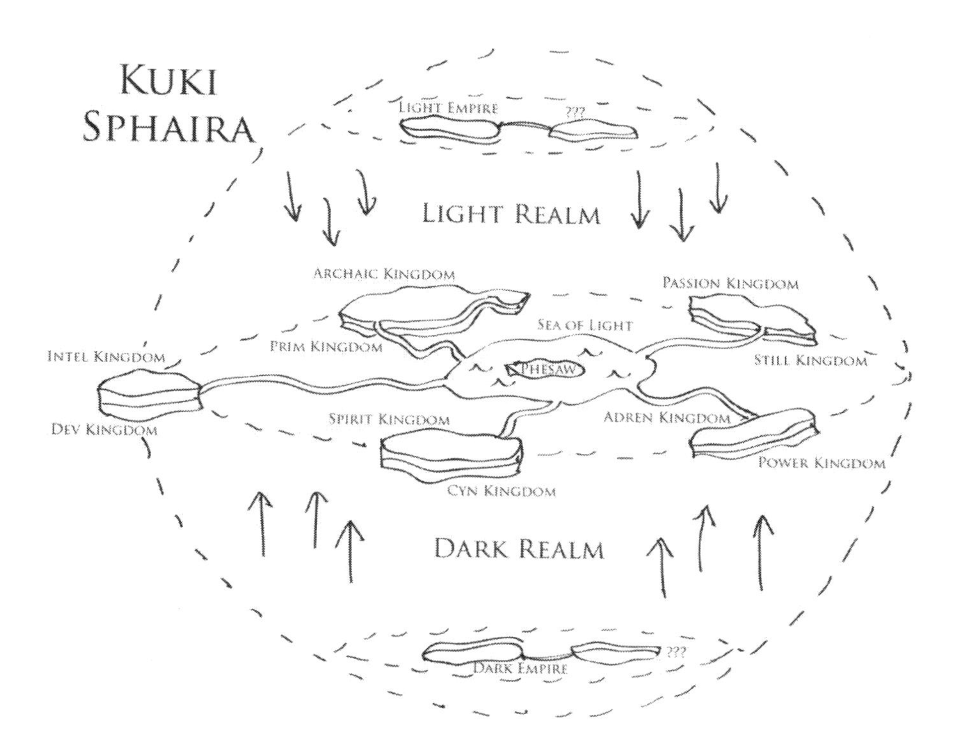

*This is a 3D diagram of Erafeen's world, Kuki Sphaira: a ball of air with floating islands and rivers. There are no landscapes or structures within each kingdom because its purpose is a full-world view. Arrows represent flow of gravity. Dev, Cyn, Power, Still, and Prim Kingdoms (Dark Realm) hang on the underbellies of floating islands. Intel, Archaic, Spirit, Adren, and Passion Kingdoms (Light Realm) sit atop. More detailed maps of individual kingdoms ahead.

INTEL KINGDOM
(LIGHT KNOWLEDGE KINGDOM)

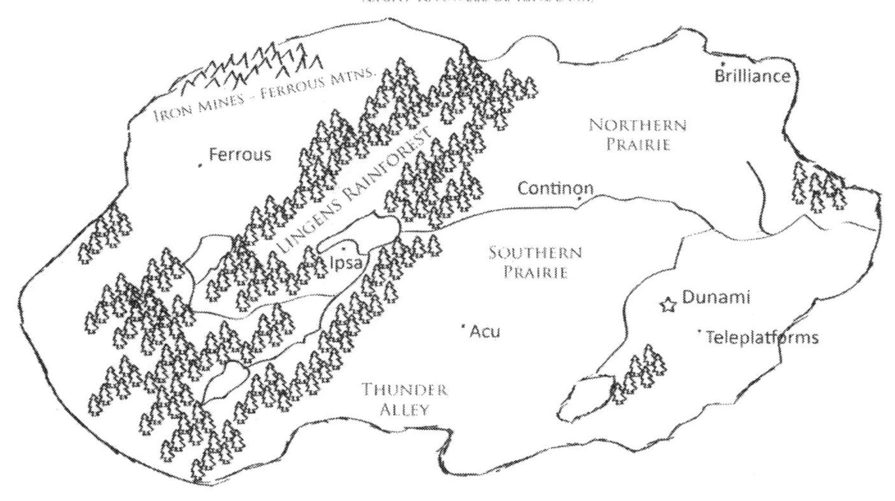

PHESAW
(CENTRAL SCHOOL OF THE LIGHT REALM)

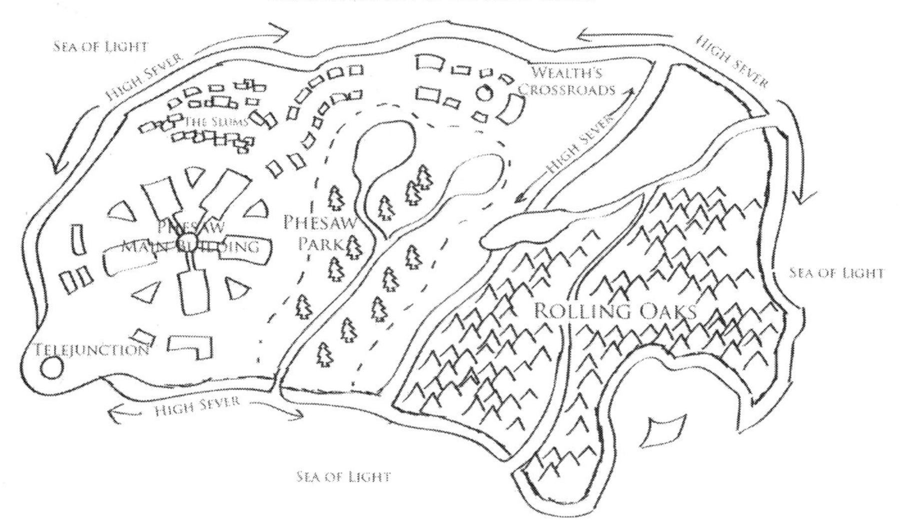

DEV KINGDOM
(DARK KNOWLEDGE KINGDOM)
Tames
TAMES FOREST
COSMOS RUINS
Cosmos
Teleplatforms
TAMES MTNS.
REGION OF
DEMONS
Shreel
Rence
NECROSIS
VALLEY
RENCE
FOREST
Cogdan
Prayoga

PASSION KINGDOM
(LIGHT EMOTION KINGDOM)

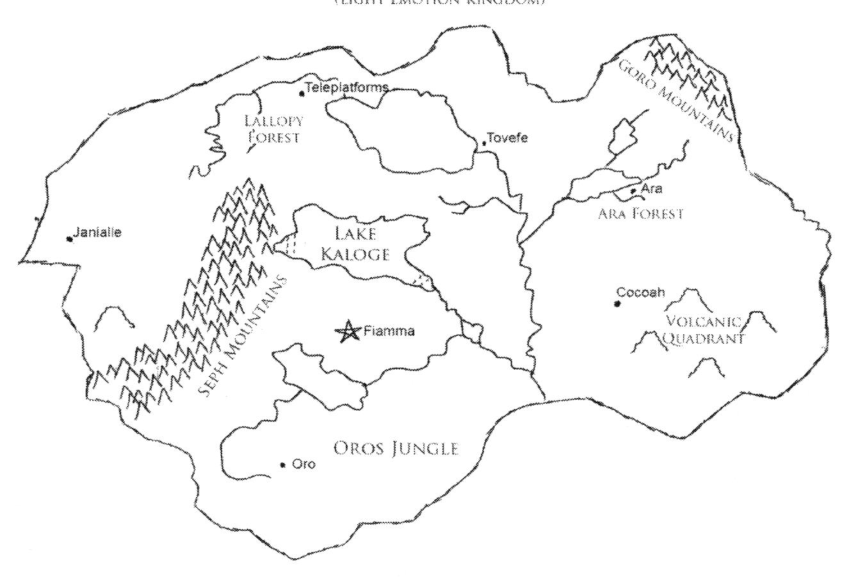

ARCHAIC KINGDOM
(LIGHT MORALITY KINGDOM)

SPIRIT KINGDOM
(LIGHT SPIRIT KINGDOM)
Reikon Gate
Teleplatforms
CHERRY FOREST
Sodai
GULF OF SODAI
SHINDO RIVER
DaiSo
Wing City
TSUBASA FOREST
Squalsh
WYNDING MOUNTAINS
CLOUD-CLEAVING BUTTES
Soulful
Windwynder

Light Realm

Intel Kingdom (mind, electricity):
Bryson, Simon, Lilu, Jugtah, Princess Shelly, King Vitio, Grandarion, Lars, Yvole, Frederick, Gracie, Limone, Jayce

Passion Kingdom (heart, fire):
Olivia, Himitsu, Director Venustas, King Damian, Fane, Horos, Rosel, General Landon, Barloe, Jannis

Spirit Kingdom (soul, wind):
Jilly, Tashami, Director Neaneuma, Queen Apsa, Wert, General Minerva, Crole, Frina, Rayne

Adren Kingdom (body, speed):
Toshik, Yama, Director Buredo, King Supido, Toth, General Sinno, Saikatto

Archaic Kingdom (mind, ancients):
Agnos, Rhyparia, Itta, Prince Sigmund, Ophala, Vliyan, Musku, Captain Gray Whale

Dark Realm

Dev Kingdom (mind, psychic):
Vistas, Flen, King Storshae, Illipsia, Tazama, Warden Gala, Jina, Halluci

Still Kingdom (heart, ice):
Apoleia, Ropinia, Titus, Garlo

Cyn Kingdom (soul, supernatural):

Power Kingdom (body, strength):
Vuilni, Warden Feissam, Queen Gantski

Prim Kingdom:

Not all characters are listed.

1
Situational Cognizance

Dev King Storshae spent most of his journey from the teleplatforms to Cogdan inside his royal carriage. But whenever he passed through a city or town, he'd ride in the front seat with a smile on his face, standing tall, waving to the citizens as they cheered.

Grand Director Poicus had been shackled to the back of a carriage and was now being pulled through the kingdom. Old, weak, and badly injured, it was difficult for him to keep pace without his cane, which was at the front of the convoy under Storshae's watchful eye.

Youth had bested Poicus back at Phesaw. He had hoped that Storshae would simply kill him but knew that would never satisfy such a man. Instead, the Dev King took him captive and decided to drag him into the Dev Kingdom via Telejunction. Any fleeting hope Poicus had of someone trying to chase Storshae down had been put to rest the moment they'd arrived at the teleplatforms, where an entire army of burgundy cloaks waited for their leader's safe arrival. The teleplatforms would have been a suicidal choke point.

Poicus had never traveled the road that crossed through Cosmos and Shreel. He had headed straight for Rence during his previous visit, opting for the quickest route to Cogdan. But these were different circumstances—he was now a prisoner.

The city of Cosmos was beautiful, although it was difficult to appreciate with the insults and objects being rained down upon him by the Devish masses. He supposed this wasn't too bad, considering the wrath Mendac had unleashed on this city decades ago. The Cosmos Ruins—just out of sight beyond the thicket of buildings—were a reminder of that.

Shreel, while still grand in size, was a more modest city. Storshae and his convoy stayed there for a couple days, chaining up Poicus in the middle of the road each night. He served as a trophy, but not one to be lauded or cared for. The soldiers who stood guard allowed civilians to shame or assault him however they saw fit. Nothing was off limits.

Poicus would die soon, his body succumbing to old age and irreparable wounds. These restless nights were only quickening the process, and soon he'd join Senex in eternal slumber. He only wished Phesaw had been his grave.

* * *

Dev King Storshae grinned as he stared out the window at the moonlit city street below. Euphoria coursed through him as he caught sight of Poicus's current state. The Grand Director had sent Mendac and Thusia after Storshae's father nearly thirty years ago. And last year he impersonated a Dev soldier, infiltrated Cogdan Palace, murdered countless men, tampered with King Rehn's coffin, and left Storshae incapacitated. The old man had a damned mountain of crimes against him.

"Please make sure the man doesn't croak on us at the wrong time."

The woman's voice caused Storshae to finally turn away from the window. Kadlest stood behind an armchair with a hand resting on its back; Toono sat comfortably in front of her with an open book in his lap. Off to the side of the room was Yama, the violet-haired swordswoman. And

Illipsia slept on a couch with her hair wrapped around her as makeshift covers.

Storshae smiled. "Let me have my fun, Kadlest."

"This isn't about fun," she replied. "This is business. Your foolishness isn't going to raise King Rehn from the grave any faster."

"Does it really matter?" he asked, taking a seat on the edge of a desk. "We're forced to wait, anyway. Until Chiefs Toth and Wert get a proper hold of the Archaic Kingdom, we're stuck here."

"It shouldn't be long," Toono said, scratching underneath the bandage circling his head.

Storshae chuckled. "Those two men are clueless, so I've tempered my expectations. Luckily, Tazama's with them."

"I think they'll operate smoothly," Toono said.

"You haven't spoken to them before, so I forgive your naivety."

Kadlest asked, "And what does this Tazama woman provide for us?"

"Besides her quick lip?" replied Storeshae. "Well, her weaving skills provide her with a plethora of talents. Not to mention her ability to flip the switch of her aura in an instant. She can be snarky, charming, or warming—whichever suits the environment she's in or the people she's talking to. She's a multifaceted pocket knife and the only reason why I'm okay with Chiefs Toth and Wert's involvement in this mission."

"Wasn't she taken by Mendac's army when he invaded decades ago?" Kadlest asked. "You weren't old enough to recognize her importance then."

Storshae sighed as he tilted his gaze to the floor. "General Ossen always spoke highly of her, which is the only reason why I knew of her existence. According to him, she was one of this kingdom's greatest losses during that whole ordeal. But, thankfully, four years ago I found out where she was after encountering one of Toth Brench's merchant ships when it docked at Cogdan's port. Since it was the first delivery his company had ever made to our kingdom, he wanted to speak to me directly. His method of communication? A broadcast aided by Tazama."

"A stroke of luck," Toono said.

"We all need a little bit of it. And given my share of bad luck throughout my life, I'd say it was long overdue."

Toono closed his book. "I'm all for powerful women, so Tazama sounds like someone I'd like to meet. Hopefully I'd be worthy of her … 'warming aura' … as you put it. I get enough lip from this one right here." He tilted his head toward a grouchy Yama, who ignored the playful attempt at a jab.

Storshae gave Yama an uneasy look. "Not quite the same."

"Another thing," Toono said. "Get in touch with the Power Queen, if you can. We must do something about her kingdom's alliance with the Light Realm. It's the most critical advantage they have against us."

"There's no severing that bond," the prince explained. "The mutual benefits between the two sides are too substantial."

"A result of your limited perception," Toono said. This resulted in a menacing glare from his counterpart. He continued, seeming not to care. "I killed Bruut Schap."

"I'm very much aware," Storshae said, seething. "You brought his body back with us. Since when do you keep the bodies of your sacrifices?"

"Because I was thinking several steps ahead," Toono said. "Enter my mind for a moment while I show you the beauty of situational cognizance—something you and Itta lacked while ransacking the Generals' Battle for Olivia. While the Power Kingdom is allies with the Light Realm, they wouldn't enter a war on their behalf. And that's because it's an alliance of commerce, not military. If, however, they had justification to join the Light Realm's efforts against us, we'd be screwed.

"And what's more justifiable than the grandson of their general being murdered by me? That'd provide them with just cause. All it would take would be Intel King Vitio to send a recording to Power Queen Gantski of Bruut's body, his eyelids pulled back, exposing the signature characteristic of someone who's died by my hands—a milky white cornea absent of iris or pupil."

Storshae's face lost its scowl as realization dawned upon him.

"But none of that happened," Toono continued, "because I brought the boy's body with us. I've dealt our side a favorable hand; now you must put it in play by contacting Queen Gantski. Account to her your witness of Bruut's death and how he was slain by Bryson LeAnce. Of course this would mean we shouldn't have his body, so don't let that slip in any way."

"I understand that," Storshae said. "But why would she believe the LeAnce brat killed him?"

"You told me that you witnessed Power Warden Feissam flee Phesaw during your scrap with Poicus, did you not?"

"Yes, leaving his Diatia behind."

"So you'll tell her that, and explain to her that Feissam can vouch for your claim." Storshae nearly interrupted, but Toono quickly elaborated. "All of this past year Illipsia scouted Phesaw for me. She brought me information on the Jestivan about their personalities, abilities, and relationships. She made it evident to me that Bryson LeAnce did not bother hiding his disdain for the Powish boy—even threatening his life. Something tells me that Feissam probably noticed this behavior.

"Don't get me wrong, I left behind a witness. Agnos saw me kill Bruut, and word will get to the royal heads. They'll then inform the Power Queen and put blame on me. But that's why this Feissam bit is of paramount importance. Gantski will likely retrieve and interrogate the warden, and hopefully that will propel her muddled thoughts to side with us."

Storshae stared at Toono for several seconds before speaking. "You're a dangerous man, Toono. You observe scenarios and process information in a way I've never witnessed before."

"Situational cognizance," Toono said.

"I've only heard stories of minds such as yours …" Storshae trailed off, then said: "Those stories being of my father."

"I admire the Oracle."

The prince grinned. "And that's why I like you."

* * *

Chief Merchant Toth Brench, wearing a fitted gray suit over his lanky frame, marched through the third-floor corridors of Phelos Palace. His attire may have been all business, but his aura reeked of unprofessionalism as he blew through archways with menace etched into his face. Behind him was the blue-haired Tazama, lackadaisically humming a tune, seemingly unperturbed by whatever was bothering Toth.

Chief Officer Wert Lamay was spending his days training his army of Adrenian and Archain soldiers, instilling respect and gaining their loyalty in the process. Meanwhile, Toth was supposed to be overseeing Archaic Prince Sigmund's progression, and severing any relationship he had with the other two members of the Amendment Order: Chief Arbitrator Grandarion Senten and Chief Senator Rosel Sania.

Toth needed Sigmund on his side. After the prince's decision during Rhyparia's Gravity Trials, it was clear that their relationship wasn't as solid as he had thought. In order to hold the reins of the Archaic Kingdom, he needed separation from Rosel and Grandarion. But he could only achieve that with Sigmund's support.

"Love, why must you worry so much?" Tazama asked. "Trust me, if push comes to shove, I'll do what needs to be done."

"I want to do this on my own," Toth replied. "I must show my worth to Storshae."

"Your worth is your business and the mountains of money it sits upon," Tazama said. "Together they allow you to hold influence over some of the most important people around Kuki Sphaira, which provides our superiors with lines of communication they otherwise couldn't obtain on their own."

As Toth finally reached the two enormous mahogany doors, he burst through without much regard for the hinges that supported them. He spotted Sigmund, Rosel, and Grandarion at the far end of a long dining table, heads bowed over their meals. They immediately turned to gaze at their unexpected guest. A few seconds later Tazama entered the hall with a tad more grace.

Toth regained his composure before calmly approaching the trio and taking a seat. A tense silence wafted over them while Tazama remained standing near the entrance.

Sigmund was first to succumb to the discomfort: "Something bothering you, Chief Toth?"

"What's with the standoffish attitudes lately?" Toth asked.

Sigmund paused and looked at Rosel and Grandarion as if he expected them to answer. Instead, Rosel asked a question of her own: "Is there merit in what Ophala says every time we visit her cell?"

Toth wasn't entirely sure what she was implying, but he could guess. Whenever he visited Ophala, she'd only strike casual conversation. "What is she saying?"

"That the Cloutitionist's Necklace was actually found ... and that you know about it."

"No. Is she still harping about that?" His answer was a calm retort. "I've never met Rhyparia's parents outside of the litigations. And the necklace was a fake, anyway. That much was made clear."

Rosel narrowed her eyes, but Sigmund's expression softened as he said, "I believe you. I had gone to Spy Pilot Ophala at the beginning of the Amendment Order's formation, but after witnessing the rapid decline of her sanity over the course of Rhyparia's trials, ending with the fiasco at the botched lynching, I realized I had put my trust in the wrong person."

Toth started to mumble a thank you, but Sigmund cut him off: "That doesn't mean I trust you, however. Chiefs Grandarion and Rosel are the only two people who have consistently displayed qualities and actions that are worthy of my loyalty. Until I see the same from you, don't expect my cordiality."

Stunned, Toth stared at each of their faces. He was upset, but couldn't show it. Rosel's glare was as stern as always, but Grandarion seemed uninterested as he twirled some noodles with his fork. Toth could feel Tazama's eyes observing him closely from afar, dissecting his conversation with her unnatural auditory range.

"I respect that," Toth said. He got up and shook hands all around. "Hopefully I can improve on our relationship as we all try to steer this kingdom down a prosperous path."

He left the table and exited the room with Tazama. She pressed her lips against his cheek as they walked. "There's the businessman I know," she said. "Losing your cool doesn't suit you."

"I'm losing my patience."

She smirked. "Take some of mine." She placed a finger against the side of her temple and extracted a wisp of mist. She then transferred it to Toth's forehead, where it passed seamlessly through his skin.

His shoulders sunk, lips curling upward. "Thank you, love."

2
Dimiours

Rhyparia could smell her own musk as she trudged down an empty dirt trail between scattered homes. They were modest, beautiful structures. Each one was a single story and constructed in the shape of a cube. And since they were dwarfed by the surrounding acreage, the village looked as if it were draped in a sea of vibrant green.

As she walked, heads of curious locals poked out of windows. She wondered if they were intrigued by her appearance. It had been over a week since she had last bathed. Layers of dirt had accumulated on her skin, tunic, and torn breeches. She had worn these since the night of her intended execution, which had been thwarted by her friends Archaic Director Senex, Spy Pilot Ophala, and Himitsu. They had risked everything to save her life.

"It's been quite some time since an outsider has come to Epinio," the round man walking next to her explained. "That's why they stare."

This boulder of a man had found Rhyparia in the Archaic Mountains. Ophala's note had said someone would meet with her, but it lacked detail.

The only reason Rhyparia trusted him was because he'd had her ancient with him—a battered umbrella. He still hadn't told Rhyparia his name.

"How long's it been?" she asked.

"Twenty-eight years. It was a momentous day. Well, we hadn't known it at the time, but now we do. We've come to appreciate them."

"And they're still around?"

He nodded and said, "There's plenty of time for you to learn about the village of Epinio. I won't answer any more questions right now. Instead, I'll show you to your humble abode."

"I get a house?" she asked, surprised.

"It's a type of house," he said.

They veered to the right at a fork in the road, following a dirt trail which led them up a gentle slope a ways before the grass swallowed it whole. Rhyparia was careful to not stumble, as thousands of roots protruded from the ground. The cubic homes were now replaced by massive willow trees, their trunks as thick as twenty stone pillars combined, hidden behind weeping green leaves and string-like branches which hung to the ground like overgrown bangs. The bases of the trees were barely visible between these natural curtains.

Rhyparia became preoccupied with the otherworldly size and beauty of the willows. Then something hard, sturdy, and rough hit her in the face, knocking her backward. She cursed under her breath, reached up to touch her temple, and felt a fresh cut.

"Pay attention, Lita Rhyparia," her companion said.

A massive, arched root was sticking out of the ground. She grasped and shook it vigorously, but it didn't budge. She ducked under it and hurried forward. "How old are these trees?" she asked.

"They outlive our timeline," he said.

Her eyes widened as she ducked, hopped, and wended between subsequent roots. They were at least fifteen hundred years old.

"Don't try to peek through the leaves," he said. "Respect the dimiours."

"Is that what you call the trees?"

"The dimiours are the beings who inhabit the trees." He turned his round face toward her and smiled. "Now, seriously, no more questions."

They eventually found a leveled-off piece of land, devoid of willows, tucked underneath a short precipice. Rhyparia could count the amount of buildings here on one hand—no more than five. The only one that stood out was the barn. The rest were homes like the ones she saw upon arriving in Epinio—only with a couple more levels to spare.

Children played in the giant dirt square located in the center of the buildings. Teenagers and young adults were scattered around the perimeter, bowed over work stations, where they were apparently practicing trades and skills. Rhyparia carefully made her way across the square, dodging unaware boys and girls that blew past. She spotted a group of people closer to her own age gathered around a whetstone in front of a house. They didn't look to be doing anything but socializing.

Then Rhyparia's mouth fell agape as someone—or *something*—exited the house with swords in his hands. She froze in her tracks, and her unnamed companion had to place his hand against her back and guide her forward. She craned her neck as she tried to etch into her memory what she saw.

Was it an animal or human? The teenagers partially obstructed her vision, but the thing was tall enough for her to see its head and upper torso. It had yellow eyes and pointed ears and teeth. It was slender and covered in red fur, but clothed in a leather breastplate.

She stammered and then asked, "Is that a fox?"

When they reached the barn, the man opened the door. He guided her inside, his hand still resting on her back.

The stench of animals and feces greeted her upon entering. The man didn't follow. He simply smiled at her. "That was a dimiour," he said, then tossed her umbrella inside and swung the door closed.

* * *

Rhyparia lost track of time while imprisoned in the barn. Before long, days began to blend together. She spent her first two days combing the windowless building, searching for weaknesses or cracks but without luck. The structure was likely reinforced with the wood from the trees she had passed during her journey through the village. She originally thought they were willows, but she now doubted that.

She spent time with the barn animals whenever she became lethargic. She'd pet the cows and horses in their pens, then find the roosters and chase them around in circles. Their presence was bittersweet for Rhyparia. While she loved the memories of Preevis Junior, the byproducts were images of the Olethros collapse and the death of her baby sister, Atychi.

When she awoke on the third day the pain in her stomach became excruciating and unbearable. The confusion she had felt as to why she was being held prisoner was now turning into panic. At first she thought this was a test to see if she would be able to refrain from using her ancient, to temper her clout. But now, with hunger stabbing at her abdomen, she had lost the ability to reason. She was living off barrels of water that sat at the barn's far end.

On the fourth day she toyed with the thought of killing one of the animals once or twice, but on the fifth day it consumed her. Firewood, flint, and butcher's tools had been conveniently provided atop a rickety table, but she had done her best to resist the temptation.

She continued to push on, reaching the eighth day with nothing to show for but skin and bone—she had no more fat on her body to be consumed for energy. She managed to grasp the bars of one of the nearby cages that contained a white stallion and pull herself up into a standing position. The pens reeked, for she no longer had the strength to clean them the way she did during her first few days.

She stood still, listening to the laughter of children coming from outside. It had to be morning. After so many days in this place she had become familiar with the pattern of the sunrise and sunset. She knew the rays of light squeezing through the tiny crevices between the planks meant the sun was starting its ascent into the sky.

She stared at the two doors that she had entered through just a week ago as if she could will them open with her mind. Then she slowly turned, using the cage as support, and eyed the tools on the table. She hadn't cooked much of anything throughout her life, let alone killed and butchered an animal. Never mind the fact that she lacked the knowledge or technique of carving, gutting, and cleaning livestock—she didn't even have the heart to do it.

As if it had read her mind, the stallion nudged its muzzle against her face. Lifting her hand to caress its forehead took more energy than it should have. She had the ancient and skill needed to collapse this building with ease, but such a measure seemed drastic and wrong.

She began dragging herself toward the water barrels but fell in a heap before she even made it halfway. As she closed her eyes, the last thing she heard was the cacophony of the livestock.

A short while later she awoke to cold water being splashed in her face. The first thing she recognized was the sunlight pouring in through the open doors. After taking a moment to readjust her eyesight, she saw where the water had come from. She scrambled backward, but didn't make it very far.

"Stop that," a large, white rabbit said. "You require more nourishment." He took a couple hops forward and then tilted a cup into her mouth. "Stay still."

Rhyparia did everything she could to not choke the water back up as she studied the creature's face. His fur was a vivid white, and his ears were as long as he was tall. He hopped around as he moved, but his posture was more erect than a typical rabbit. He also wore a hooded tunic with his ears sprouting through holes torn into the fabric.

He placed a loaf of bread in front of her. "For you, Lita."

She snatched it up, took a bite, and chewed blissfully in silence. The rabbit stared at her with a wide smile, its mouth curling around its nose. Her chewing slowed as the reality of what she was looking at sank in. "What are you?" she asked.

He frowned. "We are *who*'s, not *what*'s, miss."

"*Who* are you, then?"

He removed his hood, folding back his ears before standing tall again. "My name is Therapif. I am a healer and a dimiour."

"You're a walking, talking, humanistic animal."

His frown appeared again. "No, miss. Animals are our cousins. We protect them from humans."

That of course ignited several other questions in her mind, but she decided to hold on to them for a later time. She took another bite of her bread. "Why did you trap me in here for over a week?"

"That wasn't our decision … it was simply protocol installed decades ago." He stayed quiet for a moment, his little nose wiggling.

"So it was a test," she said.

"Basically. To see if you'd try killing one of the animals. While most of us thought this was unnecessary, we were still pleasantly surprised to see you refrained from doing so."

"Who came up with this idea?"

He smiled at her. "You'll get to meet them one day," he said. "For now, meet your new friends." He gestured toward the door.

A crowd of people stood outside the opening. There she saw children and teenagers massed behind three creatures she now knew to be dimiours.

One was the fox she had seen when she arrived the previous week. It wore three sheathed swords on its hip. There was a shirtless gray wolf, flaunting its bared teeth and toned torso, looking as though it was prepared to rip someone to shreds. Rhyparia was unfamiliar at first with the appearance of the third and had to think for a moment. She eventually deduced that it was a honey badger, shorter than the rest but just as intimidating while it stood on its hind legs.

Then a fourth creature showed itself, poking its head over the honey badger's shoulder before jumping out from behind it. It landed with its arms crossed before brushing a hand through the fur on its head. Clearly this one was a showman—an adorable weasel.

Rhyparia sat there, motionless and stunned. *Where did Pilot Ophala and Director Senex send me?*

3
Olivia's Punishment

Bryson LeAnce took a final bite of his eggs and dropped the plate in the sink. He was in the kitchen of Debo's house, where he and Olivia had spent a few weeks while he recovered from his injuries and she recovered from losses on a more personal level.

During this time, the house was quiet. Bryson didn't play the piano, electing instead to stay in bed while his wounds healed. It allowed him plenty of time, however, to practice his weaving. He was proud to say that he could now create dozens of Intelights that'd hover around his room simultaneously. He could even control their intensity and make them flicker.

Olivia was absent of Meow Meow, leaving her alone with her thoughts. Whenever Bryson walked past her room, he could see the sorrow on her face, which was something he still had to get used to after never seeing her express emotion in her life.

They didn't talk to each other—maybe an occasional few words, but nothing that'd be considered conversation. Their brains were still fried from the day Phesaw was invaded. Olivia felt guilty for the role she had played in that invasion, and Bryson was still reeling from what he had learned that day.

Olivia was his twin sister. They were the offspring of the Stillian royal first-born, Apoleia, which meant they were royals themselves—Bryson a prince, Olivia a princess … to a Dark Realm kingdom, no less. Their father, Mendac LeAnce—once considered a legend—had molested Apoleia eighteen years ago, which was how Bryson and Olivia came to be. Mendac had committed an Untenable by procreating with someone from a separate realm.

After learning all of this, Bryson had spiraled downward. His hood became a fixture over his head, and the chill he suffered from his entire life intensified over the weeks—a constant reminder of his Stillian mother. The manic depression he thought he had overcome during the past two years was once again consuming his existence. And it wasn't only the crap about his father; it was the fact that the Jestivan were splintered. They were his support group … his family.

Agnos and Tashami were busy chasing down an ancient. They didn't provide any information about where they were going. Lilu was in Brilliance with Intel Director Jugtah, using her skills as a weaver to better her future. Jilly and Toshik were at Brench headquarters in the Adren Kingdom. As for Olivia, she might have been right down the hall from Bryson, but she felt farther away than anyone else. Then there were three Jestivan who were complete mysteries.

Following the fiasco at Phesaw a few weeks ago, Himitsu disappeared in the middle of the night during the Jestivan's extended stay in the medical facility. Nobody knew where he went. The only bit of information was the note he had left on his pillow: *I'm leaving, but don't worry.* Himitsu was Bryson's best friend. Thus, naturally, all he'd done since that moment *was* worry.

The second biggest question mark was Yama, who, according to Olivia, had fled with Toono, Kadlest, and Apoleia. That was all Bryson needed to know. He wasn't surprised, but he was upset. She had abandoned the

Jestivan and likely broken Jilly's heart in the process. More important, she was now an enemy—a deadly, world-class adversary—added to the already elite ranks of Toono's hodgepodge crew.

Finally there was Rhyparia, the biggest mystery of them all. While in the medical facility, Bryson received the news that she had escaped her execution. Almost foolishly he had summoned hope before details of the true nature of the escape slapped him back into reality. Nobody had ever survived the wrath of the Archaic Mountains; they swallowed you whole. You were either preyed on by unspeakable beasts or flattened by the stone-laden avalanches.

But others had managed to lift his spirits. If Archaic Director Senex and Spy Pilot Ophala had risked so much to get Rhyparia into those mountains, there must have been a good reason. Ophala had spent years scouting the mountains with her birds while stationed in Rim. Maybe it hadn't been wasted time, and she learned something. And if that were the case, it meant Bryson could go find Rhyparia.

He was putting it off for one reason: physically, he wasn't fit to commit to such an adventure. The injuries he had sustained from Olivia weeks ago were still prevalent, and the only reason he could presently stand in the kitchen was because the hunger gnawing at his stomach was more powerful than any pain caused by bruised tissue or fractured bone.

He walked to the front of the house and peeked through the curtains of a narrow window next to the door. As the sun rose into the overcast sky, a feeble ray managed to split through the clouds. His gaze shifted to the tar-paved street in front of his yard. He looked down its path for any sign of a carriage, but all he could see were the brick-faced homes and lush green grass of his upper-middle-class suburban street.

He let go of the curtain and walked over to the piano. As he studied its black sheen, memories of his mother, Apoleia, consumed him—her face blanketed in frost, the maniacal expressions that contorted her features, and the self-induced cuts that bled across her neck. His eyes then skated across the keys along with *Phases of S*—a song he thought he had mastered … until he heard his mother play it.

Thankfully the sound of trotting hooves ripped him from the abyss of his thoughts. He returned to the window. A royal, yellow-decked lorry approached, surrounded by Intelian soldiers—on horseback as well as on foot.

Bryson called for Olivia.

A girl with long violet hair exited the hallway moments later. Bryson thought she looked naked without Meow Meow. He could tell by the look of her that she likely felt the same way. Her usual sea-blue eyes, which always put Bryson at ease, were now the color of dull storm clouds.

"Got everything?" he asked.

She nodded and walked past as he opened the door. He snatched up his belongings from the floorboards and slung a bag over his back. Just as he was about to leave the house without a second thought, he looked back, allowing the memories of Debo to waft over him. While he wasn't sure how he felt about Debo—Thusia had helped soften his anger toward him—he still understood that the man had raised him. He had taken an orphaned boy and given him a house. And over the years he crafted that house into something much more meaningful—a home filled with warmth and censure—until he performed the ultimate sacrifice by giving his life for Bryson's.

Finally he shut the door and walked down the front path. The soldiers were already patting Olivia down, searching her for weapons, by the time he reached her. They began doing the same to him—sifting through his bag, turning out his coat pockets, and flipping through the pages of the one book he had decided to bring with him: *Ataway Kawi: The Third of Five*. The contents were the same, except the cover had been vandalized and the amended title now read: *Ataway Kawi: The Third of Four.*

As far as Bryson was concerned, there was no "fifth". Mendac LeAnce was a villain of the vilest sort.

The soldiers directed Bryson and Olivia around the horse-drawn carriage while homeowners stood on their porches, their awestruck children leaning over the banisters. A steel-clad soldier knocked on the side door. A scrawny Dev servant in burgundy robes opened it from within.

"Come in," he drawled.

Bryson entered the lorry behind Olivia. "Hey, Flen," Bryson said.

"How'd you know it was me?" Flen asked.

"Tone, mannerisms, et cetera. Doesn't take much."

Flen was a Dev servant of the Intel royal family. He had an identical twin named Vistas, who was also a servant. While their features looked exactly the same, everything else about them made them polar opposites.

"Well, I'm not the only one with a twin, now," Flen said, knocking twice against a curtained window to signal for departure.

Bryson glanced at Olivia, who took a seat across the carriage. It was going to take time to adjust—simply because of the nature in which he had found out—but he loved the fact that she was his sister.

"Good morning, Jestivan."

The familiar voice beckoned their attention toward the handsome, stout man in the back of the carriage, Intel Major Lars. He held the second-highest position in the Intel military. However, considering that the position of Intel General was currently vacant due to the death of former General Lucas—at the hands of Rhyparia—it made Lars the most powerful individual by default. So much so that he had to leave his post in Rim to return home to Dunami.

Bryson harbored such spite for this man. There was a time when Bryson respected him, but his pursuit of Rhyparia over the past nine months that led to her execution—albeit stymied—left a bitter taste in Bryson's mouth … and that was putting it nicely.

"Good morning, Major," Bryson replied while Olivia mumbled something incoherent.

Lars observed them for a long moment. Bryson did the same, spending his time contemplating the idea of decking the major in his face. He didn't fear Lars and was willing to bet he could take him out. But that wasn't helpful.

Bryson decided to start the conversation. "How is it back in Dunami?"

"Conflicting."

"How so?"

"A sense of relief to be home; a sense of melancholy to know why." Lars glanced at Olivia, whose gaze was fixated on her knees. "I never would have thought it would be Phesaw to betray the Light Realm. The Archaic Kingdom, sure." He paused and his mouth thinned. "But never Phesaw."

"Nobody betrayed the realm," Bryson said. "It's not that simple."

Lars's eyebrows furrowed. "Really? What do you call a plan—created and executed by Archaic Director Senex—in which the goal is to free a prisoner who has murdered hundreds of people, children and mothers included, from the gallows?"

"Considering the circumstances," Bryson mused, "I'd call it courageous and morally just. Rhyparia was controlled by her mother. You had the wrong person's neck through that noose."

"You're as blinded as Pilot Ophala," Lars said, "ignoring the evidence that was given during the trials. Her mother didn't possess the Cloutitionist's Necklace. And, regardless of that, there's the whole ordeal of Olivia aiding the side of the Rogue Demon, Still Queen Apoleia, and Dev King Storshae in the invasion of Phesaw's campus. They struck down students!"

"Rogue Demon?" Bryson asked, confused.

Lars nodded. "Toono."

Bryson's nose crinkled. Was that the alias they were giving him now?

"I stood by my mother's side," said Olivia, dryly. "I had no part of Dev King Storshae or any of the soldiers he brought with him. My mom and I took no lives." She paused and made direct eye contact with Bryson for the first time in a couple days. "We did go to Phesaw with one person in our sights, but that ultimately fell through."

"I don't care," Lars said. "Whether purposeful or coincidental, your presence as opposition to Bryson and his Branian aided Devish efforts, allowing them to kill students unimpeded."

"Nothing you say changes what we think," Bryson said.

"Unfortunately for you, what you think holds no significance."

* * *

Bryson and Olivia trailed Major Lars through one of Dunami Palace's vaulted foyers, their footsteps against the blue marble echoing throughout. The rotunda was deep in the palace where there were no windows. Intelight chandeliers hung from the ceiling, dazzling the expanse in a thick golden hue.

Bryson had successfully avoided King Vitio for some time—five months, give or take—but now he had no say in the matter. In a few short minutes he would face the struggle of not verbally scolding Vitio for his friendship with Mendac.

They ventured into an area of the palace Bryson had never visited, and now the unease began to nestle within him. Where were they being taken? Torches replaced the Intelights, the floors transitioned into wood, and drywall swallowed them on both sides. Bryson raised his right brow, baffled by what he was seeing. Did such a place exist in Dunami, the wealthiest city in all of Kuki Sphaira?

They finally reached an ordinary door on the right side of the hall. It was absent of animal-shaped knockers or golden paneling. In fact, it was less than ordinary, flimsy and plagued by dry rot. Lars rapped three times on the wood.

It opened. The major stepped in first, then Olivia. Bryson followed but was jerked to the side upon entering. He looked over to see the other twin, Vistas. They exchanged smiles. He was one of very few whom Bryson trusted.

Bryson absorbed the new room's breadth of scope. Such a place didn't seem possible if he were to judge it based on the narrow, suffocating halls he'd just left. It was an assembly hall as big as the dining halls in Phesaw, containing six long wooden tables. Each one had matching benches that stretched along their sides filled with rows of Intelian soldiers. The walls and ceiling were made of crude, uneven stone and the floor was the dirt of the land. Torches were ablaze throughout the area. While it wasn't the most pleasant of scents, they were thankfully burning incense, which slightly masked the odor.

Every set of eyes in the room focused on Major Lars as he walked through the center of the hall. He approached the front of the room with great strides.

The block of a man that was King Vitio stood at the head of the hall. His blonde hair had become diluted since Bryson had last seen him, making way for old age's silver. His golden robes were split at his right shoulder, exposing a sky-blue surcoat embroidered with the Intelian sigil: the brain of lightning.

Queen Delilah and Princess Shelly flanked Vitio a few steps back. A spark ignited inside Bryson after spotting the leafy-green pixie cut of the princess. Like Vistas, she was another friendly presence, though a bit harsh at times.

Lars fell to a knee the moment he reached his king. Vitio gazed down at the man. "Major Lars," he said, "you entered the Intelian army at the age of seventeen. Since that day, you've served twenty years of unparalleled service to your kingdom and, more recently, demonstrated the ability to lead a city. Although earlier than previously intended, it is high time your role shifted to something greater."

Bryson's face soured. King Vitio turned, climbed a few steps to an elevated landing with its own table, and grabbed a thick white coat, accented with gold trim and adorned with medals and pins. It was the type of uniform made for a military man, but not practical for military use. It was nothing more than a trophy.

Vitio returned, holding the jacket by the shoulders with both hands. "Rise, Major, as I present to you the most coveted position for any soldier: the head of the most technologically advanced army of fighters, and protector of the wealthiest, most innovative kingdom of Kuki Sphaira's ten."

As Lars rose, so did the rest of the conjugation from their benches. He turned with his back facing Vitio. His eyes landed on Bryson. A cold menace laced through the brown of his irises as the king placed the jacket over his shoulders. It was big enough to comfortably clothe a man of Passion King Damian's size, sweeping down his torso like a cloak, but its sturdiness would never allow it to be mistaken as such. The golden epaulets on his shoulders made his head look smaller, but this somehow added to the intimidating effect.

Lars's eyes lingered on Bryson for one last moment before he turned to face his king. Vitio spoke again: "It is in this same sector of the palace that your oldest and greatest predecessors made their stomping grounds before lying to eternal rest. Here your purpose is not born anew, but rather matured as it's shaped into something more complex. Do you accept the responsibility bestowed upon you?"

"Yes, milord."

"Do you vow to protect the greatest kingdom of the last fifteen hundred years until your dying breath?"

"Yes, milord."

"What say you?" Vitio asked.

Lars wasn't facing Bryson, but Bryson felt as if the man were piercing daggers through his soul with his response: "Traitors to the realm should cower while awake or in slumber. I will hunt them with a relentless vigor unparalleled by any."

Bryson caught Vitio's fleeting glance but couldn't read much of it. "Men and women of the Intel army—" he placed his hand on Lars's shoulder and turned him toward the hall— "your new Intel General."

They responded with a deafening chant, making them sound like a pack of greyhounds. Vitio smiled. "Please enjoy a fine meal and some mead in celebration."

The door next to Bryson opened. A plethora of serving carts spilled through, struggling to roll over the packed dirt beneath them. His knees became weak as the scent of roasted meat wafted through his nostrils.

At the hall's helm, King Vitio, Queen Delilah, Princess Shelly, and General Lars stepped onto the wooden stage and approached the table, which was blanketed in a white and gold cloth. As Lars took a seat, he grinned at Bryson and Olivia.

Surprising even himself, Bryson returned the sneer. If this man thought he'd ever lay a hand on any of his friends, he had better be prepared to have them broken.

*   *   *

Bryson sat in the same cozy chamber that Lilu, Vitio, and he had occupied during his first visit to Dunami Palace a year and a half ago. That night he had witnessed Princess Shelly summon Branian Suadade—another first of such experiences. Unlike last time, though, the grand fireplace was quiet, for spring was to end soon.

During that visit all those months ago, it was Lilu who had accompanied him. He almost expected to turn to his left and see her at a forced distance at the opposite end of the couch, nervous of her father's watchful eye.

Instead it was the somber face of Olivia. This was her first time visiting Dunami Palace or meeting a member of the Intel royal family who wasn't named Lilu.

Vitio sat on a leather armchair on the other side of a carpeted expanse, while Shelly pretended to be occupied by the reading material on a bookshelf off to the side.

"These are not quite the circumstances I ever envisioned meeting you under," Vitio said in the direction of Olivia. "I always wondered when Bryson would bring you around."

"If it wasn't forced on us, it wouldn't be happening now," Bryson said.

The king's gaze shifted to Bryson. "I feel as if our relationship isn't what it once was."

Bryson's rigid glare said enough.

"Allow me to explain," Vitio said through a slow breath. "Obviously I wasn't aware as to the full extent of what your father did during his several trips into the Dark Realm. If I had known about what he did to the Still Queen, he would have spent eternity staring at the interior of a jail cell. And not because he committed an Untenable, but the method in which he did it. If they had fallen in love and fell victim to such desires, I would have turned a blind eye." Vitio shook his head gravely. "But to beat and rape a woman … damn. Forget jail; he would have spent eternity staring at the interior of a coffin." He turned around and looked at his daughter. "As a father of two girls, something demonic would have possessed me."

That was all it took to soften Bryson's rage. Perhaps avoiding the king had been a bad idea. It had caused his doubt to fester as he swam in a lake of uncertainty. If there was one thing he knew about Vitio, it was his undying love for the three women in his life.

But there was a tiny, nagging thought in the back of Bryson's mind with regard to the morning's events. He wanted to bring it to Vitio's attention. "I hope you realize what General Lars meant earlier today."

"I do," Vitio said. "And I'm afraid this will cause your disgust for me to return." Bryson's eyes narrowed as the king explained further: "I must hold certain people accountable. The people of the Light Realm—and not just our kingdom—want justice. If I go against it, I risk my people revolting."

Bryson gripped the arm of the sofa as his face twisted in bafflement. "Yes, you can. You're the most powerful man in the world."

"You're only as strong as the people who follow you. And if the Intel Kingdom resorts to destroying itself from within, that leaves us weak and exposed to our enemies abroad. Such a predicament isn't ideal in these trying times."

Vitio waved a hand in different directions as he listed off threats: "Toono, Storshae, Yama, the Dev Warden, Dev Diatia, and who knows what's happening in the Passion or Power Kingdoms. I haven't heard from King Damian in months, and Power Warden Feissam abandoned us during the fight at Phesaw. Only his Diatia stayed behind, one of whom died at the hands of Toono, according to that Agnos boy. At least I found solace in the fact that the other one acted in our interest during the invasion.

"So that is why I had to promote Lars to General, even if I was reluctant because of his thirst to hunt down most of the Jestivan. It's what my people wanted. They saw the action he took in Rim, and they want that kind of assertion and decisiveness in the military that protects them. I'm not King Itta, ignoring the desires of the populace while ruling with an unchecked agenda."

Bryson attempted to speak, but the king was unrelenting.

"I assure you, I'll keep the man in check. But that doesn't mean certain Jestivan aren't getting off without some form of punishment. While Archain soldiers are currently stationed in the foothills of the Archaic Mountains, regulating traffic in and out to only kingdom-licensed bounty hunters to track down Rhyparia, I will make an exception for Olivia. Tomorrow morning she will depart Dunami with a small group of bounty hunters and a few of my finest soldiers. She will then take the teleplatforms to the Archaic Kingdom and head to Rim. There she'll spend a couple of months preparing to enter the mountains to catch Rhyparia NuForce until next summer."

"I'm going with her," Bryson said.

"No, you're not. You have to be granted permission by a royal head and receive a waxed seal of his or her respective insignia." He paused, and then said flatly, "Which I will not do for you."

Bryson's rage swelled once again. "You're a—"

"Understood, sir," Olivia interrupted, standing tall and reaching across the glass table with an open hand. "I know what I've done, and now I must face the consequences."

Vitio paused in shock; his eyes had grown wide. But then he smiled, pushed himself from the chair, and shook her hand, saying, "My only wish, Olivia Still, is that you return home safely and healthy."

Olivia left the room without a backward glance, leaving Bryson speechless in her wake.

* * *

Bryson lay across a couch in the most breathtaking location in the entire palace—Princess Shelly's bedroom. A singular sheet of glass wrapped around the circular room and sat atop it as a ceiling. The star-spangled night sky glittered above him, and he created his own constellation of Intelights throughout the room to accompany it. He felt like he was lying amongst the stars.

Shelly walked into the room from the balcony. "I'm impressed," she said. "You've got about, what, fifty-or-so of them going at once?"

"Sixty-seven," he mumbled.

"I think even Lilu would be shocked."

"Well, what else was I supposed to do for three weeks while trapped in my house, incapable of moving my body?" Even Bryson hated the bitterness in his voice.

Shelly sat down at his feet. She was in a plain white shirt and cheap breeches, proving how comfortable she'd become with him.

She hummed, then said, "For all the complaints about your tender bones and lack of mobility, you try very hard to protect Olivia—the girl who put you in that condition in the first place. She treats you like you don't even exist from what I've noticed."

Bryson flicked his wrist, sending a cluster of Intelights soaring through the air until they formed a singular, brighter light. "She's my sister."

"I understand having a sister is new to you," Shelly said, "but if Lilu had done what Olivia had, I would expect repercussions … and I wouldn't fight it."

"If I were to chase her down, would you try to stop me?" he asked.

"I'd have Suadade stop you."

Bryson sat up and placed his feet on the carpet. "And I'd have Thusia counter him," he replied. But after taking a moment to think on it, he realized Thusia would only take Shelly and Suadade's side. He decided to change the subject. "Where's Vuilni?"

"Father freed her after interrogations. I believe she's somewhere in the city. She seems like a wonderful young lady."

Bryson relaxed, sinking into the cushions. With all the stress lately, he was glad that one weight could be lifted from his shoulders.

It went quiet as Shelly stared blankly into the distance. She gasped and smiled at Bryson. "Let's sneak out in a week and go somewhere else. We'll take Flen with us. Unlike Vistas, he wouldn't betray us to my father."

"Where to?" Bryson asked.

"I don't know. Where do you want to go?"

He looked past her into the starry night outside the glass. There were a few possibilities, some more practical than others. But there was one place he had been dying to visit for quite some time now. He refocused on her face, washed clean of make-up and lipstick yet as alluring as ever.

"Debo's hometown."

4
The Gulf of Sodai

For six days Agnos and Tashami had traveled from the Spirit Kingdom's teleplatforms to the capital city of Sodai. While the journey was long, they had nothing to complain about. In fact, they had made it there in record time. Agnos had been able to use some of the money he had made as a guide in Phesaw's Warpfinate to rent two horses from a small business in Reikon Gate, a town that housed the Spirit Kingdom's teleplatforms and served as a welcome to any foreigners.

According to the manager of the shop, the business had four other locations, each stationed in a major city across the kingdom. Upon their arrival in Sodai, they'd follow the man's directions to find the building where they were expected to drop off their rides.

Agnos felt he could manage any excursion after experiencing the multi-week trek through the gray, dead canvas of the Cyn Kingdom a year ago. The Spirit Kingdom was the complete opposite. He got to ride through Cherry Forest, an expanse of pink canopies that made Phesaw Park look like a cupboard; along Shindo River, the widest, deepest river in the Light Realm; and all while basking in an infinite cool breeze.

Agnos and Tashami had been traveling alongside the river for two days. It led to Sodai while allowing them freedom from Spirit Road, the roadway that connected the kingdom's major cities. This particular area was especially crowded, connecting the scattered suburbs to the main city. Commuters traveled it daily between work and home. But the two Jestivan hid their whereabouts at the bottom of a slope that stretched for miles, veiling them from the road by a thin layer of cherry blossoms.

Just ahead was the most breathtaking piece of natural phenomena in the entire kingdom: the Gulf of Sodai. The river widened farther as it spilled into the gulf, but it was still too far away for Agnos to fully appreciate its serenity.

His palms dug into the handles of his saddle as he spotted sails and masts impaling the sky. He gently pushed his feet into the stirrups. The horse responded with a quickened trot. He soon lost patience and sent the horse into a gallop. The gulf opened ahead, swallowing the sky with ease.

Agnos pulled back on the reins and came to a stop. Tashami approached a moment later. "Look at that," Agnos said, more to himself than to his friend.

Tashami smiled and asked, "Have you ever been to an Edge?"

"I haven't," Agnos replied. The Edge referred to the end of land. Beyond it was nothing but air, and in the Light Realm it was fenced off and tightly secured in every kingdom.

"Neither have I. I tried to get to it a couple times in my younger years since its in close proximity to Sodai."

Agnos was still focused on the gulf, scanning the opposite bank until it became victim to the horizon. "I can't even see the other side."

While every kingdom had a bay that served as an entrance, connecting a Realm River to a smaller river of the land, none of them rivaled the scope of the Gulf of Sodai. It was the reason why Sodai was deemed the hub of commerce between kingdoms and known as the Current of the Realm Rivers. It kept trade moving.

The gulf also housed Fort Rina, the main base for the Spirit Navy—the mightiest navy in the realm. The fort sat on the other side of the capital, two dozen miles east. It was most notorious for being the home of Sephrina, the *Second of Five.*

Agnos continued down the bank. Dirt and grass became golden sand created by the tides. And the hill to their left flattened out as the trees dispersed, making Spirit Road visible as it became level with the shore.

He dismounted, removed his sandals, and placed them in a pouch that hung from the horse's side. The sand molded to his feet and squeezed between his toes. He decided to walk from this point forward. He passed children splashing in the water, parents relaxing on reclining chairs, and a series of docks containing a variety of humble watercraft—longboats, canoes, rafts, and even an occasional sailboat likely owned by wealthier families.

The fun eventually came to an end upon reaching a restricted area of beach. A barred fence stood in front of them. On the other side, men and women traversed between the mainland and the shallow waters. As merchants hopped out of incoming longboats, the crewmen dragged them up the beach and away from the tide, in fear of its pull. These were members of smaller vessels that didn't have the luxury of claiming a spot at Sodai Port. Such privileges were for the most extravagant monsters of the open waters: the galleons and carracks.

Agnos could only see the far end of the port as it jutted into the gulf. A mile or two ahead, the beach veered right. The city buildings cut off most of his view, but he could see a galleon sailing toward the horizon.

A person stepped in front of him on the other side of the fence. "Do you not pay attention to signs, young man?"

It was a woman in a sailor cap, but her blue uniform implied she was a member of the Spirit Navy.

"I'm sorry, ma'am," Agnos said. "I'm not from around here."

She looked him up and down. "Get back to the main road."

They wisely obliged, retreating to the signs placed in the sand a hundred steps behind them. Agnos must have missed them while he'd been consumed with the spectacle of the gulf.

They guided their horses to the main road. The stone pavement was a real distinction of Sodai's prosperity, made even more impressive by the fact that they were nowhere near the city's heart. Their first order of business was to find the horse rental shop. It sat near the city's entrance, so they quickly dropped them off and pressed onward. In Sodai, horses were only allowed for people who not only could afford to own one, but had the financial history to qualify for a license … a strange law.

Now that Agnos was away from the water—though he could see it through gaps in the buildings at times—he was able to appreciate the man-made beauty of Sodai. Unlike the capitals of other kingdoms purposefully constructed upon flat land, Sodai was a city of subtle hills. And since the buildings were narrow and only a few stories tall, there was enough space between each one for the gulf's breeze to waft through, carrying the salty scent of the water.

Agnos could see three or four parallel streets when he looked between two buildings. Everything was evenly placed like a grid.

"I don't know how we're supposed to find this person," Agnos said while studying the plethora of buildings just on this street alone. He didn't have much to go on. Ophala's note that Himitsu had given him said only one word: Sodai.

"Well, that's what my grandma is for," Tashami said, trying to reassure him.

Agnos grinned and nodded at his friend, but he doubted the idea that the woman had anything to offer. While Tashami *called* her "grandma," she apparently wasn't at all. She was simply someone Tashami lived with during the summers away from Phesaw. He said she was a sailor, but that didn't amount to much.

After a quick bite to eat at a cheap diner—relieved to have escaped the monotonous, unsatisfying life of dried jerky—they arrived at a narrow two-story house packed neatly into a row of seemingly identical structures, the only telling difference being the color of paint displayed.

Tashami withdrew a key from his pocket as they walked up the front steps. He placed it in the doorknob, twisted it, and stepped inside. On their left a narrow staircase ran up the side wall. To their right was the living room and a hallway squeezed between the two, stretching toward—judging from the tiled floor—a kitchen in the back. While it was a small space, it was well-kept. Agnos understood that the cost of living in this city was astronomical.

"I smell dinner," Tashami mumbled. "The diner was a mistake. Accept whatever she offers you …" he trailed off before adding, "and eat it."

They made their way through the hall and into the kitchen. Candles were lit throughout, and a woman in a flowery dress was hunched over a pot that rested above a coal pit installed in the counter.

When she finally turned, she became startled, but then quickly rushed toward Tashami. "Shama-Lama!" she cried.

Agnos grinned wider than ever as he fought back a laugh. He was never going to let Tashami live that one down.

"Hey, Grandma," Tashami said, embraced in a squeeze.

She stepped back with a hand to her chest. "Sudden gale," she swore. "You blew me for a loop, there!"

Her eyes then fell on Agnos. "Hello, ma'am," he said.

"This is Agnos, Grandma, my best friend and one of the Jestivan."

"A guest?" she said, stunned. "How do you do?" she asked Agnos, pulling him toward her.

Agnos's face was squeezed against her apron. She was tall even by male standards. "Quite well," he said through a mouthful of grease-stained cloth.

"Have a seat!" she said, motioning toward a small circular table wedged into the kitchen's corner. "Looks like I'm setting the table for three!"

As they sat down, Agnos leaned over and said: "You didn't warn me she's another Jilly."

"Nobody's another Jilly," Tashami whispered under the clattering of plates. "Besides, this is the Spirit Kingdom. What did you expect?"

Agnos leaned back as the woman placed a plate of fresh green beans, carrots, and a cut of lamb in front of him—a far cry from the stale potato wedges he had had at the diner. He thought he was full, but apparently he had only tired of junk.

With no fork at his disposal, he stared blankly at the meal. This wasn't finger food. Finally she returned with chopsticks. "Ah," Agnos said. "I forgot about that."

"You know how to use them, right?" Tashami asked.

Agnos picked them up and twirled them between his fingers. "I used to eat with these when I was little and first attended Phesaw. I was fascinated by the novelty of it."

Over the next half-hour they ate, conversed, and laughed. Either Tashami's grandma didn't know about the recent happenings with the Jestivan, or she purposefully avoided the topic. It was probably the latter. Agnos didn't complain; he didn't want to think about such heartbreak.

Tashami was clearing the table and washing dishes when Agnos mentioned the reason for his presence to the old lady. *Old lady?* He immediately realized he needed a name for her.

"What should I call you?" he asked.

"Mimi."

Agnos hesitated and glanced at Tashami, who was shaking his head with a smile in the background.

"Okay, Mimi," Agnos said, ignoring the silliness of it. "Tashami told me that you've lived your entire life in Sodai, and that you once were a sailor up until a decade ago."

A shadow slithered across her face. "I was."

He paused again. "I'm hoping your extended history with this city and the gulf can lead me to a person who possesses an ancient known as Cheiraskinia."

"What a mouthful!" she said.

"That it is."

"Well, I'm not an Archain," she said, "so forgive me for not knowing names of ancients, but maybe if you tell me what it does."

"It allows someone to control sea life."

The sparkle in Mimi's eyes shifted to skepticism as she placed both hands on the table. "It's strange for someone unfamiliar with the sea to know of such a person."

"Does he or she not see land much?"

"That depends, I guess. I think the better way to put it would be: she doesn't leave DaiSo often—unless the sea calls for her."

"DaiSo?" Agnos said, shocked by the revelation of what that implied.

She closed her eyes and gave a slight nod. "That's right; she's a pirate."

Agnos rested his elbows on the table and grabbed ahold of his bangs. "That complicates matters."

She nodded, pressing her lips together. "You're right. Getting to DaiSo isn't the safest of adventures, nor is it easy. You'll require an inside source on a pirate crew who will then sail you into DaiSo's harbor, because you're definitely not going to sail up to its shore in an unmarked vessel without being obliterated by squallblasters."

"Squallblasters?"

"Talented weavers of Spirit Energy who can blast highly concentrated volumes of wind at their targets over a long range."

Agnos's forehead smacked the table. "And if I return to the river, travel a ways, and cross it? Then proceed to enter on foot?"

"Same fate, but with your limbs scattered across the ground instead."

"Then what's my best bet? Do I have any options?"

She thrummed her fingers against the table. "You wait for someone to come here."

"They allow pirates in Sodai?"

Mimi got up and joined Tashami in the kitchen, where she pumped water out of a faucet over her hands. While she scrubbed, she said, "How else would the pirates hand over any of their profits?"

His eyes narrowed as he turned in his chair. "Wait, you're telling me that the Spirit Kingdom receives some of the loot that the pirates siege from merchant vessels?"

"Yes. It's a peculiar arrangement between Sodai and DaiSo. While the pirates of DaiSo are treated as enemies of the kingdom if they try to cross the gulf or river and set food in the capital—except for a select few, usually quartermasters—they're lauded as allies by the Spirit elites when they're sailing the Realm Rivers and the Sea of Light, wreaking havoc and looting merchants that have wronged the Spirit Kingdom."

"That seems as corrupt as the Archaic Kingdom under Itta or the Power Kingdom under Gantski," Agnos said.

Mimi frowned. "Bit of a stretch, little one. I guess Queen Apsa looks at it as her receiving money that was taken from her first."

"So, karma."

"Exactly."

Tashami leaned against the counter and dried his hands with a rag. "So we have to wait for a quartermaster to arrive."

"There's likely already a few in the city, but you won't find them around these parts. You'll have to go into the grimier areas: specifically, the

Chasm—a gang-infested block of streets that is awkwardly positioned at the bottom of five surrounding hills. The sun only hits it properly at high noon. That's where the queen makes them stay, and it's where transactions occur."

It went silent for a moment, then Tashami said, "Don't worry, Agnos. We can do it. You'll have me with you."

Mimi's wrinkled eyes slowly shifted from Tashami to Agnos, whose fingers were trembling as he stared at the floor. He had already come here expecting this to be difficult, but in a way such as a game of hide-and-seek, finding a single person in a massive city with tens of thousands of people. But it turned out not to be the case at all. This would be dangerous and would force him into scenarios he didn't feel comfortable with, surrounded by thugs and criminals in a foreign, run-down sector.

He had flashbacks to his moments of weakness when he used to operate as a Jestivan: his abandonment of civilians at the Generals' Battle while he stood in shock as innocents were slain in the stands, his inability to help Rhyparia when she was being captured by the generals, and his complete lack of relevance during Storshae and Toono's invasion of Phesaw.

He didn't know how many more minutes of silence dragged by, but eventually he felt a hand on his shoulder. Tashami took a knee next to him and looked him in the face. "Remember a year ago, when we entered the Void?"

Agnos looked into his gray eyes. Tashami continued: "Do you know who steered that mission? You did. Not Yama, not Lilu, nor Director Neaneuma or Buredo. While you seemed to suffer from the Void's atmosphere more than any of us, you still managed to keep focus and lead us where we needed to go. You proved to be the strongest of the group." He paused and said with even more conviction, "*You* found me my father."

They held each other's gaze for a long moment while Mimi smiled at Tashami from across the kitchen.

Tashami grabbed the back of Agnos's head and held it steady, like a father ready to drill a life lesson into his son. His expression became stern.

"Let me find you your quartermaster."

5
To a Rival's Aid

Boredom ate at Lilu as she traveled the full expanse of the Intel Kingdom's northern prairie. The beauty of the vibrant flatlands had been breathtaking during the early stages of the journey, but that was no longer the case. She spent her time fiddling with a gray block, coursing her energy into its hollow center, working patterns to perfect her permanence skills. If there was one positive to take from this trip, it was the time allotted to training.

"We're here."

She looked up at Director Jugtah, who was peering out the front window. She threw the block aside and scampered across the lorry to get a peek of the city she had heard so much about throughout her life.

She craned her neck to see around the back of the coachman's head. A limestone wall stood erect from the prairie grass. A message was engraved above a massive gate. She read it aloud to herself: "What is seen does not leave."

"And don't ever forget that," Jugtah said. "There is technology in Brilliance that isn't even sent to Dunami. This is partly because it's unstable and needs rigorous testing—we can't risk innocent lives because of faulty inventions—but mostly it's because such technological advancements need not be seen by foreigners. Just the sight of what's contained within these walls would wage a realm-wide war."

Lilu looked above the wall. Then she moved toward the side of the cabin and looked out a different window, where she could view the extent of the wall.

"The trade gate is far out of sight so that it can't be seen from the traveler's road," Jugtah said, realizing what Lilu was searching for. "Brilliance is the Intel Kingdom's silent heart."

Lilu watched as the wall grew nearer during the final portion of her journey. Her mind raced, trying to imagine what was held within the barrier. Brilliance had no maps—at least none outside its walls—so she was walking into this blindly. Director Jugtah also hadn't said much about the city, which could be attributed to the maxim above the gate.

The coach stopped. Before Jugtah stepped outside, he said, "The guards will vet the transport—mainly to see if we're smuggling any ancients or Dev servants that could potentially record or visually document what is seen in the city. I suppose they'll ask you a few questions too."

He exited the coach, leaving Lilu alone. She ran to the front and looked out the window. A band of guards in white-trimmed yellow cloaks congregated around him. She had never seen such a uniform from any of the branches of the Intelian military. Her face twisted with bemusement as she watched Jugtah do something he rarely ever did … laugh. And not just a short chuckle, but he guffawed as he made hand gestures and ranted as if he were telling a story.

Eventually he headed back in the direction of the coach while the guards trailed behind him. Lilu hustled to her bench and adjusted the lilac in her bangs. The door swung open, allowing sunlight to come crashing into the cabin. Jugtah walked in, followed by two men. Their eyes widened.

"Milady!" they both said with shoddy bows.

It wasn't their fault, she thought. Neither had probably ever seen a royal in his life.

"Forgive me," one man said, his face turning a shameful red, "but we have to pat you down. There are no exceptions to the protocol."

She allowed this without a fuss, which caused them to relax. She was tired of the reactions she received in Dunami Palace or at Phesaw, how people would tense up around her. She would change that image here.

They searched her with delicate hands. Once satisfied, they turned to Jugtah and did the same. From her peripherals Lilu caught sight through the window of guards inspecting the carriage's exterior.

"How's the city, Travis?" Jugtah asked.

"If I'm being honest, angry."

"At what?"

"The lies that came from Mendac's son."

Lilu snapped her head around, but Jugtah pursed his lips and shook his head as a sign to not beleaguer them over the topic. "Disgrace of a son, really," Travis said.

Lilu's blood boiled, but she bit her tongue since Jugtah said no more. The carriage passed the security check and was on its way through the gate shortly thereafter.

"They really think Bryson was lying?" she asked.

"You have to understand what Mendac is to Brilliance. He's an intellectual icon, and for most people he's considered the measuring stick of theoretical and applied sciences. They glorify him so much that he can do no wrong in their eyes, even if they know he did something like capture Devish and bring them to the Light Realm as servants. But I'm guessing news that he raped a princess was simply too much for them to come to grips with."

"That is no excuse."

"And I agree."

The carriage stopped once again. They hadn't traveled very far from the checkpoint. "What's happening?" she asked.

"We've passed through the gate and now we must leave our transport so the coachman can return home. Obviously he's not allowed any deeper into the city."

They stepped onto a tar-paved road, midnight black and perfectly smooth. Lilu looked up in awe. She now understood why the exterior wall was so menacingly tall. She practically had to break her neck to see the tops of the buildings. She had grown up in Dunami Palace, one of the tallest man-made structures in Kuki Sphaira. But that was the only building in Dunami that reached such heights. She counted four buildings on this street alone that'd give the palace a run for its money. Maybe they weren't as wide at the base, but that's what made them even more peculiar. They were tall and skinny, like limestone pillars that kept the overcast clouds afloat.

She gasped as she suddenly tripped over something and fell on her rear. Her heel had hit a curb. Had she not realized she was walking backward while she searched for the top of the skyscrapers?

"Pay attention," Jugtah said. "You're in the Light Realm's most congested city, and citizens here don't have much patience." He extended his arm and helped her to her feet.

Lilu glanced down the road to her left and saw a statue extending above the crowd. "No ..."

He followed her gaze and scratched his forehead. "Yes. Like I said, Mendac means a lot to this city."

*   *   *

The lanky frame of Himitsu wobbled its way out of a pub. His mind played tricks on him as he stumbled over non-existent objects obstructing his path. It was late enough to call it early morning. This meant instead of merely receiving silent judgmental looks of disgust from passersby as he would during the day, younger people laughed at him as he reached out for a pole to aid his balance, only to fall flat on his face in a conveniently placed patch of grass.

He was thankful to Fiamma for that, at least. The random trees, gardens, and fields scattered throughout the city streets provided him with plenty of natural beds, all within easy walking distance of a pub or tavern and free of charge, which saved him money for the real necessity in life: alcohol. Tonight it looked to be this grassy square.

Thankfully, he was coherent enough to recognize the trotting of hooves coming around the block. Someone riding a horse at this hour could only mean one thing: a Passion officer.

He fumbled with the ground's handle. That action alone said enough. Unless there was a root nearby, there was no way he could have actually thought he'd find a handle in the ground. He finally managed to stand, only to keel over and vomit a moment later from a combination of vertigo and reckless intoxication. Hooves stopped in the road next to him as he heaved.

"Again, Zana Himitsu?"

The Jestivan tilted his head from its bent position. "Officer, g'day."

The woman dismounted her black stallion, the fur above its hooves a fluffy white. She stood a safe distance away. "Before I cuff you, is it all out?"

He gave her a thumbs-up. She played it safe and waited another minute before approaching. "Such a shame," the officer said as she reached for Himitsu's wrist.

But she was too slow. Himitsu snatched his hand out of her grasp and bolted the other way—more like zigzagged. He weaved a wall of black flames behind him to make up for the fact that he was moving slower than a crawling infant. Then he sprouted others, in hopes that it would throw off her sense of direction. This time of night worked in his favor, for most of the street torches were already extinguished and would remain so until tomorrow evening.

He managed to find an alleyway and then dove into a dumpster. He situated himself between the bags of garbage and thought, *this isn't a terrible bed.* The forceful breath of a horse just outside the alley made him cover his mouth. It went deathly quiet as he waited, debating when to poke his head out. Ultimately it didn't matter, as the officer's fingers grasped the container's rim and her face peered inside.

Himitsu kicked the back of the dumpster, sending the lid, which had been resting against a brick wall, firmly shut on her fingers. He lay there, listening to the woman's curses. Honestly, what good had that done? Where was he supposed to run to now?

He answered his own questions by opening the lid and climbing out. He fell back into the dumpster, landing with a bang. "I concede," he muttered.

The pity the officer had displayed earlier was wiped clear from her face. Her nose and mouth snarled, and her eyebrows became slanted. She marched forward and grabbed Himitsu's shoulder, then spun him around and slammed his face into the metal container.

"You're making it hard for me to respect you," she snapped.

*   *   *

Toshik was drowning in a sea of parchment at a desk in his father's office. Most of them were spreadsheets, organizing and detailing numbers that Toshik had no business monitoring. When was his dad going to learn that he wasn't a businessman?

He picked up a sheet and scanned down a column listing every single merchant vessel owned by Brench Crafts. Each row held numbers that accounted for a ship's weight and dimensions, the size of the crew presently on board, the amount of product being stored, and the overall value of said product. There were other numbers, too, but none of which Toshik understood.

He dropped his hand on the desk and spun in his chair with an exasperated sigh. A hundred acres of land sprawled beneath him and beyond on the other side of the singular sheet of glass. Some of it was manicured grass with a few pebble ponds or small gardens sprinkled here and there, but most of it was the forest that his mother would disappear into when he was a child.

That had once been his true love—the hunt. As a child, he was only granted a few opportunities to enter the thicket, and a part of him wished he never had. Maybe his mom and sister would still be alive.

"Toshy!"

Toshik spun around just in time to catch a stampeding Jilly as she leapt into his arms. He held her on his lap and laughed. "Hey, Jilly."

She jumped back on her feet and said, "We have to go!"

"Go where?"

"To bail Himitsu out of jail!"

His smile faded. "Do you know how long of a journey that is? Can't Bryson and Olivia do it … or Lilu? Surely *she* has the money."

"Nope and nope. It has to be us. We've lost too many friends, and I'm not losing more."

Toshik gave it some thought. He looked back at the parchment-covered desk. "Okay," he finally said, standing up and reaching for his sword resting against the window. "I suppose we can leave for a week or two. My dad has people in positions to take care of this stuff anyway—people much more suited than me. What'd he get arrested for?"

"He ran from an officer. Also: public intoxication, urination, and indecent exposure."

Toshik paused as he pushed the empty chair under the desk. "Are you kidding me?"

Jilly blinked a couple times and said, "I don't know what any of that means except that he peed a little."

He laughed and gave her a kiss on her forehead. "Let's go get the idiot." But as he exited his dad's office, sorrow wafted over him. Himitsu was grieving the absence of his mother. If anyone had the ability to relate and help him through the struggle, it was Toshik. All bad blood aside, he'd make sure his teammate climbed out of grief's abyss.

6
Escape

General Lars guided Olivia out the eastern side of Dunami Palace with his hand placed on her shoulder. They walked down a dirt path between barracks and fields where soldiers marched or trained. Musk and sweat overcame her nostrils as war cries and grunts roared through the heat. The path led to the inner wall, where a convoy awaited its final occupant.

There was a small group of men and women conjugated behind a carriage. As Olivia approached, the first trait she noticed about them was their age. She was used to operating with the Jestivan, who were anywhere between sixteen and twenty-two. These individuals, however, were no younger than thirty.

"Hello, hunters," Lars said, causing the group to split apart.

A couple of them responded, simply calling him "General," while others stared in silence.

"What an honor," grumbled one man, "for a princess to grace our side with her presence on this mission."

Olivia met his eyes, being careful to mask the sadness swirling within her. If there was anyone she didn't want seeing her weaknesses, it was this stranger. All it took was a single glance and she could tell that he had seen more in his life than most. Over a white linen shirt and trousers he wore a black vest buttoned from his knees to the base of his neck. A line of wrinkles separated his chin and the edges of his jaw. And he leaned ever so slightly against a polished black cane, which didn't manage to stifle the demand for respect his presence gave.

"Hello, girl," another man said, his brown hair knotted behind his head.

Lars's eyes darted back and forth during a stiff silence. "Well, then. Have fun," he said before returning to the palace.

The group converged once again, walling Olivia out of their conversation. She didn't mind. She had grown numb to the silence ever since Toono had taken Meow Meow from her. She edged around their pack and looked into the back of the wagon. It was nothing fancy, just an empty space with two crude benches along either side. She leapt into the back and chose a spot at the front end of one of the benches. Hopefully nobody would try to sit next to her.

She hadn't said good-bye to Bryson, and she was already regretting it. But with all of the deeds she had committed over the past year that betrayed him, it shamed her to speak to him as if she was worth his attention.

She heard a clunk from the carriage's back end. The man with the cane had boarded. He held his eyes steadily on hers before gently guiding himself onto the bench. He reached into his vest pocket, withdrew a pipe, and placed its tip into his mouth. He then rummaged in his other pocket, apparently without luck, coming up emptyhanded.

"Oi," he called out the back of the caravan, beckoning the attention of every grown man and woman still on the ground. "Which one of you lads was the fire one?" The man with his hair tied behind his head stepped forward. "Help me out, will ya?" the man with the cane said. "Seems I forgot my flint and striker."

The brown-haired man flicked his finger, and a trail of smoke twisted upward from the pipe's mouth.

"Appreciate that," he said before placing the pipe in his mouth.

Olivia watched out of the corner of her eyes as the man with the cane leaned back and expelled an amount of smoke that made her question his lung size.

Without averting his gaze from the blanketed roof, he asked, "Fancy a puff, princess?" His grating voice barely reached across the length of the space.

"No, thank you."

*   *   *

The sound of panting ripped through the air of the open field as Bryson, Shelly, and Flen sprinted through the remote grounds of Dunami Palace. Bryson led the way toward the innermost wall of defense, his speed percentage cranked high enough to not be seen by the Intel soldiers that stood in the stone watchtowers. It shouldn't have mattered much, anyway. They were probably more focused on the other side of the barrier, watching for anybody who might have slipped past the exterior wall, trying to enter palace grounds. People trying to *exit*—especially their princess—was the furthest thing on their minds. Or at least that's what Shelly had told Bryson a few days ago when they planned this. She had better have been right.

He reached the bottom of the wall with ease. He looked back just in time to see Shelly arriving and Flen a hundred paces behind. The princess put a hand against the wall and caught her breath. She was wearing trousers, an airy blouse, and a blonde wig to hide her signature green pixie cut. None of it looked right.

By the time Flen arrived Bryson was already summoning Thusia. Flen struggled to speak between breaths: "I … hate … running."

Bryson gave a nod when Thusia appeared. This whole plan relied on her abilities as a Spirit Assassin.

She smiled and leapt into the air. Bryson watched as she floated higher. She grabbed onto an errant chunk of stone about three-quarters of the way up and hung there. Then she used her feet to find grips in the wall before catapulting herself farther into the sky. This time she made it, disappearing into the top of the tower.

They waited in silence while Flen tried to regain his composure. Thusia couldn't risk exposure, so she had to be careful up there and follow Shelly's advice from days ago.

The gate inched open. Bryson, Shelly, and Flen shot through, knowing they didn't have much time. After Thusia activated the gate's lever with her wind, she was to jump to the ground immediately. But this only allowed a few seconds, for the guards would quickly remedy the situation. Sure enough, the gate rattled shut just moments later.

As Thusia returned to the Light Empire, they blew through the distance between the inner wall and the outer gate. The gate wasn't manned at all, but it was too tall and the bars too close together for anyone to jump it or squeeze through. An arrow whizzed past Bryson's ear and struck the ground ahead of him. That had to be luck; there was no way they could see him at the speed he was traveling.

"I think they're shooting at me!" Shelly screamed from behind.

Adrenaline pumped through Bryson's body and his heartbeat quickened as he saw a familiar face waiting on the other side of the gate. Its bars were bent outward, providing a gap for them to cram through. He stuck one leg through, then his shoulder and head. Alas, his carefulness was a waste. Shelly collided with him as he was about to pry himself free, knocking him forward and onto the cobblestone path.

Bryson groaned as he got up from the ground. He heard the ripping of fabric and turned around. Flen had made it, too, but now a portion of his cloak had become trapped between the construed bars.

"I know you're all winded," said the person who had waited for them on the other side, "but we should put some more distance between us and the palace grounds."

Bryson gazed at the Power Diatia. She dropped her hood, exposing her tightly woven braids and dark skin. Her hair was different from the last time he'd seen it—thick, traveling diagonally across the top of her head. He managed an exhausted smile. "Good to see you, Vuilni."

* * *

The sun was starting to rise when Bryson, Shelly, Flen, and Vuilni reached the Intel Kingdom's teleplatforms. They stepped onto the Adren platform and waited for a few other travelers to board with them. Once everyone grabbed hold of a support beam, it began to rotate, gradually reaching its maximum speed.

Bryson clamped his hand over his mouth as he tried to overcome the urge to vomit. He didn't know if it was the sleep deprivation from the restless night before or the physical exhaustion from escaping the palace, leaving the city, and reaching the teleplatforms all in the span of roughly two hours. None of it mattered, however, as they needed to get as far away from Dunami as possible. By now King Vitio was probably awake and had already found Shelly's note stating she'd be gone for a fortnight. It was only a matter of time before he'd contact Flen through Vistas.

Thirty minutes into their journey through the Adren Kingdom, Flen said, "Vistas is requesting a broadcast on King Vitio's behalf."

They scurried into position. Vuilni stood out of the picture behind Flen while Shelly and Bryson stood next to each other. Flen's right eye turned burgundy and his left eye dilated, emitting a holographic display.

"Shelly, where are you?" Vitio snapped.

"Safe with my friends," she replied, sending Vitio's livid glare toward Bryson.

"Get back here right now."

"Or what?"

"Or I'll throw Flen in the cellars," he said. Both Bryson and Shelly knew that to be a bluff.

Shelly forced a pout and asked, "But what about Bryson, Father?"

The king froze. He stammered a bit before his face softened.

"We're fine," Bryson assured him. "Our destination, Yinyon, isn't even remotely dangerous. And if—in some far-fetched scenario—we do land into trouble, we can hold our own. You know that. We also have our Branian as a last resort."

There was a pause during which the king scratched at the scruff of his graying beard. "You have two weeks," he said. "Otherwise I send Lars after both of you. I also expect daily updates through broadcast. The day I receive no word is the last day of my patience."

The display cut off. Bryson, Shelly, and Vuilni exchanged flabbergasted looks. Even Flen wore an impressed frown. "I kind of saw this unfolding differently—hoped for it, in fact. I had my fill of obscure towns when I was in Rim. There's a certain lavishness I expect in my lifestyle."

"Too bad!" Shelly yelled as they marched into some woods. "We've got exploring to do!"

Bryson laughed, but it was fleeting as he thought about their destination. He was finally going to see Debo's true grave.

7
The Chasm

Agnos and Tashami stood at the crest of a hilled street overlooking the Chasm. Cramped and covered in a thick layer of grime, this collection of city blocks was swimming in the shadows of its surrounding hills and buildings. For Agnos to descend down the street and into its depths, he'd need a push. And that's exactly what Tashami gave him.

"Come on," Tashami said as he grabbed Agnos's wrist and yanked him forward.

It was the first place in all of Sodai where the stone pavement had been replaced by dirt. There was an overwhelming stench of tobacco and liquor. The buildings were no longer vibrant and colorful, but a muddied brown. A few of them were boarded up, as if they'd gone out of business. Agnos didn't care to enter any of them to find out.

Establishments thrived with suggestive titles that hung above their doors: PURPLE PEACOCK, BREEZY BRANDIES, and DREAMMAKERS. Others were a little more straightforward and crass.

And they didn't seem to mind if their women and men solicited in the streets.

Agnos turned away, trying to focus elsewhere. "Shame on Queen Apsa for supporting an environment such as this."

A child no older than twelve sprinted past. Agnos's eyes followed him until he ran into a boisterous pub. "Where are his parents?" he asked.

"I'm guessing that any child in a place like this is parentless," Tashami said. "It's likely that this is all they know. Don't expect much in regards to morality down here, Agnos."

The Archain shook his head and marched forward. He had grown up as an orphan, hating every bit of it, but after taking a look at this he realized he had nothing to complain about.

"So what locations are we keying in on?" Agnos asked, wanting to make this visit as short as possible.

"The gambling hall," Tashami replied. "Apparently the quartermasters like to blow a lot of their money at card tables."

Agnos leaned to the left as he crossed paths with a muscular man, his hairy chest exposed behind an unbuttoned tunic. The stranger took notice and turned around with a hearty laugh. "Let's go at it, kid," he said.

Tashami grabbed Agnos and pressed forward. "I know it's difficult, but try not to show fear. It'll only entice them."

Agnos was reminded of his orphanage and the boys and girls who'd pick fights and tease him, feeding on the fear of a weaker child. He had accepted it when he was very young—four or five—because he had somehow construed it in his mind as them taking out their anger toward their teachers' lashings on them. If it made them feel better, he'd happily be their punching bag.

But when Toono had arrived at the orphanage that glorious morning, it all came to a stop. This was not because he'd cracked a skull a time or two—which he only deemed necessary in the most dire of situations—but because he was revered. There was a quality of tranquility about his aura and an intelligence in the way he spoke that caused the other kids in his age group to flock around him. Even children a few years older than him treated him with respect. And Toono even took Agnos, a good four years younger than himself, under his wing.

Tashami led the way into a building. Agnos's memories had made him forget where he was. Maybe that would be the trick to surviving this place … distracting his mind.

He stepped into a modest lobby. Conversation buzzed throughout, being interrupted every so often by an obnoxious laugh. While a man and a woman operated a bar in the back, the two Jestivan realized there were no dining tables to sit at. Instead there were card and dice tables, each one sized to fit the game it was designed for.

Tashami leaned close and mumbled, "I'll snoop around the bar, fish for information."

Agnos strolled between the masses of crowds around the tables. Most of them were spectators with mugs of alcohol in their hands. The participants sat on stools at the dealer's table. When someone would win a hand, their posse behind them would burst into cheers, splashing the contents of their mugs on everything around them—including other people. Nobody seemed to mind.

Agnos looked for anyone who appeared distinguishable. He knew a quartermaster wouldn't dress as such while in the Chasm, but maybe he or she'd have some other telling detail. Perhaps an exposed crew tattoo or a sword? Both were unlikely, however. The surest bet would be to find whichever player was risking the most money.

But that, too, was frustrating. There were awfully low bets being played. After spectating for nearly an hour, Agnos finally decided to call it quits when he saw a woman place her bra on the table as fortune. Admittedly, this caused her opponents' eyes to light up more than any coin ever did.

Agnos approached the bar. Tashami lowered his voice. "Apparently there are two other floors—each one a different tier of play. We're not going to find our quartermaster down here. He'd be playing for higher stakes."

Agnos studied the lobby. "That'd explain why the rules are so lax. Look at them hoard around the table … Cheating everywhere."

"True."

"How do we get upstairs?"

Tashami gave a hesitant glance toward a staircase hidden behind a wall. "That's the problem. You have to prove you have the money to make it to the second floor."

"I have plenty of that," Agnos said. "From the looks of this area, they'd consider me a king. We'll go back to your grandma's house, retrieve it, and then head back this way tomorrow."

"And if our quartermaster is on the *third* floor?" Tashami asked.

"We'll face that hurdle when the time comes if we have to."

They were about to call it a day when a woman seated at the bar said, "Quartermaster, you say?"

Agnos looked over at the lady. She was built as stout as a bull, but her long silver hair and scars on her face put her in her fifties at least.

"Do you know of one?" Tashami asked.

"I knew of many," she said, peering down into her mug. "And on occasion, I see a few walk up those stairs." She paused and added, "Retired captain."

They took a seat on both sides of her. She smirked. "I hope this isn't some kind of ambush."

"Have you seen any the past few days?" Tashami asked. Agnos, not fond of mingling with the brutes who called the Chasm home, let him do the talking.

"A couple. An old friend and an old rival. But they'd be on the third floor, and money alone won't get you there; you need references and a name."

"We're Jestivan," Tashami said.

Agnos glared at Tashami as the woman's eyes skated toward him. Agnos didn't want any more reasons for someone to pick a fight with them.

"I may have only heard of one Jestivan in my life," she said with a hint of intrigue in her voice. "And not because of the fact that he was a Jestivan, rather his title as *Fifth of Five*. But that's only because I've spent most of my life in DaiSo or at sea, where we don't bother with foreign news if it doesn't affect the seas and rivers. But I do know that such a title holds weight on this side of the gulf."

"So we can get to the third floor?" Tashami asked.

"While it's a start, it's not enough. You have the title, but are missing the references of names that matter."

"How do we know who matters?" Agnos asked, forgetting his own rule.

"You speak?" she asked, turning in her chair. Agnos felt embarrassed. "Here I was thinking you were a mute like the Passion King."

"I usually do the talking."

She cut into her burned meatloaf and asked, "May I ask why you're looking for a quartermaster?"

"It's complicated, but ultimately we seek someone who holds an ancient known as Cheiraskinia. A quartermaster is the first step to the process."

She instantly froze, hunched over her plate with her fork halfway in her mouth. After a few seconds, she sat back up and began chewing. "Interesting."

"You know the name?"

"I *am* a retired captain, after all. In fact, the person who wields that ancient is a fellow captain." She paused and seemed to give it some thought. "More than that. She's developed some sort of reputation over the decades. She captains the biggest ship with the largest crew, and her defenses are impenetrable. They call her Gray Whale."

It went quiet. Agnos and Tashami were likely thinking the same thing: that this mission was becoming more impossible by the second.

"Ah, don't look so glum," she said, spotting the doubt that had swept over them. "While I may not be able to help you cross the gulf and gain access to DaiSo, I still think I can be of use in a smaller way. I suppose you could return here tomorrow night?"

"Definitely," Tashami said, an air of faith returning to his tone. He looked around the lobby and asked, "Why do you hang around here if you're a retired captain? Don't you have money?"

"It reminds me of DaiSo and my life on the Realm Rivers. Being around these idiots makes me remember my crew. Besides, I don't need a mansion filled with fancy rubbish. All I need is my sailboat for an occasional taste of the open waters' salt-laced air."

Tashami nodded as he stood tall and shook her hand. "What's your name?"

"Silvia. And yours?"

"Tashami, and my quiet friend is—"

"No bother," she interrupted. "He'll tell me when he's ready."

Offended, Agnos said, "The name's—"

"Nope," she cut in once again. "You're not ready. Run along."

Tashami grabbed Agnos and pulled him away. Agnos didn't like her arrogance—or at least what his bitter mind had perceived as arrogance.

The woman yelled to them as they left the bar: "You don't have to bring the scrawny one back!"

* * *

The following day they returned, but with the sun's shadow replaced by that of the moon. It only made the Chasm darker, as torches struggled to illuminate the dirt streets. Agnos accompanied Tashami—despite Silvia's suggestion from the day prior. He'd prove himself tonight.

The Chasm was busier with the nightlife having kicked in. Agnos stayed aware of his surroundings, dodging potential collisions with passersby and gestures from pleasure-house employees. He kept his demeanor relaxed, strolling with his hands in his pockets and shoulders slacked. He had a knife in his pocket, but in reality what was he going to do with it?

He almost made it to the gambling hall without an incident until he bumped into someone. He honestly didn't know how it had happened and he had suspicion that it was deliberate. But the luxury of processing the situation wasn't afforded to him, as the man grabbed the collar of his shirt and slung him into a wall.

He yelled as a bone near his shoulder snapped. He slumped down on the ground with a hand over his collarbone. He grunted as he squirmed, pushing his forehead through the dirt. It felt like someone was sawing at the base of his neck. He heard glass shatter directly above him, followed by a shower of liquid and bits of glass that pierced his skin. The mess reeked of alcohol.

There was a roar from onlookers as Agnos pushed himself into a seated position against the building. He grimaced, watching as citizens backed away to form a crowd around a fight between Tashami and Agnos's attacker.

The man bull-rushed Tashami, but Tashami side-stepped, grabbed the back of the man's head, and yanked it down into his knee. He then raised his bent elbow into the air and swung it down upon the back of the man's neck, sending him into the ground with a nasty thud.

The onlookers had gone silent, and their mouths hung open in disbelief. Tashami stepped over the man's body to approach his fellow Jestivan. Agnos tried not to whimper, but it only made his eyes tear up.

"Dammit!" he shouted in agony.

"We need to get you out of here and find a doctor," Tashami said.

"No," Agnos replied, but then he saw the man rising from the ground behind Tashami. "He's getting up!"

Tashami turned just as a blade slipped from the man's sleeve and into his hand. His nose was bloody and crooked; a gash ran across his forehead. He flicked his wrist, sending the blade toward them at a speed Agnos couldn't visually track. But Tashami slapped the projectile out of its intended path with a casual wave of his hand. Instead it struck the hard ground.

Their assailant looked stunned, eyes bulging and lips pressed shut, while the crowd whispered around them. For Agnos, Tashami's skills as a fighter had often times been overlooked because of the amount of talent seen in the Jestivan. But in a normal setting in the real world, he was a masterful combatant. None of these people would witness such a display of weaving abilities ever again.

The man pressed forward, but Tashami was prepared. He flicked a finger, creating a bullet of wind, knocking the man's leg backward and snatching his balance away. He was falling sideways when Tashami flicked another finger, this time piercing his shoulder. Blood sprayed from his back and coated the faces of a few people standing in the crowd.

The man fell onto all fours, cursing as he grabbed his shoulder. Tashami stood still without averting his eyes from his opponent. He wouldn't make the same mistake twice.

"Are you finished?" Tashami asked, keeping his distance.

"Dammit, kid," the man grunted. "Just take this and don't open it." He reached into his shirt and then extended his arm toward Tashami, holding an envelope in his hand.

A gust of wind lifted the envelope and carried it to Tashami, who snatched it out of the air.

"Should have known what I was getting myself into if she deemed you worthy of her reference," the man said.

"What's it say?" Agnos muttered as the crowd dispersed.

Tashami flipped it over. "It's blank." He then looked at the stranger again. "Is this from Silvia?"

"It's a reference. Who it's from doesn't matter." He released a miserable growl as he pushed himself to a stand, still reaching for his shoulder. "Use it to get to the third floor. But if it appears opened, they won't accept it."

Tashami frowned. "Well, now I feel bad for kicking your ass."

"No, you don't," Agnos said.

The man snarled and walked down the street, his clothes dirtied and bloodied. Tashami turned and helped Agnos up. "We need to get you to a doctor."

"After we finish our business here."

Tashami chuckled as they pushed toward the gambling hall. "Told you you're tough as nails."

Getting through the first entry point was easy. Tashami reached into Agnos's robes and grabbed a bag of coin, which he then flashed to the bouncers at the bottom of the stairs. It felt like they had left the Chasm when they reached the second floor. Instead of weathered wood, there was a hardwood floor and polished gambling tables. The mobs turned into a few spectators who stood several steps behind the players. There was another bar at the back end, worked by two men. This one was fancier than below. Barrels of cheap ale were replaced by bottles of rum and mead, and there were cabinets to store product.

Tashami and Agnos had to walk across the room's expanse to get to the other staircase. The second floor was easier to navigate without the rowdy crowds heard below. A man with a curled mustache leaned against the rail. His scrawny frame and look of disinterest seemed unbefitting of a bouncer.

He eyed the two Jestivan with suspicion as they approached. He folded his arms, but didn't bother trying to step in front of the stairway. "A couple new faces," he said.

Tashami handed him the envelope without a word. If Agnos wasn't on the verge of fainting, he'd be impressed by his friend's composure. The man withdrew a pair of spectacles from the chest pocket of his vest and ripped open the envelope. He unfolded the inside parchment, his eyes skating left and right.

Agnos saw a waxed seal in the reflection of the bouncer's glasses, but he couldn't make out the design.

The man looked up, his gaze lingering on Agnos's shoulder. "You're good to go," he said.

They hurried past to avoid giving him a chance to change his mind. Agnos looked back down the stairs and saw the bouncer staring up at him from the second floor. A chill ran down his spine. He never realized how safe he had felt at Phesaw around people like Bryson, Yama, Toshik, Jilly, and Rhyparia. It was a luxury he now sorely missed. He was thankful for Tashami. A couple years ago he would have embarked on this mission alone, and now he knew he would have been met with failure and likely his death.

The third story looked like it could have had a spot in Wealth's Crossroads. Lush red carpet lay underneath their feet. And there were four proper dealer's tables felted in green. The only people on this floor were players, dealers, and servers—not a single spectator. There were a few servers hovering close by in case someone ordered a drink.

One of them hustled to the top of the stairs the moment Agnos and Tashami appeared. "Good evening, gentlemen," he said. "My name is Glan. What can I get for you to start off the evening?"

All Agnos wanted was a meeting with a quartermaster and a doctor, so this needed to be a quick visit. "We're fine, Glan," Tashami said with a smile.

"Okay, sir. We only have two dealers tonight, and both tables are presently booked. If you'd like, I can grab you a glass of water or warm loaf of bread."

"That sounds great," Agnos said.

As Glan disappeared through a door, they grabbed a stool at a vacant table. "So which one's a quartermaster?" Tashami mumbled.

They sat at a table behind the two active games, each seating five players. In total, six men and four women, all well into adulthood. And while they were dressed in garb, it was only a façade to blend in with the Chasm's socioeconomic status. The piles of money in front of them attested for that fact.

"Literally impossible to gauge such a distinction by staring at their backs," Agnos whispered.

The waiter returned with some bread and water. Agnos took a glorious bite. "Thank you," he said.

Glan stood there for an uncomfortably long moment. When Agnos finally glanced at him, he said, "The waiting staff appreciates any kind of tips, sir." He held a cup in his hand with a pair of coins at its bottom.

Agnos scanned Glan's attire. He wore a silk vest with a gold chain hanging from its pocket over a white button-up and a pair of black dress pants with white pinstripes. It was more than likely the only time he could dress so lavishly was at work. Tashami dropped a couple of Agnos's bigger coins into Glan's cup.

"Thank you kindly," he said before walking away.

Nobody left over the next thirty minutes, and Agnos was becoming light-headed. He could barely move his left arm and his eyelids had grown heavy. The silence in the room was lulling. The only sensation keeping him awake were the daggers impaling his collarbone.

A waitress made her rounds at one of the tables, placing a drink in front of each player: a couple scotches, a margarita, and a mug of something else. Her tip glass was filled to the rim and all because of the generosity of one player—a brawny, dark-skinned man with dreads that appeared to crawl down his back. His thick arms and broad shoulders were begging to rip free from the confines of his tunic.

Agnos had noticed this a while ago. Nobody tipped the waiting staff … except this man. Some of the other players even pointed it out. "Every time you come here, you give them more money than you place in bets," a woman complained. "Put it to actual use, Barloe. You've given each of them enough to buy a small barn house for goodness sake."

"Spread the wealth," Barloe would respond. "None of you need more money than you already have."

This got Agnos thinking; he whispered to Tashami, "Why do you think the guy with the dreadlocks is the only one handing out money?"

"He's a nice guy?" Tashami guessed.

Agnos stood on the base of his stool and leaned over the table. There were six coin bags hanging from Barloe's waist … and a sword. Agnos had to unclench his fist before he banged it on the table. Tashami also stood to grab a look, but his reaction wasn't quite the same.

"It's only a sword," he said. "Lots of people carry them."

"I wonder what's in his mug," Agnos mused. With his good arm he waved for Glan to come over. The server approached and Agnos motioned for him to lean in. "I want whatever the man with the dreadlocks is having."

"That'd be rum, sir."

"Oh, really?" Agnos said with a hint of skepticism. "Never mind. Not my taste." He turned to Tashami as the waiter left. "Rum and a sword."

"Still doesn't mean anything," Tashami said.

"Well, just *look* at him," Agnos said. "He looks like a pirate. And what about what your grandma said?"

"She said a lot of things."

"The Chasm is where the exchange of profit happens. Now in order for such a transaction to occur in a place as crowded and dangerous as the Chasm, there needs to be a controlled area that's separated from the rest. And it needs to be done in a way that's masked."

Tashami watched as Barloe dropped another handful of coin into a new glass. His eyes narrowed as he whispered, "These tips are actually a system cleverly contrived to serve as transactions between DaiSo and Sodai."

"Spot on," Agnos said. "Barloe is a quartermaster. And this waiting staff is full of middlemen that transfer the money from the crews of DaiSo to the royals of Sodai Castle."

It got quiet as Agnos sat in his thoughts. "My broken collarbone was worth it. We have Silvia to thank, for we would never have gotten up here without her."

Eventually Barloe got up from his stool. He had filled six tip cups and now his coin bags were empty. "Ran me dry," he said.

"You did that to yourself," someone else replied. "Losing a few rounds of blackjack had nothing to do with it."

Barloe chuckled. "I'll see you all next time."

"And when exactly is 'next time?'"

"Ah, whenever the tide sweeps me back."

Agnos shot another look at Tashami.

"Safe travels, friend," another player said.

And with that, Barloe walked past Agnos and Tashami and descended the stairs, his heavy boots clunking against the wood. The Jestivan left their table and went to follow, but someone called to them: "Which one of you fresh meat wants to play first? Take Barloe's spot. Not exactly big shoes to fill." He paused and pondered on that statement. "Not symbolically at least."

"We're good," Tashami said.

They bolted down the steps just in time to see Barloe's dreads disappear beneath the floor across the room. They ran toward the opposite wall and down the steps and then burst through the building's front door.

Once in the street they glanced both ways, dipping and standing on their toes to see which direction he'd gone. Agnos winced as his collarbone continued to betray him.

"I see him!" Tashami said. He began giving chase through the crowd, bumping shoulders and curling his body around lackadaisical pedestrians.

Agnos struggled to keep pace. Luckily Tashami's pure white hair was easy to keep track of in the crowd. He saw Tashami turn into one of the buildings with boarded-up windows. Agnos sighed, having had his fill of abandoned houses back in the Void.

He followed a soft glow in the back of the house, leading him to a room devoid of furniture but cluttered with junk. He froze as he saw Barloe's sword pointed underneath Tashami's chin. Barloe looked at Agnos. "Why are you following me?" he asked.

"We're seeking a quartermaster," Agnos replied.

Barloe's eyes narrowed, his sword held steady. "You were on the third floor. Who are you?"

"We're Jestivan."

"And what's a Jestivan?"

Agnos didn't know how to respond to that. Had this man never actually heard of the Jestivan? "Listen," Agnos said, wincing. "I'm in pain, so I need to get out of here and find a doctor. But my friend and I met a lady named Silvia yesterday. She got us onto the third floor in efforts to help us find a quartermaster."

Barloe dropped his arm to his side, the tip of his sword hitting the dirt. "Silvia, you say?" He chuckled unexpectedly and mumbled, "What is she doing over here?"

Barloe turned away and ignited a flame on a few wicks with a simple wave … a Passion Kingdom native. "More important," he said "why did she send you to the third floor?" He looked back at Tashami and Agnos with an eyebrow cocked. "Again, what's a Jestivan?"

"We're considered the elite students of Phesaw," Tashami explained. "Or that's how others view it."

"So you're glorified children?"

"If you call nineteen and twenty-year-olds children …" Tashami said.

"I do."

"Have you ever heard of Mendac LeAnce?" the snowy-haired Jestivan asked.

"Of course. The supposed legend of our time."

"He was a Jestivan before he became hailed as the *Fifth of Five*."

Agnos groaned and looked down the hall, back toward the opening where a front door should have been. Anxiousness joined his discomfort as he heard creaking over the crowd outside. This was a creepy building with an aging foundation.

Barloe sat down on the floor, his back against the wall. "So what is it that you want from me?"

"We seek passage into DaiSo."

The quartermaster's gaze held steady on Tashami. "You're serious? What for?"

"To find Gray Whale and her ancient."

A thunderous chortle boomed throughout the entire floor. "Did you tell Silvia that?" he asked after regaining his composure.

Agnos saw a shadow in his peripherals. He yanked his head to the left, watching the crowd march past the door in the street. Was his mind playing tricks on him?

"Silvia knows."

"Interesting." Barloe trailed off and studied Tashami. "And what is it that you have to offer a crew of pirates? Meeting such a woman requires sailing. Do you have any expertise or skills?"

Tashami went quiet. Neither of them was sure how to answer that. They hadn't planned on leaving land.

Barloe shook his head. "Well, that answers—"

"Wait," Agnos said. He reached into his pocket and pulled out his glasses. "My relic allows me to decipher any language, written or spoken."

The pirate extended his bottom lip in consideration. "That's quite something, but we rarely sail into Dark Realm waters due to the hassle of whirlpools. And that's the only place we'd need such a tool since ninety percent of this world speaks Sphairian."

At this point, Agnos wanted to walk out. He and Tashami could come back tomorrow. Finding someone to treat his injury was more pressing.

There was shouting in the streets. Agnos looked back toward the door and saw another brawl happening amongst a group of men. "A bunch of animals in this place," he muttered.

Tashami walked into the hall. "Perfect," he said. He then glanced at Barloe. "Let me show you my worth to a crew."

Barloe approached the hall and followed the direction of their gaze outside. Since they were at a strange angle in the back of the building, the doorway was more of a narrow space cut into the wall near a stairwell banister and coat rack.

Tashami lifted his hand, palm out and fingers extended. He then flicked a finger toward his palm, one after the other in rapid succession, pinky to the thumb. High-pitched whistles pierced Agnos's eardrums and suddenly the ruckus outside ceased as five bodies hit the ground.

"Don't worry," Tashami said. "I avoided anything vital."

Barloe's eyes had widened, the whites contrasting heavily against his skin. The spectators outside had no clue what had just happened.

"I can be an unconventional archer," Tashami suggested, "except I don't need equipment."

"No," Barloe said. "You're not just some archer … you're a marksman."

8
Elyol

Two ladies strolled out of a hedge garden and down a gentle grassy slope. Several guards cloaked in red were posted near the maze, but far enough away to allow the women their privacy. One was Passion Director Venustas, a woman with dirty-blonde hair tucked into the back of her robes, a presence typically seen on Phesaw's campus. The other, Queen Fiona, was a brunette, her hair tied in an extravagant bun, complete with braids.

"To think we've made something of ourselves, Fiona," Venustas said.

"I'm nothing more than a woman who married a royal head," Fiona replied. "You're an Energy Director at Phesaw."

"You could have been a doctor if you wanted, but that's not the path you chose … which is fine."

Venustas observed the Great Flame in the distance, perched hundreds of feet in the air atop a stone pillar in the center of Jarfait Meadow. It appeared to be fighting the sun for ownership of the sky.

The queen said weakly, "My medical knowledge won't mean much if Damian is dead."

They reached a fountain surrounded by a patch of flowers and a few benches. Venustas sat down with her friend. "You'll need to tell the other royal heads about his disappearance," she said. "It has been far too long."

"General Landon disapproves of such an idea," the queen said. "He doesn't want our vulnerability brought to light."

Venustas watched the water splash down the sides of the centerpiece. "The more you try to hide information from them, the worse it gets. Landon didn't participate in the mission to retrieve Rhyparia as he was supposed to. And with Marcus gone, you have no communication with the other kingdoms to even try to lie about Fiamma's condition. You've left the royal heads in the dark. I wouldn't be surprised if there are foreign spies in the capital right now. You need to come clean." She sighed and added, "If we tell them now, maybe they can send scouts to help find our king. With the Light Kingdoms withdrawing most of their troops from the Archaic Kingdom, they'll have the resources to aid us."

Fiona looked at the ground with sad eyes. "I don't know, Felli. General Landon is better suited for this. I just want my husband, and I believe Landon will do whatever it takes to find him."

"You're the queen!" Venustas snapped. "When the royal head is unaccounted for and his or her children too young, the next position of power is his or her partner—not the general … Look at me," she said, grabbing Fiona's chin. "Prove to everyone that you are more than just a man's wife."

Fiona stared into Venustas's eyes for a few moments. Finally she said, "I will send General Landon to Dunami, where he'll meet with King Vitio and set up a conference with the other royal heads."

Venustas nodded. "You *are* more than just a wife."

* * *

King Vitio walked through a sunlit corridor with General Lars at his side. They had been discussing the absence of both royal daughters, Lilu and Shelly, when Vistas stepped from a hallway ahead of them.

"Passion General Landon has just arrived, milord. He's in the throne room."

Vitio and Lars exchanged looks before breaking into a jog. The last time anyone had heard from the Passion Kingdom was November of last year. It was now July.

They entered the throne room through a rear entrance. General Landon stood at the center of the vast room. In addition to the general stood a wall of Intel soldiers stretching from the main doors to the steps that led to the throne. Vitio waved them away toward the far wall as he took a seat. Landon's eyes landed on Lars.

Vitio leaned forward. "Well, where do we begin, General Landon?"

"How about with the betrayal of my king when you nearly drove his Dev servant blind?"

Lars clenched his jaw, but Vitio nodded calmly. "Is that the cause of the Passion Kingdom's silence? While I may understand it, a complete halt in communication seems reckless and extreme."

The Passion General's gaze shifted to the yellow carpet beneath his feet. "King Damian is missing."

"What?!" Vitio exclaimed. He shot forward in his throne.

"He's been missing ever since he was supposed to return from Phelos, after the truth extraction."

"You kept this silent for seven months? He could be dead by now; we have no way of knowing!"

Landon became equally as enraged. "And what does that matter to you?"

"You'd be wise to bite your tongue," warned Lars.

"Oh, shut it!" Landon spat. "You put on a general's outfit and now you can stand toe-to-toe with me?"

"Damian has been a great ally and friend of mine for decades," Vitio said, temporarily ending their quarrel. "I would have done anything to help you find him! I know I overstepped my boundaries in Phelos. I took advantage of his trust in me because I saw no ulterior option to obtain the information I needed. But that doesn't mean I wish him harm."

Although still seething, Landon didn't respond.

"Listen to me, General Landon," the king said. "Return to Fiamma and tell Queen Fiona I'm speeding up the process of withdrawing my forces from the Archaic Kingdom. She can expect several hundred men and women arriving at the Passion Kingdom's teleplatforms within two weeks."

Landon nodded. "Understood."

"And I'll inform the other royal heads of the news, so expect search parties from your other allies as well." Vitio gave him a rigid stare and said, "Whoever is guilty had better hope we find Damian with a pulse. Otherwise a wrath unlike anything Kuki Sphaira has ever seen will be unleashed."

* * *

Chiefs Toth and Wert traveled by horse out of the city of Phelos. They had covered enough distance to reach the lake closest to the capital. "This had better be worth it," Toth huffed. "I'm not fond of baking in this kingdom's summer heat."

Wert laughed. "Doesn't even affect me anymore."

"That's because you're beet red and your skin is scabbed to the point of no sensation."

"Touché," Wert replied. "I wanted to show you the man responsible for Senex's capture."

"Why, so we can give him a medal?" Toth asked.

"He's more than just that. He's the reason why the soldiers have started listening to me."

Toth slapped a wet rag against his face, not bothering to point out the fact that Wert should have gained that respect on his own. "Is it just me, or is it getting hotter?"

"It's not just you," Wert said. "Look."

Toth removed the rag and was met with a strange sight. A sea of bubbling magma stretched for miles below the plateau they currently occupied. "What in the world?"

"You see that hut in the distance?" Wert asked.

"Yes."

"He's spent most of his time there since Rhyparia's escape."

"Why?"

"He's improving his endurance by consistently weaving miles upon miles of lava. Basically testing how much volume he can manage at once."

Toth's eyes rolled over the red and orange blanket until some of it spilled into a lake. "He did all of this today?"

"Of course not," Wert said. "Ancients and Archaic Energy don't work like the other energies. For someone like me, my wind disappears the moment I stop weaving, whereas the evidence of an Archain's ability only disappears if he chooses for it to. They can stop weaving, but their ability will stay a reality. And that's because the ability is more a product of the ancient than it is the user's energy."

Toth took a moment to appreciate the rare circumstance that was Wert teaching him something new. "It appears that all the time you've spent with the Archaic soldiers wasn't put to waste."

"I know I'm ill-tempered and not the brightest of minds, but that doesn't mean I'm completely useless. Queen Chara made me Spirit Major all those years ago for a reason."

"What's this guy's name?" Toth asked.

"Elyol Brekton, son of former Archaic General Inias."

"And he's definitely on our side?"

"He is. And he will be a huge help to the uprising."

*   *   *

Toono, Yama, and Kadlest occupied an indoor training hall in Cogdan Castle. Along one wall there were windows stretching seven stories high from floor to the ceiling. Kadlest stood on a balcony overlooking the mammoth hall while Toono and Yama were on the floor.

Toono stood casually in a bubble while Yama charged at him, her sword pulled back over her head. She swung downward, hacking at the shield, but was met with a loud clang that echoed violently throughout the hall. The handle reverberated free from her grasp, causing the sword to clatter against the floor.

"You'll never break it," Toono said. "Not even with a speed percentage like yours."

"But I saw Bruut destroy one of your bubbles."

"Not this kind. The one I threw at him was an elastic material. Still requires extraordinary strength to break, and he was the first I witnessed to do it, but it's not impossible. This, however, is a different beast, for it does not bend or fold. The problem with this steel bubble, though, is that I can't attack—or, at least, I shouldn't be able to. I've been working on a way around that."

Yama charged again with a shriek, ending with a grunt upon contact. She backed away, grabbing her wrist. "If you're resorting to such a defensive tactic," she said, "that'd mean your opponent has superior combative skills, correct? They'll just wait for you. Eventually you must leave the confines of your shield."

Toono's gaze turned lazy. Yama only wanted to fight him. He supposed he could give her that.

He let the bubble disappear, and, as expected, Yama pounced on the opportunity. Toono grabbed Orbaculum from his back as Yama burst through the hall. He swung it in front of him, creating a clear tube between them both. She slammed into it shoulder-first as a test of her speed percentage. Her momentum caused the elastic tube to give way, but it didn't break. Toono had to skip back as he saw her face pressed against the material.

Yama had to have realized how risky this move was for her. Did she have that much faith in her speed to blow through his force field? Now that it didn't work, she was in a situation where she had created a human slingshot, and she was the projectile. The stretched bubble finally rebounded, shooting Yama across the hall. In the blink of an eye, a crater formed in the opposite wall where she landed against it with the soles of her feet. She bent her knees and prepared to ricochet herself directly back at Toono.

Toono wisely formed another bubble behind the original just as Yama ran through them, successfully cutting through them with her sword extended. It slowed her down just enough for Toono to strike her stomach with his ancient. She hacked up air and spit as her body nearly crumpled, but he snared her neck with one of the loops of his staff and tossed her into a window, splintering glass in every direction. He immediately slung another bubble toward her. Fumbling with her sword, she raised it in the nick of time to deflect the bubble across the room. Yama heaved as she slid down to the floor.

"Perhaps that was a little much," Kadlest said from above.

"Shut up," Yama said. "I don't need your pity."

Kadlest's face curled into a crafty smirk. "That Jilly girl really softened you up. While Toono has improved leaps and bounds beyond where he once was, you might have stumbled."

"No more," Toono said, conjuring silence at once. He looked between the two women. "You two need to put your misplaced differences aside. I don't expect it to happen overnight, but I'll be damned if I don't see slight improvement as the months go by."

Yama glared at him, her eyebrows forming a menacing arch, as blood trickled down her chin. She pushed herself up and sheathed her sword on her hip before walking away. Toono wondered what she was thinking. Of course she missed Jilly, but did she regret following him out of Phesaw that day? Yama had never been a convoluted person, but clearly that blonde-headed Spirit Jestivan had left a lasting impression on her.

* * *

"Why are you taking me through here?" Toono asked as he and Storshae walked through the living chambers of Cogdan Castle.

"I have come to view us as close partners," Storshae said, "but sometimes I feel like the lesser man in this arrangement."

"You became that after your soldiers killed children at Phesaw," Toono said.

Storshae ignored him and continued: "You've worked hard to bring my father back—granted it's been for your own goals more than mine, but that's neither here nor there. You've killed the Prim Prince, a Cyn Diatia, Still Queen, Passion King, and a Power Diatia. That is an unprecedented list, and you've hit the halfway mark of it. So let me show you the trust I have toward you."

The Dev King pushed open a door. Toono stepped inside and recognized the room as a nursery. He spotted a crib and approached it. A baby girl lay deep in slumber. He looked back at Storshae. "You're a father?"

The king smiled in return, and, for the first time since Toono had known the man, it was genuine—birthed by the unconditional love that only one's own seed could bring. He glanced back at the girl swaddled in silk cloth. "Why show me this?"

"A token of my trust. It risks a lot, exposing such a piece of information to you."

"You're protected by the Untenable that forbids the murder of a royal first-born. If people found out you've had a child, they'd hunt you without fear."

"It's still an Untenable," Storshae said, "but yes, they'd feel safer doing so, knowing I've already passed on the first-born trait."

"And if I killed you right now?" Toono asked.

"If you had wanted to commit such a deed, you would have tried already. Obviously an Untenable hasn't stopped you before; you killed the Prim Prince. You will also need me alive when you try to coerce my father into sharing his knowledge. Something tells me he wouldn't be so inclined if he knew you had killed his son."

"True," Toono muttered. "And who's the mother? You're not married."

"Not important."

Toono shook his head and went silent for a moment.

"I'm working on gathering you a formidable force to add to your numbers," Storshae said. "The longer this goes, the bigger it gets. You'll need reinforcements."

Toono placed his finger underneath the baby's chin. "Thank you."

9
Ataway Kawi

Perhaps Bryson should have joined Shelly, Vuilni, and Flen when they walked up the stairs of the tavern after checking in. It had been a tiresome journey, and they were wise to get some sleep—even if it was still the middle of afternoon.

Yinyon was a rural town that sat as close to the Edge as Bryson had ever seen. It was on the far end of the kingdom, hundreds of leagues away from the capital, with a vast prairie and acres of forest between it and the rest of civilization. Shelly had pointed out the two oak trees atop a small hill in the distance when they arrived. That was where Debo and Suadade's graves were. But Bryson wasn't ready to visit them—at least, not yet.

Instead of going upstairs to rest, he sat by himself at a table in the tavern's bar. He took a single glance around and was pleased by the lack of activity. Better yet, it was completely empty. The only person he'd seen since entering the building was a man in the front lobby who'd nearly gone into shock at the sight of guests.

Bryson retrieved his book about Debo from his bag and plopped it on the table. He flipped through the pages in search of passages that described the town of Yinyon. There was a mention of a humble inn at one point; and seeing that this was the only inn in the entire town, he wanted to gauge the accuracies of the description.

A door was kicked open behind the bar. The sunlight implied that the door led directly outside. A boy appeared who was roughly the same age as Bryson. As he set foot inside the tavern he immediately spun around and stooped to wrestle with "something" trying to follow him in. It soon became a game of reverse tug-of-war. Bryson recognized the noise of the animal the boy was fighting … a goat.

"You're not coming in here, William!" the boy said.

Bryson smirked and looked back at his book. He was in the middle of nowhere. Farm life wasn't something he was familiar with. He thought of Simon, who would have thrived in a town such as this.

"Whacha readin'?"

Bryson was startled. The boy from behind the bar was now standing next to him.

"Just something," Bryson said.

"Name's Kolver," the boy said, leaning over Bryson's shoulder and narrowing his eyes at the open pages. "I'm the barman, waiter, butler …" His voice trailed off. "Is that *The Third of Five*?" he asked.

"Kind of. It's a biography of Ataway Kawi before he became known as the Third of Five."

"Should put that away and never show it again 'round these parts," Kolver warned.

"Why?"

"That's banned reading material in Yinyon. It's filled with lies."

"But this isn't the actual fairy tale. Like I said, it's a biography."

"Don't matter," Kolver said. "I can tell by that page alone that it's messed up."

Finally Bryson turned toward him and asked, "Well, what's the truth, then?"

Kolver sat down at the table across from Byrson. "Can't give you the full version cus I don't got the time for such an epic tale, but I can skim over the key points."

"I have plenty of time," Bryson replied.

"Well, I don't. I got animals to take care of." Kolver leaned back and chewed on some straw. "Besides, it's strange havin' visitors. I never been asked to tell the story, and now that I have, I don't know how I feel 'bout you knowin' it."

"Fine," Bryson said. "Key points, then."

"Well, the first thing you need to know is that there never was a Leo. I know your fairy tales talk 'bout one. Instead there was Leon Suadade. He was brash and young, but a skilled Adrenian, second only to the man and myth himself, Ataway Kawi. Now these two were like flies on honey. They were always together.

"They became the first citizens of Yinyon to head west toward the capital. And they did so in hopes of joinin' the Adren military. They were successful. Yinyon sat without them for years, and one day news of Ataway's promotion to Major made its way to our little town. We cheered and held festivals in their honor—even without their presence. It felt like a win for all of us. But then that fateful day happened.

"Yinyon wakes early. That's the nature of farm life. So even in the early hours of dawn, we're all working in the fields. On a certain morning, two people were seen runnin' through the prairie. As they got closer, people noticed who they were. It was Ataway and Leon. But they were much slower than normal. It was clear they had run all the way from the capital to Yinyon. It's unbelievable that they made it so far.

"Yinyon citizens dropped their farming gear and ran to meet their town's idols, but a mass of silver-cloaked soldiers and horses growing larger in the distance made them stop. Now they knew why Ataway and Leon were runnin'. The two men arrived back in the village and immediately prepared to defend the town. They gathered up any citizens willing to help fight. But in a small village like this, there wasn't much help.

"Long story short: Ataway and Leon ended up killin' over a hundred soldiers by themselves. The rest of the forces retreated back across the prairie. Another year passed in silence, but eventually the army returned again. They were met with the same results, as Ataway and Leon proved victorious.

"But the next year was different. The Adren Queen led the charge. As you know, Ataway would've beaten her too if it wasn't for her Branian … but even the Branian was put to the test, as Ataway pulled tricks out of his bag nobody had known was possible. Ultimately though, he was killed, followed by Leon shortly after."

Bryson eyebrows rose. "That sounds awfully similar to *The Third of Five*."

"On the surface it does, yeah," said Kolver. "But what does your fairy tale say the reasoning for the conflict was?"

"That Ataway Kawi and a man named Leo returned home to Yinyon to protect it from being wiped out by the Adrenian elites, deeming the village too poor and useless to exist. That Yinyon's existence was hurting the kingdom rather than helping it because nobody had the funds to pay taxes. Ataway and Leo nobly defended the poor against the greedy rich."

"That's a cover-up," Kolver said. "Ataway and Leon defended their town because when the queen discovered her major in the act of sexual relations with her corporal—both of whom were men—she had them arrested. Then she sent her army after the town that birthed them, fearing it'd spawn more like them."

Bryson believed it. He had to. He recalled the night when he and Shelly had summoned their Branian. Suadade had never said anything about a romantic interest in Debo, but it was implied. He even disappeared the moment Shelly had asked him if they were in love.

"It's a sad story," said Kolver. "If you ever wanna read it in its entirety, the mayor holds the one copy in existence." He got up and threw a towel over his shoulder. "But it's a long read, and the only way the mayor'll let you read it is if he's around. You'll be lucky to get an hour with the book every week."

Bryson closed his book and stared at the cover. "I don't have that kind of time."

"Well, maybe one day you can come back. Why you out here, anyway?"

A faint smile appeared on Bryson's face, catching even himself by surprise. Memories flooded back. "It's complicated, but I came here to see Ataway's grave."

"I see." The door behind the bar rattled in its frame as the goat on the other side rammed into it. Kolver glanced at it. "Well, I gotta go," he said. "Make sure you hide that book 'fore someone important sees it."

"Thanks for the story."

"No problem." Kolver ran toward the door. "William, you dimwit!" he shouted.

Bryson shoved his book in his bag and left the building. He looked in the direction of the two oak trees atop the hill. It would be a good jog from where he now stood. He followed the smaller of the town's two dirt paths. It took him away from the trade shops and into the acreage of farmlands. He wended between the orchards, pastures, and plantations. He'd pass a vast meadow of grazing cows only to see a wall of corn erupt immediately after. It seemed this land was capable of growing and feeding an abundant variety of vegetation and livestock.

He finally found a way to reach the hill by traversing a small gap between two separate fences. He held his breath as the stench of horse dung funneled into his nostrils. The sun had begun its descent by the time Bryson reached the hill's crest. Thankfully up here all he could smell were the flowers at the bases of headstones across the cemetery.

The oaks were enormous and serene, their leaves the healthiest of greens. Bryson crunched over acorns as he walked beneath their canopies, approaching Suadade's grave first. The dates on his headstone were 930 – 960 K.H. He had only lived to see thirty. Bryson then moved toward the other tree, anticipation flowing through him as he realized the remains of Debo were some forty feet away from him.

His eyes flooded with tears as he gazed at the name engraved in the headstone: *Ataway Debonicus Kawi*. Or as Bryson knew him … *Debo*. How could he have ever questioned this man? Even after Debo's death at the hands of Bewahr Fonos just to save Bryson's life, Bryson still questioned the good in him. Even this past month he had been filled with doubt.

In Debo's first life, when he was Ataway Kawi, he fought not just for his identity and beliefs but also his people. Ultimately he died, but not before he saved his town. Then he was reborn as a Branian of the Light Empire's Bozani before moving up a rank to a Pogu. That's when he was sent to execute Mendac LeAnce, a man who had raped and impregnated the

Still Princess just so he could test a theory. Who knew the amount of death that had been avoided because of Debo's valiancy? He even took five-year-old Bryson in and treated him like a son for twelve years.

Bryson ran his finger underneath his nose and sniffled. He took off his favorite hoodie, walked behind the headstone, and reverently placed it over the stone slab as if he were putting it over Debo's shoulders.

"I was cursed with my father's genes and was destined to be like him," Bryson said to the grave, "but you made sure to steer me down the right path all my life. You were more than just my guardian." He placed his hand on the headstone. "Thank you, Dad."

Bryson left with his eyes trained on the ground, tears rolling down his cheeks. He took only a few strides before he felt a presence ahead of him. He looked up to see Shelly—the peculiarity of her blonde wig as jarring as ever.

"Hey," he said.

She stared at him for a long moment. Bryson almost grew frustrated before she finally said, "You weren't destined to be like Mendac."

"I was. Poicus, Thusia, and Ophala have all pointed it out during the past year."

"It's likely you misinterpreted them," she said. "Yes, you can lose control over your urges at times, but those violent urges stem from something different than Mendac's did."

"It doesn't matter," Bryson rebuked. "They're still violent."

Shelly stepped closer. "You want to hurt the people that hurt your friends … make them feel what your friends felt … No, that's not quite it. You want to make your enemies feel an insufferable amount of pain that is exponentially greater than anything you've felt in your life."

"How is that different from Mendac?"

"It can be fixed; that trait can be turned into a positive," Shelly said. "Mendac was soulless. How Thusia managed to woo something human out of him is beyond me. People were nothing but lab rats to him—a sacrificial means to a scientific end.

"I'm old enough to have remembered your father. He was away from the palace most of the time, but whenever he would return from a mission in one of the Dark Realm's kingdoms, I could always tell there was something sinister in the way he would look at a person of no real value to him. And he never seemed to try to hide it.

"Just as with Debo, the Light Realm's history is full of cover-ups. They want to mask the evil contained within." She sighed and added, "My father won't be happy I'm telling you this, but … you know of Lilu's favorite flower, correct?"

"Chocolate Cosmos," Bryson muttered.

"She claims that Mendac bought a bunch of seeds for her during his stay in the Dev Kingdom, but that's false. No fault of hers, though. My father never told her the truth. The only reason that flower isn't extinct is because of Lilu's garden in Dunami Palace. It used to only be found in the Cosmos Meadows of the Dev Kingdom. The Devish even built a city close by and called it Cosmos.

"In this day and age, the Cosmos Meadows are better known as the Cosmos Ruins. The Light Realm thinks it was a natural disaster that wiped them out, but the reality of it was that Mendac did. He burned all of it to the ground, effectively eliminating hundreds of miles of pure beauty."

Bryson was silent, unable to find the words. Nothing about that revelation made him feel any better.

"I tell you this because I wanted to provide you with another example of what kind of evil Mendac was. Nobody sees that in you … *nobody*. In fact, when I look at you, I see someone who shows more love than anyone I've ever met. But remember that passion can take many forms, some less flattering than others."

Bryson put his head down and attempted to march past her, but she caught him by the arm and pulled him close. Her lips hovered near his ear as she said, "Embrace love's beauty, but tame its monsters too."

10
Weavineering

Ten days after departing from Brench Estates, Toshik and Jilly entered the Watchman Precinct in Fiamma. Toshik approached the front desk. "I'm here to bail out a prisoner by the name of Himitsu Vevlu."

The watchman chuckled. "We were beginning to think nobody was coming to get him."

"What do you expect when you make the bail ten thousand granules?"

"Well, that's what happens when you're a Jestivan. Turns out the title is more than just that. Bugger is a pain in the ass to catch. Not to mention he's been arrested fifteen times in the past month. All that hassle causes the bail to increase."

"Just get me the idiot," Toshik said.

"*Please*," Jilly added.

Toshik rolled his eyes and sat in the waiting area while the watchman fetched Himitsu. Jilly plopped onto his lap.

"Get off," he said. "We're in public."

She wrapped her arms around his neck. "*Never!*"

Someone cleared his throat. Toshik looked up to see the watchman had returned, Himitsu looming behind him. Toshik shot into the air, sending Jilly crashing onto the floor.

"How cute," Himitsu teased.

"He better not cause any more issues," the watchman said. "If we have to bring him back here, he's not leaving."

"I might bring him back myself," Toshik said.

They paid Himitsu's bail and took him into their custody.

As they joined the crowded city street outside, Himitsu asked, "Where should we go first? I know all the liveliest spots."

"We return to my estate," Toshik replied.

"I think we should find an inn for the night," Jilly said. "We've been travelling nonstop."

Toshik stopped immediately. Jilly slammed into him from behind. "Fine," he said. "Lead the way."

Himitsu laughed and then made a sound with his mouth: *Kwa-pshhh*. "Someone's whipped."

Toshik and Jilly trailed Himitsu through the city. Despite Himitsu being sober, there was an unnatural stagger to his stride. How much alcohol had he consumed over the last month? So much that his motor skills were still affected? Toshik realized this might be harder than he had originally thought. Himitsu was far gone.

Someone tugged at his sleeve. He looked down to see Jilly's sad eyes. "What's up?" he asked.

"You're going to fix him, right?"

"I'll do what I can."

* * *

Toshik hovered next to his bed the following morning before heading to Himitsu's room to make sure he was awake and ready for the journey to his estate. He studied Jilly from head to toe, tangled in a mass of blankets that she had wrapped herself in after Toshik got out of bed. Throughout hundreds of dates with women in his life, he had never waked to see this moment. Instead he'd sneak out in the middle of the night or, even better, he'd leave before his date would even pitch the idea of having him sleep over.

Jilly had changed all of that. For the past ten weeks, he went to sleep and woke up next to her. He endured kicks and punches throughout the night—she was a fidgety sleeper—only to wake up with an arm slung over his shoulder, an ankle trapping his legs, and her face pressed against the back of his neck. He had since learned the science of prying himself free from the trap after several instances of trial and error.

Toshik left the room only to find Himitsu lying down in the hall against the wall's baseboard. There was a mug sitting within his loose grip. Toshik picked it up and sniffed inside … Bourbon. He sighed. "Dammit, Himitsu."

Toshik adjusted his friend so that he was now seated listlessly against the wall. He slapped his face a few times, perhaps a little too gently. The Toshik of two years ago would have punched him in the nose for the desired result—or just walked past and ignored him

He thought of something else. "Hey, Bryson!" he shouted.

Himitsu's eyes slowly opened as he slurred, "Bryson? Yo, Bryson." He looked both ways down the hall. "Where is he?"

"Not here. Let's go." Toshik grabbed Himitsu and stood him up. "We've got a long road ahead of us."

Himitsu struck Toshik's forearm away with his palm. "I'm not going anywhere. This is my home." He looked around, absorbing his surroundings. "Or close to it."

Toshik clenched his jaw and balled up his fist. It was taking every ounce of effort to not hit this idiot in the face. "We've gotta get you away from here, man," he said, composing himself. "This place isn't healthy for you. Too many memories."

"Well, you can go," Himitsu mumbled. He then grabbed his head and groaned. "I'm staying."

"So you can get locked up again … for good this time?"

"Like father, like son!" Himitsu said with a drunken chuckle. His eyebrows rose. "Like mother, like son."

Toshik nearly punched the wall next to Himitsu's face but stopped his fist in time, mere inches away.

"Control yourself there, buddy," Himitsu said. He reached down, grabbed his mug, and thrust it into Toshik's chest. "Have a drink."

Toshik stared at the Passion Assassin as he contemplated his next move: abandon Himitsu here, drag him to the estate against his will, or stay in Fiamma with him? He took a deep breath and accepted the mug from Himitsu. He then threw his arm around Himitsu's shoulder and pulled him in, leading him down the hall toward his and Jilly's room.

"Want to hang out with Jilly and me?"

The drunk smirked and threw his arm around Toshik's back. "Of course."

"Good. Get used to our company because we're not leaving."

* * *

Lilu awoke in an environment she still wasn't used to: a twin-sized bed in a small rectangular room, complete with a dresser and a desk. This was the reality of dorm life. The lavishness of Lilac Suites back at Phesaw wasn't typical. Out of thousands, only around thirty students actually housed there.

But now she was starting fresh at a completely different school, the Intelian Weaving Academy—or IWA. Her status as an Intel princess didn't matter, which didn't bother her. Director Jugtah had warned her of this many times before their journey. If she was more like her sister, Shelly, then this arrangement would have been a deal-breaker.

It was mid-July, so the third quarter of IWA's school year began today. Unlike Phesaw, where there were two semesters and the year started in September, IWA began in January and only afforded the luxury of a week-long break between each of its four quarters. Lilu had arrived in Brilliance a couple weeks ago, during which she spent barricaded in a room in a tavern per Jugtah's instructions. It was a miserable period of time, but if she had disregarded his orders, he threatened to send her home. Peculiar that a man with no ties to royalty had such confidence to threaten a princess.

Lilu stepped into a pair of slippers and exited her bedroom, crossing into the main room of her student suite—not that it was much of a suite. It was one large space with two halves. One side was a carpeted study area with a sofa, armchair, and bookcases lined against the wall; the other was a tiled kitchen complete with counter space, a sink, and an ever-ice pantry for the storage of cold foods. The kitchen contained the front door which led to the hallway. Across the width of the room was a door identical to the one Lilu had just stepped through, which led to her roommate's bedroom.

The one aspect she adored about the suite was the sliding glass door in the study area. She approached it and opened the vertical blinds, allowing the dreary morning light to cut through. She slid the door open and stepped onto a narrow limestone balcony.

There was another edifice of limestone just a couple hundred feet across the way. Every building in this city was monstrous. She gazed at the ground some seven floors below. Horse-drawn carriages packed the main road while pedestrians stuck to the sidewalks. A symphony of neighing horses and work-day crowds sang below.

This was what she had come here for—the city life she had heard so much about from Director Jugtah over the past year. She didn't believe it when he had told her there was a city grander and more impressive than Dunami. But he was right. It was remarkable.

She spent a few minutes appreciating the subtle breeze rubbing against her calves until she heard the door behind her slide open. She turned around to see Gracie Jugtah—niece of Director Jugtah—her olive-skinned roommate with hair as black as midnight.

"Let's go," Gracie said with a smile. "You're going to be late for your first day."

"I lost track of time!" Lilu said as she hopped back inside.

"Hurry up. Do you want a turkey or ham sandwich?"

As Lilu shut the door to her room and pulled off her nightgown, she shouted, "Is there quail?"

There was a long pause as Lilu fought to get her leg into her pants. She put on the rest of her clothes, grabbed her bag, and opened her door to leave. She stopped as Gracie stood in front of her with an exasperated expression, her eyebrows flat and her head tilted slightly. There was a paper bag in her hand.

"Here you go," she said.

"That's awesome! You had quail?" Lilu asked as she looked inside.

"No. I scooped up some oatmeal and threw it in the bag."

"Why …"

"Because you asked for quail, and that was stupid. I'm an unemployed student attending IWA. How am I to obtain quail?"

Lilu hesitated. "I'm sorry. I forget."

* * *

Lilu and Gracie arrived at their class to discover they were the last two. "Nice of you ladies to join us," a man said at the front of the room. "Party too hard during your week off?"

It was the pudgy Nyemas Jugtah. "Sorry, Director," Lilu said as she and Gracie grabbed the only two available seats in the back of the class.

"I'm not 'Director' here, Ms. Intel. 'Professor' will suffice."

"I'm sorry."

Jugtah immediately addressed the class. "I see a lot of familiar faces in here from previous courses. For those of you who don't know me, I'm Professor Jugtah. I took a brief hiatus last year to teach at Phesaw, where I strengthened their weaving curriculum by updating their core courses and introducing the study of Permanence."

A hand shot into the air. "Yes?" Jugtah said.

"They don't teach Permanence over there, sir? Isn't Phesaw the Light Realm's biggest, most populated school?"

"They didn't," Jugtah replied. "But you must understand that Phesaw isn't renowned for its academic track record. It's funded by the citizens of all five Light Kingdoms through their taxes. It's a private institution that only runs because of outside contribution—which sounds strange, but it works. Children of families from all social classes can attend it. And yes, it's the mecca of what a younger person would consider campus life. If you want to attend school for the social experience, go to Phesaw."

"It's also good for learning to fight and using your energy for combative purposes," another student said.

"We're off track," Jugtah said. "The point is that I'm back here now. I'm looking forward to teaching a subject offered to only the most masterful weavers with the most potential." He extended his arm toward a young man seated at what looked to be a teacher's desk. "This is Frederick Santio, and he'll serve as a student teacher and my assistant this quarter. Now, with all of that out of the way, let's start this off."

He turned to the chalkboard, began writing three words, and said, "Welcome to Crafting and Kilning."

Lilu already had her quill in hand with its tip to parchment, ready to scribble away. For once in her life she was surrounded by minds that could rival her own while also sharing her passion. She had nothing but respect for Agnos, but what he wanted to do with his knowledge wasn't even in the same spectrum as Lilu … that age-old tale of the Mind War—the Archain pursuit of wisdom versus Intelian thirst for factual knowledge.

"We'll treat today as a refresher of previous courses," Jugtah said as he walked behind his desk and rummaged underneath it. "Pay attention because you won't have this luxury again. If you ask me a stupid question that you should already know after today, I'll ignore it and instruct you to leave."

Lilu gulped. His teaching style was the same here as it was in Phesaw—maybe harsher.

Jugtah heaved a stone block onto his desk. "Someone tell me what this is. Don't bother raising your hands; blurt it out."

"Provod," a few students said.

"Found from where?"

"The provod mines in the Power Kingdom's Malanese Peaks."

"What is the unique trait that separates it from all other natural material such as limestone, granite, basalt, and marble?"

"It deflects energy instead of absorbing it—no matter the clout or concentration used when weaving. It can withstand unimaginable pressure."

"That's right," Jugtah said. "We can carve into it with tools, but no matter how much we try to damage it with our electricity, it not only resists said damage, but it deflects the electricity in another direction. It's a strange phenomenon, and that's what makes it the most sought-after commodity in cities such as Dunami and Prayoga. It's the main reason why the Light Realm is allies with the Power Kingdom. Now what does this trait allow us to *do* with provod?"

"We can use it to store energy," Lilu said.

Jugtah grabbed a blade from his desk. "Exactly. Provod is surprisingly soft." He began carving into the block. "To create a vessel that stores energy, I must first cut a small opening in the surface. That's the "door" or the "latch"—the space for energy to enter or exit when exposed. Then I must use delicate touch and hollow out the inside, careful to not widen the entryway too much. The area of space allowed for the door influences how energy releases from its storage unit.

"Since I don't have the time to properly hollow out this provod ..." Jugtah trailed off and looked at the class. "Which reminds me, what happens if you don't groove the inside of provod correctly and try to weave EC chains into it?"

Gracie responded with an exaggerated "BOOM!" Lilu smirked, recalling the many times she'd experienced such a disaster.

"Yes," Jugtah said. "'Boom' is correct." He gestured for his assistant to approach. The assistant pulled his own provod from his bag and brought it to the desk. "While some of you were out partying last week, Frederick here was slaving over a Permanence vessel for the purpose of this showing." He backed away and motioned for Frederick to step forward. "Show us what you've got."

"Thank you, Professor," Frederick said as he placed his vessel next to Jugtah's slab of provod. "So this is a completed—and *active*—Permanence vessel. This means its hollowed center currently contains EC chains bouncing around inside. It will never disappear unless I open the door. When I do open it, the electricity will spill out of it in a way that reflects the pattern of the grooves inside and how I weaved my EC chains ... so let's see what happens."

Frederick pushed a provisional lever that he had installed on the vessel, opening a door that was carved into the provod. Lilu flinched, expecting the vessel to become volatile and explode in his face. But that was foolish. Obviously Frederick wasn't a novice like her. Instead she became flabbergasted at the beauty that ensued.

Hundreds of intelights soared through the door and into the air. They were soft enough to not blind anyone, but there were enough of them to cast a celestial light throughout the classroom.

"These intelights exist on their own. They've escaped the cramped confinements of the hardened provod and are now able to slow down in open space and hover. Any of us could weave an EC chain, connect it with the cluster that is responsible for the intelight, and then effectively sever the self-feeding loops, causing the light to disappear. Go ahead and do that."

Lilu managed to kill a dozen of them while her classmates took care of the rest. Jugtah stepped forward. "Thank you, Frederick, for an excellent demo." As Frederick returned to his seat, Jugtah addressed the class. "That is what you should expect to learn over the next year in sequential courses. While in Permanence, you learned about provod and the *concept* of storing energy, in this class you'll *apply* that knowledge and construct devices. What Frederick showed you just now is the most novice technique a weavineer will learn. On Thursday you'll finally get to carve into provod and begin sculpting a vessel. Good day."

Students left their seats with wide-eyed expressions—a mixture of excitement and anxiousness. Lilu gathered up her stuff and ran to the front to see Professor Jugtah.

"Hey, Professor."

"What can I do for you, Ms. Intel?" he asked without looking up from inspecting Frederick's vessel.

"I've still yet to learn how to hollow out provod without it blowing up in my face."

"And?"

"Is there a trick you've been holding out on me?"

Frederick stared at her as he stood next to Jugtah.

"Listen, Ms. Intel," Jugtah said. "You already have a head start compared to everyone else. I broke my own rule last year when I took you to the side and skipped ahead. I suppose the promise you showed was refreshing when around all those sluggish minds at Phesaw; but now that I'm back here, no more. You'll learn like everyone else: through normally scheduled classes or any studying you do with classmates outside of class hours."

Lilu frowned, a habit she had developed during her years as a princess whenever she didn't get her way. "So I'm getting the Bryson treatment."

Jugtah laughed. "I suppose, if that's what you want to call it." He stood straight and studied Lilu. "Look, Frederick here is also a great tool. His job is to tutor students outside of class, and he received his weavineering license a few months ago."

"I'd be happy to help," Frederick said.

Lilu glanced at him. He was short—Agnos and Yama short—with skin color a slightly darker shade than Himitsu. His hair was unkempt like Bryson, but a different texture.

"Thanks," Lilu said.

Gracie strolled to Lilu's side. "Hey, Uncle Nyemas."

"Hello, Gracie," Jugtah replied with a rare smile before leaving the room.

"He tries to keep family ties out of the classroom."

Lilu laughed. "Glad to see you get almost the same treatment as I do. I don't get the smile, though. Let's go eat."

The two ladies were about to leave the room when Frederick said, "Let me know when you're ready to jump ahead."

She turned and gave a nod. "Will do."

* * *

Lilu and Gracie explored IWA's third floor later that day. The weavineering floor was restricted to any student who wasn't in a qualifying Weavineering class, which accounted for roughly ninety-nine percent of the school's population.

Most didn't make it this far. The vetting process to get in such classes were rigorous since they were considered the pinnacle of the weaving curriculum, and if just any student was allowed access to the third floor, they'd likely hurt themselves as well as others—probably kill a few people too.

It was divided into three wings—Kilning, Permanence, and Weavineering—and each wing housed several laboratories appropriately designed and equipped for their intended purpose. While Lilu and Gracie were allowed to roam the halls, they weren't allowed entry into the labs until they completed a certain number of weeks in class without being thrown out. So they simply observed the more experienced students and lab assistants through the walls of glass.

Lilu watched the crafting and kilning laboratories in awe. This was what her class would be focusing on first. Weavineering ultimately went through a three-step process—crafting and kilning being the first. Students could be seen carving and molding their provod at work stations. Some were just beginning to shape the outside while others were focused on carving ridges within the hollow center. After they'd finish this process, they'd walk over to a slew of steel machines sitting against the side walls, open the heavy doors, and place their vessel on a grate inside.

Flames would spit and hiss when the door was opened, so students wore safety goggles, aprons, and gloves that reached their elbows. Women had their hair tied back in buns, and there were three assistants stationed next to the kilns.

"It has to be hot in there," Lilu said.

"Hot enough to make the Archaic Desert melt into a puddle," Gracie said. "And all the gear they wear only makes it worse." She paused, then added, "There's at least one incident of heat stroke every quarter."

"Really?"

"Yep."

Lilu noticed that students would strip down and leave the laboratory after placing their vessels into the kiln. "How long does it take to harden?"

"Forty hours. They'll come back in three days to find out how their provod handled the kiln. If they constructed it properly, their unfinished provod vessel will have become a Permanence vessel by the time they return." Gracie turned and laughed at Lilu's face. "Phesaw really must suck."

"I didn't realize until now."

"Just think of how far you'd be if you spent your entire educational life here."

Lilu's face plopped against the glass, and she breathed a blotch of fog onto it. "My father didn't want me to receive my education from IWA."

"Why not? You'd figure the king would want his daughter to experience the best of the very best."

"He didn't want me swallowed by Mendac's shadow."

Gracie forced a laugh. "I'd say that Bryson kid is the only one who has to struggle with that." She continued, ignoring Lilu's glance. "After what he revealed during that broadcast … man, imagine finding out your dad did such a thing … or his sister. What's her name?"

"Olivia," Lilu mumbled.

"And the Still Queen." Gracie paused for a moment in thought. "I never thought I'd find myself feeling sorry for someone from the Dark Realm."

"Yet this city carries on like that broadcast never happened. Like what Mendac did *never happened*," Lilu hissed.

"I feel your pain. The price we pay for living in a man's world … especially in this city."

"Don't ever say that to me," Lilu balked.

Gracie's dark brown eyes fluttered at the princess. "Don't' fool yourself."

"And I'll rid you of that perception soon enough."

11
Craftmasters

Rhyparia scampered between the willows, her heart pounding as she foolishly glanced behind her and tripped. She stumbled forward until her shoulder hit a sturdy root.

"Dammit!" she screamed, grabbing her nose and fighting her way out of the mess.

"I'm coming for you, little girl!" a grating voice rumbled from behind, immediately followed by laughter that sounded like wheels over gravel.

She got to her feet and hopped from root to root. The metallic taste of blood seeped through her lips as she looked for somewhere—anywhere—to hide. The obvious option was to enter the cascading branches of the hundreds of willows that surrounded this area of Epinio, but she had been warned before to never do such a thing. The dimiours didn't take kindly to such intrusions.

Instead, she dipped into a cove barely big enough to fit two of someone her size. It was formed within snarls of roots. She had to crouch to keep errant pieces of wood from stabbing her back or tangling with her hair. There was a small crevice in the cove's exterior, allowing a glimpse of the trail behind her. She didn't look away from it.

Her pursuer rounded the trail's corner and came into view. His name was Kakos—a wolf that stood on its hind legs just like the rest of the dimiours. He was shirtless, exposing his gray coat of fur. His teeth were sharp and bared—the foulest of grins. As he neared Rhyparia, she covered her mouth to stifle her breaths.

He held his nose in the air, sniffed a few times, and then came the sandpaper laugh again. "Little girl!" he bellowed.

Claws swiped past Rhyparia, tearing apart the roots around her. Quickly she dove to the side, jumped back on her feet and fled. All the while Kakos chuckled behind her. She looked back as she broke free from the willows and ran up a grassy hill. Kakos was no longer on his hind legs; he was tearing through the grass on all fours. If it hadn't been for all the speed training she had done with the Jestivan over the past two years, Kakos would have caught her a long time ago.

Her destination—the guild—sat atop the hill at the base of a cliff-side. Maybe she'd be safe up there. A cheering crowd awaited her at the top. In front of them were the guild's craftmasters: Thereapif, the rabbit; Atarax, the fox; Biaza, the honey badger; and Moros, the weasel.

What was going on?

The fifth craftmaster was Kakos, the wolf, whom she had been running from. He walked toward her as he reached the hill's crest. "That was fun," he said, laughing.

"What just happened?" Rhyparia asked, trying to catch her breath.

"I hunted you."

"For fun?!" she screamed.

"With much success."

Kakos joined his colleagues as the crowd dispersed and continued with their daily activities. Therapif hopped toward Rhyparia and grabbed her hand. "Let's have you lie down so I can treat your wounds."

As the two of them cut through the other craftmasters, Rhyparia asked, "When will someone tell me what I'm doing here?" But, like always, she was met with silence.

She had become more impatient with each passing day. She had arrived here two months ago and all she had done was learn to forage, farm, prepare vegetative meals, and smith weapons and armory.

After Therapif mended her wounds, he left Rhyparia in solitude. She got up and looked out the window toward the partially hidden sun behind the mountains. Maybe one of her fellow Jestivan was doing the same. She had spent her years at Phesaw before joining the Jestivan as an outcast. She had known solitude, but somehow she had never felt more alone than she did right now.

There was a knock on her door. "Come in," she said.

Rhyparia had to look down whenever her guests entered. Standing at around four feet tall, Biaza strolled inside with Moros on her back—a weasel riding a honey badger.

"How are you?" Biaza asked as she climbed onto Rhyparia's bed.

"Angry and confused."

Moros leapt from Biaza's back and pounced on the mattress. His stretched, narrow body jittered as he walked across the sheets. "The dimiours are scared of humans," the weasel said. "It's practically embedded in our souls to fear you."

"Why?"

"A long time ago, before the beginning of the Known History timeline, our kind was nearly wiped out by humans. Luckily we escaped."

"How old are you?" Rhyparia asked.

"Me? I'm eighty-two," Moros said, snickering. "The dimiour species, however, dates back to the undocumented territory of the timeline."

Rhyparia looked at Biaza. "And you?"

"I've lost count of the years. I'd say I'm just shy of three hundred."

"And all of you have lived here your whole lives?"

"Pretty much," Moros said. "A couple of the craftmasters grew up in the mountains as Unboundants, which are dimiours who identify more with their animalistic side than the humanistic. The origin of dimiours is what you now call the Prim Kingdom. But as I said earlier, we had to abandon our homes over a millennium-and-a-half ago as we were being hunted and killed."

"By whom?"

Moros glanced at Biaza for help. "What do they call it now?"

"Musku calls it the Power Kingdom."

Rhyparia's eyes widened because of two revelations in the honey badger's statement. "Musku?" she asked them.

Moros fell onto his back, laughing and clutching at his stomach. "Nice slip up, Biaza!"

The honey badger rolled her eyes. "Oh, well. Better she finds out now, anyway. These tests she's been put through are pointless."

"Was that charade Kakos just pulled another test like the barn?" Rhyparia scoffed.

Biaza hopped down to the floor. Moros scurried across the bed and leapt onto her back. "It was," she said, "to show you the perspective of a hunted animal. Kakos was acting as the hunter."

Moros snickered. "Acting is definitely not the word I'd use. That unboundant enjoyed every bit of it."

Biaza nodded in agreement.

Rhyparia repeated the term with confusion: "Unboundant?"

The honey badger waved off her question. "Nothing."

"I want to get out of here," Rhyparia said. "Why am I being punished for the actions of people who died thousands of years ago?"

"Oh, be quiet and let's go," Biaza said, walking across the room.

"Where to?"

"You're a Jestivan, correct? Let's meet a few of your predecessors."

* * *

Rhyparia followed the craftmasters as they left the guild's square. They stopped next to a towering waterfall after rounding a bend in the cliff-side. She frowned as the waterfall's mist dampened her clothes and frizzed her hair.

"Your ancient piece," Therapif said, handing over her umbrella.

She took it from him and then looked around. She finally craned her neck to look up. "I'm assuming that's where we're headed."

"Don't kill us," Moros said.

For once Kakos appeared uneasy as he growled, "I don't understand why we're not taking the trail like normal."

Rhyparia smirked as an idea came to mind—payback for Kakos's charade as a hunter. She opened her umbrella and twirled it. Their faces twisted in shock as their feet lifted from the ground. Even Atarax, the dry-faced fox, raised an eyebrow.

"A flying weasel! Who would've guessed it?" Moros exclaimed, twisting his slender frame and swimming through the sky as they soared higher.

The most satisfying reaction for Rhyparia came from Kakos, who was digging his claws into the side of the precipice as his feet were pulled toward the sky.

"Grow a pair, Kakos," Biaza said, teasing.

"Wolves aren't made to fly!"

"Neither is a honey badger—or a fox, for that matter."

Rhyparia sneered at Kakos. "I suppose if wolves aren't made to fly, then …"

Suddenly a portion of the cliff-side crumbled as Kakos's claws were ripped from their handle. He yelped and plummeted toward the ground like a rock, his claws fumbling with the wall.

Moros snickered. "Evil."

Just before Kakos smacked the ground, Rhyparia stopped his descent inches above the grass so he could count the individual blades. But she wasn't done. They briefly heard a cry of help as Kakos's body flew and rocketed past them before disappearing atop the plateau.

Atarax grinned while the rest of them burst into fits of laughter that only intensified when they reached the top of the cliff, where the wolf was growling on all fours. He was ready to pounce, his nose and butt low to the ground.

After Kakos relaxed, Rhyparia observed her surroundings. There wasn't much to look at, for the ground seemed to abruptly end a few thousand feet in the distance. She followed the craftmasters toward a log cabin complete with a chimney. Therapif knocked.

A latch in the door opened, exposing beady eyes. Their gaze narrowed as they looked around. "Is everything okay?" the voice belonging to the eyes asked.

"Yes," Therapif replied. "I know it's strange to see all of the craftmasters away from the guild at once, but we figured it was time you met the stranger we told you about who arrived from the mountains a few months ago."

"And that requires all five of you?"

"We believed you'd find a special interest in this particular guest. It's the girl Ophala rescued from the execution and sent to us."

The latch closed and the door swung open. Rhyparia grimaced as the stranger's face became visible. She should have been comforted by the fact that he wasn't another dimiour, but a human. Instead she was taken aback by the dozens of scars on his face that crisscrossed every which way, making his skin look like a patchwork quilt.

"You're a Jestivan?" the man asked, stepping closer to her.

She backed away. "I was."

"You still are. It's not a title you simply lose."

"I'd say I lost it."

"I never did," he said.

Her eyes narrowed. She stopped leaning back as realization dawned upon her. "Saikatto …"

He grinned. "In the flesh." He stepped to the side and motioned everyone in. "Let's talk."

Rhyparia entered a beautiful main room with a vaulted ceiling and an overlook on the floor above. Sunlight bounded off the log walls, splashing the bookshelves and rocking chairs in a burned orange. An immense rostrum sat near a window, a sheet of parchment covering its surface.

"Care for tea or water?" Saikatto asked.

"Tea sounds nice," Rhyparia said, walking around the room and reading the spines of books.

"Musku's in his study, so we won't disturb him now," Saikatto said, pouring hot tea from a kettle. "As for Rayne, she could be anywhere."

Rhyparia continued to run her fingers across the spines. "How old are these books?"

"I don't know, but some aren't readable anymore because the pages have eroded into nothing. Then there are a few written in a language not even Musku knows how to decipher."

Her mind jumped to Agnos and his glasses. He would have locked himself in this place for months until every book was read and every language deciphered. It was likely there were some hidden gems in here.

"She passed your tests," Moros said as he climbed onto the breakfast table. "Didn't harm a fly in the barn and didn't try to hide in the willows when Kakos hunted her."

Saikatto's expression became stern, his eyes hardening upon the wolf seated in the rocking chair. His gaze stayed glued on Kakos as he handed Rhyparia her tea. "And why did you have her tested?"

Moros stuck out his tongue at the wolf. "Told you."

Kakos ignored the weasel and snapped at Saikatto, "Because we test every human that passes through those mountains that way. You, Musku, and Rayne were the ones who came up with the tests in the first place! Why change it for the sake of this girl?"

"Because it's not necessary," he replied. "Ophala told us all we need to know about her. She's been used and abused her entire life, and we're not going to continue that."

Rhyparia uncomfortably took a sip of tea while the craftmaster and Jestivan argued—as if she weren't even in the room with them—over something she didn't care about anymore.

"How about we grab Musku and Rayne so we can get down to business?" Atarax said in a deep, soothing voice. "Rhyparia's been left in the dark for too long."

Shocked from hearing his voice, Rhyparia swallowed her tea down the wrong pipe. She sputtered and coughed.

"You okay?" Thereapif asked, hopping over to pat her back.

"Was caught off-guard by the fox saying something."

"He's a dimiour of few words," Biaza said.

Saikatto nodded at Atarax, who was leaning against the wall. "If that's your wish, go ahead and interrupt the man."

"Moros," Atarax said.

"Got it, boss," the weasel said before leaping onto the banister of a staircase and scurrying up to the overlook. He jumped from the guardrail to a door handle. He hung on for dear life as he twisted it, his momentum swinging open the door.

"MUSKU!" he shouted from above.

Rhyparia was reminded of mornings in Lilac Suites, when she and Himitsu would be in the lobby while Jilly screamed for Toshik to wake up four floors above them.

Biaza got up and stepped outside. "I'll grab Rayne."

Small talk passed the time while they waited for Musku and Rayne. Finally they heard Moros's feet pattering across the hardwood above. Then his tail became visible as it wrapped around the banister, tossing him into the air before landing on Kakos's back a floor below.

"Get off me!" Kakos growled. "I'm not Biaza, rodent."

The wolf spun and grabbed hopelessly at his fur as Moros skittered around his torso. He was a fast and nimble little guy.

A man Rhyparia assumed to be Musku walked across the overlook and descended the stairs. The front door opened as Biaza returned with a woman, assumedly Rayne, behind her. All three of the original Jestivan wore simple robes.

"The whole gang is here," Rayne said. Her eyes fell on Rhyparia. "And a plus-one. Wait …" She looked closer, then asked, "Is that her?"

"It is," Atarax said.

Musku reached the floor and approached Rhyparia with a hand extended. He had a sundial wrapped around his wrist like a watch. "Lita Rhyparia, a pleasure to meet you."

"Likewise," she said, trying to not stare at the shriveled left half of his face.

"Can we skip the pleasantries and handle more pressing matters?" Atarax asked with his eyes closed. "You can discuss old friends and such later—not on my time."

Musku glanced at the fox. "Of course, Atarax." He backed away from Rhyparia and began rifling through the bookcase. "What'd you think of the monstrous statue at Epinio's entrance?" he asked.

"I thought many things," she replied, recalling its resemblance to Meow Meow.

He grabbed a book and flipped through its pages. He smirked as he found what he was looking for and glanced at Rhyparia. "Let me tell you the story of Dimiourgos, the creator of ancients."

12
Dimiourgos

There was a time before ours, when the world of Kuki Sphaira was shaped differently. Instead of six floating islands, there was one massive expanse of land in the form of a ring that surrounded a sea. While the Light and Dark Realms still faced opposite directions, the kingdoms within each realm were connected. Some constructed walls and others used natural formations such as rivers, mountains, and forests to serve as boundaries.

Energy and the ability to weave were considered divine traits. These were attributed to only ten individuals, who each ruled one of ten kingdoms with an iron fist. They were considered immortal and their power was unchecked, for the commoners didn't possess energy to oppose them.

One of these rulers was different from the rest; his name was Dimiourgos, king of the Dark Morality Kingdom. Unlike the others—with smooth skin and hair that only grew on their heads—he was covered in a coat of fur from head to toe, mimicking the appearance of a lynx. In the eyes of neighboring kingdoms, he resembled an animal. But he saw no such thing, for he stood on his hind legs and carried himself like a human.

Dimiourgos was believed to be an omnipotent deity. While the energies of his peers permitted each of them one ability, his energy could transform into almost anything when weaved accordingly. He could spit fire and then breathe ice; summon lightning, then produce windstorms; or shift gravity, then raise a tidal wave. His repertoire was endless.

But such talents brought out the worst in his kingdom's neighbors, one in particular—the Dark Courage Kingdom. Their leader was a man whose name has been lost over time. He despised Dimiourgos and engaged in battle with him several times. The only problem was that Dimiourgos never fought back.

The first time the two kings clashed, Dimiourgos was killed effortlessly. It turned out that these rulers might have been immortal to time, but they could still die at the hands of an equal. The Dark Morality Kingdom grieved, but a day later Dimiourgos returned from the dead. This outraged the DC King; he refused to believe it. But he returned to the DM Kingdom to make sure. Once he spotted Dimiourgos alive and well, he killed him again.

The cycle continued six more times. During Dimiourgos's seventh life, he decided to share his ability. The functionality of Prim Energy was a mystery. It could do things that the other energies weren't capable of. He weaved different abilities into various objects across his kingdom—mementos for his people to not only remember him by, but to use to defend themselves when he was no longer alive to protect them. Today they're called ancient pieces.

But he kept one ability for himself, and that was the power of resurrection. He split its functionality into two pieces: a handful of white gems and himself. He could make use of it nine times, and it was the only reason why he was on his seventh life.

The DC King returned for an eighth visit, this time burning and killing animals on his way to Dimiourgos. And he had a different tactic entering this fight: he'd cut off the lynx's head, figuring a decapitated body couldn't possibly be resurrected.

And the world believed it to have been successful. Nobody heard from Dimiourgos again, and the Dark Morality Kingdom was overtaken by the Dark Courage. The dimiours and humans of the DM Kingdom had Dimiourgos's ancients to aid them, but without the knowledge or skill to wield them properly, they were useless. The humans were enslaved while the dimiours were slaughtered without mercy.

Only a few escaped the DC King's wrath by traversing through a hole in the ground that Dimiourgos had created throughout his first seven lives. He'd carved into the crust for thousands of miles until he reached light on the other side. But that still posed problems. If the dimiours were to jump in, they'd only plummet to a midpoint between the two realms, forever stuck floating in a void between two opposing gravitational forces until they died.

He therefore shifted the gravity inside the hole so that travelers could walk on its sides. He'd grown trees and vegetation throughout the passage, so food would be available over the course of the journey.

That hole ultimately led to the Light Morality Kingdom, behind one of Kuki Sphaira's grandest mountain ranges. It was here where the dimiours started anew. And perhaps their new home was a blessing in disguise, because it kept them hidden from the most catastrophic war of all time—the war that ended a timeline.

* * *

Rhyparia was leaning forward in earnest, elbows on her knees, fingers interlocked. Words failed her. She'd never heard of such a story, one that took place before Known History. She'd never heard of the name Dimiourgos. And she never thought of Meow Meow as a lynx rather than a silly cat. But now that she visualized him, she could see it.

Musku closed the book and gazed at her. "It's important to remember that this isn't the full story of Dimiourgos's life or the conflict between him and the Dark Courage King. It's more of a short story that reads like a fairy tale you'd tell a child before bed. In fact, that's what this entire book is—a collection of primordial fairy tales."

"If you read it to me, there must be some merit," Rhyparia said.

"There definitely is. There is truth to what's being told, but a lot of information has been lost. Based off the nomenclature used in this telling, whoever wrote this book did so between Year 0 and 842 K.H., when the only Sphairian Summit was held between the royal heads of the ten kingdoms. That's when the names of kingdoms changed to their energies. Today, the Dark Courage and Morality Kingdoms are known as the Power and Prim Kingdoms."

Musku stood and returned the book to its spot on the shelf. "This is the only story I've ever found that takes place before our timeline. It's the most marvelous piece of writing I've ever read—a crown jewel of literature."

"So I've known an omnipotent king for the past two years," Rhyparia mumbled.

"Correct," he replied with a gentle smile. "When Spy Pilot Ophala informed us of a girl with a hat that resembled the head of Dimiourgos's statue, we were unsure of how to process such news. It couldn't have been a joke because Ophala would never make light of something held so dear to this village's heart. Eventually we accepted her news as truth and rejoiced. Before that, nobody knew what had become of Dimiourgos. The dimiours believed that the DC King had been successful in killing him."

"So Dimiourgos is alive and on his eighth life?" Rhyparia asked.

"Eighth or ninth, we're not entirely sure. He could have been killed again sometime in the past fifteen hundred years."

"Toono's trying to bring the Dev King back to life, and he's been chasing down Olivia. I guess he only wanted Meow Meow."

For the first time since Musku had told Dimiourgos's story, someone else in the room spoke up: "You named our legendary deity … *Meow Meow*?" Moros asked.

Laughter erupted at the absurdity of it. Rhyparia flushed a deep shade of red, forgetting that the name was ridiculous to anyone's ears besides the Jestivan.

Musku nodded once the commotion settled. "This Toono fellow—Ophala told us about him—is likely trying to use Dimiourgos and the gems as an ancient. He wants to use the ninth life on Dev King Rehn."

"But it requires the sacrifice of ten strong individuals. There was no mentioning of Dimiourgos sacrificing lives to resurrect himself in the story you just read."

As Rayne ignited the lanterns throughout the log cabin without even waving her hand, Musku said, "Which is exactly why I said: there's a lot missing."

Rhyparia scanned the faces in the room—specifically the dimiours. Atarax's arms were folded, eyes closed as his chin was tucked into his chest. Kakos was seated on the floor, eyes slanted with resolve. Therapif stood off to the side, his long rabbit ears drooping forward. Biaza was seated calmly in a rocking chair with Moros sitting on her head.

"So I'm guessing you want to get Dimiourgos back, now that he's been found," Rhyparia said.

"That'd be ideal," Atarax said, "but not practical."

Musku gazed out a window in the direction of the monstrous statue between the two mountains. "We can't retrieve Dimiourgos. He's lodged too deeply in a present-day war we have no part of. The dimiours can't just stroll into public eye. Nobody knows such a species exists."

"So what's this mission Atarax mentioned?"

"To return to the Power Kingdom and rescue the people who are still treated as slaves. While the dimiours who weren't killed were able to flee through the tunnel, the humans who were led by Dimiourgos were enslaved and still are to this day … fifteen hundred years of slavery."

Rhyparia's eyebrows climbed her forehead. "We have a common enemy."

"Do we now?"

"My friend, Vuilni Gesluimant, was born a slave in Ulna Malen. While she was able to escape by merits of her talents as a fighter, that was an astronomically rare occurrence. She told me how slaves are treated there—the condition of their homes in Stratum Zero. It's ghastly."

Musku sighed. "I know. I studied Ulna Malen's unique structure when I was younger, before even becoming a Jestivan. I want to save those people."

Thereapif hopped forward. "We all do."

Rhyparia stood up. "Well, how are we going to do it? If you can't travel past the mountains, how will we get there?"

"This is a daunting mission we'll be undertaking. It's something we've been planning for quite some time, but there has always been one obstacle in our way. But with you here, Rhyparia, that obstacle may no longer be an issue—once you receive proper training, that is."

She stood silent for a moment before saying, "I'll do whatever it takes."

13
DaiSo

Agnos, Tashami, and Barloe pushed a canoe into the babbling Shindo River. They had traveled a few miles upstream to put distance between them and the Gulf of Sodai—a necessary strategy when operating as a small group toward DaiSo. While approaching the city in a marked pirate ship was acceptable, a canoe was a different story.

As the canoe hit depths where it could float, they jumped inside and grabbed their paddles. They heaved as they rowed against the current to reach the opposite bank … or at least two of them did. Agnos was already useless due to his weak frame, but now that his shoulder and chest were wrapped in a sling from his clavicle fracture, there was nothing he could provide besides his mind.

"What do we do when we approach DaiSo's defenses?" Agnos asked.

"It's a city of pirates," Barloe said. "Do you really think they wasted time and money building a wall? There are several entry points into DaiSo, all of which are guarded by a couple pirates from whichever crew is designated to protect those points that week."

"What about the squallblasters Silvia mentioned?"

The man chuckled. "While squallblasters are capable of some damage, they're still people. They can only do so much. Silvia was simply spreading fear."

Half an hour later they reached the opposite side. They dragged the canoe into nearby woodland, hiding it within a dense bushel of underbrush. After relieving themselves, they traveled east, heading deeper into the forest so they weren't visible from the river. Black birds soared above the canopies, flying in flocks big enough to shield the land from the sun's rays. The Spirit Kingdom was known for its population of winged creatures.

DaiSo sat ahead of them as they broke free from the woods. Like its counterpart, Sodai, it was hilly, but unique in the fact that it was one giant shade of brown. The roads were dirt, not paved in tar or stone, and the buildings were made of untreated wood and absent of any paint. Besides an ancient castle near the back of the town, nothing rose higher than two stories, making the ships sitting in the bay a beautiful backdrop.

Agnos sniffed the air and tried not to gag. Barloe laughed. "Did you expect to smell the water's salt like in Sodai?" he asked. After not getting a response, he said, "You're around pirates now. When the horses take a dump in the streets, there's no one running out to clean it up."

As if right on cue, Agnos stepped in something soft and warm. He lifted his foot and cursed.

"Might want to invest in some boots there, kid," Barloe said. "Clogs won't cut it."

They passed the pirates who stood guard with ease. "Ay, Barloe," one said.

Barloe tipped his head in silence and continued on.

Agnos tossed his clog off to the side. "I'm guessing you're a big deal, as a quartermaster."

"You're only as big as your last success. Luckily my crew landed a big treasure a couple weeks back."

"So you've been basking in that glory?"

"Nah, I didn't bother getting caught up in it, which was why I was happy to travel to Sodai. It got me away from the festivities at the crew house."

Agnos watched as a man pulled down the front of his trousers and pissed against a wall.

"Crew house?" Tashami asked.

"Each crew has their own building where they do whatever they wish when not at sea. Sleep, drink, gamble, brawl … whichever mood the rum brings out of them on any given day."

Barloe abruptly turned around, drew his sword, and placed its edge against a stranger's neck. "Give it back."

"What are you doing?" Agnos gawked, looking around to make sure nobody else tried to join in.

Color drained from the man's face as he dropped a handful of change into the dirt. "I'm sorry," he stammered.

Barloe shoved him backward and kicked the bottom of his boot into the man's chest, sending him crashing into a stack of wooden pallets. "Pick those up and pay attention," Barloe said to Agnos as he glared at him. "And put all of your money in your bag, including your spare change."

Agnos patted a coin purse at his side to find it empty. He retrieved his coins and dumped them into his travel sack with the rest of his savings.

The quartermaster shook his head as he pressed onward. "I can't believe you're walking around with a bag that literally jingles. You didn't even try to disguise it. Aren't you the smart one?"

"I suppose I could've wrapped my coins in my clothes instead of just tossing everything in."

Their walk was comprised of Barloe frequently exchanging nods with fellow pirates. Every so often an individual would garner a more courteous gesture such as a verbal greeting. Nearly everyone dressed in the same raggedy attire, making it impossible to distinguish if one was more important than another. He'd pass a brothel on occasion and spot the women in corsets through the windows, shutters open to entice entry from passersby.

They finally walked into a tavern which occupied the entire main floor. Dirt blown in from the windswept streets covered the wooden floorboards and sunlight was the only source of light for the interior, the candlewicks being absent of any flame.

Barloe approached a woman behind the bar. "What do you got open for the next few nights, Zorra?"

She stepped from behind the counter with a wet rag. "We don't provide lodging here, Barloe," she said as she began wiping down a table. "You know that."

"For old time's sake."

"Which I'd like to forget."

"Let me—"

"Get out," she said. There was nothing playful in her tone.

Barloe sighed and turned to leave. Agnos and Tashami tried to follow but were knocked to the side as he turned back around and ran toward a door behind the bar. They followed as Zorra gave chase. They burst through the door into a storage room to find Barloe embraced in an old lady's hug.

"Where have you been?" the woman asked.

"Before my last mission, your daughter left me."

She gasped and glared at Zorra. "Why would you do such a foolish thing?"

Zorra didn't even try to argue, electing to brush past Agnos and Tashami and excuse herself from the area.

"Do you have a room for my friends here?" Barloe asked.

"Of course! First I'll have Jon clean it up a bit." She smiled at them. "Food and drinks are on the house."

And with that, the two Jestivan had a place to stay and food to eat for the next four days.

* * *

On the fifth day, Barloe guided Agnos and Tashami down the beach toward the tide. Men and women came and went, dragging rowboats onto the shore. Everyone looked rugged and seasoned, making Agnos feel like a fish out of water in his robes and sandals. Still, he refused to wear boots.

Tashami held his hand above his eyes to block the blinding sun. "So which one's the *Whale Lord*?"

Agnos scanned the dozens of ships against the sky's blue canvas. His eyes landed on the biggest one. "I'm guessing that," he said, pointing his finger in its direction.

Barloe nodded. "Correct."

"Now I know why they call it the *Whale Lord*," Tashami said in astonishment.

"Not quite," Barloe said.

"And does Gray Whale stay on her ship even when it's stationed in the harbor?"

"Yes, she rarely leaves. She appreciates these breaks between voyages since it's the only time she gets the ship to herself."

"Doesn't a carpenter or boatswain stay on the ship for quality control?"

Barloe gazed curiously down at Agnos. "You know crew positions. Have you been studying during your stay here?"

"Ships have been something I've always made myself familiar with, albeit not pirate ships. My objective in life requires knowledge of sailing to get to where I need to go."

"I see." Barloe gazed across the harbor once more. "But, no, Gray Whale is fully capable of performing the duties of every crew position. She's well versed in carpentry, navigation, piloting, rigging, and most everything else … Just don't let her try to saw off your limbs; leave that to the surgeon."

"Seems like a respectable, skilled woman," Tashami said.

"She is. But of course, when the ship does set sail and the crew's aboard, she becomes one role only: the captain. The most feared captain throughout the Realm Rivers and Sea of Light."

"And why haven't we met the crew yet?" Agnos asked.

Barloe brushed a few stray dreads from his face. "Because that's the catch. In order for you to call yourself a member of Gray Whale's crew, you must be voted in by the crew's majority."

"You're the quartermaster," Agnos said. "You have authority over them. Just tell them we're joining."

Barloe laughed heartily and looked around the beach. He singled out a woman preparing to board a canoe. "You there," he said. She looked back, her expression freezing at the sight of who called for her. "What would you and your mates do if your quartermaster brought two new men on board without consulting the crew first?"

"The severity of it depends on the crew," she shouted over the waters. "But in most cases, the quartermaster would be voted off the ship, his reputation permanently squandered."

"You see?" he said to Agnos and Tashami as the woman continued her business. "Agnos, you're thinking along the lines of a naval vessel, where the captain and second-in-command rule unchecked. Pirates are very different."

"So a navy ship is operated like a monarchy while a pirate ship is a democracy," Agnos said.

"Exactly that." Barloe sighed. "The Realm Rivers weep for my return, and soon they'll have it. We depart on the grandest voyage ever in exactly one month."

"A month?" Agnos said. "Where are we supposed to stay for a month?"

He smiled and walked back up the beach toward the town. "Depending on your bartering skills, either the crew house or nowhere."

"What's that supposed to mean?"

"We're headed to the crew house, where you will make a case for the crew's vote in your favor. If the majority approves of your pitch, you'll lodge with the crew. If not, you're on your way out of DaiSo, for there's nothing I can do for you at that point."

They passed a few palm trees before stepping onto a dirt street. "Not even a warning, huh?" Agnos mumbled.

"While I have faith in Tashami's argument for why he's a valuable member to the crew, I have little in yours. You claim that you're intelligent, and while I've seen a flash of it a time or two, book smarts mean nothing on a pirate ship. So let's test your wit, shall we? And I see no better way of doing this than by springing a scenario such as this on you unannounced."

A heavy downpour had begun by the time they reached the Whale House. Like the other buildings in DaiSo, it reached only two stories high.

The difference between it and others however was its square footage. It was as wide and deep as six buildings grouped together.

Upon entry they were searched by a man in a trench coat despite the fact that they were clearly guests of Barloe. Laughter and music streamed through the many rooms occupying the first floor. Barloe was a different person here. Someone handed him a mug of ale, which he gratefully accepted, and he smacked people on the back as he made his way around the floor, laughing throughout the entire journey.

Agnos and Tashami, meanwhile, were invisible. A couple people gave the Jestivan inquisitive looks, but they dared not question their presence with the quartermaster seemingly leading them through.

When they reached a lively barroom, every table and barstool was occupied. Some people were forced to hold conversation while leaning against a wall. Agnos couldn't hear his own thoughts over the din. Even the music from the strumming bassist in the back corner was inaudible.

Barloe reached the bar and banged his fist on the counter. "Aye, mates!" The buzz softened before completely waning out. "Everyone take a seat or stand off to the side." He raised his voice louder and bellowed, "To the lot of you around the house, get in the bar!"

More people straggled into the room, doubling the previous number. Even the Spirit Kingdom's cooler temperatures couldn't combat the combined heat of this many bodies compacted together.

Agnos's stomach churned as he studied the pirates surrounding him. There were swords on almost every hip. And while his logical side reminded him that he had spent the past two years around the likes of Toshik and Yama—two people more talented with a sword than anyone in this room—the coward in him didn't care. If he had one weakness that bothered him more than most, it was the effect that physical intimidation had on him.

"I have two new potential crewmates," Barloe announced, causing every eye to focus on Agnos and Tashami. "You all know the drill. We'll let them make their case and then we'll vote."

"Aye," they replied.

Barloe glanced down at the two young men. "Whoever wants to go first, the floor is yours."

Tashami looked at Agnos, and Agnos nudged him toward the floor. Tashami took center stage in the middle of the barroom.

"My name is Tashami Patter, and I'm a sharpshooter."

"Where's your bow?" someone asked.

"I don't use bows or arrows. I'm not an archer."

"So you throw rocks?" There was a roar of laughter in response to the question.

"I shoot wind—or air—depending on how you perceive it," he said, unfazed by the mockery.

"We already have two squallblasters," someone said, "which is plenty enough for us."

"If I'm not mistaken," Tashami said, "squallblasters serve one of two purposes on a ship. They either manufacture wind to aid a ship's movement or they block a firefighter's flames in a battle between ships."

"And we have two people better suited for such tasks than you."

Tashami shook his head. "That's not my argument. I think all the rum in here has clouded your memory. I clearly stated that I was a sharpshooter."

Agnos's eyes widened as the room somehow became quieter.

Tashami continued: "While a squallblaster weaves wide blasts of wind, I weave finely threaded EC chains clustered so tightly together that the resulting wind resembles an arrow shot from a bow. It takes all of the power seen in a windstorm and concentrates it into a single point, capable of piercing any surface … including steel."

A woman in a red jacket hovering outside of a doorframe asked, "How old are you, kid?"

"Just turned twenty."

"Forgive me if I don't believe that you can do what you say, but I'll gladly ask for a demonstration so you can prove me wrong." Her eyes narrowed as she finished with a warning: "Keep in mind that we don't take kindly to lies from crewmates."

Tashami glanced at Barloe, who nodded in return. People jumped as a high-pitched noise pierced through the air and glass shattered at the back of the room, all in the blink of an eye. Eyes widened as there were now eight holes peppered into the barroom window, glass splintering around each of them.

"When I said 'resembles an arrow shot from a bow', I meant more like exponentially intensifies the effects of an arrow shot from a bow. Not only can I do greater damage, but I can direct the path of my wind bullets midflight."

As silence continued to mull through the crowd, Tashami elaborated what his purpose was: "I don't intend to steal any spots on your already established crew. The squallblasters can keep their positions. I'd never want to be the reason for someone losing his or her job. No, I'd act as a stealth striker. I could be stationed almost anywhere and be able to pick off enemies if needed."

Tashami returned to Barloe and an anxious Agnos at the bar. Agnos was proud of his friend for making such a compelling case, but now he was unsure as to how he would follow it. He should've gone first.

Barloe addressed the crew. "All those in favor of Mr. Patter joining the *Whale Lord*?"

There was a resounding "Aye!" in response.

"All those against?"

Silence.

"Welcome aboard, Mr. Patter!" Barloe yelled, thrusting a mug into Tashami's grasp.

Once the brief roars of approval ceased, Agnos was called to the floor. He knew he reeked of uncertainty, but he couldn't help it. What could he offer this crew? His knowledge of the Sea of Light and the sky's stars? They already had a skilled navigator and pilot. Or rigging? They already had a boatswain and plenty of riggers. And with those areas of his skillset not needed by them, he was useless because he definitely couldn't fight.

"Tough act to follow," a woman said.

Agnos finally managed to move his lips. "You said you don't like liars, so I'll refrain from being one." He paused. "My skillset means nothing to most of you. I have no physical strength and I've been told by Barloe that my relic holds no value to the crew. I have knowledge of ships and the sea, but this is the best crew of pirates in DaiSo, so you have enough of that already.

"So here's my desperate plea ... Make me the swab. I'll mop the decks morning, noon, and night. And if there are any other jobs deemed beneath the rest of you, I'll take over those duties as well. This has been my dream my entire life—a dream I once shared with a dear friend. I want to learn the Realm Rivers and Sea of Light not only from books, but from the experience. And what better way to do that than by sailing alongside the most accomplished men and women of the sea?"

"Flattery won't do you any favors," one man said.

"There's more to the sea than an experience," a bigger fella explained. "The problem I see with you doesn't lie in your weak frame, but rather your weak mental fortitude. I saw it in your face when you watched your friend finish his argument … cowardice. The sea can be a nightmare—inexplicable beasts and unpredictable weather, opposing crews and disease."

Agnos gazed emptily at the man. He was right. In fact, Agnos could feel the color draining from his face in this very moment. There was arrogance in the way Agnos spoke when around inferior minds if there wasn't any physical danger nearby. It was why he had gained the respect he did with the Jestivan when at school. But here, that confidence had vanished.

"No …" Agnos mumbled, recalling what Tashami had said at Mimi's house. "Cowardice? How many of you have ever visited the Void?" There were a few laughs in response, followed by someone dismissing the idea as insane. "I have," Agnos said.

"I thought we weren't gonna lie," someone replied.

"And nobody has. Not only did I visit the Void, but I stayed there for over a month." Eyes began skittering around the room. "Tashami and I are Jestivan—the same as names like Mendac, Thusia, Saikatto, Musku, and Rayne. We carry out missions from time to time. A group of us traveled through the Void's Almawt Woods all the way to Spachny while our spirit was slowly expelled from our bodies by the distant roars of the Linsani. The dead whispered and materialized around us. And the air was as thin as the peaks of the Archaic Mountains.

"And I led that excursion. Me—" Agnos pointed at his own chest—"the decrepit, cowardly orphan dressed in robes and clogs without a single weapon in his arsenal … just this tool." He lifted his finger to the side of his temple. "So don't talk to me about nightmares. I've seen a walking, breathing man stripped of skin, skeleton partially exposed; watched hundreds of innocent civilians murdered in the Generals' Battle audience;

and witnessed my fellow classmates slain right before my eyes at the hands of Dev soldiers."

Agnos's eyes glued themselves to the man who questioned his mental fortitude. "Have you ever seen children be slaughtered?"

His stunned silence said enough.

"I have more purpose in life than the majority of this room combined. And no, not money, revenge, or respect, for what drives me is far greater than anything as insignificant as those. I seek meaning to our existence. I seek answers to questions most people don't even know exist."

Agnos heaved as a fire had ignited in his chest and boiled into his head, leaving him hot and uncomfortable. He had never ranted with such intensity. People knew him as a mild-mannered individual. He and Tashami were alike in that aspect. But this situation called for something different. These were pirates. If there was one thing they could rally around, it was a fiery display of passion.

With Agnos still at the center of the room, Barloe asked, "All in favor of Agnos joining the crew?"

The response was an overwhelming "Aye!"

14
Burned Bridges

The great hulk of Power Warden Feissam had made it through the first eight stratums of the Power Kingdom's capital, Ulna Malen, with only a little bit of his stamina depleted. The city was constructed on a lone miniature mountain. Down the mountainsides were paved streets and clusters of pure white limestone buildings—not a speck of land to be seen. Ringed walls of stone divided all nine stratums, each occupying a certain elevation of the mountainside. The higher the mountain one climbed, the stratums became smaller and the people wealthier.

Feissam stood outside the white stone wall that surrounded Stratum Nine at the mountain's pinnacle. He looked back to see the lower stratums sprawled beneath him all the way to the lowest of the low—Stratum Zero. It was here that no pristine stone gleamed underneath the sun. It was a floor of shacks, mud, and dirt until you looked far enough out to see the hard, barren crust of the dead zone.

A soldier eventually met Feissam at the gate and guided him inside the castle. This was a meeting Feissam had avoided since his return, but with the Power Queen's request for his presence, he didn't have a choice anymore. He had stayed at Ipsas ever since his unexpected return from Phesaw. After abandoning his Diatia, he had spent months reflecting on his choices and worrying about the fates of Vuilni and Bruut.

But he had concluded a long time ago that he couldn't go back to the Light Realm. Surely people already knew of his selfish abandonment. The Power Kingdom was supposed to be allies with the five Light Kingdoms. It was what made their kingdom so untouchable in the Dark Realm. But had his decision severed those ties?

The soldier dropped Feissam off in the throne room before bowing and taking his leave. The warden stared down his queen as he approached. She was bald and as bulky as a wild, full-grown ox. Slender slabs of granite molded over her shoulders, arms, and chest as armor. The table in front of her, with its trailing beige cloth, caused her legs to remain unseen.

"Good day, Queen Gantski."

She bit into a leg of turkey with a scowl. After chewing for a while, she said, "My first time meeting a warden of Ipsas … such a pointless place."

Feissam chose his words carefully. "It's an honor to be in your presence, milady."

"You're a big man. You'd fit well in my army. Fourteen feet, or somewhere around there?"

"A foot away, milady."

She gulped down the contents of her goblet. "I'm in a terrible situation, Feissam. It seems that one of your Diatia has been killed."

The warden hesitated. This was his fault. He should've dragged them out of Phesaw even when they refused his original efforts. Better yet, he should never have gone there.

"Now, typically I wouldn't care. But since the Diatia who was killed also happens to be my general's grandson …" her eyes narrowed, "we have a serious problem."

"I didn't—"

"Truth be told, I received this news a couple months ago from Dev King Storshae. One of his officers visited Ulna Malen with a recording.

While it was alarming news, I wasn't sure how confident I was with his claim. He didn't have a body to show me. All he had was a verbal account of what he had witnessed that day he invaded Phesaw.

"We sent people to Ipsas in hopes of finding Bruut to rebuke his claim, but with no luck. But you and Vuilni weren't there, either, so we figured that you were still in Phesaw. I thought Storshae was simply trying to create a rift between us and the Light Realm. But then I finally received a letter from Intel King Vitio confirming Storshae's claims, in which he also mentioned some other jarring details …"

The queen leaned back in her throne. "Based off information the Intel King gathered from witnesses in the fight, he said you abandoned the Light Realm and your Diatia. Now, fleeing a battle between two realms I can understand, but deserting fellow Powish in the process is despicable."

"It was a selfish, cowardly mistake, milady," Feissam said.

"So here's the conflict I'm faced with," she said. "I have two powerful royal heads—both of whom are vital trade partners for our kingdom's provod—confirming the death of my general's grandson. That they can agree on. But the rub lies in their accusations of who did it, each trying to pin blame on the other because of the little war they're having—even if they refuse to call it that. Neither of them claims to have Bruut's body.

"I'm looking to you to tell me the truth since you spent several months in Phesaw. Intel King Vitio placed the blame on the man named Toono who's been wreaking havoc across Kuki Sphaira, but Dev King Storshae says it was someone else entirely … someone from Phesaw. Tell me … is there anyone in that school that expressed a desire to hurt or kill Bruut Schap?"

Feissam nodded. "I will say this first, milady: when I left Phesaw, Vuilni went to fight with the Jestivan while Bruut went to fight with the Dev Diatia and Storshae's men. Storshae is allies with Toono, so I doubt it was he who killed Bruut. With that said, I can only think of the Jestivan, and there are two specifically who despised everything about him, threatening his life on more than one occasion."

"Their names?"

"Bryson LeAnce and Yama."

Feissam ducked and covered his head as the queen kicked her table off the floor with enough force to send it flying into the double doors, where it shattered into pieces. Queen Gantski stood tall, nostrils flared and veins pulsing through her bald head.

"Storshae was right," she said, enraged. "I've had it! The Power Kingdom is cutting all trade to and from the Light Realm. The whole world should know by now to never trust the Intel King and the people who follow him!"

Feissam quickly dropped to a knee. "I'm so sorry, milady."

"If you ever want to walk free, you'll have to make up for the mistakes you've made," she seethed.

"Anything, milady."

"Bring me Bryson LeAnce."

* * *

After two months, Olivia spent the day walking through the streets of Rim for the last time before she would enter the mountains. It was a depressing scene; the city was a disaster. Rhyparia NuForce's failed execution had been the final nail in Rim's coffin. A few buildings had been burned to ash in riots protesting the Amendment Order while shops and taverns tried to recover from the looting that occurred during said riots.

Streets were sparsely populated, even in the morning hours. Nobody found it safe to travel. Businesses closed down as the economy collapsed, only deepening the hatred the people had for the Amendment Order—specifically three people: Chief Arbitrator Grandarion Senten, Chief Senator Rosel Sania, and Archaic Prince Sigmund. Those were the names civilians shouted in the streets or carved into the wood of buildings.

Olivia thought it'd be Spy Pilot Ophala, which still was heard on occasion. But perhaps her imprisonment had dampened those gripes. Grandarion, Rosel, and Sigmund were the three who not only declared Rhyparia's punishment as death by hanging, but decided to do it in Olethros. People blamed them for making the escape so easy.

Olivia decided to spend her last day visiting Olethros. She had refrained from doing so since arriving, opting to stay on the opposite side of the city where she had easier access to the plains for training purposes. Thankfully this was a day of rest.

She wasn't able to venture too far into Olethros because of the Archaic soldiers stationed around the perimeter of the wreckage. There were a few scientists and other scholars scattered throughout the disaster, searching for who knew what.

It resembled nothing of the sector it once was a decade ago. At least in recent years, man-made structures had been noticeable—even if they'd been poorly constructed shanties amongst the debris of a seven-year-old Rhyparia's wrath. Now molten crust swathed the land in black while jagged stones and cinder rendered the sector unsuitable for life. Olethros was now a barren wasteland.

Olivia was able to approach the platform that was to serve as Rhyparia's execution, for it hadn't been swallowed by Elyol's lava. She tried to picture what that night might have been like. She envisioned the mobs shouting with a mixture of rage and glee as they surrounded her, the guards stationed directly around the platform to ward off any reckless spectators that tried to run up the stage, and the person in charge of cutting the rope waiting in earnest.

But the most haunting image was that of Rhyparia with her head through the noose. Olivia knew that a girl such as her—and all that she'd been through—would have been calm in that moment. She would likely have accepted her fate, no matter how unfair her path in life seemed to be. In the end she had killed hundreds of people.

Olivia looked toward the mountains. What could she expect upon entering them? No entrants had ever returned in fifteen hundred years of recorded history, or so went the tales. Rhyparia was the latest victim. This massive hunt that the royal heads were pursuing seemed like a lost cause. If anything, it'd only claim more lives.

"A bit of sightseeing, aye Princess?"

She didn't have to turn around to recognize whose voice that belonged to. "Hello, Yvole. I'm reminiscing on my old friend."

He limped toward her on his cane. "The same girl we begin our hunt for tomorrow?"

"I've found myself in an unfortunate circumstance."

"It seems so." His gaze followed Olivia's to the peaks. "Have you decided on what you'll do if we find her?"

"I'll listen to my instincts and act accordingly."

Yvole retrieved his pipe and ignited it with a striker. As he put it between his lips, he said, "Ain't no other way to do it. Only a fool neglects instinct." He blew out a cloud of smoke. "I learned that lesson as a boy."

Olivia gazed up at the grizzled man, waiting for an elaboration, only to receive nothing of the sort. His eyes narrowed, lost in thought. "What is the true meaning of 'good'?" he asked himself. "Sometimes you do what the world would see as honorable and morally right only to realize it doesn't align with your own perception. That decision bit me in the ass. Instinct trumps morality in my eyes."

She studied him for a moment longer before asking, "Are you an Archain?"

He smirked. "I know my thought process sounds like one, but no. I'm the opposite." He looked at the execution stage. "Before we leave, let's get rid of this eyesore." He waved his hand and a stream of electricity blasted through the platform, causing it to collapse.

Soldiers bellowed for them to leave immediately. Yvole was way ahead of them, as he limped his way across the rubble back toward the heart of Rim.

*   *   *

A Dunami Palace courtyard was once again playing host to a training session between Still Prince Bryson and Intel Princess Shelly.

"When's your dad going to send soldiers into the Dev Kingdom?" Bryson asked as he unleashed a voltaic surge toward Shelly. "So I can go with them."

She jumped and flipped with a twirl, dodging his attack while coming down with a whip of lightning. "Not anytime soon."

He stepped to the side of her whip as it singed the grass. "Pause," he said.

She wiped a bead of sweat from her brow. "What's wrong now?"

"So we're just gonna let Toono and Storshae roam free after all they've done? Do I have to go to the Dev Kingdom myself? I've done it before."

Shelly sighed as she walked to the side of the courtyard and grabbed a glass of water from a maid. "You turn eighteen in five days. You've experienced so much these past two years, yet you're still as naïve as ever. Nobody invades a kingdom through teleplatforms. They're choke points. If we were to make a move on a large scale, it'd have to be with our naval forces."

"So send the navy."

"It would take time. For now, the most realistic option is to allow the spies we have in the Dev Kingdom to do their work. Once they contact us with valuable information, we'll plan accordingly."

Bryson groaned. "So what can I do? There has to be something."

An electric whip formed in her hand. "You train. I'm already willing to bet you could fight a royal first-born and possibly be victorious—not me of course. But what about a Gefal? If you ended up fighting someone with a Bewahr, like Storshae had Fonos, could you do something about it?"

His gaze fell to the ground, and Shelly replied. "Exactly. The heroes of the *Of Five* ..." she trailed off as Bryson's forehead furrowed. She corrected herself: "The heroes of the *Of Four* were documented to rival the skill of a Branian or Bewahr—possibly higher ranks. I know it sounds unbelievable, but it's the truth."

Shelly gathered air into her lungs and huffed as she looked to the side, as if she was debating her next words. "Listen, I might be arrogant when it comes to my skill, but even I know beings like Thusia and Suadade are more talented than I." She looked back at Bryson. "Have you ever thought about training with Thusia? Spar her like you do with me or the other Jestivan."

Bryson gave it some thought. She was right. Why had that idea never crossed his mind? He finally gave Shelly a smile. "You're a genius."

15
Role of Tazama

Toono stood outside a cell, his hand casually gripping a steel bar as he studied the elderly, crippled man imprisoned within. The torches embellished the shadows of his sunken eyes while illuminating the dirt trapped in his eyebrows that hung past his cheeks. Without his cane he couldn't walk, so the rare times he did move—usually when a bowl of water or slice of bread was placed near the gate—he dragged himself across the cold stone floor.

It was humbling for Toono to see a man as distinguished as Poicus in such condition. While he had never met the man before, he still knew of his accomplishments from reading his biographies. He learned of Poicus's history growing up—his growth through the ranks from a runt of the Archaic Kingdom's military to corporal, the third highest position in the military. He then eventually changed course, practicing the art of deception and stealth before becoming Spy Pilot underneath Archaic King Dolomarpos.

Toono respected Poicus's reasons for leaving the Archaic Kingdom after that to become the Grand Director of Phesaw. The man had desired a change in his environment, and sought a quality in himself he thought he'd almost lost: compassion. Toono's journey through life was the opposite. He was benevolent at a young age, but as he grew older he learned things that caused his heart to scab.

He left Poicus's cell and exited the prison chambers. Yama was leaning against the opposite wall with her arms folded and a foot behind her resting on the stone. She looked up with a placid gaze. "When are you going to kill him?"

Toono walked down the hall. "When I can stomach it."

"There are always other options," she said, walking slowly behind him. "I've had to listen to Storshae whine about the Archaic Prince for months because of his betrayal of Toth and Wert with his verdict. Why not make him the Archaic sacrifice?"

They rounded a corner and cut through the moonlit gardens. "Am I mistaken, or does the callous Yama pity someone?"

"I'm not callous," she said. "I don't care either way. Do what you want."

A smirk appeared on Toono's face. "I'll keep Prince Sigmund alive, mostly because he could be of use down the line, but also because nobody knows if he's capable of summoning a Branian yet. He's kept that information a guarded secret."

"How old is he?"

"Around twenty—a year past the average age of when a royal first-born awakens their Branian."

Yama stood off to the side while Toono combed through the rose garden. "I've grown impatient," she said. "You never mentioned sitting around in a castle while months pass by. When can we focus on the Adren sacrifice?"

Toono bent low and smelled a flower at the bottom of a bush. "We don't rush things. We're not invincible. If we're not calculated with our movements, then we're done for." He finally picked a rose and stood tall, smiling as he examined it closely. "Powerful people know of our names. They seek us while we try to hide in the shadows, striking only when safe.

This is a war, Yama—not a battle. Development requires time in war; it's strategic in nature.

"We must wait and rely on other pieces of our puzzle to complete their assignments so we can make a move. Right now Tazama is that piece. Without her, the next move is impossible." Toono placed the rose in an inner pocket of his jacket. "Don't worry," he said, "we'll get you to Toshik soon enough."

*   *   *

Toth stood next to a window on the second floor of Phelos Palace. He gazed outside to Archain Road, the massive cobblestone street that divided Phelos perfectly in half and connected the city's outer reaches to the palace's main gate, which had drawn his attention.

Archaic Prince Sigmund, Chief Grandarion, and Rosel stood outside the gate with a mob of civilians surrounding them. The only reason why they weren't being mauled was because of the Archaic soldiers fending off the crowd.

Toth and Wert should have been out there, but their fellow chiefs and the prince barred them from participating. They were trying to distance themselves from the two men for the sake of public image. Ultimately Toth played along with their act after Tazama had explained to him the benefits.

"Don't you notice the public's hatred for them is only growing as each day passes?" Tazama had asked. "They're keeping the spotlight on themselves while you fall into the background."

Toth had been sitting on his bed while Tazama prepared for the day in the bathroom. "You're right I suppose," he had admitted.

She walked toward the door and looked at him while brushing her wet hair. "There will come a day when it boils over, and I feel that you'll be who they run to when it does."

As Toth replayed the conversation in his mind, Tazama's prediction began to unfold before him. The mob's collective force overwhelmed the soldiers, trampling them in the process. The few soldiers who'd stayed near the chiefs and prince shielded and directed them back through the gates and onto palace grounds. The gate began to close as the staff in the watchtowers went to work, but the civilians pushed against it.

It was a fight that the public seemed to be winning. A few leaked through the small gap in the entrance only to be apprehended by soldiers that swarmed in from other areas of the palace. A few more guards tried to counter the civilians by pushing against the other side of the gate, but they didn't have enough numbers. They could have easily used their ancients to fend off the mob, but with the amount of heat the Amendment Order was already under, such a dire measure would have been political suicide.

At this point, Grandarion, Rosel, and Sigmund had retreated up the main steps of the palace. Toth glanced down and to the right, catching a new presence. His partner, Chief Officer Wert Lamay, was marching around the palace's southern wall with a full company of soldiers behind him. He lifted his hand and pointed at the gate, and his entire unit broke into a run. They closed the gate with ease, putting an end to the potential threat.

Then something interesting happened. Toth pushed open the window as Wert approached the gate that sat between him and the angry mob. He wasn't going to talk, was he? He'd ruin everything. Wert didn't know how to speak to civilians, only to soldiers—and even that was more of a bark.

As the crowd's cacophony simmered, Wert said, "Do you see what happens when we let extremists such as those three—" he swept an arm behind him toward Rosel, Grandarion, and Senten— "make decisions? They butcher your kingdom! Chiefs Toth and I wanted life in prison, so the dreaded NuForce girl could suffer under our watchful eye here in the kingdom's capital, where there'd be no chance of escape. But no, they wanted to take the girl all the way to Rim … and for what?! Poetic justice?"

The crowd roared, and Wert bellowed, "They're fools! Now Rim has become something straight out of the Void. The Archaic Kingdom's economy is on the verge of collapsing as the Intel, Passion, Spirit, and Adren Kingdoms are withdrawing their troops from your land!

"Is this what you want the royal heads to see? You've spent the past year and a half complaining and rioting about your disdain for their presence—claiming that you don't need their help. And now that they've up and left, you're proving them right by crumbling from within and burning businesses to the ground!"

Wert paused and inhaled deeply before rattling the gate with a viscous pounding of his fist. "What sense does that make?!" he shouted. "I understand your hatred for the Amendment Order at this time. I, myself, hold grievances about a few of my equals. But all chiefs aren't of the same mold. So have faith in me, the unyielding leader of an evolving military, and Chief Toth Brench, the second wealthiest man in the world!"

The citizens roared with war cries.

"Toth and I—along with the will power of you, the people—will bring the Archaic Kingdom back to its feet! The other chiefs tried to hide us after Rhyparia's escape for a reason, but I say no more! Let's rebuild this into a proper kingdom!"

Toth's lips parted as his eyebrows climbed his temple. The horde of people blanketing Archain Road weren't yelling out of rage anymore; it was passion. Wert Lamay had just rallied an entire capital with a motivational speech like no other. For the first time in their friendship, Wert actually sounded like someone from the Spirit Kingdom who instilled drive in others. And it wasn't that light-hearted essence seen in so many Spiritians, but a vigorous, unrelenting resolve that could will a flame to ignite in the middle of the sea. For once he proved why he'd been the Spirit Major.

"Impressive address of inducement from a man I thought very little of," Tazama said.

Toth turned to look at her. There were splotches of a clayish substance on her face and work robes. "I'd like to say I knew he had that in him," admitted Toth.

"He's proven useful," Tazama said, "and that's all we can ask for. Better to be surprised than alarmed." She smiled and turned away. "Come."

He followed her through the palace until they reached a door located in the depths of the dungeon. There wasn't a handle, but there was a pattern of eight squares embossed in the door's surface. To any regular person, it was simply part of the design. But to a Devish, it was a puzzle lock.

Tazama went to work—no hands were needed. The squares slid in what looked to be a jumbled mess of directions. One would occasionally lift from the surface and hover to a different spot. It was an algorithmic mechanism that was too difficult to decipher for most minds.

As the last square slid into place, the door vanished. "Quickly," Tazama said.

Toth stepped through just before the door reappeared out of thin air. He gawked at it, but quickly turned around after realizing which room they were in.

"I'm running low on provod," Tazama said.

"How many have you built?" Toth asked as he rounded the circular stone platform.

"This is the second one. But Toono requested six in total—four of them in key points throughout the palace and two more in the city's outskirts. My stockpile of provod won't suffice for even a third."

"So we wait a little bit," Toth said. "Storshae has planted seeds of doubt in the Power Queen's head. If it works, she'll gladly send us more provod than we need if it means aiding King Vitio's opposition."

"And if that doesn't work, we can ask Storshae to retrieve provod from Prayoga and send it to us."

Toth approached her and kissed her forehead. "You continue to astound me with what you can do." He looked back at the contraption. "A teleplatform … unbelievable."

16
Lilu's Tutor

Before Lilu had departed for Brilliance earlier this year, she had informed most of the Jestivan of her plans while also finding out what theirs were. She knew Agnos was chasing down Cheiraskinia in Sodai, but that's not what interested her. It was his answer to a certain question.

"Did you ever find out what the word in Bryson's dream says?" she'd asked as she packed her bags in her Lilac Suites dorm. She'd escaped her battles from Phesaw's invasion relatively unscathed.

"I did, but I don't know what it's referencing," he had replied, pulling out the parchment and scanning over it again. "*Theory of Connectivity*."

She frowned and stared off into space. "Never heard of it."

"I figured," Agnos said. "Unfortunate. If anyone would've known, it would've been one of us. We're the only ones who took advanced theoretical weaving courses."

"Director Senex might've known."

That statement was followed with silence, as they both reflected on the news they had received of Senex's death.

"It's more likely that Director Jugtah knows," Agnos said. "Mendac was a man who liked to research the functionality of weaving. Senex, on the other hand—while exceptional at weaving—didn't care about researching the theoretical applications."

Lilu threw her bags over her shoulders. "I'll ask Director Jugtah during the journey to Brilliance. If I find out anything, I'll get in touch with Bryson whenever I return."

Several months had passed since, but Lilu thought about it every time Mendac's name was referenced in a class at IWA—which was nearly every day. Director Jugtah had claimed to know nothing of the theory. But who knew if that was actually true?

She had committed to the idea of researching information that hinted at such a theory, but with the amount of homework she had received throughout the quarter, there wasn't any time for leisurely study. It was September, the end of IWA's third quarter was approaching, and her Permanence vessels were still exploding in her face. Meanwhile Gracie was on her seventh successful vessel in less than nine weeks.

As the two ladies left a kilning room and began taking out lab equipment, Gracie said, "I've been working toward this my whole life. Stop freaking out. You were only exposed to it a year ago."

"I don't care," Lilu said, brushing soot off her cheeks. "I may not have had access to provod and kilns when I was younger, but I understood Permanence. I drew up blueprints of mechanisms using theoretical techniques I'd found in Mendac's study. A lot of stuff in Dunami Palace was built by weavineers who used my blueprints."

"And you should be proud of that," her friend said, throwing her arm around Lilu's shoulder. "But imagining something is different than building it. I have faith that you can do it. Your potential is sky-high."

"I hate the word potential."

Gracie laughed. "Well, maybe you'd reach it faster if you let that sexy teacher's assistant help you out."

Lilu threw Gracie's arm off. "He has a name, and I'm not foolish enough to put myself in a one-on-one situation with him. I know what he wants. I can see it when he looks at me."

"I wish he'd look at me that way," Gracie mumbled.

"What was that?"

"Nothing."

Upon arriving at the dorm, Lilu dropped her bag on the kitchen counter and collapsed onto the the loveseat in the study while Gracie rummaged through the ever-ice pantry for a flavored ice pop. "Where are all the greens?" Gracie asked.

"That guy you had over yesterday ate at least three of them," Lilu said, plopping her head back down on the cushions.

"I'll kill him." Gracie grabbed a red pop and leaned against the counter. "What do you have planned for tonight?"

"Studying."

"Let's do something."

"Yeah, studying."

Gracie groaned. "We're doing something whether you like it or not. Or I'm telling my uncle that you've blown ten vessels to smithereens."

The princess rolled her eyes, unwilling to argue. "Fine."

* * *

That night, Lilu and Gracie walked down a crowded sidewalk underneath radiant Intelamps. Certain areas of Brilliance didn't sleep; and with the nightlife in full swing every night of the week, even the brightest of minds knew how to let loose.

The two women were dressed in the finest attire without being too frilly. As a royal daughter, Lilu's wardrobe was infinite—although somewhat limited, being away from the palace. She'd lent Gracie a pouf dress, the top half of which was ruby red and hugged her chest and lower ribs. Once it reached her navel, it became a pattern of rose pedals against a white background, splashing away from her waist and ending mid-thigh at the hem.

Lilu wore a sunny yellow high-low dress accompanied by a band of daisies above her grassy bangs.

They entered a restaurant and waited to be seated. Gracie raised her eyebrows. "Usually when men turn and look at me, they appear to be craving something. Tonight they simply looked stunned."

"Which do you prefer?" Lilu asked.

"Definitely the latter. How do *you* deal with all the attention?"

"I don't worry myself with ravenous slime balls who lack the proper decency to act as though they've seen a woman before."

Gracie frowned. "Seems a bit—"

"Don't say it," Lilu said.

"Say what?"

"Prudish, prissy, uptight."

She laughed and shook her head. "I was going to say chaste."

"I carry myself with a certain level of integrity, and I believe men should do the same."

The hostess came over and brought them to their table. Lilu glanced back toward the crowded lobby, curious as to how they had been chosen over a dozen people. She then slowly realized where they were headed. She had been set up. The student teacher was already seated at a booth, dressed in a blue button-up vest against a white shirt. He had a glass of white wine in front of him.

"Good evening, ladies," he said as they joined him.

Lilu didn't respond, but Gracie sat down and took a swig of his wine. "Hey, cutie."

He laughed and glanced down at the table—a hint of modesty perhaps? While he had his fingers interlaced in front of him, he had the proper sense to place his forearms on the table instead of his elbows. His dazzling silver cufflinks reminded Lilu of Toshik—not the most flattering comparison.

At the beginning of dinner Lilu provided very little input to the conversation. She'd say a few words when coerced by Gracie, but nothing was voluntary. She could tolerate this charade as long as the attention wasn't on her. Gracie, however, would make sure she didn't have that luxury for long.

"So Frederick, did you know Lilu's had twenty volatile vessels—all of them exploded."

Lilu shot Gracie a livid glance, as Frederick said, "I've heard, although the number was definitely lower than that." As she turned her gaze toward him, he explained. "Stuff gets around. Do you think the lab assistants in the kilning sector don't gossip with their colleagues? Eventually word makes it to the weavineering assistants."

Lilu stared emptily at her quail, and her eyes grew heavy. "So I'm the laughing stock of IWA?"

Frederick's face became grave. "Not at all. You impress people, Lilu. You may not be able to craft a proper Permanence vessel yet, but you can definitely think up some of the most amazing concepts just by mentally applying the rules of weavineering and visualizing it. The building part takes time, but once you can do it, you'll be a champion of the weavineering world."

"A bunch of words that amount to nothing but 'potential.'"

"Listen," Frederick said. "Professor Jugtah has shown some of your blueprints and diagrams for weavineering devices to licensed weavineers—people who have been in the profession for decades."

"Where'd he get my blueprints from?" she asked.

"He must've snuck them up from Dunami or Phesaw. The point is: you've garnered the attention of industry experts without even creating a Permanence vessel yet! You're a specimen."

She cringed. "Don't use that term."

"You're right, sorry."

"So this whole time you've looked at me not because of a physical attraction but because of my mental aptitude."

"Can it not be both?"

Lilu glanced at Gracie and nearly died of laughter. She was pressed back into the booth as if she was trying to disappear into the cushion, a noodle hanging from her puckered lips. There was a giddy delight in her eyes—like she was watching a play and the lead actor finally landed the girl of his dreams.

"Sit up," Lilu said, rolling her eyes.

Gracie slurped up the dangling noodle and nodded her head. "My bad."

Returning her attention to Frederick, Lilu asked, "Why'd you never offer to help me if you knew I was failing so miserably? It could have been the perfect excuse to speak to me."

"I'm not one to push if I'm not wanted. I respect boundaries, and you clearly had a wall around you as tall as Brilliance's."

Gracie looked back and forth between the two of them as she scooped soup into her mouth directly above the bowl.

Lilu studied him; her eyes narrowed. He was a trophy of class—nothing at all like Toshik. She allowed herself to smile. "The wall has been cracked. When can we begin work?"

* * *

"You're not going to pass the final exam on Friday, but that's okay," Frederick said as he placed a block of provod in front of Lilu. "You'll retake the class during the fourth quarter. Then, when December hits, you'll be ready. I'll start by observing you build a provod vessel, but I won't speak; this way I get a feel for what needs to be changed."

They were in a small lab room tucked into an exclusive corner on the third floor. Advanced students could reserve this room for hour-long chunks, but there was typically a queue as they were in high demand. Thankfully Lilu had a licensed weavineer in Frederick. And even then, they still had to get here at the crack of dawn on a Sunday morning to secure a time slot.

Lilu stared at the provod as though it were her nemesis. After sizing it up, she picked up a knife and carved a circular lid out of the surface. She then grabbed a gouge and gutted its insides. This was the easy part since there wasn't much finesse involved. Once she created a hollow center, she took a deep breath and reached for a jointed chisel. It was a peculiar contraption adapted from a jointed scalpel used by surgeons who wanted to see hidden locations inside the body.

Its base was a metal rod that was screwed into the table's surface. At the top of the rod was an appendage that jutted to the side, capable of swiveling three hundred and sixty degrees upon a synovial joint. This appendage attached to a smaller metal limb via a hinge joint before connecting to one final pin-sized limb that held a chisel and miniature Intelight. Each hinge joint had a tiny circular mirror placed on it that allowed Lilu to glance into the first mirror and see inside the provod through sequential reflections.

It was backbreaking work which required her to keep her neck craned over the device with one eye strained into a mirror, and her left hand holding the vessel steady while the other transitioning between six knobs, each controlling a different part of the jointed chisel. This method took hours to carve grooves into the provod's inner walls. There were several times when she had to step away, stretch her back, and crack her neck.

"You've got this," Frederick said, sitting on a table across the room.

There was a knock on the door. Another assistant was gazing through the window impatiently. Frederick waved him off. "We're busy."

Finally Lilu backed away, pleased with her work. She groaned and rubbed her eyes. "What time is it?"

"Half past two," he replied while approaching the station.

"Seven hours ..."

As he placed his eye over the first mirror, he said, "You're definitely a perfectionist; that's for sure."

Lilu practiced patience as he fidgeted with the knobs, inspecting every possible angle of the vessel's interior. He was a lot better at handling the device than she was, but that was to be expected from someone of his caliber.

"There's a lot of space in here," he said. "It's *too* hollow."

"Is that a problem?" she asked. "It's so it can hold more Intel chains."

He stood up and rubbed the back of his neck. "But it makes the walls too thin, which risks the vessel bursting. There's your error."

"It seems it was easy for you to spot," she muttered.

"That's a good thing. That's an easy fix. If it was something like your grooving or texturing, that'd take more time. But I saw no issues with your attention to detail." He picked up a rag and pressed it against his face a few times. "In fact, your problem lies in what I said earlier: you're a perfectionist. Why were you spending so much time on certain spots? Or why did I see you finish an area of the provod, then move on to another spot only to return to what you had just finished?"

"Because I felt I didn't get it right the first time. I felt I could carve better."

He shook his head and laughed. "That's why your walls are so thin. You continue to unnecessarily carve deeper into them. Trust your skill, Lilu."

She looked down at the floor, appreciative of Gracie's set-up at the restaurant the other night. It took someone pliable and organic like her to force a stubborn mind to change. Lilu couldn't let her know that she'd been right.

Lilu looked up. "All right, is there any more provod?"

He stared at her, flabbergasted, with his brows furrowed and lips twisted. After a moment he guffawed. "Relax," he finally managed to say. "We'll come back tonight in a few hours, but I need to eat something first … and get some fresh air."

She shrugged. "Slacker."

* * *

The two of them spent hours talking as they walked through several blocks of Brilliance's massive expanse. Topics of their conversation included weaving, kilning, Permanence, and weavineering—basically everything related to school. It was all Lilu cared to talk about. And while Frederick might have preferred a break from the mind-numbing discourse, he did well in masking it by smiling throughout.

When they reached the first intersection in Brilliance—where Mendac's statue stood—Lilu's disgust radiated from her pores. Frederick took notice. "Did you know him?"

"Kind of. I was very young."

"When you grow up here, the first man you hear about is Mendac. A lot of children have been named after him." He paused, then said, "Luckily they're too young to be in IWA."

"Why hasn't this been knocked down yet?"

"Good question."

"What would happen if I destroyed it?"

Frederick looked at her, his lips firmly flat. "You'd be locked up and put on trial for a serious offense."

She looked back at him. "You forget who I am."

"Ah … True."

They stared at each other for a moment.

"Can we find somewhere less crowded?" he asked as he narrowly avoided being trampled by a caravan. "Or at least get away from this intersection?"

Lilu absorbed every detail of the statue before nodding and turning away. Later they stopped by her dorm to rest before returning to IWA. She stood on the balcony with the glass door open behind her, so she could talk to Frederick while he rifled through the reading material in the study's bookcase.

"Is the statue supposed to symbolize anything?" she asked. "Like a specific event?"

"Not an event, but his achievements. The scroll held in his hand lists all of his most groundbreaking theories and laws. He had a lot of them, but the most notable one centered on the human body's energy system."

"You mean they're literally carved into the stone scroll?"

"Yep, but you can't see it from the ground. With the angle it sits at, you'd have to gain access to the upper floors of Brilliance's Weavineer Tower to see it."

Lilu stepped inside, sliding the glass door shut behind her. "How do we get up there?"

He turned and looked at her. "Uh … we don't."

"Why not?"

"It's for the League of Weavineers—elite scientists." As Lilu continued to stare at him, he explained further. "Top secret. Highly secured. Groundbreaking technology."

"Well, I'm getting in there," she said.

"No, you're not. The main entrance is always fully staffed with guards, including overnight shifts."

Lilu rolled her eyes and grabbed her bag. "As if guards could stop me. Regardless, we have more pressing matters to attend to for now. Let's go, then."

17
Jun and Alina Brench

Toshik, Jilly, and Himitsu chose one of Jarfait Meadow's grassy clearings to lay out a blanket and have a picnic. It was the perfect location: close enough to appreciate the beauty of the Great Flame that burned atop a massive stone pillar, but far enough away to not feel smothered by its heat.

Jilly pulled out food from the basket while Toshik grabbed a bottle of wine and poured himself a glass. His original plan to stay in Fiamma for no more than a day had perished. Today was the end of the second month in the Passion Kingdom's capital. Himitsu was three weeks clean, but more progress needed to be made for the word "sober" to be used accurately.

Many times Toshik would notice a storm cloud hanging low over Himitsu's head throughout the course of a day. It was evident in his posture, but more importantly his eyes. Then there were Himitsu's nightmares that often woke Toshik from his slumber. Jilly would get out of bed, then walk across the room to Himitsu's bed, sit there, and hug him until his crying stopped.

Most of their picnic went well. They ate, laughed, and conversed until Himitsu's shoulders eventually sunk and his gaze turned empty. Jilly and Toshik exchanged glances. Toshik decided to do what he'd refrained from doing the past couple months … tell Himitsu his story.

There were two reasons for his reluctance. One, he didn't want to vocalize it and therefore relive it. Yes, it was always in his head, but there it remained contained. There was something vaguely threatening about speaking it into existence and losing control over it. Two, the last thing he wanted to do was make it sound like his issues were more severe than Himitsu's and risk implying that he had nothing to complain about. That definitely wasn't the case. Even though Toshik's mom and sister were dead, and it pained him to know this, it had happened over a decade ago. Plenty of time had passed for him to grieve. Himitsu's heart was still freshly wounded.

"Remember in the Rolling Oaks, when you asked me about my mom?" Toshik asked.

Himitsu's head slowly turned as he blinked himself back into reality. "Yeah."

"Her name was Jun." Toshik could tell Himitsu's attention was piqued and continued. "As I told you back in the Oaks, she was the head huntress of Brench Crafts. Hunting was her passion. She loved the chase and respected the power and skill of the beasts that inhabited the different kingdoms. And she's the reason why I know a lot about animals.

"As a child, she'd tell me stories about her adventures. Spunka are the common targets of the Brench family since their spines provide the most valuable wealth and their habitat directly surrounds our estate. But there were exotic beasts she'd travel all over the Light Realm just to hunt. And then there were the ones she'd travel just to find, for even she knew she couldn't kill them—not just because she lacked the skill, but she didn't have the heart to rob the world of such rare beauty."

Toshik paused. "Gale Thrasher—that monstrous bird you rode to Phesaw—doesn't fall under any of those categories because nobody ever believed it actually existed. When I saw Gale that day, all I could think of was my mother and how euphoric that moment would have been for her.

"My mom kept a journal of her encounters. What I read in that journal was what made me want to hunt like her. It's why I picked up a sword rather than the quill my father constantly tried to force into my grasp. I wasn't going to be a businessman. I didn't care about numbers.

"My mom brought me on many trips into the edge of Spunka Forest behind our estate, but not deep enough to face any real danger. She kept me busy with rabbits, squirrels, and snakes while I watched main units penetrate the belly of the woods. The small game gave me enough of a thrill to keep a younger me satisfied for a few months, but I eventually lost patience. Seeing the hunters run past me every day inflated my curiosity.

"My mom knew this, but she made sure I didn't overstep my limits. The path from rabbits to wild dogs was a long one—roughly two years. I remember the day she finally caved to journeying deeper into the forest." Toshik smiled at the memory. "Talk about the greatest day of my life. I saw my first baby spunka. I didn't get to attack it or anything, but I got to watch my mom dance around a small clearing as she dodged fangs, spikes, and tails before cornering her target and landing a fatal blow with her sword across its neck.

"When I was nine, she allowed me to tag-team a baby spunka with her—which, if you remember correctly, are still quite vicious and huge. I did well, and she even let me strike its neck for the kill. It was euphoric for a couple reasons; I'd done my mom proud by showing her I could hunt with her, and I finally had purpose in my father's business.

"I remember dragging that beast back to the estate, where my dad waited on the back patio in his typical suit, a glass of champagne in his hand. When he saw blood coating my face and gear, he briefly panicked. But then my mom slung the spunka in front of us, saying 'Look at what Toshy did.'"

Toshik paused and breathed slowly. He knew this story would only bring forth tears, but he didn't care. Himitsu needed to hear this.

"I was so proud of myself, largely because I'd never seen my dad so proud of me. After years of failing to teach me numbers or prepping me to one day run Brench Crafts, he'd realized there was another avenue for me. And not only that, it also paid respects to his wife's greatest passion … and my dad loved that woman, so that fact alone trumped anything else."

Toshik shook his head before continuing. "So one day I had a foolish idea. I'd slain many baby spunka on my own, and only at the age of nine. I thought I was big and bad, tough enough to lead someone else into the forest and show them the adrenaline-inducing thrill of hunting … my little sister, Alina.

"She was seven, and she was always envious of my escapades with Mom. I'd tell her the stories at the end of every week when I'd return to the estate. That day I brought her with me—we snuck out right before dawn while the sky was still dark." Toshik paused as his gaze fell to the blanket they were seated on, tears rolling down his cheeks. "I never brought her back that day."

Jilly scooted next to him, placing her arm around his back. "We ran into a momma spunka—just my luck. I'd never seen such a beast in my life. It stood tall—more than twice my height—and its fangs were long enough to pierce cleanly through my entire forearm.

"There wasn't any time to think. Its paw slashed downward at a speed I couldn't see. Next thing I knew, I was covered in Alina's blood and she was slammed against a nearby tree. The momma reared back and roared before returning its front legs to the ground, its spikes standing erect at roughly five feet in length.

"It inched toward me while I backed away, tripping over a vine and having to crawl backward while my sister's mutilated body remained in my peripherals. There were no tears—at least, not yet. The adrenaline and terror coursing through me didn't allow it. I remember giving up on retreating. I closed my eyes and accepted the fate I had brought upon myself.

"The spunka roared once more, and every muscle in my body clenched in anticipation. But then I heard its wounded cry. I slowly opened my eyes to see my mother's back facing me. Her sword had sliced through the belly of the beast. I'd been saved, but no part of me rejoiced because all I could think of was my sister.

"I got up and cried to my mom that Alina was dead, but I didn't get a response. Instead she fell to her knees and collapsed limply onto the forest floor. I scrambled toward her through the leaves, grabbed her chin, and tilted her face toward me … her entire neck had been gouged. I checked for a pulse, but of course there was none. So there I was, in the middle of the forest, next to three carcasses—two of which I loved dearly.

"I ended up running back to the estate, receiving incredulous stares until I found my dad. That was a depressing moment. There wasn't any anger in his eyes when I told him, just panic and fear. But after that day, things changed between the two of us … and rightfully so. I deserved all of it."

Toshik's story was followed by a couple minutes of silence. All that could be heard were the distant sounds of children playing in the park. "You always hear about tragic deaths in theatre," Toshik mused. "The person who dies always gets at least one final sentence in before they're robbed of breath—a sense of closure. That's not realistic. I never got that. My mom and sister never had a chance to say something to me."

"Wow …" Himitsu said. "You've lived with that for eleven years."

Toshik wiped his eyes. "It was hard, and I'll admit that I did a terrible job of coping. My methods weren't exactly healthy for myself or fair to others. You brought that up when we entered the Rolling Oaks two summers ago. But the Jestivan helped, and I realized I needed to salvage some sort of a silver lining.

"It took me eleven years to realize my father had not given me a burden, but a gift when he made Jilly my charge. A way to provide a love that had been torn from my life. I'll admit, it has morphed into something a little different as of late, but I can't complain." He smiled at Jilly. "She is my healer."

Himitsu nodded, emptily gazing past them. "The Jestivan has helped us all. It seems most of us came from broken backgrounds … all we needed was a proper sense of friendship and family."

Toshik held up his glass. "To family."

Jilly and Himitsu echoed his sentiment: "To family."

18
The *Whale Lord*

The crew descended the final dirt street before meeting the sandy banks of DaiSo Harbor. Tashami mingled with a few of the utility crewmates: the squallblasters, firefighters, and seashockers. Agnos trailed the pack with a young cabin boy named Eet at his side.

"I know what it's like to be the odd one out," Eet said. "I want you to know you'll always have a friend on the ship."

Agnos faked a smile. "I appreciate that."

"There's a certain way to act, and they'll love you for it."

"My personality shouldn't have to conform to their desires."

"Huh?"

Agnos reworded it: "I shouldn't have to pretend to be someone I'm not for them to like me."

"Ah," Eet replied. "Makes sense. Well, if 'yourself' is what you showed at the Whale House then you should be great."

"That's what I'm hoping for."

They made it to the beach and approached the longboats. Agnos's heart pounded against his ribs as the cool bite of high tide crept up his ankles. He leapt into the boat with a few other lower ranks. These included Eet, a cabin girl named Osh, a couple other swabs, and a powder monkey.

They rowed after Eet, Osh, and a swab grabbed the oars. Agnos dragged a hand through the water as they glided across the harbor. Massive ships blocked the sun on both sides. He was fascinated by the intricacies of some of the helms. Extravagantly sculpted skulls covered the front of certain ships as a way to intimidate any potential threats. Pirates climbed rope ladders up the sides of ships from their longboats. Others, who were already aboard, tossed bags into the water to be brought ashore.

Agnos had never envisioned his first trip to sea in this way, but it didn't deplete the anticipation. He was excited for what was to come, even if it meant having to mop the decks to start out. He was confident he'd quickly grow out of the position once a situation presented itself that would allow his mind to shine. He just needed to stay patient.

Agnos grinned as they approached the *Whale Lord*, the grandest beast in the harbor—big enough to rival the galleons docked across the gulf at Sodai Port. It wouldn't be farfetched to assume that any kind of merchant or navy ship that encountered the *Whale Lord* would do its best to veer clear.

The *Whale Lord* was as tall and long as any other ship, but its width was roughly twice the size of most. That had to hurt it in battle scenarios requiring evasive maneuvers. It had dozens of sails—two of which extruded from the ship's sides like wings—three masts, and enough rigging to make one's head spin.

Agnos climbed out of the longboat and fumbled with the netting on the ship's side. The ladder swayed with each step, and the fact that all of them were climbing at once only worsened the instability. He had to steady his breaths once he climbed over the rail and onto the deck.

He only had a few seconds to appreciate the activity surrounding him before someone shoved a rag in his hand and dropped a bucket of water on the floor. "Get to it," the man said.

"Don't I get a mop?"

"We'll give you one when you're ready," he said. "Need to establish some tenure first. For now, on your hands and knees."

As pointless as it might have been, Agnos did as he was instructed. He got on all fours, dipped the dirty rag into the bucket, and then wiped the floorboards. He was surprised to see that it was in very good condition. It didn't look like a ship that'd been sailing the Realm Rivers for decades. Instead it appeared fresh out of the shipyard.

Rather than staring at the floor, he snuck glances across the decks in search of anyone important. Perhaps Gray Whale, the captain, was roaming around while the crew prepared for departure, but he didn't see anyone in distinguished attire. Barloe was also missing. Even Tashami was nowhere to be seen. Granted, Agnos couldn't see much due to the vastness of the decks, their varying elevations, and the crowd of pirates carrying material to and fro.

So he stuck to scrubbing. Tashami was likely doing something important … maybe even meeting Gray Whale. Agnos cursed his inability to shoot wind or strike with electricity. Such talents would make things a lot easier.

He was knocked forward as someone accidentally ran into him. "My bad, kid."

Agnos hung his head and returned to scrubbing, as flashbacks of his time in the orphanage crept into the forefront of his mind.

* * *

Night had fallen and the command was given to lift the anchor. Agnos made his way deep below decks into the ship's cargo hold, where the ruckus from the decks was barely audible. Agnos appreciated the solitude and now knew where to go if he wanted to read. Of course a few books were all that he had bothered bringing with him on the journey.

The ship's ten swabs were gathered near a pile of overturned barrels strapped to the floor by rope. A few of them joked around while others had quieter conversations, but there was one constant: they all knew each other. Agnos stood to the side. If he hadn't already been used to silence, this would have been uncomfortable.

A latch in the ceiling opened and a man with a lantern in his hand descended a ladder. Its flickering glow illuminated his grimy face and stringy gray hair, casting shadows in the depths of his hollow cheeks. He looked like he could have been the husband of the head librarian in Phesaw's Warpfinate with his permanent snarl.

As he stepped closer to the group, the ambience shifted to something chilling, causing discomfort in Agnos to his very core. Agnos didn't like it, and he'd make it a point to stay out of his way from this point forward.

"We got a first-timer this trip, so let's go over this real quick," the man growled. "My name is Farlyn. Swabbies sleep in the early evening hours—anywhere between seven at night and two in the morning. Once it hits two o'clock, you start your day cleaning whichever deck you're assigned to. You do that until eleven, when you will then move below decks and clean the interior until evening arrives. Then you can choose to spend that time sleeping or whatever else it is you fancy."

His eyes scanned their faces and landed on Agnos. "Got that?"

"Yes, sir."

"You're the rookie, which means your duties below deck will take place here, in the hold." There were a few snickers from his mates. "As for deck duties, it'll change depending on the day. But be certain that you'll have the nastiest one."

"Yes, sir."

The man's face fell, clearly not amused by Agnos's acceptance. "I'll give it three days before that confidence is wiped clean."

Once the meeting was adjourned, Agnos returned to the main deck where he spent the next hour watching the crew work, keeping an eye out for Tashami in the process. Crewmates tugged at ropes as sails unraveled, crashing down to expose an expanse of collective canvases. Every piece moved in a harmonious sequence, as the crew proved that its decades at sea were more than just talk.

He approached the rail and gazed across the waters toward the shrinking harbor. They had covered a considerable distance, and pretty soon there would only be the *Whale Lord* and the horizon. Agnos thought about the possibilities of where they were headed. Whether it was land or another ship, one thing was certain when on a pirate ship: it was something dangerous and of great value.

Agnos wasn't fond of death, but he knew there was no avoiding it. What really scared him was dying before finding a treasure beneath the sea. It was nothing of monetary value, but a book—one that could provide answers to all of Kuki Sphaira's mysteries. His mind drifted to his childhood at the orphanage, where he first met a man named Neeko. That man taught him everything he knew.

*   *   *

As dawn arrived, Tashami found himself in the ship's study alongside the rest of the utility crew. The title of "utility" hinted at lesser work, but at sea it was one of the most vital positions. While each of them served a purpose in the vessel's daily functionality, their specialties really shined during battle.

There were the firefighters, who torched enemy ships with flames; seashockers, who electrocuted the surface of the sea when opposing crews jumped or fell into the water; and squallblasters, the most important of them all. They either directed wind through the sails for evasive purposes or deflected incoming flames from enemy firefighters. The last thing a crew of pirates wanted was their wooden ship to catch flame.

Tashami was a squallblaster, but a completely different type, so much so that they created a new title for his position—a squallshooter. And ever since the crew had seen his performance the previous month in the Whale House, pressure had mounted. Expectations for the young elite were through the roof, as they imagined battle scenarios and the possibilities of what could be done with him in their arsenal.

This was Tashami's one gripe. They treated him like a weapon rather than a person, but that was his fault, he supposed. It's how he had sold himself to the crew.

Barloe stood at the front of the room, polishing a few blades that were strewn across a desk. "It'll be months before we locate our target. Gray has a lot of area to scout, so she'll be spending her time locked away in the captain's area while she sends her dolphins across the Realm Rivers."

"Not that she ever leaves her cabin, anyway," a squallblaster named Crole said.

Jayce, one of two seashockers, cursed. "Dammit. Was looking forward to some action."

Barloe peeled his eyes away from a blade he was cleaning and glanced at Jayce. "This means we'll help around the ship wherever and whenever needed. If I see any of you acting like you're royalty of this crew, I'll rat you out to Gray."

The lot of them fell silent.

"Do any of you want to become fish food?"

They shook their heads.

"All right, you're all dismissed," Barloe said. "Squallblasters stay at the ready to fill the sails. The sky is dead today."

As they filed out of the room, Barloe said, "Tashami, stay for a second."

He turned around. "What's up?"

"Shut the door." The quartermaster waited for the latch to click before saying, "Agnos is aware that the likelihood of him meeting Gray is slim to none, correct?"

"It'll happen."

Barloe smirked and swept his dreads out of his face. "You have a lot of faith in him."

"If you saw the determination he had in the Void, you would too."

Barloe stepped to the side of the desk and leaned against it, kicking a leg over the edge. "Gray doesn't leave the captain's room—not even in battle. She conducts everything from within her cabin."

"You're the only one who's allowed in there, right?" Tashami asked.

"Eet and Osh, too," he said with a nod. "The cabin kids."

"Well, you can put in a good word for him."

He laughed. "Yes, because my recommendation holds so much weight."

Tashami held the quartermaster's gaze for a moment before turning and heading out the door. "We all know it does."

* * *

Tashami searched the entirety of the ship for Agnos, having not seen him since yesterday morning when they were still in DaiSo. This past day made Tashami realize that this trend would likely continue throughout the journey. No matter how many times Barloe preached the unity of the crew, a hierarchical spectrum was definitely present. The two Jestivan were on opposite ends of it.

He found Agnos in the ship's hold, scrubbing away at the curved wall with a rag. Agnos was visibly relieved when he glanced back and saw his visitor. "Hey."

They embraced. "How is it on the other side?" Agnos asked.

"Quite boring."

Agnos motioned for Tashami to follow him toward a pile of barrels, where they proceeded to wiggle into a crevice. "A nifty nook for reading," Agnos said as he grabbed a lantern wedged within the cargo. "I come here to pass the time. If the ceiling door opens, I bolt out and pretend to clean."

Tashami smirked. "Is the morally bound Agnos settling for sly and mischievous conduct?"

"I suppose it seems that way on the surface. I'm being an educator."

"How so?"

"Eet, Osh!" Agnos shouted.

Two children sprinted from the shadows of the hold's farthest reaches. "It's the squallshooter!" Eet screamed.

Osh, a brunette girl with hair short enough to have her mistaken for a boy, expressed her intrigue by pulling at Tashami's ear and poking his shoulder.

Tashami laughed. "What are you rascals up to?"

"Story time!" Eet yelled as the two of them jumped between the barrels and onto Agnos's lap.

"Ah," Tashami said. "You'll find no better narrator."

"High praise," Agnos said. "But I do know of one better."

While Tashami leaned against the barrels, he observed as Osh held the lantern and Agnos opened a book and flipped to a page. "This is my favorite story ever," Agnos said. "Who wants to hear about the world before ours and the cave on the seafloor?"

19
Power Shift

Archaic Prince Sigmund, Chief Merchant Toth Brench, and Chief Officer Wert Lamay occupied the grand library of Phelos Palace. Wert stuck to the main area far away from any bookcases, while Toth and Sigmund strolled into the maze's depths.

"You saw how the city responded to Wert's rally cry," Toth said. "The public's loyalty doesn't lie with Rosel or Grandarion, but with Wert and I. You must pick a side."

Sigmund shook his head and replied, "Wert threw me under the carriage along with Rosel and Grandarion in his speech. Why would I follow that? Rosel and Grandarion would never do such a thing."

"You must forgive Wert," Toth said. "He can be impetuous at times …" He paused and gave it some thought. "Most of the time. But you can't deny the effectiveness of his speech."

Another silent pause.

"Remember General Inias?" Toth asked.

"Obviously. He was one of the greatest generals the Archaic Kingdom ever had and is now forever known as the Light Realm's Chief General, an honor bestowed upon him following the permanent termination of the Generals' Battle."

Toth stopped walking and turned to look at the prince. "What happened to him was a travesty … to be killed by a man whom your father allied with."

"What is the point?" Sigmund asked.

"His son, Elyol, has been training hard to be able to use the lava ancient better than his father could. And he's on our side—Wert's and mine. He wants nothing more than to see his kingdom return to its history of moral integrity and unsurpassed wisdom."

"My father is responsible for his father's death …" Sigmund said. "I see a problem with such an arrangement."

"I understand your hesitance. I've scheduled a meeting between the two of you. With the four of us—you, Elyol, Wert, and I—we can give this kingdom reason to believe once again."

Sigmund seemed to mull over the possibility in his mind as a woman appeared at the end of their aisle. Toth gazed curiously at her. "Tazama, any news?"

"A couple things," she said. "I've received word from the estate that Toshik and Jilly have been missing for three months."

"What?"

"And also, the list of entrants into the Archaic Mountains from two days ago just arrived …" She paused. "One of those entrants? Olivia Still."

*   *   *

Wert stormed through a gallery with Toth and Tazama trailing, their destination several floors below them. The man was on a verbal tirade: "Why did Vitio allow for her to enter those mountains? You'd figure he'd cherish her safety. Or you'd think he'd be smart enough to realize if Olivia found Rhyparia, she wouldn't catch her and bring her back—she'd join her!"

"The list does state that Olivia Still was ordered there as punishment for her actions at Phesaw during the invasion," Tazama said.

"I have plenty of soldiers prepared to go after her," Wert said.

"Trivial allocation of resources," Toth replied.

"What's that supposed to mean?"

"We're already preparing for prior engagements more massive in scale and significance than a Jestivan. You know we have a big undertaking ahead of us. Plus …" Toth went quiet, as if he didn't want to admit his next statement. "Olivia Still, by herself, would be a massive problem for even Elyol to fight. She'd kill anyone we send into those mountains."

Tazama agreed. "And she's accompanied by several skilled bounty hunters."

"She's a child!" Wert snapped. "Elyol would disintegrate her!"

"We're not sending anyone out of their way," Toth said. "Get word to our best hunters already stationed in the mountains. *They* can go after her."

Wert's boot squealed against the floor as he came to an abrupt halt. "I'm the Chief Officer. I command my troops how I want." He then stormed away.

"Such an obnoxious man," Tazama said.

Toth approached the side of the hallway and gazed out a window, his mind elsewhere. "Where's my son?"

* * *

Toono, Yama, and Kadlest once again occupied an empty grand hall inside Cogdan Castle, training for battles that were sure to come. This time, however, they were accompanied by a smaller guest—the four-and-a-half foot Illipsia.

Yama ricocheted around the room at one of her higher speed percentages, but she wasn't making contact with the walls, floor, or ceiling. She seemed to bounce off air, a spectacle that would throw any bystander for a loop.

Toono looked away from Yama as Storshae entered the hall with a woman in a hologram-coated robe. The two of them paused as they witnessed the impossible. Yama screamed with each change of direction, exhaustion getting the best of her as she tried pushing through for a second hour. Suddenly her trajectory pivoted, as she lost all bodily control and was sent tumbling through the air onto the floor.

"I'm sorry," the soft voice of Illipsia said as Yama picked herself up.

Toono gazed at Illipsia. "This training is as important for you as it is for Yama. If you don't get this right, a lot can go wrong in an actual fight."

"I don't know if I can weave EC clusters compact enough to support her weight and speed."

Toono's only response was: "Again."

Yama brushed debris from her shoulder and out of her hair, then shot off the ground and rebounded through the air. Toono kept his eyes on her, but noticed Storshae and the woman approaching him in his peripherals.

"Brilliant," Storshae said.

"Have you come to train with us?" Toono asked without looking at him. He quickly glanced at Illipsia and yelled, "Better!" over Yama's shouts.

"Toono, this is Dev Warden Gala." Storshae stepped away as Gala extended her hand.

Toono finally gave them his attention. He studied the warden, becoming more interested in the patterned holograms circling her robes than anything else. He shook her hand. "Pleasure, Warden Gala."

"Nice to put a face to the name," she said before turning her eyes toward practice. "That little girl over there is telekinetically suspending those tiny rocks against the swordswoman's weight?"

"Her name is Illipsia, and yes."

"How many does she have levitating at once?" she asked as she gazed throughout the hall. "The entire place is full of them—from the floor to the ceiling."

"Eighty-five."

"Fascinating …" Gala went silent, then said, "Her eyes are closed too? My goodness … A clairvoyant?"

Yama didn't concern Toono in this drill. The swordswoman had spent her life on peg courses and rock-speckled brooks. This may have been a bit different, but someone of Yama's skill could adapt. All Toono cared about was Illipsia's ability to track Yama's movements while simultaneously strengthening her telekinetic hold of whichever rock Yama's path was headed for.

Clairvoyance, itself, was already a near impossible feat for any Devish, including the most skilled and experienced weavers in Prayoga. Not even Dev King Storshae was capable of it. To ask a twelve-year-old to achieve this level of multi-weaving was absurd.

Yama soared toward a rock near the ceiling. The ball of her foot connected, but Illipsia wasn't prepared for such an angle. The rock didn't have the proper resistance, giving way beneath Yama's foot, and causing her to crash into the ceiling.

As she plummeted, Toono swung his staff to form a massive bubble across the floor just in the nick of time to catch her.

"All right, that's it," he announced as Illipsia fell to her knees. "Yama, take Illipsia to the medical wing. And make sure you get patched up too."

"Warden Gala will accompany you ladies," Storshae said, shooing her out of the hall.

Toono grabbed a broom and began sweeping the rocks that had fallen to the floor. Once only Storshae, Toono, and Kadlest occupied the hall, Storshae said, "I had a broadcast with Toth Brench today."

"How'd that go?"

"Toshik and Jilly have disappeared from his estate. They haven't been seen in months."

"Don't let Yama know that," Kadlest said from above.

"Believe me. I don't want to witness that volcano erupt. Also, they've run out of provod."

"How many teleplatforms has Tazama built so far?" Toono asked.

"Two, but there's no need to worry. I'll have some sent to her from Prayoga." His face grew grave with his last piece of information: "Olivia Still entered the Archaic Mountains."

Toono stopped cleaning and looked back at the king. "How'd she get in there? I thought they were properly manned."

"Apparently Intel King Vitio provided her with documentation that allowed access. The paperwork said she was there as punishment for her assistance with us at Phesaw."

Toono went silent. Olivia hadn't acted on his behalf in Phesaw. Her mission had been her own, dealing solely with Bryson.

"But Toth and Wert seem to have it under control," Storshae said, ripping Toono from his thoughts.

"What do you mean?"

"They've sent their bounty hunters who are already stationed in the mountains after her. She has a bigger prize on her head than Rhyparia."

"Bad move," Kadlest said.

"Are they idiots?" Toono hissed. "Have none of you realized that I don't want her hurt? Not only that, but what happens if Vitio receives word that Olivia is being hunted under orders from the chiefs? He'll send his troops right back into the capital! Such results would unhinge our plans of an uprising!"

Storshae seemed appalled by Toono's reaction. "What am I supposed—"

"*You tell them to rescind their commands!*"

The order echoed violently around the walls. For once, Toono broke character and sounded like a ruler … a dictator. This didn't sit well with Storshae, a rightful king.

The Dev King collected his thoughts and thrusted out his chest. "I don't know who you think you are, but you're definitely not a Gefal—you're not even a king. You will not *ever* speak to me like that again."

Storshae approached Toono so they were chest to chest—close enough to feel each other's livid breaths. "You need me; I don't need you. I can find myself another Archain to finish the job you've already started. I'm aligned with the kingdom that houses Archains.

"Remember this … I am a king." He walked past, ramming his shoulder into Toono's chest. "And you will always be an orphan."

Toono stood still, sights locked on the opposite wall as his mind absorbed those words. He didn't move because, if he did, he'd likely kill that man out of an impulsive rage.

Kadlest echoed his thoughts from above: "Be rational, Toono."

* * *

Intel King Vitio, General Lars, and a few advisors and high ranking officials were cramped in Dunami Palace's map room, which was essentially a smaller version of the war corridor. A detailed map of Dunami was sprawled across a table, but it wasn't the focal point. All eyes were on a topographic map of Kuki Sphaira's ten kingdoms that plastered an entire wall. General Lars stood next to it, directing their attention to certain areas with a meter stick.

"As of yesterday, we have fewer than three hundred soldiers in the Archaic Kingdom. Our military is as close to fully staffed at every city and base across the Intel Kingdom as it's been since before Itta's capture. With that said—" he whipped the meter stick against the Passion Kingdom's diagram— "we have hundreds of scouts and soldiers scouring the Passion Kingdom for any sign of King Damian, his unit, or Marcus, and we'll be sending more."

He glanced around the room. "Any questions?"

"Rumors are circulating that the Archaic Kingdom is already crumbling after Rhyparia's escape, sir," Major Peter said, who had recently been promoted from corporal. "Should we be withdrawing so many troops?"

Lars glanced at his king at the back of the room. Vitio considered that his cue: "The Amendment Order knows what they're doing—specifically Chief Merchant Toth Brench. As everyone knows, Brench Crafts is a powerhouse in the business world. Their stranglehold of the bladesmith trade is permanent and has made the Brench family one of the wealthiest behind mine. He has the ability to cause an economic boom in the Archaic Kingdom and has already instilled plans to boost the process."

Vitio nodded toward Lars, giving him the floor once again. "Brench Crafts has offered a sale unlike any other to each of the Light Realm's kingdoms. They've always had bulk sales, but not like this. None of the royal heads could refuse it."

Lars reached toward his waist and drew a long, slender blade. "Everyone knows that Brench Crafts specializes in swords made from spunka spines. They practically own the forest the beasts inhabit. Each of the royal heads has accepted the sales terms offered by Brench Crafts, which means we'll be coughing up more coin than ever. But in return, we'll receive enough spunka swords to arm one out of every three soldiers in our army."

"We can't discuss the financial specifics," Vitio said, "but let's just say Toth Brench will have more than sufficient funds to rebuild the Archaic Kingdom. Each of the royal heads will be sending hefty deposits in the coming months."

"Interesting …" an advisor mused, "an Adrenian trying to be an ambassador of the Archaic Kingdom."

Someone knocked on the door. Peter opened it a tad, his head disappearing behind it. He looked back. "It's Vistas."

Lars approached and exchanged whispers with the Dev servant before shutting the door with an envelope in his hands. "What is it?" Vitio asked, noticing his general's bewildered face.

Lars approached and handed the envelope to Vitio. It was sealed with the Power Kingdom's insignia—two massive fists pressed against each other. Power Queen Gantski had written this personally. Typically the only written communications with the Power Kingdom were invoices written up by the trade and economic departments.

He opened it and unfolded the parchment held within. His eyes skirted through the letter, and a fury ignited in his chest the more he read. "Everybody get out except for General Lars," he said.

After they filed out of the room, he read through it again, this time aloud:

Intel King Vitio,

In March, you informed me of the death of Bruut Schap, grandson of the Power General. You claimed that you took the other Power Diatia, Vuilni Gesluimant, into custody for questioning, but what am I to believe with no proof? You also claimed that a young man by the name of Agnos told you that Toono defeated Bruut in battle.

I regret to inform you that I've recently received news that opposes your claims. And I have reason to believe it. I know who killed Bruut Schap, and it wasn't Toono. And I know why Power Warden Feissam fled Phesaw.

Let me make this clear: there will be repercussions for the Light Realm's actions against the Power Kingdom. This is official notice of my kingdom's withdrawal from its alliance with the Light Realm.

Spirit Queen Apsa, Adren King Supido, Passion King Damian, and the Amendment Order will each receive similar letters. The differences lie in the details of our specific commerce arrangements.

To the Intel Kingdom, keep your iron. We have ceased all exports of provod into the Light Realm.

I demand every Light Realm kingdom withdraws their naval forces from Power Kingdom waters. You have a timetable of one month. Otherwise retaliation is certain. I also suggest leaving the Dark Realm altogether, seeing that I cannot guarantee your safety across the Dark Sea and its rivers.

It seems you're all replicas of that vile Archaic King Itta. You've made an enemy out of the Powish. Fight with might, and good luck.

Gantski Power, Queen of Fists

Vitio's eyes met the general's. A brief moment of uncertainty wafted over both of them, followed by panic.

"Their allegiance is more than ending, it's shifting," Lars said. "I guarantee it. This does not bode well, milord. This gives King Storshae a lot more power."

"And significantly hurts us," Vitio added. "Our economy thrives off of the technology Brilliance produces. If it stops receiving imports of provod, the weavineers and their ability to innovate will regress."

Lars walked toward the map on the wall and examined the massive river that led into the Power Kingdom. "And what do we do about our ships?"

"We'll discuss that after I get in touch with the other royal heads and find out their courses of action. But I'm definitely in no rush to retreat." Vitio paused and glared across the room. "We need to find King Damian, and quickly. War is on the horizon."

20
Sundial

Rhyparia stepped out of the log cabin that housed Musku, Rayne, and Saikatto. She followed Musku and Atarax to a river that had no source. It simply began out of nowhere, sputtering from the ground until it flowed toward the plateau's precipice and crashed to the ground below as a waterfall. They approached the edge and observed the billowing mist below.

"Well, you two have fun," Musku said, looking apprehensive. "I'll take the trail. Besides, I have to make a stop somewhere. My presence has been requested by someone important."

Atarax smirked at Rhyparia, which was a strange gesture from the normally dry-faced fox. She had learned that a thrill was the one thing that could bring such an expression out of him.

They dove off the cliff, a blast of excitement and fear overcoming them before being caught by Rhyparia's lighter gravity. They sunk to the rocks bordering the base of the waterfall. She fumbled with her footing against the slick stone, but eventually steadied herself and took a seat. They stayed silent even as they were continuously sprayed by the crashing water.

Rhyparia's gaze landed on the swords sheathed at Atarax's hip. "Why do you carry three swords?" she yelled over the roaring falls.

He tore his eyes away from the statue of Dimiourgos in the distance and looked back at her, his reddish fur drenched. "Because I fight with three swords!" he shouted back.

"I've never heard of such a thing!"

"You've never met such a swordsman!"

Rhyparia wanted an elaboration, but Musku had finally arrived. He stepped past and carefully traversed the rocks. "Follow me," he said.

She waited to see where he was headed before following his instructions. Her eyebrows rose as Musku penetrated the waterfall and disappeared behind it.

Atarax nodded for Rhyparia to enter first. As she stepped through—her knees buckling under the force of the falls—she wondered where she was being led. A cave with rows of unlit torches stretched into shadows on the other side, but it grew brighter as Musku stepped from torch to torch, igniting each one.

"Be wary of rattlesnakes," he said, sending her gaze skating across the ground.

The three of them ventured deeper into the cave until finally reaching a chamber. "Do *not* move," Musku said. "Give me a second."

He followed the chamber's wall, igniting more torches as he went. As he gave the room light, a bottomless cavity became visible in the ground. No wonder Musku was moving as delicately as he was. There wasn't much space between the edge and the wall—a mere ledge.

Rhyparia got on all fours and crawled toward the hole. Atarax strolled to the edge and gazed down. An entire forest grew sideways out of the cavity's walls, although it resembled more of a desolate wasteland after centuries of unuse. Dead trees bent at the base, drooping into the obscurity of the bottomless pit.

Musku finally circled his way back to Rhyparia and Atarax. "There are many factors that make the Realmular Tunnel difficult to navigate. The forest that Dimiourgos had built fifteen hundred years ago died out over time without natural light, making life unsustainable. If one was to travel through the abyss, they'd have to pack months' worth of food—and that's not practical even with normal gravity. Here one would have to jump from tree to tree in order to make it anywhere. And imagine trying to do that with a month's worth of supplies tied to your back."

Rhyparia shook her head. "Tough."

"And then there's the biggest problem—the reason why traversing the abyss is impossible."

Rhyparia nodded. "The gravity."

"Dimiourgos temporarily altered gravity to make the escape from the Dark Courage King's wrath possible, but that's it. He never dreamt of the dimiours trying to get back."

"So you want me to float everyone through the hole like Dimiourgos?"

"No. That wouldn't work, and Dimiourgos didn't do that. You'd have to be in a constant weaving state throughout the entirety of the journey, and that's impossible. Eventually you'd falter, and that'd result in natural gravity taking over once again."

"And a plummet to our death," she concluded. "So what's the plan?"

"The same that Dimiourgos had when he constructed this abyss: make the walls the ground."

"How?"

Musku knelt next to her. "You've always thought of your ability as shifting gravity up or down, but have you ever thought of a lateral gravitational force?"

"Sideways!?" she asked.

He laughed. "Yes, sideways."

"Can I do that?"

"With a lot of time and some masterful weaving."

"How much time?"

Musku gazed across the abyss as he seemed to ponder on it. He hummed to himself before answering. "Twenty years."

Silence followed. Rhyparia's expression dulled as she glanced over at Atarax. "Is this a ruse?"

"It is not," Musku replied.

"I'm not waiting twenty years. We might as well march through those mountains right now."

"But it will only take one year," he said.

She groaned. "Make up your mind."

Musku tapped the sundial on his wrist with a grin.

Rhyparia groaned again. "Make up your mind." She froze with a dumbfounded expression. "Err … Talk about déjà vu."

"You're not even aware that you just repeated yourself."

"I did?"

He nodded and showed her the sundial on his wrist. "I rewound you by two seconds while keeping Atarax and me in the now."

"I'm in the past?"

"Not really … my ancient doesn't work like that. I simply rewound you." His eyes narrowed as he looked off to the side. "Even for me, it's tricky to explain."

"That's amazing," she said. "And kind of invasive."

"It's why we can turn twenty years into one … if you're up for it."

"There has to be a catch."

He nodded. "There is. As the ancient's wielder, my body and mind will experience sixty years compared to your twenty."

She got up and retreated through the cave. "Nope, we're not doing this. We'll go through the mountains and deal with roadblocks that are actually manageable."

"I've come to grips with this decision," Musku said as he and Atarax chased after her. "As an Archain, there is no higher honor than to sacrifice one's self for moral justice. Let me honor my beliefs."

Rhyparia planted her foot and spun around. "How old are you to think that you can just throw away sixty years of life?"

"Fifty-one."

"You'll die!"

"And save thousands in the process," he said.

She paused and gathered her thoughts. This was insane. Playing with time wasn't safe. According to Musku, however, his ability didn't alter anyone's time but the wielder and target.

"So what will happen to me?" she finally asked.

"You'll experience twenty years of training in one, which means by October of next year, your weaving skills will be leaps and bounds ahead of where they are now."

"And the negatives of such a tactic?"

"You're losing twenty years of life. And then the final effect is either negative or positive, depending on how you take it. You'll physically age twenty years."

"I'll look like a thirty-eight-year-old woman …"

"Exactly."

Rhyparia mulled things over in her head. She would become unrecognizable to her friends at Phesaw, but what did it matter if she'd never see them again? She would face death sooner than intended, but that was selfish thinking coming from someone who had already cheated it.

She began to think of Vuilni, her hoodie over her head and braids crashing down her shoulders. The slaves were treated like something less than human by the higher stratums and Powish elites. Vuilni told stories of her home that made Rhyparia's childhood sector of Olethros seem like a royal palace. And Rhyparia had vowed that she'd accompany Vuilni whenever she decided to return to Stratum Zero. Then the two of them could make a difference however they saw fit.

Rhyparia nodded to herself and glared at Musku. "I'm in."

21
The Commissioner

Toshik awoke to the sound of shattering glass a floor below him. He rubbed his eyes and gazed toward the window above his bed to see the moon hanging high in the sky. As the commotion downstairs loudened, he sat up and put on his slippers.

"What's happening?" Jilly asked.

"I don't—" Toshik paused as he noticed Himitsu's empty bed. He shot up and grabbed his sword, not even bothering to throw on a shirt. He poked his head out of his room and looked toward the stairs. Someone was hollering from below.

"I'll have you locked up for years!"

Toshik hustled down the hall, a lethargic stagger in his steps, with Jilly behind him. He had hoped to descend the steps, peek over the banister, and not see Himitsu. But that would have been too convenient.

Himitsu hurled glass mugs across the bar into the wall, wobbling throughout the room and flipping tables as he went. He tossed chairs and dumped plates of leftover food onto the floor. And he did all of it with laughter.

Toshik stormed down the remaining steps into the bar. "Himitsu, stop!"

The Passion Jestivan did as he was told. He nearly lost balance as he spun to see Toshik. He hiccupped and chuckled. "Numbness is bliss," he said.

"Alcohol doesn't make you numb, idiot! It makes you apathetic! Look around you! Look at what you're doing!"

Himitsu lost his footing as he whimsically twirled, collapsing into an overturned table.

Toshik marched toward him until they were only inches away from each other, continuing his rant: "Your drunken apathy doesn't change the fact that your parents are locked up!"

Himitsu clumsily pushed himself to a stand, his eyes wavering between Toshik and the girl on the stairs behind him like a ship being rocked by the waves of a storm. "You sleep with the enemy!" Himitsu bellowed, the perfume of alcohol pounding through Toshik's nostrils. "You kiss the enemy!"

"How is *she* the enemy?!"

"Her father imprisoned my parents!" Himitsu shouted, tears pouring out of his eyes. His smile was gone.

"And so did mine! But we're not our parents!"

The bartender begged for them to calm down, fearing what this might turn into. Two Jestivan known for a history of rough quarrels were currently in the middle of their biggest yet. Jilly joined his efforts as she entered the room.

"Stop it, guys," she said. "You're friends. There are other people in this building."

Himitsu's voice lowered. "So you wouldn't mind if I choked the life out of them?"

Toshik's fist struck Himitsu's face, sending the assassin stumbling backward until he tripped over a barstool's legs. Blood spilled from his nose as he lay still.

Jilly's eyes spread wide, but she turned and headed for the stairs. "*Everyone get out!*" she screamed, sprinting up to the second floor. Heavy thuds were heard as she pounded on every door in the building. The barman wisely fled outside.

Himitsu rose and kicked a stool at Toshik. He turned, allowing it to shatter into pieces against his back. Himitsu charged, grabbing Toshik around the waste and tackling him into the counter.

Toshik dropped his elbow onto Himitsu's head then sent it sideways into his ear. He sprung away from the counter and struck the staggering drunk with his sheathed sword. Himitsu swept his arm as he fell backward, sending a wave of black flames across the room. Toshik leapt over it, fighting the impulse to draw his blade.

Residents of the tavern evacuated the building while Jilly protected them, conjuring gusts of wind to slap away errant debris from the fight.

Flames sprouted throughout the bar, burning the wooden furniture to ash. Toshik needed to end this quickly. He had been trying to subdue Himitsu without excessive force, taking into consideration the fact that the young man was drunk and suffering. Clearly that had been a foolish desire.

Toshik cranked his speed percentage to its maximum. In the blink of an eye, he was behind Himitsu with his right arm wrapped around his throat. He pressed his left hand into the back of his neck and flexed his choking arm with all his might while Himitsu struggled to break free. Toshik slid against the side of the counter until he was sitting on the ground. Slowly, Himitsu's body relaxed in Toshik's lap until he was rendered unconscious.

The swordsman heaved for air as he made a visual assessment of the damage done. The flames were gone and thankfully they had claimed only furniture as their victim. A few dents from thrown projectiles blemished the walls, but at least the foundation was still intact.

He shoved Himitsu off and noticed the amount of blood on his forearm that wasn't his own. The lower half of Himitsu's face was covered in red from a broken nose. Toshik sat there without the energy to move. Physically, mentally, and emotionally, he'd been drained. Not even the sight of officers walking through the front door made him want to run. He only wanted to drown in his misery along with Himitsu.

Jilly stood off to the side as the officers stepped through the debris. What an image the Jestivan were painting for themselves. Yama was a traitor; Rhyparia, a mass murderer; Olivia and Bryson were royals of the

Dark Realm; Himitsu, a depressed alcoholic with criminal parents; and Toshik, a man who had just rendered his best friend unconscious.

An officer checked Himitsu for a pulse and then picked him up with the help of another. Two more came to yank Toshik up by his armpits. He glanced at Jilly as he was dragged toward the door. Her cheeks were streaked with tears.

The officers pulled him into the frigid streets, where other officers in red coats were pushing onlookers away from the scene. He had worked so hard to help Jilly move on from Yama and realize she wasn't at fault. He thought he could help Himitsu too. But the reality was that Himitsu's problems struck too close to home. Toshik couldn't help his fellow Jestivan if he still hadn't forgiven himself for what had happened in the forest behind his estate all those years ago.

He hadn't fully healed.

And he never would.

* * *

Lilu, Gracie, and Frederick entered IWA's third floor on the final day of the fourth quarter. Frederick split off from the group and wished the two ladies good luck while Lilu and Gracie headed for the kilning laboratories. This was Lilu's second time taking this exam. She'd failed her first time a few months back.

For Gracie, this was her first attempt. When she'd realized Lilu wasn't going to pass last quarter, she pretended to have fallen ill for two weeks so that she'd be absent for the remaining classes and exams. It was the reckless move of a loyal friend.

They stepped into a ready room, where they put on the necessary safety equipment and tied back their hair before entering the human furnace that was the kilning lab. These days it was nothing to complain about, as it was a welcome change from the cold December weather.

Lilu should have expected it from her last exam, but she was still caught off-guard by the presence of a Dev servant in the far corner. After all, she thought they weren't allowed in Brilliance. When asked, Gracie told her that professors and weavineers were watching the students through the servant's recording. It made Lilu's nerves stand on edge, knowing that Professor Jugtah was eyeing them down, quill in hand, making note of every observeable detail.

She stood at a station with her name on it while Gracie walked to the far end of the lab. Of course they had to be miles apart, and it was likely Jugtah's doing. As she stared at the block of provod resting on the table in front of her, a montage of explosions played through her mind … *Not today*, she thought.

"All right, students, you have two hours to get your provod vessel into the kiln." The lab assistant gave a friendly smile. "Good luck. You may begin."

Lilu snatched a blade and cut into the surface, carving out a circular chunk. She placed the lid to the side and used a gouge to hollow out the core, moving at lightning speed she'd never matched before. It was the beauty of not doubting her technique—something Frederick had spent months fighting out of her. Throughout her life, her fastidious mind had always been her biggest enemy.

Within ten minutes she had a mountain of provod shavings on her table. Now that there was enough space inside the vessel, she could put the most daunting tool to work—the jointed chisel. Its complexity came from its mechanical functionality, but she had become a savvy operator after watching how Frederick handled one over the months.

She rotated it on its axis and then dipped the third limb into the hollow core. Now it came down to spinning nobs and adjusting handles as she stared into the tiny mirrors. She felt herself smiling and didn't bother hiding it. The grooves she carved into the inner walls were lining up perfectly. She even worked some fancy detailing while hatching certain areas.

"Time's up."

She straightened up and rubbed her neck as she admired her handiwork. That was two hours? Felt like half that. Proud that she hadn't succumbed to carving over surfaces she had already grooved, a sense of confidence ignited within her. Not once had she second-guessed herself.

"When I call your name, carefully make your way across the room and place your vessel into the kiln. Please do not drop it. If you do, we're not going to let you remake one. You'll fail and retake the class next month."

One by one, students brought their provod vessels to the kilns. Lilu turned and smiled as she caught Gracie's eye.

"In three days, you'll return to the lab to see if your vessel hardened properly. Then each student will fill their Permanence vessel with a basic weaving pattern of Intel chains. If the vessel reacts the way it's supposed to, the professors will then grade you. If the vessel is a dud or breaks in any way, it's an automatic failure."

Lilu had flashbacks of the first time her vessel exploded. It was not something she ever wanted to experience again—not in this setting, at least. It was embarrassing.

The assistant nodded. "See you on Monday."

* * *

Three days later Lilu retrieved her hardened Permanence vessel from the kiln with a pair of thick gloves. She brought it back to her station and inspected every inch, her face close enough to nearly singe her eyelashes. Its surface was absent of cracks—a good sign that her walls weren't too thin. That would have led to a volatile vessel, risking eruption if too much pressure was stored within.

Unfortunately this emanated other worries that were in direct opposition to explosions. Maybe—and this was something she used to never have to worry about—she had a dud. If she didn't hollow out the core enough, that meant her walls were too thick and had not been able to fully harden in the kiln during the given timespan. This would spell doom for the Intel chains she'd eventually weave into the vessel, for they wouldn't effectively rebound off the inner walls. They would bounce a few hundred times, slowing with each collision until they withered out.

The assistant first walked through the stations, inspecting each vessel for any obvious issues that would deem them unfit for testing. By the time he reached Lilu, he had already sent two students out of the lab—one of them wiping tears from his eyes. Her pulse quickened as he studied her vessel with more due diligence than the others. Perhaps he didn't want a repeat of last time. She exhaled with relief as he walked past her, moving on to the next student.

The assistant returned to his steel lectern and instructed them to weave Intelights into their Permanence vessel, nothing else—a necessary safety precaution.

Lilu readied the lid over the vessel's doorway. She pointed a few fingers into the hole, weaved several hundred loops of Intel chains into the core, and then quickly shut the lid.

She instinctively backpedaled into a classmate's station as she shielded her face, but that ended up being her mistake because the explosion came from behind her. She yelped as provod pelted her back, causing her to dive onto the floor and cover her head.

Lilu's ears rang as she stood up again. Welts formed on her back, but she was able to ignore them at the sight of her intact vessel. Once the station behind her was cleaned and the student escorted out, they were instructed to lift their lids.

Anxiety clawed at her chest as she reached for the handle. She lifted the latch. Glowing orbs spilled from the container, brightening the laboratory and joining the rest of the class's Intelights. It wasn't a dud!

As the students cheered their success, Lilu slumped forward and rested her forehead against her folded arms, her eyes watering with happiness. A hand was placed on her back, and she heard Gracie's voice: "Good job, Lilu."

* * *

Lilu and Gracie left the ready room amongst a raucous crowd of students. This exam had represented more than a milestone; it was a lifetime of work paying off for most of the group.

For Lilu, it proved that she belonged. She had spent her entire life doodling devices that she could imagine and understand, but couldn't build. In fact, the platform that served as the entrance to Shelly's room back in Dunami Palace was a concept of her own, built by a weavineer her father had hired.

But there'd never been anything beyond sketches and blueprints for her, for the palace didn't have weavineering labs. Any technology in Dunami that involved Permanence required the outsourcing of jobs to weavineers in

Brilliance. What Lilu learned of the subject came through dusty textbooks in the untouched corners of the palace library.

The only reason why she had discovered such a concept existed was because of Mendac. She had seen him reading in his study during one of his rare month-long stays in the capital—he was always abroad. She had slipped into the room after he left and read through some of the pages. That was when she learned there was a depth to weaving that most people didn't know about … All of this at the tender age of five.

"You, me, and Frederick need to celebrate tonight," Gracie said, giving a passing classmate a high-five.

Lilu couldn't stop her voice from shaking. "I can't wait to get our vessels back from the professors. I'm going to experiment like a lunatic."

"Give yourself a break," Gracie replied. "We just finished the last quarter of the year. We have three free weeks through the new-year until our lives disappear forever. The curriculum beyond the horizon is killer."

"I suppose I'll enjoy the festivities … see which city brings in a new year better, Brilliance or Dunami?"

Lilu began to wave as Frederick rounded the corner ahead of them, but he froze with a wide-eyed stare above them. She frowned and spun around as footsteps approached.

Three men came to a halt. One was Professor Jugtah. The other two she didn't know. Both were dressed in slim-fitted trench coats, buttoned with gaudy gold circles. Matching gold strings accented their hems and cuffs, while a silvery glint hung from their wrists and necks.

"Lilu Intel," the blond man said.

"That's me."

"I've heard a lot about you," he said. "Would you like to visit Weavineer Tower?"

"And who are you?"

He smiled. "Forgive me. I'm the commissioner of the League of Weavineers, Wendel LeAnce."

22
Weavineer Tower

"I hope you're not going anorexic on me," Gracie said while Lilu stared at her plate of mashed potatoes and steak. She added, "Frederick doesn't want skin and bone."

Lilu didn't care enough to respond to her shallow comment, but Frederick spoke up for her: "Doesn't matter to me."

They were having a night on the town once again. Lilu was spending her money on both of their dinners. Gracie refused to use her uncle's money but had no problem burning Lilu's. Frederick could fend for himself, but he ate very little when compared to the appetite of most men she'd known in her life … or Jilly and Thusia.

Lilu looked up from her food and finally mentioned what had been weighing her down all day. "I didn't know there were other LeAnces."

Frederick and Gracie exchanged looks, communicating with not-so-subtle gestures as to who should speak. Gracie caved.

"'LeAnce' is a family name that doesn't leave Brilliance. It's more of a cult than a family—even if they are related by blood … except for Mendac. He was an orphan, but he inherited their last name at a young age. Or that's how the story goes."

Lilu shook her head; that didn't add up. "But people outside of Brilliance have known of the name for decades ever since Mendac joined the original Jestivan."

"Correct, but nobody knew of anyone else who had it, nor did they know the significance behind it." Gracie paused and stabbed her fish with her fork. "Want to know something juicy?"

"Go on," Lilu said, playing into Gracie's need to be prodded.

"Brilliance used to be a city of *only* weaving. There was no weavineering until Mendac returned from the Dev Kingdom with a discovery. The details are frustratingly vague, but he is credited for everything: provod, kilning, Permanence, and weavineering. His discovery—whatever it was—changed the course of this city."

"And you're telling me nobody knows the specifics of how he discovered such a complex concept?" Lilu scrunched up her face in disbelief. "Something tells me he likely stumbled upon it and stole it."

"The LeAnces know," Frederick said. "How many of them are alive? Not sure. The city knows of one, and that's the commissioner. But people believe there are a few others who hold seats in the League of Weavineers."

"Sounds dubious."

Gracie shrugged. "Well, if a man like Mendac was a product of such a family, I'd say 'dubious' is too endearing of a word."

Lilu stared emptily at the table. "I'm gonna go tomorrow."

Gracie tilted her head and raised an eyebrow. "It's one of two possibilities. They either want to recruit or murder you."

Frederick dropped his fork onto his plate as Gracie said this. He glanced at his wristwatch. "I have to go," he said, deflated. He slid out of his booth and wiped his mouth with a napkin.

"But *whyyyy*?" Gracie whined.

"I'm tired." He smiled at both of them. "Good night, ladies."

Lilu continued to stare at the table as he walked out. Gracie pouted at her friend. "I hate how oblivious you are."

"I'm not oblivious," she replied, which wasn't a complete lie. A better word would have been "distracted." Her mind was on a certain other LeAnce, wondering what antics he was getting into … She missed him.

*　　*　　*

Lilu climbed a broad set of stone steps that led to Weavineer Tower's main entrance. Once she reached the entryway, she stopped and stared at a contraption that looked and behaved like no door she'd ever seen. There were four glass panels connected at their hinges in a crosslike pattern within a circular room no bigger than a closet. She watched as people entered and exited the building. They'd step into a pocket between two of the doors and push a handlebar, walking in step with the rotating mechanism until their pocket opened up on the other side.

Someone bumped into her. "Excuse me, miss."

She decided to give it a whirl. Everyone else made the timing of it look easy. She took a leap of faith and almost lost her arm in the process. Once inside the building, she glanced back at the monstrosity as her heart hammered against her ribcage.

She regained her composure and turned, only to be blown away by the opulence. The stylistic design of the architecture was unique to this building only. It didn't have the expensive polished gold seen in the foyers and rotundas of Dunami Palace. The wealth screamed in a quieter, more naked way.

Like everywhere in Brilliance, Lilu's gaze was pulled upward. A wall of glass stretched from the oiled wooden floor to the angularly vaulted ceiling a hundred feet above, providing an unprecedented view of the carriages and crowds in front of the edifice.

There was a sea of floor space and a busy check-in counter against the back wall. There were sitting areas with black leather furniture placed against walls short enough to look over. She could just see a bar through an archway in the distance. And if she looked to her left across the expansive lobby, there was a lounge. Was this a place of business or recreation?

As she approached the front desk, she noticed something else … a musical harmony. She scanned her surroundings and spotted a woman seated at a parlor grand piano. This triggered a couple memories for Lilu—both of which were conflicting. She pictured Bryson, a handsome and tenacious young man as he exposed his more vulnerable and expressive side. But then she saw a frozen Apoleia in the Lilac Suites lobby, hammering away at the ice-capped keys.

Lilu turned away and approached a woman at the desk, a sudden chill biting at her skin. "I'm here to see the commissioner."

The lady glanced up from some parchment. "In all my years here, that's the first time I've heard such a statement." She looked down and scribbled something on a note before handing it over to another woman, who then disappeared through a doorway in the back wall. "I guess it pays to be a princess—even in Brilliance."

"Excuse me?"

The woman looked at Lilu with a bored gaze. "Have a seat in one of the waiting areas. I've sent word of your arrival. Someone will be down to get you shortly."

Lilu bit her tongue and found a vacant sofa. A couple men in suits sat nearby in the same area. They both were young, but one seemed fidgety as he continuously adjusted the knot of his tie.

"Name's Arrogo," said the more composed gentleman. "Are you here interviewing for the Weapons Weavineer position?"

"That's a thing?" she asked.

He paused, clearly surprised by her cluelessness. But then he grinned. "Playing it cool … I see."

"I actually have no idea what you're talking about."

He looked her up and down. "You're dressed up for an interview …" he trailed off, his head tilting with a thoughtful expression. He then raised a finger. "Unless you have a job here already, but then why would you be seated in the waiting area?" His eyes widened. "Unless you've been planted here to observe us while we wait!"

Lilu went from baffled to amused, as she delivered a wry smirk to spook Arrogo. The young man straightened his posture and placed his hands on his lap, which only made him look stiff.

A lady in a gray dress skirt and white button-up met with Lilu and escorted her out of the lobby. As she traversed the first floor, she realized just how deceptive the exterior of this building had been. It was clearly the widest and tallest tower in the city—from what she had seen—but this journey felt more like a voyage, for there was a never-ending depth to the structure.

They stepped through a doorway and into a compact, rectangular box—barely big enough to fit more than five people. Next to the door, a lever extended from the wall with a column of numbers running down its side. The lever presently sat in its highest position next to the number one. The last number at the bottom of the lever was 126.

"Is that the number of floors?" Lilu asked.

"Yes, milady."

"Don't call me that," she said, forgetting what it was like to even be addressed in such a way. "I'm sorry," she added. "I appreciate the etiquette, but I don't want to be known as a royal here."

The woman's frown turned into a smile. "Understandable. I'm guessing this is your first time on an Intelevator."

"Kind of," she replied as she gazed around the cramped space. Her escort yanked the lever down, rattling out a series of clicks until it stopped next to the number 119. Lilu felt the floor lift underneath her feet as the box jarred upward. It was reminiscent of the platforms in Phesaw's auditorium stage, but completed with walls and a ceiling. On one hand, she felt more secure because of it, but on the other, not having a visual of where they were headed was unsettling.

During the lengthy ascent, she mentally constructed the complex Permanence vessel needed to perform something of this scale. The vessel had to be immense and able to store billions of EC chains within it. It also needed to be segmented into one hundred and twenty-six compartments—a doorway between each of them—to match the number of floors it served. The amount of floors someone needed to travel would determine how many doorways in the vessel needed to be opened. With each floor they passed, a corresponding compartment must have opened.

This left one question. Where would one store such a massive, intricate piece of Permanence? She lodged that question into her memory bank for a more opportune moment.

Several minutes passed by the time they reached the 119th floor. Her escort didn't step out of the Intelevator with her. "This is as far as I can go," she said. "Speak with the gentleman at the desk. Good luck."

The door shut. Lilu felt stranded, as if she was in the northern prairie alone. She approached the man at the desk. He greeted her with a pleasant smile, handing her a piece of parchment in plastic with her name scribbled on it: *Lilu Intel.*

"Hang it around your neck for identification purposes," he said.

Fantastic. The last thing she wanted was for people to know her last name. He guided her through a few halls until they reached an office walled by glass sheets and veiled by closed blinds. He knocked. "Ms. Intel is here."

The door opened to reveal the commissioner. He had blond hair like the only other two LeAnces she knew: Mendac and Bryson.

"Come in," he said.

Lilu stepped inside, stranded once again by an escort's genuine aura. While windowless, the room was lit exceptionally well. The Intelights glowed brighter than any she'd ever seen, casting a white light instead of a flickering gold. She wanted to meet whichever talented weavineer had been responsible for them.

"Have a seat," he said with a level of enthusiasm that reminded her of her father when he'd see Bryson.

Wendel used his forearms to push the contents to the left and right sides of his desk. He then grabbed a rolled up scroll from his drawer, unraveled it across the desk, and slapped his hand on top of it. "Amazing," he said.

Lilu leaned forward for a better look at the contents of the scroll. "Those are some of my earliest blueprints. I drew those when I was seven. Not my best work."

Wendel chuckled quietly. "I'm not sure if you're being foolishly humble or naïve."

She raised her right brow and glanced at him. "I'm a little appalled that Professor Jugtah brought these up here from Dunami without my permission … then proceeded to just hand them over to you. These concepts were automatically licensed to me the moment I drew them."

"Oh, believe me, I know," Wendel said, giving a frantic nod. "And that's why you're here. Nyemas brought you to Brilliance because it's the only city with buildings high enough to match your potential." He placed his hands on the desk and leaned in. "I want you to leave IWA and study here, directly underneath the best of the best. We'll give you your own laboratory stocked with its own equipment—top of the line, mind you. And you'll get your own assistants."

Lilu's lips and eyebrows flattened dully. "My father put you up to this?"

He released the same chuckle as before. It made her feel uncomfortable. "Lilu, your father doesn't pester me. He knows I make the majority of this kingdom's money. That hospital in Dunami is a product of the work done in this building."

"But all I did was pass a crafting and kilning class. Now you want me to work in Weavineer Tower?"

"I know it sounds ludicrous, but seriously … appreciate what you have here," he said, gesturing toward the diagrams on the desk. "Look at it from a perspective outside of your own. *This* can't be taught. *This* is creative and innovative design, which—at its core—derives from critical thinking. This isn't memorizing *what.* It's asking *why* and knowing *how*, only to ask again … *what if?*"

Lilu flushed red. That was high praise coming from a person of elite status. She almost forgot about his last name.

"You have a rare mind that topples pretty much every weavineer in this building. The only leg up they have on you is their ability to actually build the devices, but even that's because you haven't had the time they've had to learn the craft. Dunami and Phesaw stifled your aptitude."

"You said I'd get my own assistants?" she asked.

"Yes, and we already have potential suitors."

"Not the right word choice."

His nose wrinkled as he squinted. "You're right. My apologies. We have many candidates."

She stood up as tall as she could make herself. "I will only do this if I get to place two of my own on the team." she said.

"Done," he replied without hesitation. As they shook on the deal, he asked, "So who is it you're looking at hiring?"

"Gracie Jugtah."

He smiled. "Of course. And the other?"

"Frederick Santio, a newly licensed weavineer who works as Jugtah's assistant at IWA."

"Hmm …" He reached for a stack of parchment sitting on the edge of the desk. He withdrew a sheet after briefly perusing through it. "It seems he applied last night for a position as a Weapons Weavineer … very last-minute. He's going through the interview process right now. Judging by his résumé, he won't get the position—not enough experience or credentials. If you're vouching for him, however, then he must be worth something. Consider it done."

Lilu tried to contain the excitement building inside her. "When do I get to see my lab?"

He rolled up the blueprints and shoved them back in the drawer. "No better time than now."

* * *

Lilu and Wendel boarded the Intelevator and descended to their destination. She tried asking him about the location of the Permanence vessel that powered it, but he refused to divulge any information. They stepped off the Intelevator at the 88th floor, which happened to fill the space of four floors because of its height.

Wendel pulled another lever outside the door. Hundreds of white Intelights illuminated the room, forcing Lilu to shield her eyes until they could adjust. They were standing on a walkway suspended in the air by cables strung from the ceiling. It was an observatory bridge that split into two separate paths just ahead until reconnecting across the room.

A grand laboratory sat underneath them. Nothing in IWA compared. The floor was a stark white. There was a plethora of work stations stocked with crafting tools and an entire wall of kilns. She spotted odd devices she'd never seen before. One of them resembled a jointed chisel, but instead of jutting out of a desk, it was bolted into the floor and likely bigger than Lilu herself.

The most eye-catching component of the lab was a pit located in the middle of the room. Searing coal lined its walls, and flames danced at the bottom. A circular platform hovered at the center of the pit, as two walkways connected it with the main floor for safe travel by weavineers. Safety rails lined the edges of the pit, and wisely so. If anyone fell into that, they were done for.

"Is that a massive in-ground kiln?" Lilu asked.

"A kilning pit, yes. It's for the larger, more intricate provod vessels you'll be creating. You'd simply lower them into the fire."

She gawked at the size of the platform. "What exactly will I be working on?"

"I think you know the answer to that. You forget that I've seen all of your designs …" He trailed off and smirked. "That includes your more innovative ones. At times, the weapons you'll build will require multiple people crafting a single provod vessel. That's why you see mobile stairs and so many architectural contraptions."

"So the people interviewing as Weapons Weavineers are trying to land a spot working for me?"

"That they are."

Lilu smiled and leaned against the metal rail, admiring the dreamland below. "So surreal."

"One more thing …" He looked toward the steel wall on the far end of the lab and bellowed, "Open it!"

The wall split at the middle, and the two halves began sliding apart. "Now, I understand your feelings toward Mendac," he said, "so don't look at this as us telling you to admire him or anything along those lines. We want you to use this as a reference area. It's basically a library filled with incomplete research essays, lab manuals, and failed experiments."

Lilu's eyebrows raised a notch as the room expanded to twice its original size. Wendel continued: "It's a treasure trove of hypotheses, theories, experiments, and data …" He paused and sighed, "Mendac LeAnce's personal lab."

23
Hunted

Bryson leapt from stilt to stilt on the peg course of his backyard, dodging Thusia's gales as she somersaulted and twirled with a feathery disposition. A year ago he had struggled to simply make it to the top layer of pegs. Now he was dancing on them like they were solid ground.

"You're not ready," she said, throwing another blast. "This is a poor showing, Bryson."

He dove left, grabbing and spinning around a peg before tossing himself back onto a shorter one with the ball of his foot. He clapped his hands together, and a pulse of electricity appeared next to Thusia with a deafening pop. He did it twice more, forcing her to skip backward as voltaic blasts peppered her area.

"A new trick," she said. "I like it. It's more unpredictable and difficult to track."

She grinned as though she had something devious planned. She thrust forward both hands, palms out, as a flurry of wind pellets sliced through the air. Bryson contorted his body in efforts to dodge them with some success, but he couldn't avoid the attack in its entirety.

He was in the midst of a flip across a peg when he saw Thusia's leg rise and slash down. A blast of wind swept through the course. Bryson redirected his flip toward a higher peg and desperately latched onto it. The wooden pole vibrated in his grasp, but at least he hadn't been blown away.

Then Thusia's knee rammed into the middle of his back. He yelled as a sharp pain shot up his spine, but he alertly grabbed her by the foot, released a stream of electricity up her leg, and threw her into a nearby peg.

Holding onto the pole with one hand, he grimaced as he reached for his back. He bit down on the wood to smother a whimper. Thusia had bruised his spine.

The Branian groaned as she lowered herself to the ground with a gentle breeze.

"You just whined!" Bryson said. "I win!"

"No, I didn't!"

He released his grip on the peg and plummeted until his feet crunched upon the frigid grass. "Let's get out of the cold," he said.

Once inside, Thusia collapsed on the sofa while Bryson grabbed some milk from the ever-ice pantry. "I feel useless," he said. "It's January. Two more months and it'll have been a year since Toono and Storshae invaded Phesaw. How is it that nobody has heard from them since?"

"There's nothing you can do," Thusia replied, rubbing her leg. "They made a bold move and now they're letting the dust settle before they strike again—just like after you chased down Storshae and took Olivia back. I'm sure they have plans in motion, but you can't do much to find out about them. That's what the royal heads should be doing."

"I have no faith in them," he mumbled.

"You've been training non-stop for six months. With Phesaw closed for the year, you haven't had classes to distract you. And not only that, but you've been training against me."

Bryson sighed. "Olivia's been in those mountains for six months, and she *still* has six left in her punishment."

Thusia turned toward him. "Your sister is fine, trust me."

*　　*　　*

Olivia climbed a pile of rocks alongside Yvole and Jannis. They were the only three hunters left in a group that had originally started with seven. Despite the legends of the Archaic Mountains, it wasn't death that claimed their comrades, but boredom and exhaustion. A couple of them had left two months into the mission, deeming the reward not worth it. Then the other two followed suit a month later. As for the likelihood that they had made it back safely to Rim … Olivia liked to think they did.

Of course the greater possibility was that they were still aimlessly wandering the mountains or dead. Even Olivia wasn't sure how she'd get back. They were entering their eighth month here, and they had stopped leaving tracks a while back.

There were a few reasons why Olivia, Yvole, and Jannis hadn't fled like the rest of them. The most obvious was that the duration of Olivia's punishment lasted a year, so she still had four more months to live like this. Then there was Yvole's determination to receive his bounty, but Olivia had begun to think it was something else. He was standoffish and rude to most of the team. He mostly stuck to that mantra with Olivia too, but there were moments when something softer tried to kick its way through his shell.

As for Jannis, he was an ass in his own way. He was boisterous and arrogant, but cowered any time Yvole made a sudden movement—even if not directed toward him. She couldn't blame Jannis for it. After witnessing Yvole's capabilities when faced with the many dangers that had been presented in these mountains, most would be wary. He truly was a frightening man—the kind who carried himself with nothing to lose, and the entire world to gain.

It was another hot night in the mountains, or at least in the foothills. The three of them tended to stick to lower elevations to escape the thin air. Once they cleared the rock pile, a green valley presented itself. They had seen it a few miles back and decided to reach it before setting up for the night. The best part of this location? The stream that ran through it.

Before entering the mountains last summer, Olivia had questioned the water supply necessary for a year-long stay. The Archaic Mountains showed no signs of water on maps, but the soldiers who stood guard outside the mountains reassured entrants that there were several streams held within.

Olivia picked a spot in the grass and lied down, hands behind her head, as she stared at the stars. Yvole headed for the stream to retrieve water while Jannis sparked a fire with his Passion Energy.

Moments later Yvole staggered against his cane with a heavy pot of water in his free hand. He placed it over the flames, waiting for it to boil and rid itself of harmful bacteria. They had no tents or mats for comfort, only nature.

Jannis was the first to break the long silence: "Care to tell us a bedtime story, Yvole?"

"Not particularly," he replied as he grabbed a ladle from his tattered travel sack. He handed it to Olivia so she could take a scoop of water.

"Come on," Jannis said. "No political rants of disdain for your king?"

"He's weak … that do it for you?"

"I don't get you," Jannis replied. "You despise Mendac LeAnce—one of the most notoriously aggressive men in history—but hate King Vitio for not having that same mindset?"

"Mendac did things for the wrong reasons. He didn't operate out of defense; he was the aggressor, as you said. But now we're in a time when a leader needs to make a statement and counter the evil running around our realm." He shook his head. "You'd think the most powerful man in said realm would be the one to do so. Instead he's punishing princesses and hunting down little girls."

Olivia glanced at Yvole as she passed the ladle over to Jannis.

"You think he's scared to call it what it is … a war," Jannis said.

"You call a spade a—" Yvole was cut off by movement in the distance. He grabbed his cane and stood up.

Olivia and Jannis glanced over their shoulders in the direction of his gaze. It was the hill of stone they had just crossed, glowing white under the moonlight. "Saw something?" Jannis asked.

"I'm not sure …"

Just as he said this, Olivia spotted a blur of color approaching at a speed only capable from an Adrenian. "Move!" she shouted.

She and Yvole managed to avoid the attacker, but Jannis wasn't quick enough. He had dodged to the side, but the swordsman had already severed Jannis's arm at the elbow. He released a bloodcurdling scream, but Olivia and Yvole couldn't tend to him.

They spread out as another blast of wind swept over them. Olivia just caught a glimpse of the speedster and dove to the side. The man banked a turn against a stone and bore down on her again. This time, however, she confronted him head-on, grabbing his wrist and spinning him around until she lifted him in the air and slammed him into the ground.

Yvole put a hand on his hip, impressed. But then he was knocked off his feet as someone's boot connected with his chest. There were multiple enemies.

Olivia tried to stomp on the Adrenian, but he rolled and returned to his feet. He forfeited running and instead tried his luck with a joust of sparring. He swung his sword with the grace of a butterfly's path during flight. He swiped downward with two hands gripping the handle, only to transition to one hand as he slashed across his body. Olivia hopped back, ducked low, and even leapt from the ground as she felt the wind from his sword sting her skin.

Yvole, meanwhile, was using his cane to bat away kicks and punches from a man who stood over a hundred yards away, his limbs stretching as if they were rubber.

"What in *thunder's mind*?" he cursed in anger. "I couldn't get the normal one?"

Olivia undercut one of the Adrenian's swings and struck upward into his wrist with the inside of her palm, knocking the sword free and breaking several carpal bones in the process. He roared as she quickly transitioned into an elbow strike to his sternum, expelling all air from his lungs. That was followed by a left hook that shattered a few ribs. As he fell to his knees, Olivia kneed him in his chin, rendering him unconscious as he collapsed in the grass.

She left Yvole to the rubber man and ran toward a squirming Jannis. He was bleeding profusely into the grass. A whistling sound grew louder on her right, and she turned just in time to snatch an arrow out of the air inches away from her face. A line of archers peeked above the stone rubble—twelve of them, perhaps—their bows drawn and loaded.

They released their grips with a snap, sending a volley of arrows at both her and Yvole. She prepared to dodge, but a burst of red flame danced in front of her, illuminating the moonlit expanse and turning the arrows into ash.

A crevice formed in the infernal wall. She glanced over at Jannis, his face pale as life drained from him. "Go!" he shouted. "I'll have your back!"

Olivia's foot formed a dent in the sod as she pushed off, her legs bulging with each step. The archers peeked again, releasing a flurry of arrows. She caught two, but a wave of heat washed over her as three fireballs rushed past and took care of the rest.

She leapt in the air, soaring toward the rubble until she pounced on top of it, breaking stone and sending debris in every direction. Two archers were wiped out by a chunk of rock that collided with their heads, plastering them against the ground. With a sharpshooter's precision Olivia threw the two arrows she had caught earlier into the skulls of two other archers. Then she stampeded through the rubble, effortlessly disposing of the rest of them with powerful blows. They weren't foot soldiers after all; this wasn't their specialty.

The fight settled, and she combed the area to count the bodies … she saw eleven. She looked up and scanned the scattered forests and rocks that climbed the many mountainsides. She watched as a woman fled into the woods, but Olivia didn't give chase.

She sprinted back toward her teammates, but slowed as she noticed Yvole seated calmly with his legs crossed next to a motionless Jannis. He didn't bother looking up when Olivia arrived. His gaze stayed on Jannis, whose severed arm was lying a few feet away.

Yvole reached into his cloak and withdrew his pipe, while Olivia took a seat on the other side of the fresh corpse. He placed the tip in his mouth and struck up a fire. "You were the best flint a man could ever ask for," he grumbled, extending his pipe as if he were giving a toast at a dinner party.

Olivia pulled her legs close and placed her chin between her knees as she observed the first confirmed casualty of their time spent in these mountains. But this had been unexpected—at the hands of unlikely opposition. She began to wonder … who actually had a bounty on their head?

Yvole took a puff and narrowed his eyes, watching Olivia for a long moment. "Someone's not happy you're here, Princess," he said.

She didn't respond, so he removed the pipe from his mouth and stared at it. He then extended his arm over Jannis's body and offered it to her. "You're eighteen," he said. "Here, for the tension."

Olivia gave it some thought, but eventually took it from his grasp. She studied it with apprehension before pressing her lips around it and inhaling. Her lungs responded by coughing it out of her, but all the same … she inhaled once more.

Yvole tapped his fingers against his cane's handle. "You'll get the hang of it."

* * *

Three hours had passed, during which Olivia spent digging a sizeable hole in the ground with nothing but a jagged chunk of stone. She grunted with each hack at the sod, sweat trickling from her eyebrows into her eyes. Once finished, she slumped to her knees with the back of her hands in the dirt as she looked up at the stars. Even for her, this punishment Vitio had given her had taken its toll.

The worst part of it was the psychological warfare being waged within her. Whether it was Bryson's forlorn shock as she pummeled his face against the bar in Lilac Suites or the teasing visuals of seeing Rhyparia appear unharmed out of a cluster of trees, every night a different person took her dreams hostage. The worst was the image of her mother's disgusted face after her daughter's betrayal.

Olivia stood tall and leapt cleanly out of the pit, landing with both feet in the grass. She bent her knees and scooped up Jannis's corpse, his dismembered arm lying on his stomach. She sat at the grave's edge, her legs dangling down the side, and did her best to gently lay the body to rest.

Her eyes caught something peculiar in the near distance. Yvole stood in the babbling creek, both legs of his trousers rolled up, and his cane serving as a brace against the slow-moving currents. She'd never seen him expose his legs, and while he was presently washing the fresh wounds on the left one, it was the right leg that caught her attention.

Gashes spiraled up his shin and calf, eventually stopping at his knee. It looked like his body had tried to heal, but clearly such an injury was too much. He turned and stepped out of the stream, hobbling against his cane. He dragged his foot limply across the ground. It appeared to hang from his ankle like a flag from its mast on a windless day. He placed his good foot in a boot with ease, but the other took some guidance and force by his hand.

Olivia altered her gaze toward Jannis as Yvole sat on the pile of dirt dug out from the ground. There was a moment of silence before he said, "I was born in Ferrous."

She looked up in shock, but quickly glanced down again, fearing eye contact would make him uncomfortable. "I haven't met anyone from there," she said.

"It's a secluded town—far away from Dunami and the teleplatforms—but arguably the most important town in the Intel Kingdom."

"I thought that title belonged to Brilliance," she replied.

"Of course not. Ferrous is the reason why the Intel Kingdom has ties with Dark Realm kingdoms. We supply iron to them. Without it, we can't trade for the Power Kingdom's provod or Still Kingdom's ever-ice."

He drew his pipe once again and inhaled. "The citizens of Ferrous are proud, hardworking people—religious zealots at times, but hardworking. At the age of seven, I worked in the deepest iron mines in the Ferrous Mountains. I wheeled barrels of the rock in and out of those caves from dawn 'til dusk without a peep. It didn't matter if you were a child; there was no crying or complaining about the backbreaking work—even if the little pay you earned didn't go to you directly, but your family. I'd be lucky if I got a sucker when my mother took me to the town's only shop."

"Very small town," Olivia muttered.

"More cathedrals than outhouses," he replied. He lifted the pipe and inspected it. "Anyway, it's why I smoke from this thing all the time. It's the sucker I always wanted but could never afford." He closed his eyes and continued: "The mines had many restricted areas that were considered unsafe. Rational minds blamed it on nature's erosion; cynical minds deemed it the work of thunder's deity. There were rogue crews that'd reap the rewards by taking the risk. If you mined from these areas, you didn't have to hand it over to the company that owned the mines, effectively eliminating the middleman and increasing profit.

"One night my friend, Psya, and I were in the depths of said area—pushing wheelbarrows as usual—when the ground reverberated beneath our feet. I heard echoing shouts through the tunnel behind me, where miners were busy hacking away at iron. Meanwhile the roof was crumbling, as bits of rock and dirt rained down upon me.

"Psya and I dropped our wheelbarrows and ran for it, but the tunnel ahead was closing. I sprung over the pile of rubble, but Psya struggled. Naturally, I risked everything and turned around to help pull her over amidst the destruction. She wouldn't have made it had I not done so. As she cleared the rubble, she sprinted away to safety while the roof collapsed onto my leg. And I, who had originally made it through unscathed, was now trapped.

"I was stranded … for hours I was a pinned rat. On one side was a wall of broken rock, the dull shouts of fellow miners traveling through. On the other, a clear tunnel with an exit somewhere in the distance. I didn't panic, confident that Psya would return shortly with help. We were best friends, after all—practically siblings. We were neighbors. Our families frequently shared pastures and livestock.

"But eventually a cold reality dawned upon me. She wasn't coming back … she didn't want her family to know she'd taken an overnight job in forbidden mines. And because of the secrecy of this job, nobody would have known to go check on the mines if she didn't tell anyone. So I began trying to tug my leg free of its rocky entrapment."

Olivia found a lapse in the story's details, so she asked, "You mean to tell me nobody had the wits to leave one person at the entrance?"

"Well, there was one, but I suspect he fled when he heard the collapse." Yvole shook his head and chuckled. "Cowards and such. Anyway, my family didn't know I had gone in the middle of the night, so they didn't know where to look. It was impossible to gauge time, but a couple days had to have passed by the time I finally mustered up the courage to drag my leg out of the wreckage. The craggy rocks shredded not only my skin, but layers of muscle. It was a slow, excruciating pain.

"But even that wasn't tantamount to what was next. My foot proved more difficult to dislodge from the debris since it was at such an awkward angle. A good while passed before I finally committed to twisting my ankle within the rubble, completely breaking it …" Yvole's gaze was empty as he stared at the ground, lost in his memory. "I howled, Olivia. Noises came out of me that weren't human. But I still managed to pull my listless foot free.

"I pushed myself onto one good foot and, using the wall as a crutch, I trekked through the rest of the tunnel with my injured foot dragging behind me. I was able to make it back to an active mining site with only a couple of hours to spare before my body would have given up on me from a combination of dehydration, starvation, and shock."

As he ended his story, Olivia looked back at Jannis's body under the moonlight. "What's the lesson?"

"Sometimes it's better to be selfish than moral," he replied as he pushed himself off the dirt pile. "Most importantly, I wanted to offer Jannis a parting gift. He was always prodding me about my past." He kicked some dirt into the grave. "Come on … let's cover him up, Princess."

24
A Declaration

Passion Director Venustas was alone in a Fiamma Palace medical room; the naked cadaver on the table didn't count as company. Its chest and abdomen were cut open, her gloved hands submerged in its organs. She felt around while craning her neck to read an open book on the stand beside her. It had been a while since she had done something like this, but ever since returning to Fiamma for the first time since her studies, she had reacquainted herself with the practice.

There wasn't much for her to gain from this body, however, considering it had been dead for some time. She was simply revisiting a murder case that had been swept away years ago after doctors concluded he'd died from natural causes. But it wasn't much of a conclusion if there wasn't any data or evidence to support it.

Venustas stopped digging around as soon as she heard someone knocking on the window behind her. She turned to see Passion General

Landon with a grave flatness to his lips. She left the room, preparing herself for some sort of terrible news.

"I have word regarding King Damian," he said while Venustas removed her gloves and scrubbed her hands under a running faucet.

"And what is it?" she asked behind her mask.

"A group of teenagers who were swimming in Lake Kaloge found dozens of dead soldiers tied to bags of sand on the lakebed."

Venustas froze, heartbreak wafting over her. Landon continued: "Nearby scouting units were informed, who then traveled to the lake and dove to its depths to pinpoint the king's body … and they did indeed find him."

"What did Queen Fiona say?" Venustas asked, pulling down her mask.

"She doesn't know."

The director straightened up and glowered at him. "You told *me* before the woman who *loves* him?" she hissed.

He didn't flinch. "I figured she'd receive the news better from you. Besides … you seem to have taken the wheel of the kingdom since your arrival. I almost feel as if I should be bending the knee right now."

Nostrils flared, Venustas's temper spiked at his wry jab. For him to bring this out of her was not an easy feat. She—much like all of the Energy Directors—had a good handle of her emotions. And this was especially important for her since she was a Passionian. Nobody wanted to see her erupt.

"Get out of my face," she said.

He matched her glare before turning to leave the chamber. As the door shut behind him, he said, "Milady."

She turned toward the medical room and slumped against the glass panel. How was she to deliver this news? More important, how would the realm respond?

*   *   *

Venustas entered the throne room to find her queen standing in front of the steps that led to the throne. Fiona didn't turn upon her entry; her gaze stayed glued to the royal chair. Venustas walked down the length of the hall, between the extravagant fireplaces that lined the two walls. Each was ablaze, bathing the room in a rippling heat.

She stood next to Queen Fiona and studied the throne with her. While the Passion Director saw only a chair, it was likely that Fiona was staring at the ghost of her husband.

"Milady," Venustas said.

Fiona's eyes finally met hers. "What is that tone?" she asked.

Venustas made sure to hold her gaze—the queen deserved that respect—as she said, "They found Damian's body." Fiona lifted her hand to her mouth as her eyes drowned in tears. "He was at the bottom of Lake Kaloge and—" Venustas was cut short as Fiona fell to her knees and slumped against the stairs, her wails echoing throughout the room.

A door opened, and the innocent freckled face of Prince Pentil—a young boy of ten—peeked inside. Noticing his mother's cries, he ran inside, confused and alarmed. Venustas could do nothing but sit on a step and absorb the sorrow that seemed to be swallowing the realm.

* * *

Intel King Vitio occupied his royal chamber with Vistas standing at the center—one eye burgundy, the other dilated—as he projected a display in the air. The hologram switched between a different face each time someone talked. There was Adren King Supido, Spirit Queen Apsa, and a wide view of the Amendment Order seated at a table. But they were waiting for the person who had called for this broadcast.

A new channel appeared, occupied by the face of a young woman with rosy cheeks and dirty-blonde hair. "Good afternoon, royals," she said.

"Hello, Felli," Chief Senator Rosel said.

Venustas gave a nod, her face absent of cordiality. "Do you have news?" Supido asked.

"I do. Passion King Damian's body was found at the bottom of Lake Kaloge … along with many of his soldiers."

A bottomless pit formed in Vitio's stomach as the broadcast fell silent. This was the tipping point; everyone knew it.

"It was Toono," Vitio said.

"It could have been Still Queen Apoleia," Supido said. "She was also at the Passion Kingdom's teleplatforms during one of the incidents. She killed a soldier."

"No," Venustas said. "Vitio was right. I have yet to see the body since it's still being transported to the capital, but reports indicate that his eyes were completely white—no pupil or iris present."

Queen Apsa nodded. "So now he has his Passion sacrifice."

Vitio shook his head, realizing something didn't add up. "He was able to wipe out a royal first-born in his forties and an entire military unit?"

"I don't find it shocking," Supido said.

"Scouts are also telling me that the soldiers' bodies had burns similar to what was described of the Prim Prince's wounds two years ago," Venustas said. "Like something had eaten at their flesh and muscles. A few even had damage to their organs."

"Who do we know that sides with Toono and can use flame?" Vitio asked.

"From what I'm hearing, it doesn't sound like fire," Venustas said. "I'll have to inspect the bodies when they arrive."

"So Toono's tally is up to five sacrifices," Rosel concluded. "The kingdoms he still has left to target are Archaic, Spirit, Intel, Adren, and Dev."

"And if we're to assume he has Grand Director Poicus as a prisoner—" Apsa paused, and then said, "Well, let's be honest. He's probably dead already if that's the case. That'd make his tally six, so we can cross the Archaic Kingdom off the list."

"And we can also assume that he and Storshae already have someone lined up as the Dev sacrifice," Vitio added.

"So it's our kingdoms that must worry at this point," Adren King Supido said, referring to himself, Vitio, and Apsa.

"Do you think we should hide the people we think Toono would target?" Vitio asked. "Clearly his targets are talented individuals. There shouldn't be many we have to hide. The royal first-borns must stay within palace walls. Honestly, all family members of the royal heads should—generals too, as well as any of the Jestivan."

"I whole-heartedly disagree," Venustas said.

Vitio's eyes narrowed. "Forgive me, Director, but you don't hold a position that allows you much of a voice. Where is Fiona? She should be the one in this broadcast."

"She asked me to step in. As one could imagine, she's not in a proper state to deal with this."

Vitio gave a remorseful nod, and then adjusted his tone. "We must hide any and all elites."

"Your response to this madness is to cower?" Venustas asked, her nose curling up at the very notion. "Nobody knows where most of the Jestivan are. Surely you have Bryson under your wing, but you sent Olivia into the mountains. And Lilu is in Brilliance—luckily that's already the most secure city in the realm. As for the rest of them, they could be anywhere. A plan of action needs to be made, royal heads."

Queen Apsa voiced her approval: "We do need to strike eventually. Since the Generals' Battle, every terroristic event has been directed at us from Toono and Dev King Storshae. We took care of Itta, but it's been made clear that he wasn't of much importance to the real operations."

"So what do you suggest?" Supido asked.

"Oh, you pretend to want my advice now?" Apsa asked. "I recall a lack of cooperation when I presented information to you and King Vitio months ago."

"Because it was preposterous," Vitio said. "Why would you believe anything that woman tried to tell you? She's locked up for a reason."

Toth's eyes narrowed, taking this opportunity to speak up for the first time. "What are you talking about? I don't recall the Amendment Order being part of such a meeting."

"Matters involving the three remaining royal heads of the Light Realm," Apsa explained. She paused and muttered, "Which doesn't include you, Mr. Brench. Are you a king? Do you control a kingdom?" As he stared in silence, she answered the question for him. "I think not."

The broadcast went silent as they mulled over their thoughts. Toth's posture had stiffened since Apsa's comments, although nobody took notice.

"Our naval forces departed the Power Kingdom's waters a few weeks back," Apsa said, regaining her composure. "Now they're searching for whirlpools to be returned to our realm. Let's alter that plan."

"You want to send our combined fleets toward a kingdom's coast?" Supido asked.

"No, that'd be suicide," she replied. "Let's hover. In the Dark Sea there's a cluster of monstrous stalagmites that jut from the surface between the Prim and Still Kingdom's rivers. This city of spikes stretches for hundreds of miles."

"I know of the Stalagmite Sea," Vitio said. "But not even the Dark Realm kingdoms traverse that area for fear of wrecking their ships … and those are *their* waters. We simply cannot risk it."

A look of resolve painted over the Spirit Queen's face. "King Vitio, my capital is known as the Current of the Realm Rivers for a reason. We are the hub of commerce, and our navy is the scariest of them all. Do you not think we've studied the Dark Realm's rivers too? We conduct trades with their kingdoms almost as much as we do with the Light Realm." She paused. "You always trusted my mother. Now trust me. I have a captain down there who can lead ships through the sea stalagmites. They're perfect for cover and ambushes. Nobody would expect it."

Vitio contemplated her proposal, trying to rid himself of the image of the tiny princess he once remembered just two decades ago. She was now a leader with conviction.

"I have faith in Queen Apsa," Supido said.

Vitio nodded and asked, "What do you think, Prince Sigmund?" He wanted to make sure he didn't make the same mistake with the Archaic Prince as he had with Apsa. They were both royal first-borns, and needed to be treated as equals.

Sigmund quickly sat up, surprised to be included. He glanced around his table within the broadcast. "I think it's a smart idea if the Spirit Captain can pull it off."

"He can," Apsa said. "Jacob Bizen is my best captain. It's why he's in the Dark Realm."

"All right, each of us will give word to our fleets in the Dark Sea," Vitio said. "Outside of a few spies, they're all we have beyond enemy lines, so let's keep them there. As for how we'll handle the safety of elites such as generals, royals, and Jestivan, I suppose each royal head can make those decisions on his or her own. One more thing, before we end this broadcast … Mr. Brench."

Toth turned his head, his mind seemingly still jumbled from Apsa's earlier vague remarks. "King Vitio."

"How's your merchant ship making out across the waters? Does the Brench Hilt near arrival?"

Toth smiled. "It is—although it's not as simple as a straight path. We're forced to move erratically to throw off our scent. Thankfully I have nothing to worry about with King Supido's finest naval forces escorting my merchant galleon and the deposits across the Sea of Light and Realm Rivers."

"Well, that's a large amount of money you're carrying in one shipment," Supido said. "Unheard of."

"Whatever gets the money here faster so that I can rebuild the Archaic Kingdom."

"That commitment is exactly what we need," Vitio said. "With where Kuki Sphaira is headed, we'll need the Archaic Kingdom at full strength to help fight the Dark Realm."

Toth agreed. "This is war, milord."

* * *

"Two broadcast meetings in one day?" Vitio asked later that night, this time only with Queen Apsa and King Supido involved. He sighed. "What is it you want to say, Queen Apsa?"

"Everything I said earlier today about the sea stalagmites was a ruse. We should redirect our forces just out of sight of the stalagmites in open water. I guarantee you that word will reach Dev King Storshae about what was said in our earlier broadcast. Let's catch him by surprise."

Supido shook his head. "Is this about Chiefs Toth and Wert, again?"

Vitio echoed his frustration. "We've already gone over this, Apsa. We're not going to take the word of Ophala Vevlu over those two men. They've done nothing but put their all into helping the Archaic Kingdom rebuild, not only after Itta's disastrous reign, but now during the economic depression caused by the woman you're trying to get us to listen to! A woman who failed at discovering King Itta's traitorous schemes, planted fake evidence on a witness, lied about it during testimony, sabotaged the execution, and betrayed the realm!"

"But Spirit Director Neaneuma—one of the most decorated captains of the Spirit Navy during my grandmother's reign—is certain that Ophala was correct in her convictions," Apsa said.

"Neaneuma is an Energy Director at Phesaw now," Vitio retorted. "While I understand her past, it doesn't overshadow her present occupation and who she mingles with."

"What does that have—"

"It has everything to do with it!" Vitio bellowed.

Apsa's lips pursed. Even Supido's eyes widened a bit. While the Light Realm's royal heads were on cordial terms, such a tone was considered crossing a line.

Vitio, noticing the shift in the meeting's atmosphere, calmly explained, "Grand Director Poicus fought us on every decision we made last year. He's oftentimes rebellious and disrespectful. Archaic Director Senex was one of the keys to freeing Rhyparia from her noose; he died accomplishing it. Now Passion Director Venustas is trying to play queen of the Passion Kingdom. That trend isn't a coincidence. The Energy Directors think they're above the royal heads."

"What say you, King Supido?" Apsa asked.

"I say we stick to the stalagmite idea," he replied. "I think you hit the nail on the head with that tactic."

Apsa closed her eyes and shook her head. "If this comes back to bite us in the ass, it's on the two of you idiots."

* * *

Toshik and Himitsu occupied neighboring cells. Toshik hadn't been bothered at first. He figured he'd be out of the facility within a couple days because of his reputable last name, or at least someone from the estate would come to bail him out. But after a week silently swept past, he became annoyed. Had the officers or Jilly not alerted his father or the employees back at the estate? Why was he still in this place? True, this wasn't a maximum security chamber shoved in the dungeons of a castle, but it was still behind bars—not something a high-maintenance gentleman such as Toshik should have had to tolerate. And there was a certain comfort he'd gotten used to the past several months: a partner to sleep next to. But that, too, was now gone.

On the eighth day, the two rivals finally acknowledged each other's existence. "Where's your daddy?" Himitsu asked.

Toshik stifled the urge to respond rashly. He had an easy comeback that would have regarded Himitsu's mother, but instead he said, "Shut up."

"Nice."

And that was the extent of their conversation. It took a month before an officer came to inform them that someone was on their way to pay their bail. *Good,* Toshik thought. *Jilly finally made something happen. She probably got lost somewhere between here and the estate.*

"I'm sorry," Himitsu said.

Toshik sat with his back against the wall that divided their cells. He stayed silent at first, but he eventually replied, "I'm not the one you need to say that to. Knowing her, she'll forgive you, but I don't think I'll be able to. That girl is a part of me now, and while she's molded me into a kinder person than I once was, I can't pretend that what you said to her was okay—I can't excuse it."

"There was a time when you made a lot of awful accusations about Bryson," Himitsu said.

That was true. Toshik's head slumped. He gazed at the floor between his legs.

"After the Generals' Battle and Olivia had been taken," Himitsu said. "Bryson stopped hanging with the team. He even skipped mandatory meetings. Jilly and I felt bad, of course. He missed his best friend. But you … you called him weak and pathetic, said he'd never be captain in your eyes. You said you wouldn't show compassion for a weak-hearted man."

There was a pause, and then Himitsu said, "Those were cruel accusations that didn't sit well with me."

"I remember," Toshik said. "That was our first fight … on the bridge in Phesaw Park. We wanted to rip each other's head off."

"And look how far we've come," Himitsu replied. "I understand it'll take some time, but hopefully it's sooner rather than later. You won't forget—of that I'm certain. But I do seek forgiveness."

Footsteps carried down the hall as two people approached. An officer led the way, but the lady behind him wasn't someone Toshik had expected. The look on her face shamed him.

Passion Director Venustas stood outside their cells. The familiar smile she used to walk the halls of Phesaw with was replaced by a mask of disappointment.

She sighed. "Long time no see, boys."

25
War Begins

Chief Merchant Toth Brench sat at his office desk with Archaic Prince Sigmund seated across from him. Tazama stood in the back corner of the room, serving as a proctor. This meeting was vital. It was his final shot at winning over Sigmund, but it would require a cleverly contrived story of lies. Thankfully he had a mind like Tazama to plan this out for him.

"Do you see the lengths I'm going to for your kingdom?" Toth asked.

"It's become clearer to me over the months, yes."

"I don't think you're seeing everything," Toth said as he reached for a model ship on his desk and placed it between them. "This ship is what you do see. This is the *Brench Hilt*, my company's lord merchant vessel—a galleon big enough to dwarf a navy warship. And you know it's currently transporting millions of granules toward the kingdom right now. That's an obvious act of support on my end. But what about the lengths Rosel and Grandarion are taking? What have they done?"

"They've taught me a lot about bureaucracy," Sigmund replied.

"They've dismantled your kingdom and set you up for failure."

"How so?"

"What kingdoms are they native to?" Toth asked.

"Grandarion is from the Intel Kingdom; and Rosel, the Passion Kingdom."

"And which two kingdoms do we know in the Light Realm have always been the closest?"

Sigmund thought about it and then said, "Intel and Passion."

"And which kingdom has been the Intel Kingdom's enemy for fifteen hundred years … to the point that a name was given to the silent feud: *The Mind War*?"

"Archaic … mine."

Toth raised his eyebrows. "So it's only natural that the Passion Kingdom back the Intel Kingdom when it comes to their opposition, correct?"

Sigmund's eyes widened. "True …"

"What happened in Olethros last year wasn't an accident—and not because of Ophala. She was a pawn in a plan contrived by the royal heads of the other Light Kingdoms. Let's face it, Sigmund; the fiasco at the Generals' Battle was massive in scale and catastrophic in damage. Do you really think imprisoning and killing Itta was satisfying enough retribution for them?"

The prince didn't respond, but the expression on his face said it all.

"Why else would Rosel and Grandarion bring the execution all the way to Rim? And why did the royal heads not send at least one or two of their high-ranking soldiers? Even Intel Major Lars, who'd spent an entire year leading that city, didn't show up. They had planned for it to fail, knowing it would result in hysteria across the kingdom. And it did. Citizens revolted and the economy crashed. And then what did the other kingdoms do when this happened?

"They withdrew their troops!" Toth said, pounding his fist on the table. "Now we have a couple hundred from each kingdom in the capital, but that's it—just enough to keep watch. The low point for Archains wasn't when Itta was captured, but now. How much longer do you think Rosel and Grandarion will stick around before their royal heads tell them their job is done and they can return home? They've left us to fend for ourselves while a war is brewing between the two realms!"

Sigmund's jaw clenched as his brows furrowed. "You're right ..."

"And who has tried righting the ship? Wert and I!" Toth hissed. "He's been fortifying the military while I've been relocating my business and redirecting its profits into the Archaic Kingdom. We seem to be the only chiefs who care."

Sigmund glared at the desk. "I want my kingdom back."

Toth glanced at Tazama in the background. She wore a proud smile. He rose from his seat, rounded the desk, and placed his hand on Sigmund's shoulder. "We'll take it back."

* * *

Toono and Kadlest entered Cogdan Castle's throne room, where Dev King Storshae was waiting. He stood behind the throne as usual, not believing that he deserved it. His father had been taken too soon in his eyes.

Rage bubbled within Toono as he approached. He hadn't forgotten that day of his and Storshae's quarrel, the harsh words that had been tossed his way. The rift still existed—even if they tried to ignore its suffocating presence.

"Toth has contacted us with new information," Storshae announced, skipping the pleasantries.

"What are we looking at?"

"Damian's body has been discovered. A meeting between the royal heads of the Light Realm was held—including the Amendment Order. They've declared war."

"It took them long enough to recognize it for what it is," Kadlest said through a chuckle.

"They thought they had remedied the problem by disposing of Itta and implementing the Amendment Order." Storshae paused and then said, "It was never that simple."

"Do we know their first move?" Kadlest asked.

"Those fleets that Power Queen Gantski forced out of her waters and were supposed to be heading back to the Light Realm via whirlpools … well, they've decided to keep them here."

"Foolish," Toono said.

Storshae stepped around the throne. "They believe they're safe in Stalagmite Sea, which is true to a certain extent. I'm definitely not sending my ships into there. I've already talked it over with Power Queen Gantski, Still Queen Apoleia, and Cyn King Zisha-Li."

"You got in touch with the Cyn King?" Toono said, unable to mask the surprise in his voice. "And he agreed to assist us?"

"I did," Storshae said, an air of smugness inflating his chest. "Since the Light Realm doesn't know that we have an inside source with Toth and Wert, they're thinking we'll innocently sail a vessel past the stalagmites—maybe even a pack of them. And they'll strike. But since we know of their plan, we'll still do exactly that.

"We'll send a few ships near the stalagmites and bait them into a pursuit. And what will we have waiting for them in the distance? Our own collective fleet that'll surely dwarf the measly numbers they have down here. Their guerilla tactics won't mean much."

Toono was impressed, and it must have shown on his face because Storshae seized the opportunity to say, "Don't forget that I'm the son of Rehn, the Oracle."

"And I, the son of no one," Toono said. "Yes, you've made sure I don't forget that."

Storshae's smile fell—perhaps from a sense of guilt? Toono didn't care for the king's remorse. He'd said enough already. Instead he shifted focus. "The Prim Kingdom is still staying neutral in this whole ordeal?"

Storshae shrugged. "Well, you did kill their prince and general."

"The euphoria of that night," muttered Kadlest through a grin.

"My ships are being prepared as we speak. In a month, they'll be deployed. Also, provod has reached Phelos, so Tazama's been continuing work on the teleplatforms. She's built four."

Toono turned and left the throne room. "Keep us updated, son of Rehn."

Kadlest grabbed his shoulder and pulled him toward her. "We're getting closer and closer," she mumbled. "It starts with the uprising."

* * *

Toono pressed his face between the bars of Poicus's cell. He had stalled for long enough. With the Light Realm finally wising up and taking action, it was time to provide another dagger to their already wounded pride.

Poicus slowly lifted his head. He was weaker than he'd ever been in his life. A child could have disposed of him at this point.

Toono swung open the gate. "You may not know it, but you had taught a younger me so much. I only wish circumstances allowed me to stay in that mindset."

"Do it quickly," the old man wheezed.

* * *

Ice and snow covered the grounds of Kindoliya's frozen palace. Still Queen Apoleia and her younger sister, Ropinia, stood next to a tram-ram outside of the barracks as they awaited someone's arrival. Frost speckled their violet hair, and they wore powder blue dresses embroidered with crystal.

Two soldiers guided a man down a path from the main grounds. His heavy combat boots crunched in the ice, but he didn't don the uniform of a soldier like he once did nearly two years ago.

Apoleia's smile spread beyond her cheeks as the man approached. "Good morning, Garlo," she said.

Garlo, the former Still General who had served Apoleia's mother before her death, squinted at her without a response.

"Not used to the sun after months of rotting in the dungeons?" Apoleia asked with a wry smile.

"Why am I out here?" he asked. "I was expecting the gallows, yet I see none."

Apoleia snatched and squeezed his jaw with menacing might, providing just enough force to teeter between agonizing pain and breaking his jaw. "*Manners*, Garlo."

He tried to say something, but Apoleia was having too much fun feeling his bones tremble beneath her pressure. She thrust out her hand, causing the man to stumble backward. "Let's try that again," she said sweetly.

He rubbed his jaw and readjusted himself. "What can I do for you, milady?"

"You're going to help Toono," she said, a tone of business taking over. "I'm sending you to Cogdan." Garlo started to open his mouth, but Apoleia's livid eyes stopped him. "You'll traverse across the Diamond Sea by tram-ram with a few soldiers. You'll then be escorted through the teleplatforms and across the Dev Kingdom until you arrive at the capital."

She paused, stepping closer to him and leaning in. "Let me make this crystal clear. If I learn that you try to flee, you will die the most uncomfortable of deaths." Frost coated Garlo's face as she spoke. "If you achieve everything asked of you, I'll grant you passage home to Kindoliya as a servant in the palace."

He glanced between the sisters. "Of course, milady."

* * *

Toth strolled through the dungeons of Phelos Palace. He'd been down here many times over the past year since Spy Pilot Ophala's imprisonment, but it wasn't his familiarity with the layout that allowed him to traverse the maze of corridors so easily. It was the woman's whistling that led him to her cell.

Having prisoners of elite status in the dungeons wasn't a normal routine. Usually they'd be in the secluded tower chambers like Itta used to be and Horos was now, but Ophala was a special case. She may have not possessed her ancient anymore, but that didn't mean she couldn't communicate with birds. She simply couldn't control them.

Toth stood a couple feet away from the bars once he arrived. "Ophala."

The woman paused while absentmindedly braiding her hair on her mattress. "I look forward to these visits," she said. "It's lonely without my birds."

"I come today on a somber note."

"Am I to die soon?"

"Yes."

"Will I get to see my husband beforehand?"

"You will."

"That's nice." She finished her braid and finally looked over at Toth. "Are you looking forward to seeing it?"

"I will avoid the show like I did with Rhyparia."

Ophala nodded, looking back at the wall as she started another braid. "A good man who lost his wife, then lost his way … unfortunate."

"Why are you so accepting of this outcome?" Toth asked.

She frowned. "Who said I've accepted it?"

"Your demeanor, your tone, and your choice of words."

"I was trained in the art of being a spy at a young age. I can be someone else when I need to."

Toth's eyes narrowed. "Should I be questioning who you are right now?"

"Mr. Brench," she said with a smirk. "You waited entirely too long to ask yourself that question."

He gripped a cell bar and scowled. "That's somewhat smug advice, coming from a woman trapped in a block."

"You sound like Wert … very unbefitting for you. Allow me to wish you a good night. Thank you for the company."

* * *

Toth gazed out the window of his bedroom while Tazama lay in bed with an open book. "There's a sense of complacency in her that unnerves me, Tazama."

The Dev servant turned a page. "Ophala has intrigued me ever since the Amendment Order convened for the first time. I've always told you to be wary of her, for she is formidable. Even while imprisoned, she's a bigger threat than Rosel and Grandarion. It's likely that her plan extended far beyond the events at Olethros, and now pieces are moving without the need of her supervision."

"You think that she thinks she'll get out of this?" Toth asked.

"Or maybe she's actually accepted her fate, but can do so peacefully because she thinks we'll fail in some way," Tazama explained. "The people of the Archaic Kingdom used to be known for their minds—just like the Dev and Intel Kingdoms. But such a strength perished over the past several centuries as their royal bloodline became more corrupt."

She paused, then said, "She's a rare exception—one of the old minds." The room fell silent, and Tazama looked up from her book. "What else bothers you?" she asked.

"I don't know where Toshik or Jilly are," Toth said. "My business is in the process of moving to Balle, and those two were supposed to be part of it. I need them both here before lines are drawn."

Tazama closed her book and placed it on the nightstand. "I fear it's too late, love. The uprising will happen as scheduled, and we have no control over that fact—Toono and Storshae do."

"You think I've lost my son."

Tazama's response would eat at Toth for eternity … "You lost your son when you lost your wife."

*   *   *

Bryson chased Intel King Vitio around Dunami Palace, desperately pleading for allowance into the Archaic Mountains. Each time he was met with a firm no, something he wasn't used to from the king. Usually Vitio was eager to aid Bryson in any way.

"How do we know if she's alive?" Bryson asked.

"We don't."

"She's my sister."

"I'm fully aware, Bryson, but it's still a no."

They climbed a staircase. "If Lilu was in trouble, you'd do anything to go after her."

Vitio shook his head. "There is no connection. Lilu didn't commit heinous crimes. This is a timed punishment. Olivia must serve her time."

"Mendac never served his!"

Vitio turned. "Mendac's punishment was death!"

The king huffed and continued up the stairs. Bryson stood, flabbergasted. Of course he knew this fact, but how did Vitio know? Did he simply word that incorrectly?

Bryson sprinted up the stairs to catch up. "What are you talking about? He died protecting Shelly from an assassination attempt, according to his story."

"You're right."

"No," Bryson said. "What did you mean?"

Vitio whirled around once more and grabbed Bryson's shoulders. "I understand you're grieving the absence and uncertainty of your sister, but I have too much on my mind right now."

"You mean the war."

Vitio sighed. "That daughter of mine and her big mouth …" He stepped into a room, closing the door behind him. "I'm not a bad guy, Bryson."

26
Rats Aboard

Agnos shivered under the moonlight. Rain hammered his back as he scrubbed the main deck. This was an unnecessary task, but Farlyn, the head swab, forced it upon him. None of Agnos's peers were on the decks. They took the night off since the rain would do the job for them.

Agnos couldn't feel his hands, making the task harder than it already was. The combination of it being March, them being at sea, the rain, and twilight hours made for an insufferable experience. A flash of lightning lit up the night sky, followed by thunder's roar seconds later. But Agnos kept his head down in fear of the stinging needles that fell from above.

They had been at sea for months without a single taste of confrontation. Several ships had been spotted, but apparently none of interest. There were even a few naval vessels that sported their kingdom's emblem on their sails, but for some reason none of them ever initiated pursuit of the *Whale Lord*. Tashami had explained this phenomenon to Agnos at the beginning of the voyage.

"Nobody wants to start a battle with Gray Whale," Tashami had said as he leaned against the rail next to the ship's helm.

Agnos had been assigned to scrubbing the quarter deck that night, and Tashami had decided to neglect sleep in order to keep his friend company. "Nothing about this ship—besides its size—strikes me as ferocious," Agnos had said.

"I don't quite understand it either." Tashami replied as he scratched at a spoke on the wheel. "I guess the crew's firefighters, squallblasters, and seashockers are that talented."

While replaying the conversation in his mind, Agnos noticed blood sloshing within the rainwater, so he checked his knuckles and saw that they were raw and bright red. His extremities were so numb that he couldn't feel the skin tearing from them. He fell back on his butt and scooted backward to a rail. He slumped, keeping his head down. He gripped himself from the cold, releasing sporadic breaths as if he was in the midst of a seizure.

He looked up as footsteps approached. Farlyn snarled, rain dripping from the hairs of his patchy beard. He grabbed Agnos by the collar and tossed him across the deck. Agnos tumbled and then lay still, glowering at the wooden planks as if they'd been his oppressor. The footsteps grew nearer once again. This time a balled up rag was tossed into the back of his neck. "Get on with it, boy," Farlyn grumbled.

Agnos grabbed the rag from his neck and began scrubbing again, wincing in pain as he now had a cut in his shoulder from being thrown. He glanced up to see the light from Farlyn's lantern disappear underneath the deck. As he wiped the floor, he released a roar that not even the thunder could silence.

*   *   *

The following evening, as the sun set, Agnos spent his rare bit of free time accompanying Tashami, who was adjusting the rigging.

"Any news from the inside?" Agnos asked.

Tashami tugged on the rope, grunting with effort. "Nope. Barloe hasn't mentioned anything about a change of plans or new intelligence from the captain. Same crap, different day."

Agnos studied the decks for any important faces. Unfortunately, Farlyn stood out amongst the rest. He appeared to be in his own world, paying no mind to the rest of the crew, as he walked around with a rigid structure to his jaw.

Tashami stopped pulling the rope for a second as he followed Agnos's gaze. He then looked back up at the sails and continued work. "Has he been treating you any better?"

"I think it's gotten worse."

Tashami shook his head. "Still don't want me to say something to Barloe?"

"The last label I want for my reputation is a rat."

"That man goes against everything this crew is supposedly about. I don't think anyone would mind if you exposed his actions," Tashami said.

Agnos's eyes narrowed as he asked, "Have you heard about who we're chasing down? Any hints at all?"

"In the words of Barloe: 'the biggest haul the world has ever seen.'"

"That must come with some protection."

"I'd bet on it."

Agnos stretched and let out a massive yawn. It may have been only seven o'clock at the latest, but for him, it was time for bed after a long day of cleaning duties.

Far below decks, Agnos nestled into a cranny between a couple overturned barrels in the orlop. He propped a pillow against the curved wall and retrieved one of his lighter reads from a crevice—something that he didn't mind falling asleep to. Tonight that was a book about the Cyn Kingdom's Linsani, a species of ghostly wyverns made of bone. He put on his glasses since it was written in Cynnish, although he had improved on his understanding of the language without them.

Agnos dozed off, but awoke a short while later to the sound of murmuring. He muffled a yawn, and once his mind escaped sleep's lull, he recognized the sound as the hum of a tune. Someone was pacing nearby, but Agnos couldn't see the culprit while this deep in the pile of barrels. And he didn't want to risk movement—otherwise the whole structure might collapse.

Occasionally the man would sing a lyric amongst the hums, but the moments were sporadic. There were three lines that stood out:

The sea claims me,
The sea tames me,
The sea takes me.

Agnos tried to think of any poetry or songs that he had learned of sea life lore, but nothing linked.

The man walked past Agnos's hiding spot, causing Agnos to unnecessarily shrivel into the darkness. It was too dark down here for someone to see him. He watched as the man walked past again. This time Agnos recognized him to be Farlyn. He waited for the head swab's footsteps to grow distant and the door to shut.

Agnos readjusted himself, not investing much in what had just happened. There were plenty of reasons for a swab to visit the orlop, and the song was just one of many sailor tunes that could be heard hummed around the ship. So he allowed himself to drift off to sleep once more.

Hours later, a clap of thunder woke Agnos. Fear overcame him when he realized he might have overslept. He crawled out of the crevice and tucked his belongings between the barrels. He stood still a moment to gain his balance while the ship swayed against the stormy sea.

He managed to climb multiple ladders between the floors until he was on the main deck—once again being pummeled by rain. Outside, the decks were mostly deserted except for a few crewmates who manned overnight positions. Agnos had no idea what time it was, but judging by the moons and stars, he had just beat the two o'clock deadline. Hoping it'd put him in Farlyn's good graces for the night, he began swab duties early.

A couple hours crept by, and Agnos became confused about Farlyn's absence. There weren't any other swabs outside, but that was to be expected during torrential storms, for they didn't have to work. Instead of relief, Agnos felt only unease. Farlyn always made it to the decks at two o'clock sharp to make sure everyone was accounted for and at their proper station. He had *never* missed a day.

Agnos was reminded of Farlyn's visit to the hold earlier in the night. He hadn't thought much of it at first, but perhaps there was something to it. The man had been pacing uncomfortably, despite the humming.

Thus Agnos did the unthinkable; he siphoned some courage and left the deck. He crept down the steps, their groans swallowed by the cacophonous storm. He wended his way through the hammocks occupied by resting crewmates in search of Farlyn, but with no luck.

He searched every inch of the ship that he was allowed access to, but saved the orlop for last. He got on all fours and paused next to the square door in the floor. He waited for the sound of another thunderous boom outside before opening it a crack. He peered inside, but it was too dark to make out any shapes. He took advantage of the symphony of howling winds, bruising waves, and cackling thunder in order to slip into the orlop undetected.

He questioned his cautious movements. Why would anyone be down here? So he picked up his pace, but remained slow enough to not stumble in the blackness. Then he heard a whispering dialect that sounded like a mixture of a snake's hiss and a wolf's howl, except softer.

Agnos's heartbeat fluctuated between rapid and slow, unsure of how it should respond. The foreign whispers made his heart rate drop unnaturally, but the shock from hearing it on a ship in the middle of the Light Realm forced it to simultaneously spike. He knew that language—it was Cynnish.

He understood most Cynnish because of the practice he'd obtained over the last three years, but that was mostly in writing. He had a decent grasp of spoken dialect, but he couldn't follow the fluidity and speed at which this person spoke. He needed his relic.

Luckily he was only a few feet away from the crevice where most of his belongings were stored, but they were lodged so far deep into the barrels, it would require finesse—something he didn't possess—to reach it without making any noise. But perhaps with the aid of the storm he could risk it.

So Agnos took a few more steps, and then lifted his foot to step up and into the nook. Whoever had tied these barrels down before the ship's departure months ago had done a fantastic job. Agnos never appreciated it until now, as a wave of relief washed over him.

He made it all the way to the wall, where he reached behind a barrel and retrieved a bag with his glasses. Another crack of thunder sent his heart into his throat, nearly shoving a yelp out of his mouth. He rested the back of his head against the wall while releasing a slow breath and putting on his glasses. He sat there without any luck, for the whispers had become inaudible.

He crawled forward and slipped out of his hiding spot. He could hear the whispering once more. Agnos had to steady himself as memories of his visit to the Cyn Kingdom seeped to the forefront of his mind—the disfigured Unbreakable and the children hanged from the banister. He inched his way closer to the end of the barrels and peeked around the corner.

A pair of glowing burgundy eyes floated within the darkness—a Devish.

What in the world?

Agnos snapped his head back as he made sense of what he was hearing and seeing. There were two people down here. A Devish was recording while a Cynnish was speaking … Two Dark Realm citizens on a pirate ship in the middle of the Sea of Light. How was he supposed to process this?

He listened closely while his glasses deciphered bits and pieces that weren't silenced by the sea's wrath: *Switching course to the northwest … intercept you … bottleneck … clueless …*

They were directions. Someone was leaking information, but to whom? Toono, Storshae? No, that wouldn't make sense. They were speaking to whoever it was Gray Whale was chasing down.

Agnos decided to get out of there, not wanting to overstay his welcome and risk getting caught. Once back at the hammocks, he debated on who to wake: Tashami or Barloe. Ultimately he decided on the quartermaster. He could do more with this knowledge since he was one of three people on the ship who conversed with Gray Whale—the other two being Eet and Osh, the cabin kids.

He reached the main deck and risked pounding on the door to the higher ranks' quarters. He continued to do so until one of the firefighters opened the door. "Something like this takes some massive balls, swab," she said, rubbing her eyes.

"I need to speak with Barloe!" Agnos shouted over the storm.

"I don't think so!"

"It's urgent. There's a traitor on the ship!"

The woman paused, teetering between amused and baffled. "Come again?"

Agnos shoved his way past her and, with no knowledge of which door led to the quartermaster's room, began to shout: "Barloe! It's Agnos, and I have urgent news!" He continued walking aimlessly through the hall, the firefighter marching behind him. "Wake up, Barloe!"

A door at the end of the hall jarred open. Agnos was happy to see the quartermaster's dreads against the light of his lantern. "What is it?" Barloe asked.

"You have two people on your ship who aren't from the Light Realm."

Barloe's eyes widened. "Show me the way," he commanded without a second thought.

The two of them descended through the floors. This time Agnos didn't bother easing open the trapdoor; he yanked it open. "In the hold, past the cargo," he whispered.

He followed the burley quartermaster down the steps. This time the trip proved easier with the lantern's light guiding the way. They reached the end of the barrels and turned the corner, but nobody was there. Barloe swirled in every direction, arm extended so the light reached the hold's depths. He gazed back at Agnos, who was already prepared for a verbal lashing. His entire body had tensed.

"What did you see?" Barloe asked.

Agnos's muscles relaxed. That wasn't the reaction he'd expected. "Not much … a pair of bright burgundy eyes and a man speaking in Cynnish."

"Did you have your glasses on? What did the man say?"

After Agnos repeated the bits he heard, a fury ignited in Barloe's eyes as he tromped away. Agnos ran after him and grabbed his massive bicep. "Wait, wait!"

"Get off me."

"Don't say anything to anyone."

Barloe turned as more thunder roared. "Why not?"

"You'll only alert whoever they were, and then we'll never be able to catch them in the act again."

"You don't betray your crew," Barloe growled.

"I understand that, but we need a plan to expose them in the act. And here—" Agnos quickly poked around and grabbed a bag of flour before handing it to Barloe— "Bring this upstairs so that it looks like this was what you came down here for … in case someone's watching from the upper decks."

Barloe huffed and gave it some thought. "Meet me in the navigation room at first light," he said before leaving the hold with the flour bag slung over his shoulder.

Agnos waited before ascending the two floors. He was intercepted by Farlyn, who grabbed him by his armpit and yanked him toward the stairs to the main deck. "Where have you been?" the head swab asked.

Agnos could have asked him the same question, but he wisely held his tongue. As he was thrown back onto the deck, he pondered that question: Why wasn't Farlyn outside when Agnos began his shift earlier?

* * *

Agnos was relieved to be able to abandon his swab duties early in order to visit the navigation room. He stepped inside as an older woman opened the door for him. A detailed map of the Sea of Light lay on a table near a back window, while dozens of other maps plastered the walls. But Agnos's eyes were drawn to the three-dimensional human-sized module of Kuki Sphaira that hung in the far corner of the room.

He began walking toward it until Barloe stopped him. "We're not here for that."

Agnos stared at it a moment longer before returning his attention to the quartermaster. "Sorry."

Barloe went on to introduce Agnos to the lady who opened the door for him as Graft, the ship's navigator. She was the first person of importance—besides Barloe—who Agnos was able to formally meet. That was progress.

"I was surprised when you believed me without question," Agnos said.

Barloe nodded. "Well, I had reason to."

"Why?"

"Agnos, the *Whale Lord* has pursued and caught almost every target it's ever had during its existence. And even if the target wasn't caught, we at least found it. But there is one powerhouse that has evaded us twice in the past. And what makes it even more frustrating is that this person has roughly a hundred ships that are constantly sailing throughout the Realm Rivers and Sea of Light."

"So why can't you find them?" Agnos asked.

"A great mystery," Graft said. "I've been on this crew longer than Barloe, and even I've never understood."

"Who is this target?"

"I can't tell you," said Barloe. "None of the crew knows who Gray Whale is chasing right now—except me. Usually we would have given up on the hunt by now, but she swears this time is different. We need to be more persistent. She speaks gravely—a lot rides on this."

Agnos mumbled, "Well, clearly someone besides you knows who it is we're trying to find."

"We need to weed out the rats," Barloe said. "Who are the most suspicious on the ship?"

"My first suggestion would be Farlyn," Agnos said.

Barloe glanced at Graft, and then gazed back at Agnos with a raised eyebrow. "The head swab … really?"

"Every night he checks attendance of swabs on the decks," Agnos explained. "His absence last night was the whole reason why I went searching through the ship. I couldn't find him anywhere, so I checked the hold because I had seen him down there earlier in the day."

"What was he doing down there when you first saw him?"

"Pacing back and forth, humming a tune. He didn't know I was there because I was in my makeshift hideout between barrels."

"So you think he was in the hold that night …" Barloe tapped his fingers on the table and scratched at his beard. "As the Devish or Cynnish?"

"I couldn't tell."

"That's fine," Barloe said. "I guess I can think of a few other shady individuals on the crew … people that have rubbed me the wrong way. What about you, Graft?"

Graft shook her head. "You know I don't mingle much with those idiots. I wouldn't have the slightest idea."

"Well, now you know why your target has been able to avoid you for so long," Agnos said. "If they know where you're traveling at all times, then they can steer clear of your path. You must dispose of the spies as quickly as possible."

"We can interrogate Farlyn," Barloe said.

Agnos approached the table and inspected the map. "I have a better idea. We'll lure them out again." He spotted the Spirit River. "Let's turn the ship around."

"But we're trying to reach the Archaic River in time to intercept our target," Barloe rebuked.

"Let's retreat. You said you've given up on pursuing this target twice before, so it wouldn't be a surprise if you do it again. Turn this thing around, and that'll mean the rats will have to inform whoever it is they're talking to about a change of direction … and we'll be ready for it."

Barloe glanced at Graft. "What do you think? How long can we risk retreating before we lose our chance to catch the target?"

"Depends. If we make that new squallblaster fill the sails, this ship could move at a speed I would have previously deemed impossible. He's a talent."

Agnos couldn't help but smile at the compliment of Tashami.

Barloe placed both hands on the table and gazed down at it. "All right, let me inform Gray of the decision. See if she gives us the go."

* * *

Agnos was carrying a bucket of water across the deck and about to descend into the lower floors when he heard a command shouted from the quarterdeck: "Drop the kedge! We're heading back to DaiSo!"

He looked up to see Graft standing next to the wheel while the skipper began to turn it. The crew didn't know how to respond at first. Agnos thought the entire ship had frozen in time. "Get on with it!" Graft shouted.

The kedge was one of the ship's smaller anchors. If dropped into the sea, it would serve as a weight, causing the ship to pivot in a different direction.

Pirates began hustling to their positions. They pulled on ropes and climbed shrouds to release the necessary sails. Since it wasn't a battle or evasive maneuver, the crew's motions were efficient rather than frantic. It felt like a surrender—an abrupt end to an arduous voyage … and they had absolutely nothing to show for it.

"Squallblasters fill the sails south!" Graft bellowed.

Tashami and two others took their spots on the poopdeck and began to blow winds into the sails at the required angle.

Agnos watched in awe as all of these moving parts came together as one. But he needed to get below deck, so he took his bucket downstairs. He waited on the berth deck for any sign of Farlyn. But after thirty minutes of nothing, he dropped down to the utility deck. He even made sure to check the orlop, but nobody was down there.

Had the culprits taken advantage of the crew's distractions up top and already informed their counterparts? Or would they wait for the dead of night when most were asleep, and utilize another stormy night to drown out their voices?

Agnos returned to the main deck. Barloe stood on the quarterdeck, carefully observing the crew beneath him in search of suspicious behavior. He made eye contact with Agnos and nodded his head toward the forecastle. Agnos spun around and scanned the crowd on an elevated platform at the front of the ship. There was Farlyn, standing peacefully as he stared at the sea.

Farlyn turned and faced the main deck with a look of calm. Whereas others in the crew seemed agitated with the fact that they were giving up on the mission, he seemed to accept it. But one could chalk that up to his position as a swab. It wasn't as if he would have gained a large portion of whatever prize it was they were chasing. Purely out of spite, however, Agnos wanted this man to be one of the people he'd witnessed in the hold.

*   *   *

Three more nights passed without any suspicious behavior from Farlyn or any others. Barloe had reassigned sleeping locations of certain crewmembers, spreading out hammocks to cover more space. These men and women were to serve as a sort of night-watch. They pretended to sleep, occasionally keeping an eye on every inch of space that was visible to them.

Agnos was stationed alone in the largest area of the ship—the orlop. He would stay in his crevice lodged deep within the barrels for the night's entirety. He got away with missing swab duties because Farlyn believed he was in the surgeon's quarters. Someone had informed Farlyn that Agnos was suffering from scurvy and wasn't likely to make it.

It was early evening when Agnos heard someone enter the hold from above, which wasn't an alarming occurrence. People frequently visited this area of the ship to retrieve supplies or seek privacy for more personal acts. It wasn't exactly pleasant for Agnos, but he had learned to pick up a book and stuff his face in that as a distraction.

But this time he heard a familiar tune. There was humming, then the song he'd heard nearly a week ago:

The sea claims me,
The sea tames me,
The sea takes me.

He caught glimpses of Farlyn walking past a couple times. He heard doors shut and items shuffling about. Was he gathering supplies or inspecting the area? Agnos was lucky it was as dark it was down here, or else Farlyn would have seen him in his peripherals while brushing past the barrels.

Once Farlyn left, Agnos wiggled free of the crevice, threw on a hooded cloak, and hunted down Barloe. The few pirates standing guard on the other floors knew who was under the cloak, and they'd give signals of which way Farlyn went so that Agnos could avoid running into him.

Agnos made it into the higher ranks' quarters above deck. He entered Barloe's room and removed his hood. "Farlyn was just in the hold rummaging around—suspicious if you ask me. I've caught him doing that once before, and it was the same night I saw the Cynnish and Devish down there too."

Barloe wiped his hands with a towel. "We're approaching storm clouds. So it seems as if there was a night for them to make a move, it'd be tonight. Did you get a sense of what Farlyn was trying to achieve down there?"

"I couldn't leave my spot; otherwise I would have been exposed. Like I said, just a bunch of movement and opening and closing of doors. He was humming the same song again."

"What was it?"

"He'd only annunciate a few lines," Agnos said, who then went on to mimic the swab.

Barloe paused, and then placed the towel on a rack. "Wow, it *is* him."

"How do you know?"

"Those are three lines from a hymn that pays ode to the sea. It's an ancient song, but a well-known one amongst sailors and pirates. Just don't ever get caught singing it."

"How come?"

"Because it's a hymn that asks the sea for forgiveness of future sin. You only sing it if you're going to commit a deed that is mutinous to your crew. As you know, there is a code to the sea: You never turn your back on your family."

"So we prepare for tonight?" Agnos asked.

"Correct. Return to your post."

* * *

Agnos waited in his hideout as the storm raged. He made sure he was better equipped tonight, cloaking himself in black cloth rather than his white robes. He couldn't listen for the door to open or footsteps because of the storm, so he simply waited for someone to walk past or the sound of close-by whispers. Last time he'd found the rats in cahoots already, so he didn't know exactly how they would enter the hold and comb the area. He only hoped they'd gloss over the barrels.

A waning glow appeared outside of his crevice. Someone had arrived with a lantern. He tucked his mouth into the collar of his cloak to stifle the breathing—unnecessary but habitual. This could have been a random crewmate trying to loot supplies.

But then the lantern swept past the gap, and Agnos resisted the urge to tense up. He noticed Farlyn's gray stubble and hollow cheekbones against the light, followed by another gentleman that he couldn't recognize. They inspected the entire floor, but they didn't pay attention to the perfectly built mountain of overturned barrels. It was likely they didn't suspect anyone to fit within the crevices, so it didn't even cross their minds.

For once, Agnos thanked his tiny, feeble frame. His appreciation for Director Senex increased tenfold.

The light disappeared, but Agnos never saw the two men cross back the other way. They were still down here and probably on the other side of the cargo. There was a lull in the storm, absent of thunder and occupied by a gentle downpour. The waves were minor disruptions, but Agnos could hear the Cynnish tongue.

He crawled between the barrels, having to adjust his shoulders every now and then to make any progress. Eventually he slipped out and equipped his relic. He placed his back against the bottoms of the sideways barrels and shuffled toward the two men.

"Yes, Captain," whispered the Cynnish man. "You should be okay now."

A different voice responded, forcing Agnos to peek around the cargo. The voice came out of the face of the glowing burgundy eyes, but he knew it didn't belong to the Devish presently recording. It belonged to whoever was on the other side of the transmission. "Good job, Farlyn," the man replied, letting Agnos know that Farlyn was the Cynnish. "This was the most important job you've had since first boarding the ship decades ago."

"I will get to return home, then?" Farlyn asked.

"Yes, when you and Rotel arrive at DaiSo, return to Sodai and someone will be waiting to escort you back to your kingdoms. You've done well."

Farlyn's voice shook as he said, "Thank you, sir."

"Your job isn't over. Let me know if there are any changes …" the voice trailed off as the Devish's burgundy eyes landed on Agnos.

Agnos yanked his head back, his heart ready to explode from his chest. Had he been seen?

The voice answered his question. "There's someone there!"

27
Gray Whale

Agnos ran the moment he heard the accusation. He tripped and became tangled in a bundle of rope that had been carelessly thrown across the floor. The lantern was ablaze once again. He foolishly glanced back only to see the two men bearing down on him. He stood up and tried to wrestle his ankle loose from the rope. Meanwhile the Devish's cloak began throwing projectiles at him. He screamed as a blade impaled his thigh.

Farlyn didn't seem to be attacking, but Agnos noticed the wood underneath the two men was inexplicably rotting before his eyes. Agnos became frightened as the unfamiliar phenomenon crept toward him. He managed to rip his leg free just before it could reach him—or, at least, he thought he did. A burning sensation ripped through the fingers on his left hand as if they'd been dipped into a frozen lake, but it felt insurmountably worse.

Fortunately, at that very moment, the trapdoor opened above him. Light spilled down as several crewmembers rushed into the hold carrying lanterns in one hand and swords in the other. Agnos collapsed, squirming while he pressed his hand around the dagger in his leg.

A woman leapt down from the floor above and sent a wave of electricity across the hold, skimming over Agnos and making the hair on his head stand tall. The blinding blue light illuminated the orlop, and suddenly Agnos was no longer being pelted by telekinetic attacks.

Tashami rushed down and knelt next to Agnos, observing the wound in his leg. Farlyn and the Devish man were jittering on the floor. The wood had returned to its normal state, which reminded Agnos of the sensation he had felt in his hand. He examined it and found no evidence of damage. Had he hallucinated?

"Get the surgeon!" Tashami yelled at the bystanders.

Agnos squinted in pain and shouted, "Turn the ship!" He then released a howl. "Whoever was on the other side of the transmission saw me. They're going to make a beeline toward their destination. We need to either catch them from behind or intercept them."

A crewmate said they'd inform Graft. Barloe and a couple of the utility crewmates grabbed the two Dark Realm residents and dragged them toward the stairs.

Agnos removed his shirt and tossed it toward them. "Blindfold the Devish man. His eyes mean everything to our target."

Tashami and Agnos sat quietly in the orlop while, through the ceiling, they heard orders given from above. "Get up, lads! The voyage is back on!" Heavy thuds vibrated the floorboards as the crew went to work.

"Why do you keep staring at your hand?" Tashami asked. "Your leg seems to be what requires your attention."

"Farlyn did something to it, but I don't know what. I could swear my skin was burning. And he made the wood rot too."

"Was he the Cynnish or Devish?"

"Cynnish."

"Cynergy is an obscure energy," Tashami said. "Maybe it mocks the atmosphere of the Cyn Kingdom—rotting and sucking the life out of anything or anyone."

Agnos finally looked away from his hand and back at his wounded thigh. "Maybe."

The surgeon hurried down into the hold with a lantern and a box of supplies. He found Agnos and Tashami and observed the injury. He shook his head. "I can't do much down here for that." He looked at Tashami. "Do you think you could carry him up to my quarters?"

Tashami scooped Agnos off the floor without a second thought. For the thousandth time in his life, Agnos felt hopeless. He tried holding back whimpers as the blade wiggled within his muscle. Instead he ended up biting a good portion of Tashami's shirt as he groaned into his chest.

"Hang in there, bud," Tashami said as he climbed the stairs to the main deck.

Pandemonium swallowed the decks as men and women shouted over the storm. Despite the poor weather and frenzied crew, they were managing to turn the vessel.

As Tashami tried to enter the specialty quarters behind the surgeon, Barloe called down from the quarterdeck. "Tashami, we need you to counter the waves!"

Agnos opened his eyes as rain drenched his face. Tashami looked down at him, uncertain of what to do. "I've got this," Agnos said.

"Agnos can limp his way back!" Barloe shouted over the din.

Tashami gingerly placed Agnos on his feet before sprinting across the deck. Agnos pushed the door open and entered an empty hall. Sadly, he was more useful in here than he was out there.

* * *

Tashami dashed across the main deck before hopping over the long boat located in its center. He weaved a gale that caught him mid-jump and tossed him onto the shrouds that climbed from the ship's rails up to the tops of masts. He grabbed hold and braced himself against nature's violent winds. He was beginning to think that this was more than a mere thunderstorm—this was a hurricane.

From high in the shrouds, he looked down to see the ship rock left and right as water crashed onto the decks. He couldn't decipher wave sizes since the lack of light transformed the sea's surface into an infinite black canvas.

He continued to pull himself up while the netting shredded his palms. The ship jerked, causing him to lose grip as well as his foothold. He dangled from the sky with the strength of only one arm. The hurricane's winds jostled the shrouds, rippling them like flags, trying to wring him free.

A wave crashed over the edge of the ship, sweeping up a large amount of crewmembers with it. Some remained rigid as they pulled at the rigging. The skipper was leaning all the way into the wheel, trying to hold it steady as he banked the ship against the waves. And Barloe's eyes were on Tashami, as if the quartermaster knew he was the most integral part to them escaping this disaster.

Tashami grunted and swung his flailing arm up to the next row of holes in the shrouds. He yanked himself up, regaining his footing in the holds. Then he climbed even higher despite the altitude's vicious gales. This time he refused to look down.

Once he pulled himself into the crow's nest, he observed the sea from a bird's eye view. Having already established that the water was indistinguishable at this height, he half expected to be met with no luck. He was surprised, however, to see thousands of Intelights circling the ship, hovering atop the waters. Tashami would have preferred something a little brighter, but this would suffice.

He kept a keen eye both on the sea below and in the distance. He couldn't afford to miss any drastic stirrings in the water's currents, otherwise the entire ship—even one of this magnitude—would go under.

Terror consumed Tashami as he realized the ship had already begun climbing a wave that was still forming. The water rose in front of them, and the *Whale Lord* was headed for its lip. He needed to accelerate the vessel in order to break the wave's crest before the path became too vertical and flipped the ship backward.

So he thrust both palms forward, weaving a barrage of wind into the three foresails. The ship gained speed in response. Slowly it neared the crest. He continued his efforts, knowing that if he failed, the voyage—and all lives—would meet a catastrophic end. There was no time to rejoice as the ship's front half broke the wave's lip, for now came the difficult part. The bow and keel would lift from the water before crashing back into it as the back half cleared the wave's crest. This would be a devastating blow to the ship's foundation and render it useless, so Tashami needed to remedy this potential disaster.

He redirected his wind so that it'd hit the sail from above at a downward angle. Hopefully his energy's clout and thrust were mighty enough to counter the ship's weight as it became suspended in the air.

It worked. The ship practically curved over the crest, its front half gently placing itself back into the sea. And all of this had been accomplished while the ship was turning.

Tashami fell to the floor as the *Whale Lord* escaped the storm. He leaned against the curved wall of the crow's nest and tried to catch his breath as his body began to weaken. His energy canals were withering away as energy depletion kicked in. Before he knew it, he blacked out.

* * *

Tashami awoke to whispers. The storm he had remembered was gone, replaced by an unexpected quiet. How many days had he missed?

"He forced this hulking ship down?" someone asked. It sounded like Crole, a fellow squallblaster.

"That's what Barloe told me," another person replied. Tashami recognized that voice immediately. It belonged to Agnos. "We'd be on the seabed if it weren't for that extraordinary maneuver."

"Unbelievable," Crole said. "Makes me feel like less of a squallblaster."

Tashami turned over in his hammock. "Agnos … Crole."

"The hero's awake!" Crole said, hurrying around Agnos's hammock to pat Tashami's shoulder.

Crole was one of the crew's younger members—in his early twenties, a couple years older than Tashami and Agnos. He had a mullet of jet-black hair and sideburns that ran down the length of his jaw, disappearing where they reached his chin.

He pulled up a stool. "Well, one of two heroes," he said.

"How long have I been out?"

"Not too long … a little under a day."

Tashami looked past Crole at Agnos. "How's your leg?"

"Didn't have to lose it, so that's good," Agnos said with a smirk. "No infections, just a lot of bandages."

Tashami gazed around the room. "Still in the surgeon's room?"

"Yes, but we have an important meeting later today," Agnos said.

Crole's eyebrows climbed his forehead. "You get to meet the woman and myth herself … Gray Whale."

Tashami looked at Agnos once more. "I'm glad you proved this crew wrong. I knew you'd do it."

The surgeon reentered the room and shooed Crole out. "Off you go, lad. Go play a game of chess or something."

As the squallblaster left, the surgeon peeled back Agnos's bandages to inspect the healing process. "Not bad," he said, turning over a bottle of fleepshire into a rag. "You two need to go back to sleep. Especially you, Tashami." As he dabbed the rag against Agnos's wound, he said, "Barloe will be here later to wake you."

* * *

That afternoon Agnos, using a crutch, limped his way through the specialty quarters behind Barloe and Tashami. They reached a lone door at the very end of a hall. Barloe knocked. "Ophala's boys are here to see you," he said.

Agnos narrowed his eyes at the quartermaster. They knew Ophala?

A voice carried from within the room: "Come in."

The door creaked as Barloe opened it. They stepped inside the luxurious great cabin. The walls may have been old and worn down, but the rest of the ship paled in comparison. It rivaled the size of the main deck and had as many full bookcases against the wall as the study. Agnos wanted to run and grab as many of the books as possible.

In the front of the room a lady stood gazing out the grand window at the trailing sea. Her hair was long and silver and splashed around her shoulders, which were nearly as broad as Barloe's. She wore a gray trench coat that looked in desperate need of a wash. Without turning, she said, "I think you're ready to give me your name, scrawny one."

Agnos had heard that before, but couldn't place his finger on it. "Name's Agnos."

She turned around and grinned. Her face was scarred, skin wrinkled tight. Agnos and Tashami had met her before … in a gambling hall in the Chasm back in Sodai. "Silvia …" Agnos said.

She shook her head. "Not here. Call me Gray Whale." She glanced at the young man with white hair. "Hello, Tashami. I've heard all about you during the voyage."

"Nice to see you again, ma'am."

"*Captain*," she corrected. As the two Jestivan stood still, she said, "Well, come in and have a seat."

Barloe left the room. Tashami and Agnos sat across from Gray as she took a seat and continued devouring a half-eaten meal.

"I thought you had retired," Agnos said.

"I had," she replied with a mouthful of meat. "But then it turned out to be only an extended vacation … once I caught wind of a potential mission. I knew I'd have to return to the sea for one last hunt. There is much to gain from this voyage."

"Such as?"

She chuckled and leaned back in her chair. "None of your concern, Anus."

Tashami's cheeks turned red as he placed his hand over his open mouth. Agnos's eyes dulled. "It's Agnos, Captain."

"My apologies, Anus," Gray said over Tashami's muffled laughter. "So I hear you're an expert on the sea."

"I simply have a lot of book knowledge, but not much beyond that. I was hoping to gain experience from this trip, but really all I've been doing is scrubbing floors."

"That will end soon," she replied. "Your role will expand, now that you've proven useful. What you did—capturing those two men—was vital. During my life as captain of the *Whale Lord*, I never once could understand how a fleet has been able to avoid me."

"Do you remember when and how they joined your crew?"

She shrugged. "I'm never really privy to who joins the crew. I leave such matters to Barloe, but he does give me a list of any newcomers before a voyage. Earlier today I dug through my paperwork from the past few decades and found their names from before even Barloe's time on this ship. Both Farlyn and Rotel joined the crew between my first and second voyage as captain, which makes sense."

"Isn't there a vetting process to weed out any undesirable members?" Agnos asked.

"It's a matter of judgment, really. But yes, usually we ask what they'd provide for the ship. For most, it's experience and knowledge. For a few, it's their weaving abilities. Then there are some who simply end up being grunts. They get on the ship because their friend might be a veteran of the crew who vouches for them. Those are the people who become swabs until they work their way up the ladder."

"Who vouched for these two guys?" Tashami asked.

She raised an eyebrow. "Honestly, nobody. And that's no one's fault but mine. My first voyage as captain was on a small ship. I embarked to the Dark Sea …" She paused at the look on Agnos's face. "Yes, I didn't bother starting off easy. I traversed a whirlpool with a crew of roughly thirteen. Then I pursued a vessel five times the size of my own—and I do mean that literally—caught it, and destroyed it."

Agnos's eyes narrowed. "You just 'destroyed' a vessel of that size? How …"

Gray laughed and leaned forward. "Listen, I have quite a story—how I came to be the power that I am—but because I'm a pirate, you won't find it written in any books. My presence doesn't exist outside of the sea."

"So tell me the story," Agnos said.

Gray glanced at Tashami, who said, "He's quite fond of stories."

"No," she said, shaking her head. "The point is, once I returned to DaiSo, word had already spread to the pirate town. Suddenly my crew was treated as aristocrats. I was dubbed Gray Whale, and a group of carpenters built me a ship, naming it the *Whale Lord.* The town even granted us residence in DaiSo's biggest crew house, which is now called the Whale House.

"With such fame came eager and overzealous applicants. And, of course, I was willing to take almost all of them in. I needed the hands, since I now had a ship that dwarfed the most daunting naval vessels. I'd also carry out missions that'd make my first pale in comparison. I took on roughly three hundred people during that year between the first and second voyage. It was easy for Farlyn and Rotel to slip through."

The three of them sat in silence, except for the creaking of the wooden ship as it rocked gently in the water. Agnos's gaze was fixated on his knees when he asked, "So Farlyn stayed a swab for thirty years?"

"I guess he felt it kept him off of the crew's map." Gray tapped her fingers and raised her eyebrows. "And he was right. Nobody's worried about a damn swab."

"Where are the rats now?" Tashami asked. "Did you kill them?"

"No. Two firefighters are keeping watch over them in the brig. Rotel had a compass on him, so we took that. We also kept him blindfolded for obvious reasons … that Devish wizardry."

A thought jumped into Agnos's head. "Do you know Spy Pilot Ophala?"

Gray went silent as she studied Agnos. "I only know *of* her. But she does know me. Then again, she knows most people in this world. That comes with the territory of being an eye in the sky."

"You knew we were coming?"

Gray smiled before getting up. "Not much longer before we run into our target," she said. "Hopefully our little three-day maneuver back toward DaiSo didn't hurt us too much. Tashami, I'll need you filling the sails every day to the best of your ability, but don't deplete your energy again. Anus …" Her voice faded as she turned to look out her window … "You will spend most of your days with me, allowing me to teach you about the sea and how to run a crew of pirates."

His eyes spread wide as he pushed himself out of his chair. "Really?"

"And eventually you'll tell me this story of a cave on the seafloor. I've heard Eet and Osh rave about it all voyage long."

28
Weapons Specialist

Lilu strolled through her lab, wending between equipment as she inspected her assistants stationed throughout the room. Yesterday she had given them an assignment to be completed by the end of the week. They were each tinkering with a chunk of provod, carving and grooving it into a vessel that mimicked what was drawn on the wheeled chalkboard at the center of the lab.

It was a diagram of a weapon Lilu had drawn many times throughout her life; conceptualizing weavineering technology had always been a hobby of hers. She had called it the volter; and, in theory, it was perfect. Without the skill to craft it, however, she couldn't prove it.

The volter's design contained a horizontal pipe called the "cannon," which extended from the top-half side of a rectangular permanence vessel—or the "supply." EC chains were stored in the supply. A springboard rested in its base, which had to be crafted separately and placed inside the supply before kilning. There were a number of different levers and switches on the device's exterior, all of which served their own purpose.

A small doorway separated the supply from the cannon, but the other end of the cannon was unobstructed, serving as the weapon's discharge point. Lilu had a theory about how springs could affect a vessel's release of energy, and now that she had a lab and proper weavineers at her disposal, she could test it.

After checking in on Arrogo and Limone's progress, Lilu approached Gracie's station. Her jet-black hair was tied back in a bun.

"How's it going?"

Gracie heaved an exaggerated breath. "Meticulous doesn't even *begin* to describe this. Why'd you put me on this team if you knew we'd be doing crafting techniques as advanced as this?"

"Because you're talented and my friend."

"I thought we'd gossip and drink."

Lilu smirked. "That's what our evenings are for." She leaned in and inspected Gracie's volter. Right now her supply was cut in half so she could insert her springboard. "Make sure your crosshatching is impeccable when you reattach the top and bottom half of the supply, and really smooth out the exterior wall—no creases."

"I know, I know." Gracie readied her best Lilu impression, straightening her back and lifting her chin. "Crosshatching makes sure the two halves lock into place when they're hardening in the kiln, while smoothing the exterior stabilizes the interior EC chains afterward."

Lilu nodded, ignoring her mockery. "Also make sure the spring is lodged deep in the supply's base. It's the most important piece of this device."

"Go flirt with Frederick or something," Gracie replied, rolling her eyes.

Lilu stuck out her tongue, but then headed toward Frederick without even realizing it. Her mouth stalled as she neared him. After a long moment of awkward hovering, Frederick finally glanced away from the mirror on his jointed chisel. His progress was impeccable, as he was much further ahead of everyone else.

"Hey, Lilu," he said, standing straight and brushing off his hands.

"You're doing so well," she said.

"That's it?" he asked, his hand meeting the back of his head. "I'm trying really hard on this."

"No, no, it's actually amazing—even better than my draft."

He looked down at the device. "I can't believe you thought of such a concept … Truly innovative."

"Well, it won't amount to much if it doesn't work. It's a fun idea, but we know the reality of theoretical experiments …" She sighed. "They tend to fail."

"True," said Frederick as he continued to carve his vessel. "We saw that when we rummaged through Mendac's essays. Thousands of hypotheses, and ninety-nine percent of them failed when experimented on. And even most of his theories couldn't be conclusive as law."

Lilu's thoughts drifted to the Theory of Connectivity. After countless hours of scouring Mendac's lab for a mentioning of the theory, she'd come up empty-handed. Perhaps it was time to inform Frederick of her hunt; it would help having an extra set of eyes.

Most of her team had left by the end of the day. Frederick and Gracie were the typical stragglers. Nobody had finished crafting their vessel except for Frederick, who had just placed his in the kiln. Since the volter was more complex than the simple blocks made in Lilu's crafting classes when she first arrived, it would take longer for the heat to harden the provod. She estimated three to four days.

It was well into evening when Gracie decided to escape the lab's confinements and salvage what little bit she had left of her night. While she and Lilu held jobs in Weavineer Tower, they were still students enrolled at IWA. They had classes in the morning.

This left Lilu and Frederick alone in an awkward silence. Lilu pretended to study her diagram, writing random words down as if she was contemplating adjustments. The reality was that she was trying to distract herself.

She risked a glance back at Frederick to discover he had other plans. He had leapt into the cockpit of a gigantic machine bolted into the floor. It resembled a jointed chisel, but it was the size of a shack. Lilu had yet to put such a tool to use. She couldn't even fathom a provod vessel big enough to require such machinery—at least not at this point in their experimentation.

Frederick took a seat and grabbed a handle. The contraption released a dissonance of grinding gears and belts as it spun to the right. He pulled a lever and continued to spin the handle. Now it moved faster.

"Don't break something!" Lilu shouted.

"Me? Break something?!"

As if right on cue, the end of the jointed appendage collided with the wall that separated Lilu's lab from Mendac's. Her shoulders recoiled as she thrust her hand over her eyes. "You're an idiot," she sighed.

Frederick's wide-eyed expression said enough. He leapt out of the cockpit, skipping the use of the ladder. "We'll blame Gracie."

"You're definitely not getting my niece in trouble for such buffoonery."

Lilu and Frederick, visibly startled, looked up at the observational bridge. Professor Jugtah was leaning against the rail. "Came in to see how things were going," he said. "Didn't know this was a playground."

Lilu's face turned scarlet. "We just got done with our work for the day," she explained. "We were about to leave."

Jugtah's eyes darted to the kiln as it hissed. "I see …" He walked down the length of the bridge to get a better look at the chalkboard. "Ooh, quite interesting. Jumping straight into your more complex designs, are you?"

"Not really … I have ones that are much more intricate."

"Ah, yes," said Jugtah with a nod. "Is your team ready for such inventions?"

"Frederick definitely is."

Jugtah smiled at his student teacher. "Yes, that I can believe. Not the best weaver, but definitely a top weavineer."

Frederick was unsure of how to respond. "*Err* … thanks, sir."

"Have you put Mendac's lab to use? Applied any of his findings to alter your own diagrams?"

Lilu's face soured. The last thing she wanted to do was use Mendac's research, but she was already guilty. Instead she asked Jugtah a question of her own: "Are there any other areas in Brilliance that Mendac operated from?"

He pushed his golden spectacles up his nose. "Someone's still hunting for an explanation to the Theory of Connectivity?"

"I am."

He paused, gave it some thought, and then said, "Mendac still stands guard."

"What?"

Jugtah walked down the bridge and returned to the Intelevator. "Keep up the good work, you two."

* * *

Lilu rummaged through stacks of folders and binders that rolled like sea waves across a table. She stood on one side while Frederick perused the material across from her.

"What time is it?" Lilu asked. Her eyes were bloodshot from hours of reading Mendac's shoddy penmanship.

He checked his wristwatch. "Approaching midnight."

"This is hopeless." She stood up and took a bite out of the last bit of sandwich that Gracie had packed for her earlier that day. "Find anything promising?"

"Not really, but this is a lot more fun now that I know what it is you're looking for. What has you so eager to learn about this vague theory?"

She crumpled up her paper bag as she thought about Bryson. Something stopped her from mentioning him to Frederick. Instead, she said, "I think it'll answer a lot of questions that pertain to someone I know."

* * *

Lilu hadn't taken more than two steps into her suite before Gracie berated her with questions: "So how'd it go? Who made the first move? Percentage-wise, how far did you get?"

"Gracie, shut up."

She frowned, placing her hand against her chest as if she'd been disrespected. "You've been gone for six hours!"

"Doing research," Lilu said. She sat down on the couch and began shuffling through her blueprints.

"Anatomy lessons, eh?"

Lilu tried to ignore her tease, but a smirk still managed to slip onto her face.

"There has to be a reason why you haven't given Frederick the time of day," Gracie said. "And it's not something silly like he's ugly, stupid, or dry—he's definitely none of those. Quite frankly, he is the full package."

"He's not my type," Lilu said.

Gracie laughed mightily, smacking her hand on the kitchen counter. "No, no, no, Lilu. He's your type. Only one thing could be making you stall like you are—" She paused for dramatic effect— "There's a boy waiting for you in Dunami, isn't there?"

Lilu hesitated, which was a mistake. Seizing the prolonged pause, Gracie said, "That's what I thought." Gracie's footsteps traveled from the kitchen to her room. She opened her door. "For your sake," she said, "I hope he's doing the same."

Lilu closed her eyes as Gracie's door clicked shut. Maybe she was right.

* * *

Lilu and her team were back in the lab the next day. Frederick didn't have much to do since his device was already in the kiln; so he proctored Gracie, Limone, and Arrogo as they struggled with the detailed crafting.

Lilu was busy sketching some blueprints for a new invention she'd thought of last night. It was something bold and a little bit unbelievable, but it just might work if she could wrestle through the complicated mechanical design.

"Lilu!" someone yelled.

She looked over to see Frederick standing next to Limone, a doughy-eyed, pudgy-faced assistant. Frederick waved her over.

As she approached, Frederick said, "Show her, then."

Lilu watched as Limone's shaky hands readjusted a mirror so that it faced the cannon's mouth. She then leaned in and observed the grooves he had etched into its inner walls.

"Your grooves are spiraling up the length of the cannon instead of straight like instructed," she said. "What's the thinking behind this?"

"Well, milady …" When Lilu sighed, he froze and then quickly corrected his mistake. "I mean … it's only a theory, but you know how talented archers twist the feathers in their arrows so that they're flight's path is more direct?"

Lilu puckered her lips as she realized what he was getting at before saying it. "Yes …"

"Well, I figured the same would apply to this device. It's supposed to function as a weapon that shoots projectiles long range—in this case, Intel chains. But if the grooves in the cannon are straight, what's to stop Intel clusters from breaking off in an errant direction when meeting open air? Why not make the chains—and thus the electricity—twist around each other, giving it a straighter path."

Lilu stared at Limone as he finished his explanation. She hated herself for not realizing this before, but she hid the shame. Instead she smiled. "Good job," she said.

"Should we change our grooves too?" Gracie asked.

Lilu walked over to the chalkboard and began drawing Limone's concept on an empty spot. "No. Continue what you've already started. Then next week, when everyone's provod has finished hardening in the kilns, we'll compare the designs. But logic tells me Limone's innovation will prove superior."

After she finished drawing the new cannon, she decided to give a name to the carving technique. She wrote two words on the board above the sketch then turned around. Frederick pat Limone's back, whose face lit up with joy as he read its name: *Limone Lining.*

*   *   *

Later that night, Frederick and Lilu finished another hopeless hunt through Mendac's lab. Frederick gazed around, absorbing the full expanse of the room. Its immense size was one thing; the clutter was an additional hurdle. "It'll take us weeks to cover every parchment in here," he said.

They gathered their stuff, closed the wall that separated the two labs, and bunched together on the Intelevator. Following a long descent to the first floor, they strolled across the deserted main lobby, walking through the revolving doors and onto the quiet streets.

It was another overcast night in Brilliance. Despite the city's seclusion from the rest of the kingdom, that signature facet remained. Besides a few waning lights, most Intelamps didn't fuction at this hour. The only signs of life were the distant crowds of IWA students at the bars and taverns a couple blocks down. Meanwhile, Lilu and Frederick treated each other to a silence that had once been awkward weeks ago but was now comforting.

They approached the intersection that housed Mendac's statue. As always, she stared up at it in disgust. Frederick stayed quiet as he followed her gaze—he had learned not to press the conflict since meeting her.

They continued onward, but Lilu stopped just as they were about to walk down another street. She turned toward the statue once more as Jugtah's cryptic words dawned upon her.

"What is it?" Frederick asked.

She shook her head and pressed forward. "Are you willing to break the law with me?"

"Would we be hurting anyone?"

"Only Brilliance's ego."

29
Departure

Passion Director Venustas led Toshik and Himitsu through Fiamma Palace. The palace in Phelos had been their only prior experience of royalty living, so this was a new experience. The majestic edifice mirrored its city, designed with an organic, free-flowing theme. Almost every foyer or grand hall had an indoor pond bordered by fresh flowers in colorful potting beds. It was a far cry from the ancient, eroding stone and dingy halls of the castle in Phelos.

Their journey came to a halt in the most magnificent room of them all. They stood in a massive rotunda stretching a few stories high with a kaleidoscope window installed in the ceiling, allowing sunlight to bounce in every direction. There were two balconies that circled the room above them, each serving a different floor.

But then there was the masterpiece which sat at the center—a sturdy oak with vibrant green leaves, its branches reaching for the second and third-floor balconies. It sat in a patch of grass encircled by a moat-like pond. Four waterfalls spilled into the moat from the upper balconies, providing the rotunda with a gentle din of falling water and a pleasant floral aroma. It must have taken a genius to contrive such an intricate design.

"So where is she?" Toshik asked.

"You know her better than anyone, Zana Toshik," Venustas said. "Where in this room would you think she might be?"

Toshik gazed toward the tree and, sure enough, a girl fell out of the canopy and landed on a lower branch with a squeal. The branch bent under her weight before flicking her across the pond. She soared through the air while giggling maniacally—her sunhat trailing from her neck—until she landed on the marble floor in a ridiculous fighting stance.

"What do you think about *that* as a battle entrance?" she asked. Her eyebrows crumpled and her mouth displayed an austere frown that came off as more of a pout.

"Not sure it's practical," Toshik replied.

Jilly tackled him around the ribs. "I missed you." She immediately backed away. "Wait— I'm mad at you."

"You're mad at me, not him," said Himitsu.

Jilly's eyes shifted to the assassin. "You're right," she said. "We're going to have a serious talk about what happened, mister." Her eyes darted between the two young men. "The both of you. We're going to hash this out."

Toshik tilted his head and whined. "I don't know if that's—"

"You should listen to the girl," interrupted a new voice. "She's smart, that one there."

As a figure entered from the opposite hallway out of the balcony's shadow, Toshik and Himitsu both said, "Fane ..."

"Are you two done being children?" he asked.

"How've you been?" Himitsu asked.

"Stressed," he said. He looked at Jilly and added, "But thanks to her presence the past few weeks, I've been allowed moments to escape reality."

"So what are we all doing here?" Toshik asked as he looked at Venustas. "Specifically you, Director."

"Well, I'm here for reasons unknown to the public. I'm serving as council to Queen Fiona."

"Where's King Damian?" Himitsu asked.

She hesitated and then mumbled, "Dead—murdered by the Rogue Demon, we're assuming."

"Toono killed a royal head?" Himitsu asked.

"It's nothing to worry yourselves with," she replied. "I've brought all of you here for other reasons. There is more at play here than just Toono. He and Dev King Storshae have sculpted quite a force. The Light Realm will need all of its power players in its arsenal to combat what those two men have built. With that said, that means we need Olivia, but she's currently wandering the Archaic Mountains under the orders of Intel King Vitio."

"What?! Why?" Himitsu shouted, enraged. "We already lost Rhyparia to that monstrosity!"

"King Vitio did it as punishment," Venustas replied, "but he seemed to have forgotten that he holds no power over her. And he did this without consulting the kingdom she belongs to, nor did he hold a trial. I don't care if he couldn't get in touch with King Damian; he still should have held off on his actions. But now that I know he's done this, I've decided to take matters into my own hands. Queen Fiona won't do it, fearing the backlash for undermining the great Intel family."

"What are you going to do?" Himitsu asked.

She looked at Toshik and Jilly. "I'm going to grant the two of you access into the Archaic Mountains to retrieve her. I'll give you the proper documentation with the Passion Kingdom's royal seal."

Toshik made a noise with his mouth as if she was crazy. "I'm not going in those mountains—especially for a girl who I witnessed stand on the side of my enemies."

Himitsu brows furrowed. "You know it was a lot more complicated than that."

"Really?" Toshik spat. "I remember, quite clearly I might add, Olivia literally helping our opponent."

"And you know why!" Himitsu yelled, turning around and standing within inches of the swordsman.

"*STOP IT!*" A blast of fire erupted between the two zana, singeing their eyelashes and forcing them to dive backward. They gazed up at a livid Venustas as her eyes pierced their souls.

"I'm going to find her," Jilly said, unbothered by the confrontation.

"That's the spirit," Fane said.

Jilly looked down at Toshik. "You're reverting to your old self. That needs to stop."

Toshik's menace morphed into fear. The last thing he wanted to do was lose Jilly because of his stubbornness. He stood up and rubbed his watering eyes, sensitive from the previous heat. "All right, when are we leaving?" he asked.

Venustas reached into her cloak and pulled out a sealed envelope. "Travel to Rim and take it to a guard in the foothills of the mountains. Make sure you're adequately supplied and mentally prepared … I advise you say a proper goodbye to Himitsu. It might be a long time before you see each other again."

Toshik slowly looked over at the Passion Jestivan—one of the few people who matched his towering stature. "Why isn't he coming?"

"He has other matters to attend to."

The two men eyed one another, contemplating how to go about this. Himitsu was first to extend his hand. Toshik grasped it firmly and shook. "Good luck," Himitsu said.

"Maybe we'll operate better when separated."

Himitsu smirked and patted the handle at his waist. "You'll always be attached to my hip—remember that."

This siphoned a smile from Toshik as he replied, "Cheers, pal."

Jilly stepped forward and burrowed her head into Himitsu's chest. He wrapped his arms around her. "Annoy the mess out of him for me," he said. "Make sure he doesn't get killed trying to slay some beast with his stick."

"What was that?" Toshik asked.

Jilly laughed, then said, "Make sure Fane eats plenty of fiber."

Fane chuckled and shook his head. "Will do," Himitsu said.

They separated, and Jilly and Toshik left the rotunda before disappearing around a corner down the hall. With them entering the Archaic Mountains, would this be the last time he'd ever see them again?

"All right," Venustas said. "Now time for the information only you need to hear."

Himitsu refocused on his director, wiping a tear from his eye.

"Before Senex was killed—actually, between Rhyparia's first and second trial—he informed the Energy Directors of Vliyan NuForce's relic, the Cloutitionist's Necklace. He sent news by letter through Ophala's carrier falcons since he didn't have a Dev servant at his disposal. He was certain that he'd win the trial for Rhyparia. Thus we were surprised when it was revealed during Vliyan's questioning that she possessed a fake rather than the real thing."

Venustas gravely shook her head. "But Archaic Director Senex wouldn't make such a blunder. He was too knowledgeable of ancients and had experienced too much throughout his long life. Something was amiss. Somehow his plan had been foiled, and based off other information he put in his letter, we had ideas of who the culprits were … and this is why I couldn't say this with the other two here."

She lowered her voice. "Vliyan NuForce, Toth Brench, Wert Lamay, and a woman named Tazama."

"Toshik and Jilly's dads?" Himitsu asked. The name of Rhyparia's mother didn't garner the same reaction; he already knew her to be rotten.

Venustas nodded. "Yes. And with all of this information, we knew that Ophala and Horos were wrongfully imprisoned."

"What a surprise," muttered Himitsu. "The bad guys win again."

"Boy," Fane said with a rigid face, "where's this pessimism coming from? Is this what I have to look forward to after experiencing the elation that is the company of Jilly?" He paused. "Let's go get your mom and dad."

* * *

Bryson stood while thumping his forehead against the wall in a random hallway in Dunami Palace. He wanted to tear the building to the ground, light the city on fire, and purge the kingdom of all life. He was on the verge of snapping Vitio's limbs in half and shoving them so far down Lars's mouth that he'd choke on them. His body temperature was spiking to a point that his head and chest wanted to explode—impressive for someone as unnaturally cold as him. It took all of his power to not punch through this wall right now. The only thing holding him back was the thought of his father—a man he wanted no similarities with.

Bryson took a deep breath and pushed himself away from the wall. The little sanity he had left remained stitched together because of Princess Shelly. Her presence kept him grounded—her subtle sass and the way her short green hair curled around her cheek. Or perhaps it was her confidence, something Bryson always lacked. She filled that part of him. He envied the way she carried herself.

He grunted and smacked his hand against a wood panel. Why was he even thinking about her? It was Olivia who had consumed him lately … all the uncertainties of her location or if she was even alive. Shelly had refused to entertain his ideas of going after his sister, which led to his current tantrum. How many times would he have to hear Vitio say no to his pleas? Then listen to Shelly support her father?

He just experienced this same routine for the thousandth time over dinner, followed by a verbal confrontation between Vitio and Bryson, during which Shelly joined and sided with her father … *The nerve of that woman.*

Bryson bottled his rage and swept through a doorway into his guest room—which now felt like his own. He had lived here for nearly a year. And even before that, he had spent more nights in this palace than at home when away from Phesaw … ever since Debo's death.

As Bryson sat at the edge of his four-poster bed, gripping himself from another chill, the door handle clicked. Shelly entered in a shamrock green nightgown that barely reached her thighs. Did she really just walk through the halls in that?

He leapt off the bed and shook his head. "Get out of here."

She closed the door behind her and stood a safe distance away, observing him with unreadable green eyes.

"I'm tired of you and your family!" he said, his voice shaking. "My sister is gone! She's not off prancing around in a walled city like yours! She's likely dead!" He stomped toward Shelly, ready to grab her by the shoulders and force her out of his room.

Her single finger against his lips stopped his tirade. Her gaze didn't change. She smelled of lilies with a note of plum. Her eyelashes were naturally long and thick, and she wore a faint silver band in her hair.

She gently pushed Bryson back. Halfway across the room, the warmth of her wet lips interlocked with his. She placed him on the bed, pressing both her hands down on his shoulders, then continued kissing him.

Bryson and Shelly had already committed the deed a few times during the past several months, but this was different. From the pace at which she moved, the delicacy of her actions, and the look on her face, there was more depth involved than simple lust. The chill subsided, consumed by a fiery passion. As Bryson placed his hand against Shelly's cheek, he felt only love.

* * *

"I was selfish."

The voice made Bryson groan and roll over in his thick blankets, as he was trapped between dreamland and consciousness.

"I've been keeping you here for two reasons—it only used to be one." There was a pause as Bryson lay peacefully with his eyes closed. "Just make sure you come back." Someone kissed his cheek and whispered into his ear. He mumbled something incoherent in response.

The mattress rose underneath him. The door clicked shut a moment later, leaving Bryson alone in his bed.

* * *

Bryson awoke the following overcast morning, expecting to see Shelly next to him. Instead, seeing that the bed was empty, sadness wafted over him. Propping himself up on his elbows, he reflected on the previous night … and not because of its glory, but because of its *meaning*. There had been more there than a physical rush.

He was about to get out of bed when something caught his eye on the pillow next to him. Two envelopes were resting side by side with a note lying on top. The small message read: *The second one is for Vuilni. Don't go looking for me to say goodbye, and make sure you leave the palace quickly.*

His eyes widened as he snatched the two envelopes. He flipped them over and saw that they were sealed with the Intelian insignia. His mouth formed a dumbfounded smile as he pressed his hand into his forehead and grabbed a fistful of his bangs. There was no way Vitio had allowed this … This was all Shelly.

30
Stirrings

Chief Merchant Toth Brench and Tazama rode in a veiled carriage through the outskirts of Phelos. It wasn't their first journey here. In fact, the last time they visited the outskirts was to meet the same person.

The carriage came to a stop, and the door opened. A cloaked woman stepped inside. She was round and squat. As she unveiled herself, Toth said, "Good to see you, Vliyan."

"Not entirely sure I share those sentiments," she replied as she took a seat across from him in the lorry.

He nodded. "I assure you we're moving as fast as we can."

"I want my necklace."

"And when we've gained control of the kingdom, you'll have it back … as well as a cozy room in the palace and a place on the high council. You've been one of the most important pieces to our success."

She raised her chin into the air, accepting the flattery. "So what are we waiting for?"

"Tazama here is working on a method of direct travel into Phelos from the Dark Realm. She's almost finished. Then we'll begin the uprising."

"I think I'll get started on it now," Tazama said, getting up and descending the steps out of the carriage.

"I hope you have a good plan," Vliyan said.

"It can be a great plan if you accept the job I'm about to offer you."

Her brow arched. "And what is that?"

"Well, there's really only one person who I feel can sabotage the uprising—Prince Sigmund. I don't think he has it in him to do what he says he will."

"Of course not." Vliyan chuckled. "He has a weak spine … How a glorius man such as King Itta produced such a disgraceful spawn is a mystery."

Toth ignored the comment. "Sigmund is supposed to keep Chief Senator Rosel and Chief Arbitrator Grandarion trapped in a dining hall during dinner. They'll know something is happening in the capital, but Sigmund won't allow them to do anything about it."

Vliyan laughed again. "He'll succumb."

"Probably," Toshik said, nodding. "There will be a lot of death and destruction that night, and his conscious will overpower his rationality."

Her eyes narrowed. "So you want me to make sure he stays true to his word by keeping them locked in a room?"

Toth leaned toward her, dropping his voice to a mumble. "One better." He reached across the lorry and dropped a few strands of hair into Vliyan's hand. He then pulled a silver necklace from within his suit and handed it over as well.

The woman grinned something twisted and foul as she hissed, "*For Itta.*"

* * *

Grandarion sat across from Rosel in her office, leaning back, balancing a glass of scotch in his open hand. Rosel sat scribbling across a sheet of parchment behind mountains of others. Even with her feverish writing, her posture was as straight as a lead pipe.

"Do you think we've lost the boy for good?" Grandarion asked.

"I don't think it's the boy we need to worry about," she replied. "We must pander to the public in order to get to the prince. The whole reason he's distancing himself from us in the first place is because he sees how his citizens are responding to us."

Grandarion stared at the rim of his glass as he twirled it. "To see how Wert rallied those people …"

Rosel paused in her writing and glanced at him over her spectacles. "Frightening."

"It's a tactic that has worked many times over history," the arbitrator said.

"By tyrants," she noted. "His message is fueled by fear and hate—just like Itta. And with the condition the kingdom is in, it's working. The people believed they were giving hope a chance with the Amendment Order, and it's failed them."

"I suspect that's what you're working on right now—" Grandarion followed her racing quill— "some kind of proposal or bill to put into action and right the ship."

"I'm a politician. That's what I do."

"And Wert's a warrior," he rebuked. "Remind me what it is that they do."

"They fight."

After a pause, Grandarion asked, "And how will your bills fair against a blade?"

Rosel put down her quill and glared at her fellow chief. "That bonehead wouldn't resort to violence. There are still Spirit, Adren, Intel, and Passion soldiers in the palace and District Four … and he'd face the wrath of the rest of the Light Realm if he committed to something so foolish."

"I think you underestimate his resources," Grandarion said.

"The man has no one."

*   *   *

Outside Elyol's hut, Wert stood staring at the sea of lava before him. He wiped his face with a rag. In the distance a plateau jutted into the sky, and the top of Phelos Palace even farther away. At this distance, however, it looked like a bug ready to be squashed.

Elyol stepped out of the hut, carrying an apple. He joined Wert in his sightseeing. "How many square miles is District Four?" Elyol asked.

"Roughly thirteen," Wert replied.

Elyol took a bite of his apple. "Manageable."

The Chief Officer chuckled as he shook his head at the magma. "You don't say?"

"How many soldiers make it their base?"

Wert gave it some thought before answering: "Close to a thousand, all of whom belong to the other kingdoms—or most of them at least. I know there to be a few Archaic soldiers who aren't with me."

"That's a lot of people," Elyol said.

"It's understandable to feel unease about this," Wert said. "You'll accumulate quite a kill toll when the night comes, but it will serve a great purpose by bringing the strength of the newly formed Lamaylian Army to light. Green and orange will swarm the capital."

"I'm not nervous, Chief," Elyol said through a mouthful of apple. "I'm restless."

*   *   *

In the throne room of Cogdan Castle, Dev King Storshae stood behind the throne while Toono, Kadlest, Yama, Dev Warden Gala, Jina, and Halluci sat on the steps which led up to it. Illipsia was sitting on the floor, looking bored, and picking at a scab on her knee.

The doors opened and a man entered. His full snowy-white beard connected with his sideburns, framing his rugged face in a perfect square. His eyes were the same beady black that Toono remembered. The last time he'd seen this man was two years ago when he had infiltrated Kindoliya Palace and killed Salia, the former Still Queen.

Garlo's strides slowed upon recognizing the slew of faces scattered across the steps, stretching from one side of the room to the other. His eyes froze upon Toono.

"You're Garlo, former general of the Still Army, aren't you?" Storshae asked.

"Yes, sir."

"Good. I'm Dev Prince Storshae. Don't worry about the others seated in front of me, for their names are not of importance to you at this moment. You'll learn them with time."

"I know Toono," Garlo said, his jaw tightening. Clearly there was resentment, and understandably so. He had been duped, attacked, and entrapped by Toono, which led to a free path for his queen to be murdered.

Storshae laughed. "So I've heard. The timing of your arrival isn't ideal, but better late than never. Most of us will be leaving for the Archaic Kingdom in a few weeks, and you'll be tagging along. Thus, you'll be training with Toono and Yama every day as preparation. They'll also fill you in on the details of the uprising."

Garlo growled. "Must I be around that man? Let me fight the girl," he said.

"The girl?" echoed Toono, his interest piqued. "That 'girl' would do you more harm than I would. Whereas I allowed you life back in Kindoliya, if it had been her, a coroner would've had to put your body back together like puzzle pieces. And don't you come from a kingdom that preaches the power of women? You should know better. I'll do you a favor," Toono said. "I'll grant you your wish. I won't train against you at all … I'll watch. Yama needs a good slicing bag anyway."

Garlo smirked wryly. "This isn't the Still Kingdom anymore. I don't have to pretend that I'm inferior because of my gender."

A rush of wind blew through the throne room. Garlo clenched his teeth as a gloved hand lifted his chin, and a sword was placed across his throat. Yama stood behind him. Even Toono hadn't seen her move.

As Storshae's chuckle turned into a hysterical laugh, Toono said, "You never were pretending."

*   *   *

Once again, Toono spent his time scheming, contemplating methods of acquiring the remaining sacrifices that stood between him and the rebirth.

He had killed many powerful individuals, but perhaps what should have been the simplest of them all plagued his mind the most. The uncertainty of the Dev sacrifice's identity bothered him. Storshae kept such information a close-guarded secret.

A structure in Toono's peripherals caught his attention as he passed by windows in a corridor. He approached one and gazed outside. A perfectly square edifice of gray sat a few thousand feet away from the palace, but still within the grounds' wall. It was a peculiar building—not a single window or door to be seen.

There weren't many things in the world that stumped Toono, for he had learned about most. Neeko had made sure of that. This, however, was a mystery. What was held within those walls?

31
A Spy's Game of Chess

Bryson roamed Rim's market square, buying supplies and food suitable for the Archaic Mountains. He had embarked on daring adventures before, but wondered if what lay ahead could compare at all. When he'd entered the Rolling Oaks, he had had Ophala watching from above at all times. And while the Oaks were mysterious and vast, the Archaic Mountains not only covered more area but were exponentially more colossal in size.

Bryson handed over some coin in exchange for an armful of jerky. He then headed to a fabric shop and bought a few cloaks. The rest of what he needed he had already taken care of before leaving the Intel Kingdom. He had returned to his house and retrieved a knife and a pot for boiling water. Supposedly there were streams in the mountains.

Vuilni was also browsing the square. Bryson easily spotted her across its expanse—strange for early morning. Markets usually thrived at this time, allowing little to no sight of any individual in the crowds. But this pitiful scene of sparse consumers was the result of the Archaic Kingdom's withering economy.

As Bryson and Vuilni reconvened at the edge of the market, he couldn't help but notice the amount of stuff she was carrying. On her back she had a bag, as tall and wide as Bryson, equipped with pots and numerous tools which hung from its sides. He now felt ridiculous for even thinking his legs might buckle under the weight of his own gear.

They journeyed through the city after agreeing beforehand that they'd steer clear of Olethros. Neither of them had ever visited Rim, but they felt like the destruction of Olethros was already engrained in their minds after watching Rhyparia's litigations last year. They didn't need—or *want*—to see the proof.

They traveled west out of the city, keeping their distance from the mountains' foothills for now. Bryson's cooking pot rattled against his hip as it hung from his bag, but it was nothing when compared to Vuilni's ear-rattling medley of trinkets. Her bag stretched from the back of her thighs to above her head, yet she walked as if there was nothing there.

They passed dozens of stationed guards, but didn't stop until they reached their desired location. Once there, they approached a woman donned in sandy brown clothing and handed over their envelopes.

She took them, but her eyes were glued on Bryson. "Mr. LeAnce, correct?"

"Bryson," he replied. "Bryson Still."

Her eyes narrowed as she broke open the seal and withdrew the documents. "Yeah, I'm not calling you that. You are, and always will be, the son of Mendac."

"I am not my father, nor do I condone his actions."

"I don't care about that," she said after reading over the parchments. "You're a mutant child. I'm not calling you by the last name of a Dark Kingdom's royal family. You are not that woman's son … you're Mendac's."

Vuilni glowered at the woman while Bryson hid his anger. "Are we allowed through?" he muttered.

Her eyes narrowed. "Not as easily antagonized as your father? I was hoping for a display of … *lightning*." She smirked and stepped to the side. "Go on, mutt."

Bryson swept past and began hiking up the craggy slope. Vuilni hesitated, but eventually fell in line. She caught up to him. "You handled that very—"

A deafening crack sounded behind them, ringing their eardrums. Vuilni spun around. Where the woman had stood was now a circle of ash, her body jittering in a crumpled heap at its center.

Bryson continued climbing with a dead expression. She had wanted a taste of Mendac's son. What she got was Apoleia's instead.

* * *

The day passed, and the stars and moons replaced the sun. Bryson and Vuilni had rounded a mountainside and were now officially cut off from any and all civilization. They called it a night amongst a cluster of broken boulders. Bryson accepted the reality that it'd be a night of twists and turns—maybe knocking his head into the jagged corner of a rock a few times—but Vuilni had other ideas.

She bent down, scooped up a wedge of rock, and, lifting with her legs, leaned it upright against another boulder. She repeated this process for ten minutes until she had formed a makeshift home. She then spread a cotton blanket across the ground. Bryson stood speechless, his mouth agape.

"Brilliant," he said, crawling under the shelter and tossing his bag against the back wall as a pillow.

Vuilni entered after him, but she dragged a final boulder toward the opening at the front to serve as another wall. With the absence of the starlit sky, darkness swallowed the room.

"This thing won't collapse on us, right?" he asked as he felt Vuilni situate herself next to him.

"No. It's secure. And I disguised it as just another pile of rocks. I know my way around architecture." She fell quiet for a few seconds before she added, "Well, nothing fancy. I just know how to build crude structures with whatever dismal material happens to be lying around."

"A skill developed from home life?"

"Not much of a home life," she said.

Bryson rolled over on his side, deciding to save his questions for another day. "Good night, Vuilni."

* * *

Bryson awoke to his face rattling violently against the ground. He bolted upright. Bits of sunlight streaked through the cracks of their shelter, but those cracks widened as the stones began to shake and become dislodged. Vuilni got on all fours and charged the front stone, ramming through it and opening a doorway. Bryson rolled her bag out; he definitely couldn't lift it—at least, not while on his knees. Then, just as the structure collapsed, he escaped with his own bag.

Once outside, the ground continued to shake beneath his feet. He gazed up the mountain to see thousands of rocks tumbling down toward them. They both turned and sprinted down the mountainside. The fact that they were already halfway up made it that much more difficult. Bryson flew down the slope, taking full strides between errant rocks that jutted from the surface. It was just like the peg course back home.

He looked back and saw Vuilni a considerable distance behind. She didn't have his speed, but even worse, she didn't possess his nimble feet. The avalanche of stone bore down on her from behind. As she lunged for an awkwardly angled chunk of stone, her ankle rolled, sending her crashing into a pile of rocks.

Bryson planted his foot against a stone, banking a turn back up the mountain. Once he reached her, he grabbed her entire forearm and tried to help her stand—an impossible feat with the baggage on her back. She grimaced as she put her weight on one of her legs.

"Is it the same one that Yama broke?" he asked over the roaring avalanche, remembering Vuilni's injury during the tournament a year ago. She gave a slight nod. "We've got to move!" he screamed.

She began running again, but entirely too slow. The tremors grew, almost knocking Bryson off balance as he tried to slow his pace. But as he looked back, he realized Vuilni's speed wouldn't suffice. "Drop your stuff so I can carry you!" he yelled.

She shook her head and, instead, began observing the rubble around them.

"We don't have time!" he bellowed. Bits of fragmented stone pelted their heads and backs as it rained down from above. Dust filled their nostrils, forcing them to cough violently.

Vuilni hopped to the side and yelled, "Get off!"

He looked down to see a relatively flat surface of stone. He leapt to the side. Vuilni threw off her gear, grabbed the stone's edge with two hands, and heaved, hoisting the massive rock as big as a royal lorry out of the rubble. Bryson bent down and helped by grabbing the other side. They managed to stand it up at an angle before shuffling underneath, keeping their backs against it to hold it up.

The tremors sent splintering shockwaves through Bryson's feet and up his legs as the brunt of the avalanche arrived. His knees buckled as debris showered upon their cover, sounding like one endless drawl of thunder that overwhelmed his agonizing screams. He lifted his head and gazed down the mountain while the avalanche rolled into a narrow, rugged valley. He just wanted it to end.

He fell to a single knee as his strength depleted, still trying to keep hold of their roof. When he glanced toward Vuilni, he was floored to see her on the balls of her feet, squatting low enough for her butt to be touching the ground. A rigid determination was carved into her face. With each impact, all she let slip was a squint.

The quakes eventually subsided, relieving the immense pressure on his back. He dropped to all fours and gaped at the rubble.

"Please move," Vuilni said, still holding up the stone slab.

Bryson crawled forward and sat against a pillar of rock while she quickly rolled to the side, allowing their improvised shield to slam into the ground.

A couple minutes of ragged breathing tore through the stillness of the aftermath. Nature was such a deceptive beast. Bryson had always been preoccupied with human threats that he never thought much of it. But after what he had just witnessed, he now understood. The power in that avalanche had been indescribable. The closest similarity he could have made was Rhyparia's gravity alterations.

Vuilni gingerly rotated her ankle. "That's a good sign," Bryson said.

"A slight sprain," she said. "It's manageable … especially after the injury I had last year. This pales in comparison."

Bryson gazed at the peak. "I can't believe we just camped out halfway up a mountain notorious for avalanches and earthquakes."

Vuilni released a weak laugh and plopped her head back against the rock. "Not only that, but I decided it'd be a good idea to trap us in a room of boulders." She paused and gazed at Bryson. "You didn't have to come back for me, and you actually made the situation worse. I had it handled."

"I know. It's a force of habit."

"You don't need to be a hero, Bryson. You forget the level of talent that surrounds you."

Bryson sighed and dropped his head. "I try too hard to be the opposite of my dad."

Another moment of silence blanketed them. "You don't have to try; you just are." Her eyes softened. "Believe me."

Bryson held her gaze for a second before glancing away. "I don't know. I kind of fried that guard yesterday."

Vuilni giggled. "You held back considerably. She's alive. Besides, she deserved it."

He smirked. "I agree."

"I know neither of us is known for our brains," Vuilni said, "but that means we're going to have to work even harder at being smarter. Maybe if we combine our two minds, we'll be as smart as Agnos." As Bryson's eyes dulled, Vuilni said, "Okay, maybe I'm a bit delusional."

* * *

Toshik and Jilly followed a stream through a rare valley of grass—the Archaic Mountains were mostly rock. Jilly led the way, with Toshik straggling behind. "How many years do you think it'll take to find her?" he asked in a bored tone.

"I think today's the day, Toshy!" she shouted back.

He had heard that same statement every day for the past week. It was her method of keeping faith, and faith kept her going. Toshik didn't have the heart—or the energy, quite frankly—to shoot down her spirit.

Toshik examined his bandaged left wrist. A few days ago they had been attacked by a brown bear while sleeping in their tent. Luckily it was only a bear, so he was able to kill it quickly. Most animals weren't much of a threat to a person who had hunted spunka at a young age.

While distracted by childhood memories, Toshik collided with the back of a motionless Jilly. "What's wrong?" he asked.

He followed her gaze toward the stream's bank, where a body lay, pale and wet. The robes clinging to his decomposing flesh were a sandy brown, and the four-pointed star on his shoulder symbolized his enlistment in the Archaic Kingdom's military. Burns and bruises peppered areas of exposed skin, but even his clothes were tattered. This man had died in a struggle.

"What was it?" Jilly asked.

"Definitely a matter of *whom*," he muttered. "Either fire or electricity, judging by the burn marks. There's somewhere around eighty bounty hunters in these mountains right now, so there's no telling who did it. The real question is why?"

"They're supposed to be looking for Rhyparia, not killing each other," Jilly said with a frown. "Rhyparia definitely didn't do this."

"Well, let's search him."

"For what?"

"An ancient," Toshik said, kneeling next to the body and sifting through layers of wet cloth. "I'd assume it was either lost in the stream or taken by whoever killed him, but it's worth a shot."

Jilly went quiet, looking along the bank in both directions. "I'll search elsewhere."

She left, leaving Toshik to his thoughts once again. If there were hunters in these mountains killing other people, who was to say he and Jilly weren't targets? Nature's wrath and wild animals weren't the only elements to be wary of. What if it wasn't another hunter, though, but someone who called this place home—and likely did so for centuries? Toshik and Jilly were infringing on its territory.

To ease his nerves, Toshik decided it must have been a dispute between two quarreling hunters who had tired of each other. It made sense, and his relationship with Himitsu could attest to that. There were several times the two of them could have ended up in a situation such as this.

Toshik's eyes widened. He ripped the man's cloak to find a steel emblem engrained between his pectorals. Four limbs extended from a circular center, curling in a way that mimicked a snake. He had heard of ancients like these from his father a long time ago, for the man had once been a connoisseur of expensive and rare treasures. Ancient pieces fell into many different classifications, but only Archains really studied them.

This was a distortion ancient. Its ability involved morphing the body in some way. Unlike other ancients that were held, worn, or equipped, these were absorbed. Grand Director Poicus, Archaic Director Senex, and apparently this dead guy were all users of such ancients. But Toshik didn't know what this one did. As an Adrenian, it wasn't something he had ever studied.

Toshik reached out and touched it, then quickly yanked his hand back. The emblem rose out of the cadaver's skin while the curling, snake-like appendages snapped into the ancient's center. A metal egg sat on the man's chest before rolling down his abdomen. Toshik quickly caught and observed it.

"What's that?" Jilly asked, giving up on her search.

"An ancient."

"Doesn't look very scary."

Toshik rolled it between his fingers and tucked it away in his pocket. "If we ever see Agnos again, we'll have to ask him about it."

"Or Rhyparia!" Jilly exclaimed.

Toshik stood up, rolling his eyes in the process. Jilly was never one to be realistic. "We're looking for Olivia, not Rhyparia," he said.

She hugged his waist while they walked. "We're going to find them both," she said.

He smiled as he held her against him. "You're right."

*　　*　　*

Fane had done the impossible—he had found an inn that housed no alcohol. Himitsu had been convinced there was no such thing. It had taken them a while, but apparently such a travesty actually existed. As Fane gave the host two fake names to put their room under, Himitsu sneered at his bar-deprived surroundings … a parlor, small breakfast area, and a room full of boxes. He would burn this place down before nightfall.

Himitsu stepped up to the escritoire and asked, "Where do you stash your alcohol?"

"This is a clean space, Mr. Vale," the hostess replied.

Himitsu, momentarily forgetting the fake name given to him, nearly corrected the woman. Instead, he sulked and slumped behind Fane. Her eyes narrowed. "You know, if you had longer hair, you'd resemble that Jestivan boy who was brought down as a witness during that wretched Rhyparia's trial."

Venustas's idea of a haircut before departing Kindoliya had paid off. "I get that all the time," Himitsu replied. "It's really annoying—being mistaken for one of those disgusting people who tried to vouch for the murderer."

The host shook her head gravely. "A shame what happened out there in Rim."

"Tell me about it," Fane said, placing his quill in his ink-stained inner pocket after signing some paperwork.

"Then to hear that two of the other Jestivan are demonic children of a Dark Realm wench …" The woman made a noise of disgust. "Horrible."

Himitsu imagined the woman's head on fire as Fane nodded. "Truly awful."

"And then that Yama—"

"Good day," Fane said, stepping past and heading up the stairs.

Once they reached the second floor, Himitsu finally released his anger. "How dare she?!"

"Keep it down."

"I hate this city!"

"At least wait until we get into the room." Fane said under his breath.

Once they reached their room on the third floor, Himitsu immediately dropped his bags and sprawled out onto one of the two beds. "Is that how the world views us now?" Himitsu ranted. "As evil?"

Fane untied his bag and began putting his clothes in drawers. "They don't know you guys, so yes. They're making judgments based off actions seen on the surface. Not to mention it's in their nature to doubt people in power—whether that be the royals, Amendment Order, or the Jestivan."

Himitsu plopped both hands over his face. "But to call Olivia and Bryson demons because their mother is from the Dark Realm? That is deplorable, Fane!"

"Stop screaming my name before I get your mom to ground you after we break her out."

"I don't get it," the young Jestivan whined.

Fane sighed and sat on the edge of his bed. "I agree," he mumbled. "If anything should have appalled that woman downstairs, it should have been Mendac's past actions. But it just goes to show you this world is twisted and ignorant. We're still in this ancient mindset that someone is evil simply because they live in the Dark Realm."

"I've met quite a few people from the Dark Realm who are morally superior to most of the people up here," Himitsu said, thinking of Vistas and Vuilni.

"Yes, and it works both ways. And the same applies to the kingdoms. Just because someone is an Intelian, doesn't mean they have to be smart."

Himitsu grinned. "Look at Bryson for example."

Fane chuckled. "Is that the respect you give your captain?"

"*I'm* allowed to insult him." Himitsu got up, rounded his bed, and gazed out the window toward Phelos Palace in the center of the city. "How exactly are we going to get into that building, find their cells, and then escape? I feel as if we're in over our heads."

"There's always a way," Fane said.

"So what's the plan?"

"The plan has been in motion for a long time," he replied. "Do you really think your mom had nothing worked out after her capture? That night of Rhyparia's escape was simply the resolution to one-half of the plan. She had set up other pieces of the puzzle the night before. She had her falcons fly letters to a few people—Felli and I being two of them."

"So what'd she tell you?" Himitsu asked.

"She had spent most of her time as a member of the Amendment Order scoping out two men: Chief Merchant Toth Brench and Chief Officer Wert Lamay. While she never gained hard evidence to convict them of anything and bring to the royal heads' attention, she still gathered bits of information that could be pieced together. And when she added it all up, she was able to assume a couple of their objectives."

"So we're working off assumptions here," Himitsu said with a hint of skepticism.

"Ophala is a wonderfully intelligent woman," Fane said. "And a masterful spy when not blindly trusting people she *wants* to believe. Thankfully she learned her lesson after her blunder with Archaic King Itta. Now she believes a takeover is in the works—an overthrow of the current regime, the Amendment Order. The problem is, we don't know when it's going to happen; but she also said to expect for its timing to align with a certain shipment of goods across the sea.

"There's a merchant vessel being guided across the Sea of Light right now by an Adrenian naval fleet. It's said to be carrying an unimaginable amount of money—a combined deposit from the Spirit, Adren, Passion, and Intel Kingdoms. So if Ophala is correct, a revolt is looming."

"How do you know all of this information about where the ship is right now?" Himitsu asked.

"Felli has been in broadcast meetings with other royal heads, where it has been a topic of discussion."

Himitsu returned to his bed. "Toth and Wert are waiting for the shipment to arrive in the Archaic Kingdom before committing anything rash. If they ransack the palace too early, the Adren Navy would likely board the merchant ship and turn it around—"

"And then Toth and Wert wouldn't get their money, which they'd desperately need with the current condition of this kingdom," Fane said.

"All right, so what's our role in this?"

"*You* won't do anything for the time being," Fane said, standing up to resume folding his clothes. "You'll sit here and practice. Meanwhile, I'm scheduled to meet with an officer in District Four. They believe I've been sent by Passion Queen Fiona to replace a member of their assassin unit stationed in Phelos. In reality, Felli sent me."

Himitsu lurched forward. "I'm not just going to sit here."

"You shouldn't have to for too long," Fane replied, tossing socks into a drawer. "Once that ship arrives, the countdown begins to something catastrophic."

"Why didn't Director Venustas inform the officer guy that there would be two of us coming to supplement their ranks?"

Fane gave him a quizzical look. "Because we can't risk you being recognized. While a haircut might fool the general public, a high-ranking officer would spot a Jestivan from a mile away."

"Who else got a letter from my mom?" Himitsu asked.

"Besides Felli and me, who knows?" Fane mused. "Your mother tends to ration information and delegate tasks so that whoever's receiving it only knows what she wants them to know. She's the Spy Pilot for a reason. All I know is there's an overarching strategy at play."

Himitsu grinned, appreciating his mom's intelligence. She had orchestrated all of this to happen while locked away in a cell—a prolonged game of chess that required extraordinary patience.

Fane pulled off his cloak. "Businessmen have this saying: *Put your money to work for you.* A man like Toth Brench probably practices that maxim every day." He looked at Himitsu. "Your mother has a similar belief, but altered to better serve a spy's purpose: *Put your data to work for you.*"

32
The Brench Hilt

"We've crossed into the Archaic River!" a woman shouted from the crow's nest.

Agnos ran to the side of the ship to see if he spotted any differences in the water between the river and the sea, but it all looked the same—an infinite expanse of blue. He supposed it made sense, for the Realm Rivers—while labeled as *rivers*—were as big as any sea, but because of their elongated shape, they received the name that they had.

Tashami joined him in his sightseeing. "It really is astounding how vast the waters are."

Agnos nodded. "Makes the kingdoms feel tiny."

"Makes me feel silly for swimming to the bottom of Phesaw Park's lakes with you all those times …" Tashami trailed off and laughed. "Like such a plunge would prepare anyone for this."

Something collided with Agnos's leg and latched on. He glanced down to the see the smiling face of the cabin boy, Eet. "What's up, little guy?"

"Grannie Gray says there will be a big fight soon!" Agnos paused, as his face fell. "What's wrong?" Eet asked.

Another child tackled his other leg. This time it was Osh, the young cabin girl. Tashami laughed and asked, "Sure those aren't your kids, man?"

Agnos wasn't even sure at this point. For some reason, it just now dawned on him that this crew was headed for a battle with two children on their ship. Where was the logic? There was no way the crew was arrogant enough to risk the lives of the youths. He was particularly disgusted with Gray Whale; Eet and Osh were her grandchildren—or so they claimed.

"After we win the fight, can we go on your mission, Agnos?" Osh asked, hopping up and down on her tiptoes.

Eet echoed her desire: "Ooo, yes! We'll find the cave at the bottom of the sea!"

"Mr. Patter!" They all whirled toward the quarterdeck, where Barloe stood next to the wheel. "Fill the sails!"

"Up the mizzenmast I go." Tashami sighed and trekked across the deck.

Agnos crouched low with a smile. "Our mission will come soon," he said. They clapped with pure unbridled joy on their face. "Now I need to talk to the quartermaster, but later tonight I'll read you a new story about Sephrina Jordan, the *Second of Five*."

After a quick hug, Agnos ascended the steps to the quarterdeck. He stood next to Barloe and watched the crew at work. "What happened to scrubbing floors, Agnos?"

"I still do my job when needed," Agnos assured him. "But I'm taking advantage of the freedom granted to me by Farlyn's imprisonment below decks."

"It's always the ones you'd most expect," Barloe said, tapping a finger against the rail.

"That's not how the saying goes."

"Perhaps not in your world. With pirates, the more suspicious the person looks, the shadier they tend to be."

After a short pause, Agnos asked, "Is Gray going to kill them?"

"No."

"So she's a merciful pirate?"

Barloe released a hearty laugh. "Not quite the word. If we kill, it's out of defense or for a greater good."

"Since we're currently on the offensive, hunting someone down, I'm guessing this mission is for a greater good."

Barloe's mouth stiffened. "Deductive reasoning would say so. For a lot of people, this may very well be their last days."

* * *

Agnos knocked on the great cabin's door and announced his name.

"Come in." As he stepped inside, he saw that the captain was in the middle of reading a book.

"What can I do for you, Anus?" Gray asked.

The purposefully butchered name was still jarring to hear, but Agnos had learned to not correct her. Instead, he asked, "The Devish and Cynnish in the brig … what do you plan on doing with them?"

Gray closed the book and set it aside. "What do you think I should do?"

"Let them return to their homes."

"Is that your true desire? After all, they did try to kill you."

"That's only because they'd been caught and were desperate to not ruin their only chance at returning to their kingdoms where they belong. They haven't killed any crewmates during their tenure, right?"

Gray shook her head.

"So violence or ill-will was never their goal; it was to simply complete tasks asked of them in order to be granted the opportunity to live with their people. They were hostages to whomever it is we're chasing."

"And as for Farlyn's unfair treatment of you as a swab?" she asked.

Agnos groaned in frustration. "I was being a baby. He wasn't asking that much of me."

Gray's austere gaze veered into a smile, as if she was amused. "Don't worry, Anus. I was going to have them sent home anyway—if they make it through the voyage."

"Glad to see even pirates have compassion."

Gray's smile vanished, replaced by a dreadful frown. "Not everything we humans do—and this goes for pirates, politicians, royals, or average citizens—is ethically justifiable." Her eyes hardened. "I need to know that when this fight begins, you won't bother me or anyone else with lessons of morality … because this is deeper than what it will appear on the surface."

Agnos looked concerned. "What is it we're about to do?"

"Listen," she said. "I've met a few people like you in my lifetime—especially Archains. They speak of moral righteousness like it's so easy to understand … like it's grade school mathematics. When we reach our target—" she swept her hand across her neck— "save the speeches. Nobody wants to hear them. You'll be next to me in this room when it all goes down. When that happens, just know that I'll give you answers after the fact."

"You're asking a lot of me," Agnos said.

"Ophala didn't contact me just to mention you," Gray said. "In fact, that bit of information was the last thing in her letter. No, she wanted my help. I may not be going about things exactly how she would have expected, but I have no choice. My hands have been forced by stubborn royal heads."

*   *   *

Agnos sat in a hammock next to Tashami, who had just awoken from a much needed hour-long nap. Since Tashami's clout and weaving abilities were vastly superior to his squallblaster companions, he had been used excessively the past few days in order to push the ship. Gray feared the worst—that her target would reach port first.

"It's nothing too bad," Tashami said through a yawn. "I can manage sleep deprivation."

"Who's filling the sails now?" Agnos asked.

"Crole and Frina."

"Hopefully we finish this voyage soon," Agnos said, his stomach grumbling. "We're running low on supplies, and rations are becoming more and more meager."

Tashami pinched his pointer finger and thumb around Agnos's wrist. "That isn't good news for you," he said, teasing. "You'll turn into nothing."

Agnos knocked his friend's hand away with a laugh. "Shut it."

They glanced at the ceiling while a ruckus thundered throughout the deck. Residue from the wood spilled down as boots pounded against the floorboards, reacting to the raucous commands shouted across the ship. Something was happening. Agnos and Tashami pried themselves from their hammocks and sprinted toward the main deck.

"Barloe's looking for all utility personnel!" one crewman said to Tashami. "Our target has been spotted!"

Once outside, Tashami forced his way through the tangled web of people while Agnos followed closely behind. They burst into the specialty quarters before splitting. Tashami entered Barloe's room to hold a quick meeting with the utility crew while Agnos pushed toward the great cabin. He barged in without warning.

Gray whirled around from her spot in front of the window. "What happened to etiquette?"

"I'm sorry, Captain," he said, heart racing. He then thought, *pirates have etiquette*?

She turned and refocused on the trailing sea. "The frenzy has gotten the best of you. How is your body reacting?"

Agnos held himself steady against a bookshelf. "Not sure," he panted. "Can't really … put it into words."

"Well, from what I've heard of your past, you should be familiar with anxiety."

"How far are we from them?" Agnos asked.

"You mean, how far are they from us? You may have noticed that Tashami has received a generous break the past couple days from filling the sails. That's because he had executed his role to completion. When we entered the Archaic River, I already knew exactly where our target was and decided on a maneuver to get ahead of them.

"I essentially bypassed our target by increasing our speed and flanking them while staying far out of their sight. Then, once I felt we were a comfortable distance ahead of them, I had the ship veer back on course, in line with our target. For the past twelve hours the *Whale Lord* has been moving at a snail's pace, allowing our target to catch up to us from behind."

Agnos's mouth fell open. "I haven't heard about preparation for what seems to be this voyage's impending climax."

"Not much to prepare for," she stated, dismissively.

"Are you kidding me? What's our target? If they've done so well at avoiding you for decades, I'm sure they're formidable!"

"Calm down, Anus," the captain muttered. "The crew knows what needs to be done. Now come here; stand next to me."

Agnos approached, his stomach churning with unease. He looked out at the Archaic River—no end in sight in any direction.

"Look closer," Gray said. "Toward the horizon."

Agnos squinted, pressing his hand against the glass to block the sun's glare. "What is that?" he asked. "Are my eyes deceiving me?"

"No, they aren't. Twenty Adrenian naval ships approach. Only about seven can be seen right now, but as the rest of the group clears the horizon, we'll get to see it in its full glory."

Agnos scoffed. Dozens of towering masts and hundreds of sails penetrated the sky. And it wasn't just the sheer number of vessels, but the size of each of them. They were all mighty galleons. They weren't as big as the *Whale Lord*—the biggest ship in the sea—but when combined, they'd dwarf a town.

"Why is our target the Adrenian Navy?!" he shouted.

"It isn't."

Agnos stumbled over words as he tried to form a sentence—a first for the quick-tongued Archain. "What are we doing?!"

Gray's eyes bore into him. "If you want to lead a mission in the future, learn to compose yourself. While I may be heading this ship, I'm acting based off intelligence provided to me by Ophala. Don't you trust her?"

His head tilted. "I'm not so sure now."

Gray pulled out a looking glass. "I'd say another three hours before contact is made. They won't even bother trying to avoid us at this point, knowing I'd be able to track them down with ease. They'll commit to this head-on, which is what I was hoping for."

"I don't think they're as scared of you as you think they are."

"And they have every right to possess such confidence," she said. "They'd be foolish not to. If you enter a battle hesitant, you're not leaving it with your heart still beating."

Agnos stood in silence while Gray turned and sat at her desk. He was about to die. He knew it. Twenty naval battleships … *twenty*? And if they weren't the target, then that must mean they were protecting something of great value.

"The naval fleet," Gray said, "is serving as a protective wall to a single merchant vessel at its center. That vessel is our target."

"So we're going to bulldoze our way through the wall."

"Precisely the plan."

"Then when are we turning around to prepare for a head-to-head collision? Our rear is exposed!"

"Oh, we're not turning."

"You're letting them mount us from behind?"

Gray cackled hysterically. "That's the phrasing you choose? Swell, coming from someone named 'Anus.'" She wiped a tear from her eye and said, "Relax. Grab a book and read a bit. In two hours, I'll show you what's going to happen."

Agnos neared the bookcases and browsed the spines, but without interest. Instead, he thought about the force that was about to run through this ship like a whale through a school of minnow.

A couple hours of pessimistic thoughts passed, and Gray called for Agnos once again. The fleet had closed the gap on the *Whale Lord*. All twenty ships could be seen at varying distances, but the one that stood out the most was the merchant galleon at the center. The sails were stamped by a symbol of two swords crossed in front of an array of spunka spines.

"Brench Crafts?" Agnos muttered in disbelief. "That's Toshik's family company. His father owns it."

"Hence the reason I never told you or anyone on this ship about our target."

"Now I'm even more confused …"

Gray walked over to a wardrobe in the cabin's far corner. She opened it, stepped inside, and dislodged a weapon from a latch. It was a magnificent war scythe, its pole made of fish scales. A gently curving blade sat at the top, its spine encased by a large shell pulled straight off a deep-sea animal's back.

As Gray returned to the window, she asked, "Have you ever wondered why this ship is called the *Whale Lord*?"

"I have. I assumed it was named because of its size."

"Fair deduction, but incorrect." She inhaled slowly.

Agnos was beginning to make out individual shapes of people aboard the navy ships. Ten ships began to turn, setting themselves up so that their sides faced the *Whale Lord.* Meanwhile ten others charged forward between the stationary vessels.

Someone pounded on the door. "Now?!" Barloe shouted.

"Turn the ship!" she bellowed back.

As Barloe's footsteps disappeared, Agnos asked, "A little late, don't you think?"

"Pay attention," she said.

Agnos watched as the most daunting display of power bore down on him. This was scarier than anything he had experienced in life—right up there with the Generals' Battle and the Unbreakable's house in the Void.

Hundreds of men and women in silver cloaks leapt onto the rails of the enemy ships. They crouched low with a hand at their hips. They weren't squallblasters, firefighters, or seashockers, but old-fashioned warriors. If they had been from any other kingdom, it wouldn't have been as frightening. But they were Adrenians, and they could likely reach the *Whale Lord* in a split-second with a single push-off ... even at this distance.

The *Whale Lord* began to turn just as the ten advancing navy vessels passed the other ten that formed a stationary wall. "They're going to board us if we get any closer," Agnos said with a hint of skepticism.

"That is inevitable. My job is to cut down their forces severely."

Agnos was about to call out the flaw in her supposed job, but he was silenced at what came next. A navy vessel's hull was obliterated after the sea's surface had been disrupted by a monstrous splash. Splintered wood filled the sky and rained down into the Archaic River as the ship instantly began to tip. The hole that had been created was massive, allowing sight into the ship's interior. Adrenian sailors rolled across the decks, clawing at the broken ends of surfaces before losing their grip and plummeting into the river's rough waters. Then the same ship was hit from the opposite side, quickening the sinking process.

"That was a warning shot," Gray said. "Now pay attention to that ship there—" she pointed in its direction— "observe the lower left corner of its bow, where it disappears beneath the waters."

Agnos eyed it closely. He caught a glimpse of a bluish-gray animal in the water just as it burst through the surface and lunged at the ship's bow. Once again, it smashed a crater into the ship's foundation.

"This is a battle at sea. Look down and watch what happens."

Agnos gazed below, toward the rudder. His eyes spread wide as he witnessed fifteen blue whales deploy from underneath the ship and race through the waters toward the enemy. They were gigantic creatures that swam as though they were a quarter of their size. Within seconds they had reached the blockade, claiming thirteen more ships as victim.

As the river became more volatile with each whale attack, it became tougher for the approaching ships that hadn't been hit to navigate the waters. Scattered chunks of wood fluttered through the air and bodies crashed into the water while galleons stood upright in the river, nose-first, as they began their plunge to the riverbed.

In this brief moment, it felt as if all death and destruction was focused on this one section of the world and nowhere else.

A firm expression had settled upon Gray Whale's face. "Welcome to the *Whale Lord*."

33
Pilot, Captain, Director, Queen

Tashami watched in awe from the crow's nest as fifteen ships plunged into the Archaic River, sucking their crews down with them. He couldn't believe they were doing this to navy vessels flying the silver Adrenian flag. Now he understood what all of Barloe's cryptic messages truly meant throughout the voyage ... *Just know that this is necessary. We tried all other means; Nobody would listen.*

The merchant galleon in the wreckage's backdrop veered eastward to avoid the battle, likely putting faith in the battleships to do their job. But from what Tashami had witnessed, this battle of twenty versus one wasn't favoring the side it should—if logic was involved.

But there was the rub ... a contingent of blue whales wasn't logical at all.

Tashami adjusted his directional weaving to help steer the *Whale Lord* toward the arching path of the Brench Craft vessel, assuming that was the target—not the Adrenians. Four naval ships remained, following the annihilation of one more a minute ago. As Tashami filled the sails, he glanced below to the battles on the deck. Somehow men in silver cloaks had made it onto the ship.

He looked back at the Adren Navy. Their vessels were too far for anyone to board, yet they seemed to be doing the impossible. How? The water between the two forces was empty of swimmers, which was expected, considering the fact that every ship had seashockers onboard ready to fry anyone in the water.

The rails surrounding the battleships' decks caught Tashami's eye. Crewmen jumped onto them, only to immediately disappear. Tashami strengthened his focus, now knowing what he was supposed to be looking for. Adrenians reached the *Whale Lord* through the use of their push-off and speed percentage, morphing into blurs as they darted through the air between ships. Bryson and Yama had always talked about the importance of the first step. Now he was seeing it in action.

Tashami glanced across the masts and saw Crole in the mizzenmast's fighting top, filling the sails. He stopped for a quick second and made a signal, as if he were mounting a crossbow on his shoulder.

Tashami nodded. He stopped filling the sails, leaving that to his fellow squallblasters. It was time he did the job that properly served his purpose in this crew. He leapt onto the nest's low-rising wall and held himself steady against the winds with the mainmast. A blast of fire erupted from a naval ship toward the *Whale Lord*, a wave of heat brought with it. Frina, who was in the foremast's fighting top, dispersed the inferno with a timely gale. Apparently, even Adrenian ships had utility personnel from other kingdoms.

Barloe was fighting three Adrenians simultaneously on the quarterdeck. The silver-cloaked speedsters whirled around him, and all the quartermaster could do was encase himself in a fiery orb to keep them from striking him too frequently.

Tashami flicked three fingers in rapid succession from his perch. Three wind-woven bullets connected with each Adrenian's head. After they collapsed—blood pooling from their wounds—Barloe looked up and shook his fist as a thank you.

The Spirit Jestivan continued his sharpshooting from the nest's wall. He struck five enemies at once, sometimes seven or eight. Adrenians were charging across the ship only to stumble forward and fall listlessly on their faces as wind bullets connected. Eventually, a few of them noticed, and word quickly spread.

Some took to the netting, climbing it at a speed that surprised even Tashami. Apparently their speed wasn't limited to their feet. Tashami hopped back into the nest and began weaving bullets from behind the wall. He shot a few adversaries, sending them tumbling down the shrouds and into the river. But the sheer amount of them who climbed was too much at this distance, so he altered his weaving technique.

He stood up and swept both arms downward, releasing a blast of wind comparable to the gales he used to fill the sails. It proved effective, as every Adrenian cascaded down the netting—some fell into the river, others splattered against the deck.

"*ARCHERS!*"

The warning that was bellowed sent Tashami's gaze to the sky, where a barrage of arrows soared skyward. They hit the crest of their flight and the arrowheads flipped direction, ready to rain down upon the *Whale Lord*. He had noticed it too late; his winds wouldn't stop them all. He still tried, but an electrical bolt surged through his body and halted his efforts.

As he jittered, the volley of arrows showered the ship. One impaled the top of his right shoulder, just barely missing his head. He slumped to the floor and cried out as he clutched at his wound, hands still shaking from the unknown electrical attack. He gingerly pulled himself up so that he could peek over the wall. Alas, another flash of blue caused him to duck. He was trapped.

He sat still for a moment to allow his body to calm down. An occasional aftershock would rock his nerves, but it had slowed. He had one option.

He grimaced, sucking up the pain before leaping out of the nest to catch hold of the shrouds. Another electrical attack whizzed past, striking the netting where his hand was. The rope practically disintegrated. He lost his grip and slipped down the shrouds, his hands blistering as he tried to regain control.

He finally caught a notch, scurried across the width of the shrouds, and leapt toward a free-swinging rope. He grabbed hold with his good arm, and the rope began to sink as he swung directly over the decks. He shot at Adrenians during his flight until another flash of blue caught his eye. This time he reacted fast enough to weave a gust that redirected his path out of harm's way.

He crashed onto the deck, landing not quite as gracefully as he had planned. The pain in his shoulder intensified; but he stood and advanced through the dozens of swordfights and elemental duels, casually blasting holes into Adrenian sailors as he stepped over fresh carcasses. Sweat, blood, and burning skin filled his nostrils, while clashing swords, grunting warriors, and dying screams swarmed his ears.

He found the Intelian enemy responsible for his shoulder disguised in a silver uniform. As Tashami marched toward her on the forecastle, he leaned his head sideways as she expelled an electric strike from her finger. She released another wave, but he dodged it just as easily. He flicked a finger from his hip. A whistling sound cut through the air, and a hole formed in the woman's chest. Blood quickly rushed out and stained her vest while she toppled backward over the rail.

He brought his attention to the rest of the ship. Bodies littered the decks—a lot of them crewmates of the *Whale Lord*. As disheartening as that was, the fact remained that there was only one naval vessel afloat. Gray Whale's crew was winning.

That final ship, however, wouldn't go down without a last hurrah. Just as it was struck by three blue whales, another volley of arrows swallowed the sky, segmenting the sun's rays. Tashami started to weave a gale powerful enough to reach them, but it abruptly died out. He had exhausted his energy. Luckily, two of the firefighters at the back of the ship torched the sky, burning every single arrow to a crisp.

Tashami lay wounded across fresh cadavers, too exhausted to move. He hadn't kept count of how many people he had killed, but he knew it was high. And now that he had time to think about it, he hadn't a clue as to why. With the moment's adrenaline dissipating, he now questioned everything. He used to temper his clout; fighting had never been something he desired. Ever since finding his father in the Void, however, Tashami had changed.

*   *   *

Agnos gazed out of the cabin's grand window alongside Gray Whale. The river's surface was a wasteland. Debris littered the water for miles, and sailors were trying to grab hold of anything floating.

"How many people did you just kill?" Agnos asked.

"North of a thousand." Gray paused, then whispered, "It's unfortunate what war does … Innocent people unknowingly fighting for the wrong cause."

Agnos shook his head. "I need answers right now."

"Tonight, when we board the *Brench Hilt* and retrieve the money, you'll get your answers." She turned and headed for the cabin's exit. "It sounds like the ruckus has died down outside. Let's go."

Agnos followed her through the hall. "Is this your first time leaving the specialty quarters all voyage?"

"It is."

They stepped outside and were met by a floor of bodies. Piles were denser in certain areas. Agnos covered his mouth, nearly gagging at the sight. And the worst part about it all? The bodies were being tossed overboard by the crew.

Heads turned as Gray Whale headed up the stairs to the quarterdeck where Barloe stood. He didn't appear to acknowledge her presence. They gazed out in front of the ship, toward a lone galleon with a white flag raised. With its navy escort annihilated, the *Brench Hilt* had surrendered.

Once parallel to each other, the two ships dropped their anchors. Gray, Barloe, and Agnos jumped onto the merchant vessel. There wasn't a single warrior aboard. In fact, every single occupant looked like an aristocrat dressed entirely too lavish to be simple merchants.

They went below decks to find an abhorrent scene. Slaves were chained throughout the entire floor, from the tail of the ship to the front, packed together like a herd of sheep.

"This is what happens on a Brench Crafts ship?" Agnos asked, aghast.

"No," Gray said. "Just this one. And this is the first time. It looks like Chief Toth Brench wanted to provide his future regime with not only a mountain of money, but a group of slaves to work difficult jobs for no pay."

"Akin to Ulna Malen in the Power Kingdom?" Agnos asked.

"Exactly like that," she replied.

Agnos was followed by hopeless gazes of malnourished men and women shackled to beams. Gray instructed Barloe to begin releasing them from their confinements. She then picked up a couple oil lanterns from the floor next to a trap door. She ignited them both and handed one to Agnos before descending the ladder into darkness.

They extended their arms, allowing the light to fill the space, bathing it in a bright glow. "Sweet Pratizina," Gray mumbled, observing the sea of bags that occupied the floor. "Be careful jumping down."

Agnos leapt from the ladder and landed awkwardly. He wasn't sure why he had expected a soft impact; after all, it wasn't as if these bags were stuffed with feathers. Instead, he heard a crunch as his knees banged onto the bumpy surface. "All of this is money?"

"A combined deposit from the Spirit, Adren, Intel, and Passion Kingdoms."

"How much are we talking about?" Agnos asked as he stepped through the mountains of money bags.

"Billions."

"So we're stealing billions of granules from the royal families?"

"We're returning it."

"What are we—"

"Agnos," Gray said, cutting him off and saying his name properly for the first time. "I'll explain everything to you tonight."

Over the next few hours, Gray commenced a plan to return to DaiSo. The two ships would travel side by side. Gray would captain the *Whale Lord* while Barloe led the *Brench Hilt.*

The wealthy occupants of the ship had turned out to be exactly what they looked like—aristocrats. There wasn't a single Brench Crafts employee. They were interrogated mercilessly and would continue to be for the entirety of the voyage back home. Luckily, they were selfish noblemen, so they ratted out the ship's Dev servant immediately. The servant reassured Gray that she hadn't recorded any of their faces, but the captain blindfolded her and threw her into the brig regardless.

At the end of the night, after stopping by the surgeon's room to check in on a resting Tashami, Agnos sat across from Gray Whale in the great cabin. A bottle of rum sat on the desk between them. Gray had taken a few swigs, and Agnos declined each offer. He desired only an explanation, for it was long overdue.

"All right then," Gray said, reaching into a desk drawer. She dug around for a moment before tossing a scroll in front of Agnos. "Read it."

He unraveled it, surprised by the length.

Gray Whale,

You do not know me, but you know of me. My name is Ophala Vevlu, Spy Pilot of the Archaic Kingdom's stealth division, and I'm writing this with only a few hours until mine and my husband's capture at the hands of the Amendment Order.

I have a favor to ask. Kuki Sphaira is in grave danger, but I cannot go to the royal heads because I've lost their trust. Anything I try to say to them would fall on deaf ears, which is my own fault … I've botched many plans over the past few years.

But that ends today.

Chief Merchant Toth Brench and Chief Officer Wert Lamay of the Amendment Order are conspiring to overtake the Archaic Kingdom, and at this point it's nearly inevitable. They have the influence, charisma, money, and, most importantly, powerful people behind them. But that doesn't mean we can't make the process more difficult for them.

I've done a lot of spy work on the two men over the past year. Recently, they've talked about a future shipment of money that is unprecedented in scale. It'd be their way of funding future bureaucratic programs to boost the kingdom's economy for the upper class. They also mentioned another 'good', but their vernacular was too obscure to decipher—something leads me to believe that it may pertain to people, such as slaves.

I don't know how they're planning to obtain such a glut of money, but they seem confident. I do know that their plan to overthrow the current hierarchy likely follows the safe arrival of such funds.

So this is my proposal to you. The first option is simple. Besides you, I've sent letters to three others. Two I won't name here because they're their own pair with a separate mission. But the third is Spirit Director Shea-Ley Neaneuma, and I need you to visit Sodai to meet with her. I'm sure you're familiar with the name since she was once a renowned captain in the Spirit Navy.

This connection will allow you an audience with Spirit Queen Apsa. She won't turn down one of her grandmother's most beloved captains. When the two of you obtain the queen's attention, present to her my information. The ideal scenario is that she believes it or, at least, considers its merits enough to discuss it with the Light Realm's other royal heads. If everyone heeds my advice, they'll put a stop to Toth and Wert's plan beforehand—hopefully even refrain from withdrawing troops from the Archaic Kingdom.

Alas, the more likely scenario is that either Queen Apsa or the others don't believe me. If that's what unfolds, take it upon yourself to hunt down Toth Brench's most beloved galleon, the Brench Hilt. By whatever means necessary, don't let it reach the Archaic Kingdom.

While Toth and Wert have established power, I still believe them to be puppets to names such as Dev King Storshae and the Rogue Demon, Toono. Together, they're trying to form a super-alliance between the Dark Realm and Archaic Kingdom.

We cannot have that. You made your name as the rookie captain who toppled the most ruthless pirate crew in the Dark Realm. End your career with a history-defining stamp.

Sincerely,
Ophala Vevlu, Pilot of Spy and Sky

P.S. Be on the lookout for a young man by the name of Agnos—scrawny kid with shaggy black hair, white robes, and clogs. He has a fascination with the sea, but more important, Marigium. I may have tipped him off about its location—I left your name out of it. He's a good kid with a good heart, according to my son.

Agnos looked up from the scroll. Gray was leaning back in her chair with a plate of meatloaf on her lap. She stabbed at a slice while reading a book.

"That's why you were in Sodai," Agnos said.

"It's the only reason why I'd ever step foot in that city. When we met in the gambling hall's bar, I'd already spent a week in the capital. Earlier that day I'd received news from Queen Apsa that there was nothing she could do, for the other kings basically called her worries nonsensical … they weren't going to believe the words of a liar such as Ophala."

"Did you know, at that point, that you'd commit to Ophala's second proposal of doing whatever it took?"

"I did," Gray said. "I believed Ophala. Brench Crafts has been known over the years to conduct a rather unethical working environment on their ships. The company's also been known for scamming lower profile customers. It's why I've tried chasing them twice before."

Agnos glanced back at the bottom of the scroll. "And when you ran into me and Tashami, you helped us find Barloe, knowing that if we made the crew, we'd be embarking on this voyage."

Gray pried a slice of meatloaf from her fork and nodded. "Yes, and that's why I didn't let anyone know our target. I couldn't let the two of you find out we were hunting the company of your friend's father."

Agnos shook his head. This had been a terrible plan. "What are we going to do to when we arrive at DaiSo's harbor? News has likely already reached the royal heads and Amendment Order. The Dev servant aboard the *Brench Hilt* definitely alerted everyone the moment they'd spotted the *Whale Lord* before the battle even ensued."

"There's nothing to worry about," Gray said. "Nobody will attack us. The Spirit Navy already has battleships lined up in the Gulf of Sodai to protect us."

"Why?"

"Because this voyage wasn't entirely my decision," Gray said, matter-of-fact. "Queen Apsa said there was nothing she could *directly* do, but that didn't imply she couldn't force the hands of her fellow kings by other means."

Agnos gave her an incredulous look. "She'd risk crossing all of the kings?"

"You seem surprised," Gray said. "Tired of being disregarded and overpowered by the bravado of the kings, Spirit Queen Apsa decided to make a statement. I might have retired if it wasn't for that young lady's resilience."

*   *   *

It was past midnight when Fane finally arrived at Himitsu's room in the inn. He sighed as he entered, plopping onto the sheets of the empty bed.

"I love how punctual you are," Himitsu said with lazy sarcasm in his voice.

Fane rubbed his eyes. "Look, it's not exactly easy to escape a military sector—even as an assassin."

"So what's the news?"

"Not too much really. Daily drills and jobs … the typical routine."

"Did you see Wert again?"

"Yes, he visits every day." Fane grabbed a candle and used its flame to light a few others. "He walks the streets and meets with a few soldiers each time. As for what he's up to, I'm not sure. When I ask around, people tell me that he's always asking about loyalties."

"He's trying to find out who he can trust," Himitsu said, "recruiting foreign soldiers. He wants less opposition for whenever he and Toth decide to make a move."

"Seems like it," Fane said. He eyed Himitsu carefully. "You've been going over your mother's plans, correct?"

Himitsu heaved an exasperated sigh. "Every day."

"You never know when this will all go down. What's the most important step of the plan?"

Himitsu turned in his bed and gazed out the window toward Phelos Palace's ancient towers piercing the night sky. "Get my father first," he mumbled.

34
An Acidic Revelation

Toth Brench was seated in his office when Tazama strode in. "Unfavorable news," she said. "Lots of it."

"What is it?"

"We've received word that four new hunters were granted access into the Archaic Mountains: Bryson Still, Vuilni Gesluimant, Jilly Lamay, and Toshik Brench."

"Who allowed my son passage!?"

Tazama seemed unfazed by the outburst. "The documentation had been sealed by the Passion Kingdom and signed by Queen Fiona."

Toth's hands went to his face as he seethed.

"Even worse news," she said. "The *Brench Hilt* has been captured."

Toth took a long, deep breath. After a moment, he bellowed, "*How?!*"

"All twenty Adrenian naval escorts were annihilated in battle by the *Whale Lord*."

A fist pounded the desk and swept across, sending quill stands and miniature ship models into the wall. "*What is happening?!*"

Tazama stayed calm. "I've already informed Dev King Storshae. He isn't pleased. He's likely informing Toono and others right now." She paused, observing Toth as tears of rage glossed over his eyes. "As for Toshik and Jilly, this could work to our advantage."

"And how is that?" he replied, his head drooping toward the carpet.

"We didn't know where they were before," she said. "Now that they're deep in the Archaic Kingdom, we can send someone to retrieve them in Rim upon their exit of the mountains. You wanted them here for the uprising; now they're here."

*   *   *

The door to Toono's room slammed open, jarring him awake. "Get up," commanded the voice of Storshae. "It's already ten o'clock. What are you doing in bed, anyway?"

"Trying to rest as much as I can before next week," Toono mumbled into his pillow.

"Well, I hope you're rested," Storshae said, grabbing some robes from a drawer and throwing them on the foot of Toono's bed.

Toono sat up. "Why? What happened?"

"Chief Toth's ship has been seized and is now headed in the opposite direction."

Toono placed his feet on the ground and rubbed his eyes. "Wait a minute. Did the royal heads catch wind and back out of Toth's proposed deal?"

"Nope, the *Whale Lord* found them."

"I thought Toth said he had that covered," Toono said.

"I told you those two men are unreliable."

"And the twenty Adrenian ships that guarded it?"

"Presently? On the seafloor."

"I see," Toono murmured. "Well, that simplifies things."

"It certainly does," Storshae said as he turned to leave. "Meet me in the throne room. Gather Kadlest, Yama, and Illipsia. I'll get the rest."

* * *

Storshae stood at his usual post behind the empty throne of his dead father. Toono and Kadlest sat on the top step while the rest stood on the open floor, gazing up at the Dev King.

"I'll spare you the details as to why," Storshae said, "but the uprising's commencement has been bumped up. Thankfully, one of our associates in Phelos completed her task of building the teleplatforms, so this slight alteration shouldn't matter." His gaze slid to four others. "Dev Warden Gala, Jina, Halluci, and Garlo; the four of you head for the teleplatforms today with a unit of two hundred soldiers. It'll take a few days to reach them if you travel uninterrupted. Once there you'll continue northeast from the normal teleplatforms to a secret cluster built by Tazama. You'll then be teleported—in groups of ten—to an abandoned building in Phelos's 62nd District. From there you'll travel southeast in those same groups to the Archaic Kingdom's teleplatforms, where you will then wait. The reason for the small groups is to lessen suspicion."

"But, Prince Storshae," Gala said, "once we arrive at the Archaic Kingdom's teleplatforms, will an ally of some sort will be waiting for us?"

"Correct," he said. "That person will hide you until the time comes to spring into action. It should be easy pickings. Understood?"

"Yes, milord."

"Good. Get to it, then." As the four of them exited the throne room, Storshae directed his attention to the rest of the group: Toono, Kadlest, Illipsia, and Yama. "Illipsia, you will stay here in Cogdan."

"I want to go with Toono and Kadlest," she said.

"Where everyone is headed is not safe for you."

"Let her go," Toono said.

Storshae chuckled softly. "You'll change your mind once you find out where you're going."

"What do you mean?" asked Toono, standing up. "I'll have slipped into Phelos Palace and out of harm's way before the uprising begins."

"I left out some information when I woke you earlier," the king said. "I didn't want to spill the beans while our dearest Yama wasn't around."

The swordswoman's head tilted up with calm intrigue.

"First of all, Bryson LeAnce and Vuilni—that Power Diatia—are in the Archaic Mountains."

"How is that relevant to me?" Toono asked. "I'm not chasing them."

"No, but I know a couple other names that would change your mind. Somehow, someway, Toshik Brench and Jilly Lamay also gained access into the Archaic Mountains without their fathers finding out until it was too late."

Yama stood, but Toono glanced back at her and held up his hand. His gaze fell to the steps with rigid concentration, while Yama grew impatient. "This wasn't in the plan," he mumbled.

"You said the moment we have a chance to pursue him, we'd take it." Yama climbed to the top step and glowered down at Toono. "This is that chance."

When Toono didn't respond, Storshae said, "I've told Toth that I'd send two of our best—the two of you—after the lovebirds in the mountains to retrieve them safely and return them to Phelos. When I said this to him, he really seemed to relax. I think it increased his trust in us, and now he feels even surer about this uprising." The king grinned. "Of course he doesn't know Yama's true motives in regards to Toshik."

After more silence, Storshae added, "And, honestly, your presence in Phelos isn't necessary, Toono. We have more than enough firepower on our side to accomplish the revolt. This is an opportunity not worth squandering for the both of you. Yama would satisfy her thirst for vengeance, and you'd gain another sacrifice. Kadlest can stay back and aid Chief Wert's efforts in Phelos."

"Did Bryson and Vuilni enter separately from Toshik and Jilly?" Toono asked.

"Affirmative. Toshik and Jilly entered the eastern end while Bryson and Vuilni entered the western. I suggest you take your leave now. Searching the mountains will take time."

Toono looked at Kadlest. "What do you think?"

"You need an Adren sacrifice." She turned toward Yama's hardened face. "And she appears to be itching to kill something."

Toono's head dropped as he stared at the marble steps. He'd vowed no more reckless missions like his stint in the Void. But perhaps he had been too naïve. With six sacrifices already under his belt, the remaining kingdoms were now on high alert for the man they called the *Rogue Demon*. Everything he'd commit to from this point forward would involve risk.

He sighed and glanced up at the little girl, her raven hair wrapped around her wrists. "You'll be coming with me and Yama."

"Intriguing," Storshae said.

"We'll need her clairvoyance," Toono explained, descending the few steps and walking across the burgundy carpet toward the door. With Illipsia and Yama on his heels, he called out: "Good luck in Phelos."

*　　*　　*

Intel King Vitio sat at a long table surrounded by elders in a meeting room. These meetings typically involved an agenda of routine topics involving public affairs: unemployment and poverty rates, highest grossing businesses, incarceration numbers, and etcetera. But as of late—ever since the declaration of war—matters had become more urgent. Unease festered not only in this room, but throughout the entire kingdom. The last time Vitio recalled such pressure was following the murder of Archaic General Inias at the Generals' Battle—but even that paled in comparison.

"Any news from Brilliance on their reserve of provod?" Vitio asked, fumbling through the sea of parchment in front of him in search of the logistic charts from the weavineers.

"They should be fine, milord," a woman said. Her scalp was shaved bald and was much smoother than her wrinkled face. "Wisely, they've stockpiled enough provod to last three years if they continue their current manufacture rates."

"And what if, let's say—" Vitio placed his elbow on the table and waved his hand with a thoughtful frown— "we ask them to increase their speed? After all, we are in a war; we do need to start seeing these technological breakthroughs they've been speaking of."

"Well, milord, clearly you'd risk depleting your kingdom of its most valuable resource," she replied. "Perhaps, we should practice restraint. Like you said … this is a war, so let's treat it as such. We're in it for the long haul."

Vitio nodded with a grumble, glancing down at the parchments. His momentary thoughts were disrupted by Vistas, a new addition to these meetings as of a couple months ago: "Po'Deelé just contacted me, milord. He says Adren King Supido requests an emergency broadcast between the royal heads … He also says he's never seen the king so livid."

Vitio stood up. "I guess we'll cut this conference short for now," he said. "We will reconvene tomorrow, same time. Leave us the room, please."

The elders rose from their chairs and bowed to their king before collecting their things and exiting the room. As Vitio sat back down, Vistas approached the far end of the table and displayed a holographic screen from his right eye. The servant's other eye shifted from beady black to burgundy, fixing itself on Vitio.

"The *Brench Hilt* has been seized," King Supido announced the moment he appeared.

Vitio leaned forward, glowering as his eyebrows slanted at the fiercest of angles. "What do you mean?! How is that so?!"

Another face entered the broadcast. This time it was the delicate features and high cheekbones of Spirit Queen Apsa, an air of business replacing her usual sweet smile. "I made a deal with a renowned pirate by the name of Gray Whale and had her hunt the ship down."

"You crossed us!" Vitio bellowed.

"An unfortunate but necessary play," she said calmly.

"That isn't the half of it," said Supido. "What do you think happened to my naval fleet that was escorting the *Brench Hilt*, Vitio?"

The Intel King went silent before he shook his head. "No."

"They've all been sunk!" Supido exclaimed. "Twenty naval battleships and over a thousand of my sailors wiped out by Gray Whale under commands from Spirit Queen Apsa!"

"I did not command her to wipe out your ships," Apsa said, raising her voice to be heard, but not so much to be boisterous.

"You *knew* I had ships surrounding the merchant vessel that'd do anything to protect it!"

"And that's your own fault," she retorted whimsically, as if this quarrel was a non-factor. But that couldn't have been further from the truth. The Light Realm's alliance was crumbling right before Vitio's eyes. Apsa collected her breath and asked, "Did I not tell the two of you to turn that ship around?"

"Under suspicion cast upon you by the liar, Ophala!" Supido shouted. By this point, he was no longer seated—instead, he stood behind his desk, leaning over it with his fists planted on the surface.

"You will see," Apsa said, closing her eyes and nodding her head slowly. "You will see."

"*No we will not!*" he roared. "From this point forward, the Spirit Kingdom is an enemy of Adren!" Vitio, who had been a silent bystander throughout the spectacle, became alert once again. Supido continued his threat: "Your kingdom, Apsa, will be alone not only against the Dark Realm forces that are stirring, but the combined powers of the Adren, Intel, Passion, and Archaic Kingdoms!"

Vitio wanted to speak up, but how would he justify a counter to Supido's threats? He wanted to provide a rational mindset to the discord, but the Adren King wouldn't care about that in his current state—and understandably so. A considerable chunk of his navy had been annihilated by a crew of pirates under Apsa's orders ... Supido had every right to be irate. But it'd prove to be unnecessary to voice his concerns after another face entered the broadcast.

Queen Apsa brushed a hand through her maple brown hair and sighed. "Ah, finally. I hope you don't mind the presence of Felli Venustas in this broadcast, for I invited her."

"She isn't a royal head," Supido said, his aggression somewhat dissipated, but the rigor still holding his tone firm. "Stop including her in these dealings. Passion Queen Fiona or Prince Pentil must step in to fill King Damian's shoes."

Venustas replied, "My queen has placed me in this role, so you'll have to accept that decision."

"So what's the point of this?" Supido asked.

"It's to make clear to you that you're not as secure as you might think," Apsa said. "Felli is on my side. If you are to retaliate, just know that you're only further dividing the Light Realm. I'd assume Vitio would aid your kingdom, but the Spirit and Passion Kingdoms would stay strong together." While Supido's face contorted with rage once more, she continued. "And soon you'll also learn that you don't have the Archaic Kingdom. And a Light Realm with such division would only perish against a united Dark Realm."

Vitio could no longer sit idly by. After much time processing all of the information he'd consumed, he said, "That cannot happen."

Supido punched his desk and asked, "What are you saying, Vitio?"

The Intel King released a cathartic breath. "I'm saying you must stand down."

"You are out of your—"

"At least until we reconvene with the Amendment Order and research the Spirit Queen's claims. If she's willing to go to these lengths, it must be to protect us from something even more catastrophic than what she, herself, committed."

"I appreciate you finally coming to your senses, Vitio," Apsa said. "But while I may have put a hiccup in the plans of Chiefs Toth and Wert, it won't stop them—only hinder them slightly in the long run. For now, their mission is well underway. I guarantee you that it's too late." Her gaze turned cold as she said, "The Light Realm will lose the Archaic Kingdom."

* * *

Passion Director Venustas had returned to a surgical room following the tumultuous broadcast meeting between the royal heads. She wore a facemask, gloves, apron, and head cap, her hair folded within. She stared off into space as she waited for the body's arrival, her mind murky with the possibilities of what Himitsu and Fane were up to at this moment.

A door opened to her left. Four nurses wheeled a narrow, transportable bed into the sterile space. Once they placed it at the center, they quickly filed out.

Venustas eyed the blanketed cadaver from a distance. She didn't want to see the man underneath, as if that meant he was alive in theory. Alas, the swollen belly area was telling enough. She stepped forward and took a deep breath before peeling back the sheet from the head.

She closed her eyes, her heart sinking at the sight of her king. He was completely unrecognizable, his skin discolored and pruned. And he had been submerged for so long that he was well past the stage of bloating. As she unveiled more of his body, she realized he had served as a feast for lake animals. There wasn't much evidence for her to gain from this—if any.

She routinely poked around his skin with gloved hands, not really expecting to find anything. But as she made her way from his shoulder to his left bicep, his hand caught her attention in her peripheral vision.

She skipped down to it and gently picked it up. It was the only body part completely absent of skin. His skeleton was exposed halfway up his forearm. From there, it was shreds of muscle that had deteriorated. This wasn't the work of natural decomposition or carnivores.

The distal and middle phalanges of his hand had also eroded. She reached backward and grabbed a magnifying glass from the tool stand. As she gazed through it and studied the pattern and texture of the eroded bones, she developed a theory. And when she linked it to the wounds of the soldiers—the holes in their chests—or the Prim General nearly three years ago, it made even more sense …

King Damian had imprisoned his Passion Assassins when he had heard about the Prim General's murder, fearing it was their flames that burned the holes in his chest. Nobody had ever contemplated the possibility of acid.

35
'Vandals'

Lilu watched as Gracie, Limone, and Arrogo retrieved their hardened provod from the kilns. Frederick was already at his station with his volter on the table, ready to be tested. He had finished his days ago.

As they returned to their workplaces and eyed their devices, Lilu asked, "How's it looking?"

Gracie and Arrogo responded positively, but Limone hesitated. "I'm not sure."

Lilu frowned and approached him, knowing that he was likely over-exaggerating. Despite his brilliancy with his idea to spiral the grooves in the cannon, he was a young man with low self-esteem—reminiscent of Rhyparia during the Jestivan's infancy. But this test would help put that unease to rest. Lilu knew Limone's suggestion was correct.

She looked over it before rising with a smile. "You'll be fine."

She returned to her post a few dozen paces away from her assistants. "So now we'll find out who was successful. I see no cracks in anyone's vessel, so that's good news. A volatile Permanence vessel is the last thing we want with a device of this power. You'll see a brick at each of your stations. Go ahead and place it in your cannon's path, but a few feet in front of it."

They each did as instructed.

"The quality of your device will determine the brick's fate. If you break or damage it: success. If your device misses or is simply too weak to deal any damage, you fail. A miss would imply failure in the grooving of the cannon. A weak discharge implies one of two things: the volter's supply didn't fully harden due to insufficient hollowing of the provod, leading to thick walls, or the springboard has malfunctioned. Of course all of this depends on the accuracy of my hypothesis. If my blueprints were wrong, none of them will work regardless." She approached Arrogo. "Let's see how you did first."

As she opened the panel set in the supply's surface, he asked, "You're filling it?"

"Yes, I'll be weaving into everyone's supply. Since this experiment is focused on weavineering and not weaving, the variable that must remain constant is the weaving. We're not worried about weaving patterns and how they'd affect the machine—at least not for now. We only care about the craftsmanship and kilning of the weapon."

She began filling Arrogo's supply with Intel chains. "And while I'm the least skilled weavineer of our group," she said, "I'm still the best weaver. I'll make sure these things pack a punch."

She shut the latch and walked away. "Safety goggles on," she instructed as she pulled her own from around her neck. "If you want to duck behind your station, go ahead. Arrogo, since you're right next to it, you duck anyway. That is an order." She paused and gathered herself. "Whenever you're ready."

They braced themselves as Arrogo's finger flirted with the lever. He flipped it. His device responded with a sound similar to someone grinding two rocks together—slow, grating, and unpleasant. Sparks trickled out of the cannon, dying out before reaching the brick. Most of it probably died while still in the cannon.

"So what went wrong with Arrogo's volter?" Lilu asked as her face relaxed.

"Well, that awful sound came from its supply," Gracie said. "He didn't mold his springboard to be perfectly shaped to the supply's interior, so what we heard was the springboard scraping against the supply's wall. That created friction, which didn't allow the spring to fully release its stored energy and expel the Intel chains from the supply and into the cannon. The measly sparks that did expel from the volter were simply your chains working on their own, and they withered before making it to open air."

Lilu winked at her friend. "But even with only my Intel chains doing the work, they still should have expelled with much greater force. The fact that they didn't also implies Arrogo's supply wasn't hollowed out enough. His walls were too thick, so they didn't fully harden in the kiln in the time allotted. My chains didn't have a solid surface to bounce off of and keep their speed."

Arrogo shrugged. "Or maybe your invention isn't as good as you think it might be."

Lilu stared at him with a rigidness she had learned from her mother. Swiftly, she turned and approached Gracie. "The only way to find out is by testing others."

She opened a latch, filled the supply, and walked away. She nodded as a signal to Gracie. The niece of Professor Jugtah flipped the switch, and a stream of electricity belched from the cannon. Some of it collided with the brick, knocking it backward, while stray strands branched out and missed the target. It wasn't perfect, but it was proof that Lilu's blueprints weren't wrong.

Gracie held up her brick with a smirk. Cracks splintered across its surface.

"I'd call that a success," Lilu said.

While Arrogo scowled, Limone voiced his congratulations and Frederick reached over Gracie's table to give her a high-five.

Frederick's volter wound up even better than Gracie's. His brick not only cracked, but chunks of its edges were blown apart. Still, he seemed disappointed.

Lilu strolled toward Limone for the final test with a smile. Over the weeks, she had come to realize that he performed better while in a positive environment. If he thought—even for a second—that he had disappointed Lilu, he fell into a rut for days.

"Let's see what *Limone Lining* can do for the volter," she said as she filled his supply and walked away. This time she put considerable distance between her and the device.

Limone pulled the lever. There was a flash of light and a bang, forcing Lilu to cover her ears and look away. It was followed by a prolonged squeal as the stream continued. She turned back around, slack-jawed.

The brick was gone, blown into thousands of tiny pieces across the table and floor. The blast had been loud enough to create a pounding in Lilu's head. Even Arrogo had stopped leaning against his station, forced upright in shock.

"You managed that much power with that tiny volter?" Lilu asked. She had never imagined such destruction from something this size. These were miniature prototypes. Sure she had aspirations of creating larger, more innovative weapons … but now she was scared to even try those.

Gracie laughed. "Look at the wall."

Lilu spun around and gazed across the extensive width of the laboratory. A circle of black, matching the size of the cannon's mouth, blemished the opposite wall. Not only did the blast destroy the brick, but it traveled the expanse of the room without losing its concentration or thrust.

"Archers have nothing on that," Gracie muttered.

*   *   *

Lilu, Gracie, Frederick, and Limone celebrated the volter's success at Clout & Thrust, one of Brilliance's livelier taverns, later that evening. Arrogo had declined the invitation, for today had not been kind to his ego.

"To the greatest weapons specialist in Brilliance!" Gracie shouted as she thrust a shot glass into the air.

Lilu rolled her eyes. "You mean to the *only* weapons specialist in Brilliance."

Gracie shrugged. "We don't know that for sure." She then pointed a finger at the royal daughter. "Listen here. Today you introduced new technology to the world of weavineering. You've sculpted the way wars will be fought in the future. It won't be manpower, but tech-power. You've sparked an evolution!"

Lilu laughed and sighed. She couldn't blame Gracie for her naiveté, for she had never stepped outside of Brilliance's walls. She's never experienced the power of elites like the royals and Jestivan—or, even worse, the Bozani and Gefal. No creation of weavineering could counter such talents. Bryson would have sidestepped the volter blast in the lab like it was nothing.

"What's on your mind?"

Lilu escaped her thoughts and looked at Frederick. "Nothing." Why did her mind always run to Bryson?

Gracie's gaze glued to Limone across the table. "Hey, Limone," she said with sly eyes. "Your cannon was impressive … had a real nice stream."

Frederick and Lilu nearly choked on their potato wedges. Limone's gaze fluttered down to the table, clearly unsure of how to respond.

"Care to head back to your dorm later and test it out again?"

"You're drunk," Limone said. "So, no."

Gracie leaned back with a pronounced frown. "Impressive. A genius and a gentleman."

Lilu smirked. She couldn't help but love Limone more and more with each passing moment.

"What about you two?" Gracie asked, glancing between Lilu and Frederick.

The two of them made eye contact, but Lilu brushed it off. "What are you talking about?"

Gracie was about to respond, but a ruckus near the bar made her turn in her seat. A group of ten men and women seated at the bar began pounding mugs against the countertop in a rhythm, humming a harmonic tune.

Frederick groaned and closed his eyes. "Let's get out of here."

"Good idea," Gracie said, rising from her seat.

Lilu was not as eager to leave. She brushed away a hand that tried to guide her out of her seat. "Stop."

"You don't want to hear that," Gracie grumbled. "They're drunken idiots."

"Swell, coming from you."

Gracie's hand slipped from Lilu's shoulder. "Fine, then."

The group's humming turned into words:

Mendac, Mendac, attack, attack!
Their land and pride, ideas hijacked!
The Fifth of Five,
Immortal to time,
Carried through ages,
LeAnce survives.

Lilu sat speechless, processing the vile chant. These people were celebrating a man not just for his accomplishments, but what Lilu could only assume to be the method of how he achieved them. *Ideas hijacked?* That was the secret to Mendac's knowledge? He had to infiltrate foreign kingdoms and steal their intelligence?

Lilu shot out of her chair and marched through the bar. Gracie, Frederick, and Limone all stepped in front of her. "Move … right now," she commanded, her voice trembling with furor.

"You'll ruin everything if you commit to something so irrational," Frederick said. "All the hard work you've put in since you arrived here will be erased."

"I don't care!" Lilu shouted, as the people at the bar continued the chanting. "I want to shut them up! We're in Brilliance! These people are supposed to be intellectuals, not barbarians!"

"Mendac's legacy is cemented here in Brilliance," Gracie said. "It's a man's world."

"No it's not, Gracie!" Lilu shrieked, her eyes pooling over. The chanting stopped, and nearly every face turned to the group of four. The tavern fell silent as Lilu's heart pounded in her ears, adrenaline pumping through her. "And I'll prove it you," she mumbled, turning to leave the bar with her friends hot on her heels.

"Where are we going?" Frederick asked.

"Gracie's going back to our dorm to rest until she's sober tomorrow. But we're headed to the lab. I want six volters crafted within the next two days."

"For what?"

"Justice."

*   *   *

It was over a week later when Lilu, Gracie, Frederick, and Limone carried six volters out of the lab. They descended on the Intelevator and exited on the first floor.

"This isn't going to work," Limone said.

"It will," Lilu replied with an air of confidence even she didn't believe.

They crossed the main lobby of the Weavineering Tower. It was well past midnight, so the building was mostly deserted except for a few guards that stood near the front of the lobby. While their job was to keep unauthorized visitors from entering the building, they were also supposed to pay close attention to whoever was leaving. And since it was a rule that employees couldn't bring company material outside of the premises, they would definitely say something to Lilu and friends, who were clearly carrying something unordinary.

"Whoa, there," one gentleman said. "That looks like provod."

Lilu glanced down at the material. "Permanence, but, yes, I suppose."

"You can't leave the building with that stuff."

"Do you know who I am?"

His eyes scanned her face. "I'm assuming you're an employee here, ma'am. But policy is policy."

"Let's go," Limone said, turning the other way.

"Come on now," Lilu teased. "Green hair, green eyes, signature flower pinned to the bangs …"

His eyes widened. "Princess Lilu."

She smiled as the other guards bowed. She had hoped to escape such treatment here in Brilliance, but she would suffer through it for this one night. The end result would prove worth it.

"Now may I please pass?"

He stood up, his face flushing red. "I still cannot, milady."

Lilu's face turned an even deeper scarlet. "You risk denying the daughter of Vitio Intel?"

"We work for Wendel LeAnce, who scares us a lot more than the Intel King."

She tried her best to mask her genuine bewilderment. How did this Wendel guy hold so much influence while keeping his name contained within these walls?

"Do you enjoy your work?" she asked, altering her approach.

"I like this shift," he replied. "Just my coworkers and I hanging out. Not much to worry about."

"What's your name?"

"Semmi Slat."

"Well, Semmi, how would you like being able to just hang out whenever you see fit?"

"What do you mean?"

"I can persuade my father into letting you and your friends live the rest of your lives without work, and you'd still be paid and housed." She paused. "You'd have to leave Brilliance to live in Dunami though."

The guard pondered for a moment. "How do you reckon you'd get us out of here? We can't exactly walk out of the city."

"He has a point," Frederick said.

Lilu snapped her head around. "Shush." She inhaled, frustrated with the amount of questions. "I'll be leaving Brilliance to visit my family soon. The four of you can come with. Since I'll have Nyemas Jugtah with me, you'd be allowed to leave under the strict supervision of Jugtah. When we arrive in Dunami, I'll arrange a meeting between you and one of my father's advisors."

Semmi's eyes drifted from Lilu to her friends, then to the volters in their arms. He looked back at his fellow guards. "What do you think?"

"I've been behind these walls for thirty-seven years," a woman replied. "I've always said the moment I got an opportunity to get out, I'm taking it." The others nodded in agreement.

"But, Jenna, we'll most certainly be fired," Semmi pointed out.

"Doesn't seem to matter," Jenna replied as she looked at Lilu.

"It doesn't," Lilu said.

After the other pair of guards nodded in agreement, Semmi sighed and stepped to the side. "Go ahead."

"Where can I find all of you?" Lilu asked.

"Room 582 of the West Creek apartment complex," Semmi said. "That's my room. Now hurry up and get out … milady."

The group stepped outside under the murky gray night sky swallowed by clouds. They threw their hoods over their heads. Most of the Intelamps lining the road in front of Weavineering Tower were off at such an ungodly hour. This proved useful for Lilu, as well as the fact that they were dead smack in the middle of a string of business-centric city blocks. Thus, witching hours were the deadest of them all.

"So is your father actually going to do what you said?" Gracie asked.

"He'll have to."

They descended the stone steps toward the sidewalk, where they then turned left and walked a couple blocks. The journey had been mostly silent until Frederick said, "Don't tell me …"

"Deal with it," Lilu snapped.

Gracie frowned. "What are we doing? And why'd I agree to something I know nothing about?"

"Because you're my best friend."

"Oh, yeah."

They reached the intersection that held Mendac LeAnce's monument. It sat between the business districts and recreational blocks, so nightlife was somewhat audible.

Lilu stopped, pivoted, and began rattling off instructions: "Limone, you take a volter down this road; Gracie, this way with one; and, Frederick, that way with two. I'll head down the main road." As she pointed out directions, Limone's face fell. "Once you've reached the distance between you and the statue equal to the width of our lab back in the tower, stop and ready your volters. You'll also see escape routes closeby."

"I can't do this," Limone croaked. His head sunk into his shoulders as a group of adolescents walked past.

Lilu looked him in his face. "Do you envy rapists, Limone?"

"Not at all."

"Or just as bad, do you sit back and stay quiet while others envy rapists?"

His answer wasn't as quick. In fact, he deflected it altogether. "It's illegal to vandalize property—city, public, or private. I don't want to break the law and be a criminal."

"What weighs more in your mind, Limone? The law or morality?"

He stammered … "Morality."

The princess relaxed and backed away to give him some space. "Listen," she said. "I know we're Intelians, but that doesn't mean we can't learn a thing or two from Archains. I knew a man at Phesaw—Archaic Director Senex. He'd always tell the Jestivan: 'Morality and law aren't mutually inclusive.'"

Limone looked up at the stone Mendac. His fearful disposition slowly morphed into something a little more concrete as his lips flattened. "All right," he muttered, turning to head down the street. "Let's do it. I suppose we'll signal each other."

Gracie, Frederick, and Lilu split ways. Once they reached their spots, they placed their volters on the tar-paved ground. There were still a couple people scattered a ways down the streets, but not close enough for them to notice anything suspicious. She gazed across the intersection to see Frederick waiting with his hand in the air on the opposite side. She raised hers. Gracie and Limone were likely doing the same thing, although she couldn't see around the buildings.

Frederick dropped his hand, and they both bent over and flipped their levers. A bluish-white flash lit up the entire block, but then all that could be seen were electrical streams that pummeled the statue from all four sides. The blast lasted for only a few seconds, but the volters had done their job. The statue collapsed, its lower legs disintegrated from the voltaic surge. It hit the ground with a bang before falling over on its side, breaking into several large chunks upon collision.

Light began filling the windows of the nearby apartments. Between the voltaic blasts and crumbling stone, it was enough to wake people throughout the surrounding blocks.

Lilu snatched her volter and bolted into an alleyway. She had given herself the most difficult path of escape, considering her alley was a dead end. The two years of training with the Jestivan had provided her with the speed, strength, and skill needed to navigate such a route.

She leapt into the air and clung to the bottom rung of a metal ladder that hung from a stairwell running up the side of the building. She clambered up to her knees with one arm, careful to not drop the wonky device cradled in the other. She zigzagged her way up the stairs until she reached the pinnacle, where she then hopped over the rail and onto a ledge that barely jutted out from the building's side.

She shuffled her feet, keeping her back glued to the limestone. A gentle breeze swept her cloak's hood from her head and tossed the lily from her bangs. She yanked her hood to conceal her face and, this time, kept her hand glued to its hem, pinning it against her forehead as the wind jostled her cloak around her knees. Nature was trying its best to throw her off balance.

She slowed her pace and recalled Intel Director Debo's speed training lesson in his backyard from years ago. An image of a lanky pair of hairy legs extruding from high heels popped into her head. He had run around in those heels to prove a point. It was one of the most peculiar deliveries of a lesson she had ever received, but its essence was vital. If he had the ability to move in heels without sacrificing speed and balance, he could navigate any terrain under any circumstances. This was a great time to apply such a lesson.

She relaxed, making herself lighter on her feet. She was glad to have a moment to put her training in heels to use. She increased her speed just in time, as someone stepped out of their apartment and onto the metal staircase. "Leave me be, old man!" the woman shouted back into the building. "I heard something!"

As the lady turned toward her, Lilu leapt from the ledge and landed on the roof of a shorter building nearby, dropping her volter mid-flight. It shattered against the roof as she rolled out of her landing and sprung to her feet, not bothering to slow down.

Her lungs stung with each intake of air as she tried to keep her speed percentage as high as possible, skipping between segmented rooftops until she reached an alley a few blocks over. She traversed enough alleys to have put a safe distance between her and the pile of rubble that once was

Mendac. Once she could run no more, she fell back into a dumpster with her hand against her sweat-lathered forehead. The getaway's adrenaline had been replaced by a blissful feeling of accomplishment—perhaps a bit of relief, too. Not because she had escaped punishment, but a different kind of liberation.

She would no longer feel suffocated whenever she walked past that intersection. The monstrosity that haunted the city was gone. For all the unfortunate victims throughout Kuki Sphaira, this was a liberating night.

* * *

Lilu and her weapons team stood outside a barrier of stone roadblocks, which were placed on each of the four streets that led into Brilliance's busiest intersection. Cavalry was stationed within the barrier, serving as another wall of protection while city officials searched the wreckage of Mendac's monument.

"Why would someone do this?" Arrogo asked, appearing distraught ever since he arrived at the scene.

Lilu glared at him from the corner of her eye. She'd given him vacation time the past week for this very reason. "I'm wondering why it took so long," Lilu said.

"Stop believing that Bryson kid's lies," he said.

"That 'Bryson kid' is a great friend of mine."

He sucked his teeth. "Which explains your partisan perspective."

Lilu was about to begin a verbal tirade when someone placed a hand on her shoulder. She looked back and saw Frederick slowly shaking his head.

An officer stepped through the horses, approaching the barrier from the other side. "If anyone has any information at all regarding the events that unfolded last night, you can either come forward now or stop by the precinct later as an anonymous witness if you fear for your safety."

Lilu watched anxiously, waiting to see if anyone would step forward. Her stomach dropped when a young lady with wavy almond hair broke ahead of the crowd and passed the barriers. The officer cradled her shoulder and led her toward the intersection.

Lilu and Gracie made eye contact, uncertainty swimming within them. She then looked back at Limone and Frederick, who shrugged in turn. Had someone butchered their escape or revealed their identity? Lilu closed her eyes and cursed internally. It was probably that fleeting moment when her hood had been blown off.

A teenage girl in front of Lilu asked her friend, "What was the point?"

Arrogo butted in, giving his two cents on the matter. "People trying to erase history."

"That's what a textbook is for," Lilu replied as the girl turned around. "You don't need a monument to preserve history. If that's your argument, it's flawed. Monuments are meant to glorify."

"So you're siding with the criminals," Arrogo said.

"And you're siding with evil incarnate!"

Arrogo gave her a suspicious look. "I'm starting to think *you* might have done it."

"I wish I had."

"Well, Mendac is the essence of Brilliance's weavineering culture, and I'm proud of my city," Arrogo said. "That's all I'm saying."

Before Lilu had a chance to counter, Gracie—of all people—punched Arrogo in the jaw. Shouting erupted around them as a scuffle broke out. Arrogo charged Gracie, but Frederick stepped between them, stopping Arrogo in his tracks.

"Get out of the way," Arrogo said.

Frederick stepped forward. "Relax."

Arrogo shouted over his lab partner's shoulder, "Got Frederick protecting you, Gracie! You've always been right! Men do run the world! Can't stand up for yourself; taking a cheap shot!"

"Oh, I'm not protecting her from you," Frederick said. "I don't know if you've seen the look on Lilu's face right now, but I'm the only reason why you're breathing."

Arrogo glanced at the princess, who stood a considerable distance away with a dreadful scowl carved into her face. "She's scared to even stand too close to us!"

Frederick sighed and stepped away. "Suit yourself."

Lilu stepped off, turning into a blur with lightning coating her forearm. Arrogo's body folded as her fist slammed into his stomach, simultaneously expelling the air from his lungs and jolting his entire nervous system. He flew backward before skidding across the ground and tumbling into a building, where he then lay unconscious. There was a vast difference between the strength of a Jestivan and a scrawny IWA student.

The intersection went silent as every set of eyes were either on Arrogo or Lilu. The crowd split, making way for three officers as they grabbed Lilu's wrists and locked them behind her back. She could have offered them the same fate, but there would be no reason for it. She deserved this, but Arrogo did too. She regretted nothing.

*   *   *

Lilu woke to the clattering of her cell gate as it opened. She turned over in her cot to see Professor Jugtah standing there. "Let's go," he said softly.

They walked through the station in silence. Both Lilu and Jugtah filled out some paperwork before finally exiting the building. Their stroll through the city streets were also absent of conversation. She expected heads to turn and look her way, but was pleased to not receive any such reactions. The wall of buildings to her left was replaced by a tall gate, composed of vertical black bars. They followed alongside it until turning down a cobblestone path bordered by two patches of lush manicured grass—nature, a rarity in the city of Brilliance.   The moment they entered IWA, the stares finally came her way. But she didn't avoid eye contact, for she stood by her actions. Jugtah led her into a sector of the building she had never traversed, filled with faculty offices. She stepped past professors and administrators with her head held high and not an ounce of remorse on her face. She was stoic until she entered Jugtah's office and saw Arrogo seated in front of the desk.

She froze just inside the room, her face growing red hot. At least he looked equally displeased.

"Have a seat," Jugtah said. As Lilu approached an armchair in the room's back corner, he elaborated. "Next to Arrogo, Ms. Intel."

The two students exchanged disparaging looks as she plopped down in the chair.

"I need both of you to apologize to each other," he said.

"No," they replied in perfect unison.

"If not … Lilu, you'll be sent right back to jail, and Arrogo, you'll be expelled from IWA and barred from ever stepping foot in any establishment that hires weavineers or weavers. Now Lilu, you'd likely be taken back to Dunami under orders from your father, but you'd never be permitted in the city of Brilliance ever again. And Arrogo, that'd mean you'd spend your life in a career very unbecoming of someone of your status—" he frowned, waving his hand without concern— "perhaps, a store clerk or janitor."

The two of them held Jugtah's unwavering gaze as he added, "Let's hear it, then. You first, Arrogo."

"I'm sorry," Arrogo said.

"For what?" Jugtah asked.

"For my comments, which were out of line and uncalled for. I was antagonizing you and Gracie, and it was tasteless." After a moment of silence, Arrogo said, "Well …"

"Well, nothing," Jugtah said, standing up and pointing toward the door. "Get out."

"But what about—"

"Her apology?" the professor asked, eyebrows unnaturally high. "How about you go home and apologize to your mother for the man you've grown into … Now get out of my office."

Arrogo sat there, clearly outraged, as a vein in his temple pulsed. He then shot out of his seat, toppling it backward in the process, and stormed toward the door. Just as he was about to step outside and swing the door shut, Jugtah said, "And I've spoken with Wendel. You're no longer on Lilu's team."

The door slammed shut with a deafening bang. Lilu studied Jugtah as he calmly sat back down, placing his face in his hands and running them through his graying hair. "Did you destroy the monument?"

"I did."

Unsurprised, Jugtah turned and gazed toward an open window. He appeared exhausted, as if he hadn't slept in a couple days. "Sometimes I question my decision to have brought you here, but then I remind myself that you're young. And these issues you speak about and the measures you take to address them are done with a good heart—one that only younger generations fully understand.

"When you get older, you get stuck in your ways. You expect people to accept the world for how it is … to simply ignore the unflattering. But that's precisely the problem. I understand what you did; I respect it. But that needs to be the last of it. I want to keep you here for as long as possible, but I can't if you make it difficult for me to divert Wendel LeAnce from your scent."

"I don't need you to do that," Lilu said. "I want him to know. I want the world to know. I'm not scared of my decision. Throw me in jail. I don't care! At the end of the day I'm not the one who has to live with the burden of being a spectator."

Jugtah removed his gold-rimmed glasses and leaned in with sincere eyes. "I need you here. These weapons you're creating … all of this was my idea. I lobbied to Wendel for months so this could happen. You haven't become a weapons specialist to craft weapons used for invasions or offensive maneuvers. You're doing this because the Intel Kingdom needs to be able to defend itself when it becomes the war's focal point—which many feel will be the case eventually.

"Our kingdom has been spoiled for far too long. I don't know if you realize this or not, but our complacency as the powerhouse of Kuki Sphaira is about to backfire. King Vitio has grown too confident in the influential privilege that has been handed to him by a long line of decorated predecessors. Now, the Intel's need help from the LeAnce's."

Lilu straightened her posture, offended by the professor's remark. "My dad has led this kingdom with—"

"Do you know of all the things Mendac has done?" Jugtah asked. As Lilu froze, he said, "Neither do I, but I know more than most. And it was all done during the reign of your father. Even if the king didn't order him to commit such atrocities, he'll still be held accountable by enemies. What happened at the Generals' Battle two-and-a-half years ago was just a pin that punctured the inflated Intelian ego; what happens when it is ripped open? Who will be able to defend our land?"

The princess scoffed. She didn't know what to say.

"I like everything about you," Jugtah muttered. "Everything. Your passion, intelligence, morality, and even a fearlessness that I've seen blossom since I met you when I arrived at Phesaw. But now that you've toppled the monument, I need you to promise me that you'll focus on your job. You may not know it yet, but you're more than just a weapons specialist."

Lilu tapped her fingers against the arm of her chair. "I can't put it behind me when people are chanting Mendac's supposed accomplishments in establishments across the city."

"Give it time. Culture doesn't change overnight." His eyes narrowed. "But I will make sure it does. Your father understood what it meant when he allowed you to come here. And you'll understand soon enough, assuming you buckle down and focus."

"All right," she said, deciding not to fight him any longer.

"This means no more wasting provod. Each successful weapon or device you create must be followed by something even better. If any of your assistants prove to be inadequate or a distraction, cut them loose. And that includes my niece."

Her eyebrow arched. "Is it really that dire?"

"The Power Kingdom has severed all commerce with the Light Realm—specifically its exchange of provod for the Intel Kingdom's iron. Thankfully, Wendel and the League of Weavineers have made a habit of ordering more than they need over the years, so there is a massive warehouse stocked full of excess material. Still … we must be frugal in our use."

"What happened to the alliance?"

"It ended the moment the Power Queen believed it to have been Bryson who killed Bruut."

Lilu scoffed. "What has happened while I've been in Brilliance?"

"A worldwide war."

36
The Calm Before the Storm

Bryson and Vuilni stood outside a hollow cove in the pouring rain, staring into its blackened depths as the sun descended beyond the mountains. Bryson weaved two Intelights and pushed them inside. They followed the light source, remaining aware of anything unusual while staying close to the exit. This cave would serve as shelter for the night. Rain was a welcome rarity in the Archaic Kingdom, but when it came to Bryson's sleep, he preferred a dry environment.

"This is probably a terrible idea," Vuilni said.

"Nothing tops our first night."

She chuckled. "True."

They threw a few cloaks on the ground as cushion and lay down. Bryson propped himself onto his elbow, twisted his torso, and stared back into the darkness. "Wonder how deep it is."

"Well, it could be as long as the mountain's base," Vuilni said. "Maybe there's another side."

"Maybe Olivia's in a cave."

"Maybe …"

Bryson glanced at Vuilni. "Want to explore it tomorrow?"

She looked back into the abyss. "Perhaps. We shouldn't travel too deep, though. We might not be able to get back out."

"We'll see."

"When do we decide to leave the mountains?" she asked. "I've lost track of the days, but I believe Olivia's punishment ends this month. Maybe she's already back in Dunami."

Bryson fluffed his travel bag underneath his head. "We're going to stick it out for a while. I'm not giving up on my sister."

"Understandable. I did the same for mine."

His eyes widened as he turned toward Vuilni. "What's that?"

"Nobody makes it out of Stratum Zero," she said. "If you're born there, you live there until you die—in a land where mud and feces are the same, where sewage from the upper stratums spills from pipes installed in the mountainsides, and where everything is the same shade of brown. Even the fair-skinned slaves are smothered in dirt."

Bryson tried his best to not make a disparaging expression in response to her description. It proved difficult, for such a life of poverty was foreign to him. He had been provided for his entire life, spoiled by the income of his wealthy guardian, Debo. Even when Debo died, Bryson had somehow managed to keep the house while also gaining free access to Dunami Palace … Now that he really thought about it; he had been handed everything on a silver platter.

Well, except for respect. That he had earned.

"My family was no different," Vuilni continued. "My father wasn't ever home, for he was a provod miner in the Malanese Peaks, slaving away for no money. That left me, my sister, and our mother alone in a place not kind to weaker women, which sadly was a common theme in Stratum Zero … no fault of their own. They had grown up believing they were weak, essentially training their mind and spirit to be weak. Belief can affect reality, if powerful enough."

Bryson frowned. "You're so unbelievably strong, though."

"And I knew it," she replied. "For whatever reason, I knew about myself what others couldn't see in themselves. I could fight back."

She paused. Bryson allowed her a moment before she said, "Of course there were Power soldiers all over Stratum Zero. They walked around in long trousers and knee-high leather boots as protection from the sewage-lathered dirt. Most of them weren't terrible, if I'm being honest. While they may have acted like elitists, looking down on us and paying us no mind, it was exactly that kind of behavior we reveled in. It beat the alternative …

"There were a few soldiers who were notorious for seeking out a fight. Most times they were the initiator—and most times they won. One man, known as Gesich Piesche, was feared more than any, so much so he was given the title of the Slave Wrangler. I'll spare you the details of his tactics, but one day he came after me and my family."

When she became silent, Bryson turned over. "And?"

"And he'd never make that mistake again," she said, her gaze fixed on the cave's ceiling. "Honestly, I thought I'd die because of what I did. I was scared my family might too. Instead I was taken from the stratum of slaves and brought to Stratum Nine, the highest of them all—the stratum that overlooked all of Ulna Malen. I then met the queen, general, and a few other men and women of importance—including Bruut. I was offered the opportunity to join the Powish military while also attending school at Ipsas."

"That's incredible," Bryson said.

"I declined it," Vuilni said. "But that didn't matter, for they then forced my hand by threatening my family's safety. At that point, I was able to barter one thing. I told them I'd do what they wanted without resistance, if they allowed my family to leave the Power Kingdom and take up residence anywhere else—and do so without the Powish elite's knowledge of where."

"Where'd they end up moving to?"

"I don't know," she muttered. "That was the last time I saw them. I'm just happy I ended up making that deal. Because if not, I'm sure Power Queen Gantski would have killed them by now out of spite for my recent actions while at Phesaw."

"How would she even know?" Bryson asked.

"Either Warden Feissam or Intel King Vitio."

Bryson sighed. "You must miss them. To not even know where they are … While I never knew where my mother was, it didn't bother me as much because I never even knew *who* she was."

Vuilni stayed quiet while the rain grew heavier. After a moment, Bryson said, "I can't believe the Light Realm allies itself with such a despicable kingdom."

"Provod talks, I suppose."

"What's provod?" Bryson asked.

She shrugged. "My dad simply mined it. Nobody was privy to an explanation as to why it was so important. Possibly it's a rarity outside of the Power Kingdom."

After that, nothing else was said. Both Bryson and Vuilni accepted the day's end, falling asleep to the melodic pattering of the rain against the stone.

They awoke the next morning as daylight spilled into the cave. They gathered their supplies and stepped into the scorching sun of the clear sky. "I wouldn't have minded a light drizzle and some clouds," Bryson said.

They walked for some time across the mountainside, desperate to escape this area. There was no plant life at all—just a desolate expanse of smoothly eroded gray stone that swallowed their entire existence.

He was about to turn and head up the mountain, but Vuilni's arm blocked his chest. "Down there," she said. "You can't miss it."

Bryson followed her eyes downward and found a giant of a man ascending the mountain. Such an unmistakable frame belonged to one person only: Power Warden Feissam. "What's he doing here?" Bryson said. "Didn't he return to the Dark Realm?"

"That's what I thought."

"He might have come to find you," he said. "Maybe Vitio discovered Shelly sent us here, and he told your queen, who then told Feissam?"

"I doubt it," Vuilni said. "And that makes no sense. If he's here, it's not good news. If Queen Gantski sent him, it's not to rescue me. Bruut was the Power General's grandson. If they found out that I fought alongside the Jestivan against him …"

She was right. There was no way Vitio would have told the Power Queen, even if they were allies. Bryson looked around in an effort to find a hiding spot, but that seemed impossible in this barren valley.

"Let's get back in the cave," Vuilni said, tugging at Bryson's sleeve.

They hurried back, careful to avoid the warden's eye. But since they had covered so much ground in the past hour, this plan was flawed. They didn't have to look to realize they had been spotted. The tremors from Feissam's stampeding feet signaled his hurried movements. Bryson and Vuilni scurried across the mountainside, slipping frequently against the slick surfaces. Feissam was gaining on them, but luckily they occupied higher ground with a small cliff between them.

Just as Bryson thought they'd make it to the cave, Feissam leapt and grabbed hold of the precipice. Debris crashed below as he clambered the crumbling edge. An entire chunk of mountain collapsed, catching Bryson and Vuilni in the cascade. Bryson flailed within the falling rubble until he smacked the ground below, the destruction's remnants pummeling him like hail until he was buried.

He groaned as he struggled to push himself out of the wreckage. Just as he managed to break free and breathe unobstructed air, he looked forward to see a fist the size of his chest barreling toward his face. Bryson braced his body for absorption, but Vuilni appeared in front of him and caught the massive fist with both hands. A blast of wind erupted from the contact, and her feet slid through the fragmented stone, carving a wedge into the pile as Bryson dove out of her way. *How powerful was that punch?*

Vuilni roared, tossing Feissam's fist to the side with enough force to twist his body. Bryson weaved a concentrated bolt of electricity from his hands that struck the warden's chest. Vuilni followed with a mighty kick into his knee that snapped it at an awkward angle.

Feissam's resulting outcry reverberated like thunder through the mountains. He swiped at Vuilni, but it was a desperate attempt. She dodged it with ease as Bryson unleashed a voltaic array upon the giant, refusing to subdue the stream. The giant jerked and howled until Vuilni finally turned around and yelled, "*Stop!*"

Bryson's assault subsided, and Feissam collapsed with a thud that shook the ground. Bryson realized he hadn't stood throughout the entire ordeal since falling from the cliff above, and there was a legitimate reason as to why. He grimaced, pulling his knee toward him to observe a gash in his skin that exposed a white sliver of bone.

Vuilni studied Bryson from afar. "We need to get back to civilization," she said. "Who knows who else might be in here?"

* * *

In the foothills of the Archaic Mountains, Toono, Yama, and Illipsia handed their documentation over to an officer, signed and sealed by Chief Merchant Toth Brench. The man's eyes narrowed as he read through the parchment. "Never heard of such names. Novice hunters?"

"Trying to get our business off the ground by landing a big target as our first," Toono said.

The officer's gaze fell to Illipsia. "And you've brought a little girl with you …"

"Is that a problem?"

He scanned over their faces once more. "Well, the reward only lasts for another month, so remember that."

"Got it."

He looked at a long sheet of cloth that was bundled around Toono's ancient on his back. "What kind of weapon do you use, young man? Looks bulky."

"War hammer," Toono said, trying to keep the conversation as short as possible.

He grinned. "I admire that. Haven't seen anyone cross through here with one of those yet." He nudged his head backward. "Good luck," he said, "and be careful. There are some formidable men and women in there."

Toono trudged forward. "If only you knew."

* * *

Toth stood to the side while Tazama unlocked the eight-squared puzzle on the dungeon door. This was the second time in three days he had taken a trip down here, for this was where he met their high profile guests. Most of the reinforcements that had traveled from the Dev Kingdom did so through the two teleplatforms in the outskirts of Phelos, but the bigger names couldn't risk it. They needed to penetrate the palace without having to do so from outside the walls. This dungeon was the trick.

The door unlocked, and they stepped inside. Tazama flipped a couple switches on a wooden lectern, sparking her makeshift teleplatform to life. Moments later it began to spin. At its maximum speed two people appeared, until slowing down and coming to a stop. Dev King Storshae stood at the platform's center while a brunette woman looked to be purposely standing off to the side—almost at the stage's lip.

Toth bowed. "Quite an honor, Prince Storshae."

Storshae stepped off the platform without an introduction. "May I ask how you managed to botch the transfer of goods across the sea with an entire naval fleet at your disposal?"

"A couple spies of mine were compromised, sir. I do apologize." He relieved himself from his bow. "They'd gone decades without being caught."

Storshae's eyes narrowed as he removed his gloves and stuck them in his pocket. "It seems your opposition has a better spy than you do. Have you vetted your friendlies recently?"

"I didn't leak the information about the merchant ship to anyone. I only told the royal heads, and of course none of them would let word slip. They had a lot of money on that ship."

The woman stepped off the platform and asked, "Can you show me where we'll be staying for the night? I must get away from this insufferable man." She gestured toward Storshae.

The king glowered. "You're far too comfortable with me. You're lucky you're Toono's precious cargo."

"And who are you?" Toth asked.

"Kadlest."

Tazama stepped from behind her board of switches and levers. "I'll show you to your quarters. But fair warning: your room will be more of a chamber … at least until the dust settles tomorrow night."

Storshae's eyes followed the Dev servant as she walked past. "Tazama," he said.

She gave a slight nod, lips firm. "Prince." She then exited the room with Kadlest behind her.

As the door closed, Storshae said, "Is there somewhere we can talk that also provides seats?"

"Of course, sir."

As they swept through the suffocating halls, Storshae asked, "Are all the dungeons like this? Naked?"

Toth glanced between the stone walls. "Back before Spy Pilot Ophala's suspicions of mine and Wert's behaviors, she'd discuss a lot about the Archaic Kingdom with me—mostly Phelos and this palace's history. Most of the dungeons are used today for the building's utilities, or they house prison cells, but even those aren't used anymore … well, except for Ophala. Her relationship with winged animals has made it impossible to hold her anywhere above ground."

They proceeded down a narrow set of stone steps, traveling deeper underground. "This area of the dungeons, however, is separated from others not only by a wall, but by layers of dirt. It was an addition to Phelos Palace in 1438 by Archaic King Dolomarpos—Itta's father. He had designed it to serve as a place where prisoners went to be taught a lesson."

As Toth fidgeted with a lock and opened a door to a small chamber, Storshae said, "In other words, torture."

Toth stepped inside after the king. "Correct," he said. "Which was why it received the name 'Agony's Lair.' And, as we all know from the stories, Dolomarpos was an even bigger monstrosity than Itta. The only thing he had going for him in the eyes of the other Light Realm kingdoms was that he didn't direct his rage at them. Instead, his own citizens were the victims. The other royal heads could turn a blind eye to that."

As Toth lit a few candles around the chamber, he added, "Of course, we all know Dolomarpos was betrayed, his life ended by former Archaic General Inias's mother. This gave power to Itta, who then changed his father's philosophy. While he still was ruthless in his desire to be the sole judge of all crime—no matter how petty it might have been—at least when he sentenced someone to death, it was a quick execution. And it wasn't done by his own hand."

Storshae sat on a backless wooden bench while Toth slid down the wall to the floor. "But that also proved to be his grave mistake. He had redirected all that rage and hunger for power from his citizens to his supposed allies in the Light Realm. And, as you know, that's how you and he became a pair, attacking the Intel Kingdom during the Generals' Battle."

Storshae shook his head with a stern glare. "The wretched Intel Kingdom didn't mind if it were the Archains being tortured and slaughtered, but the moment they became victims, it became a problem. It's no surprise a monster like Mendac was a product of such a place."

Toth rested the back of his head against the wall and asked, "Do you not feel that way about yourself?"

There was a pause, as Storshae seemed to reflect on the question. But he ignored it and instead said, "I noticed you stopped addressing me as 'sir' or 'milord' the moment we left the teleplatform and you became comfortable. You're not in a position to forget your etiquette yet … not until tomorrow is over. If the uprising succeeds, only then can you act so cordial with me."

The chief met Storshae's gaze. "I understand, milord."

"You do that, and come two days' time, you'll have others bowing to your feet." Storshae grinned. "How does that sound … 'King Toth Brench'?"

*   *   *

District Four was the heaviest militarized area of Phelos. It sat in a peculiar location for a military base, as they were typically seen on palace grounds or somewhere separated from the public. It stretched for miles outside the southwestern wall of palace grounds, at the heart of the capital and sandwiched between civilian districts. There were no walls around it—not even a fence. If it weren't for the soldiers that stood guard at every city route entering the district, civilians would have wandered in thinking it was just another city street.

District Four hadn't always been a home for soldiers. It had once been a rundown sector of buildings ravished by former Archaic King Dolomarpos, who had raided the homes and eradicated families when the district proved it couldn't keep pace with the tax demands of its king.

Adren General Sinno had taken advantage of its vacancy during his temporary placement in Phelos as an interim leader between Itta's arrest and the Amendment Order's formation. With the Archain public's negative and violent response to the stationing of Adren soldiers on their land, Sinno needed a place that would keep the two sides separated and as docile as possible. Now it was being used for not just Adren soldiers, but Intel, Spirit, Passion, and Archaic—a melting pot of ideologies.

Fane sat in one of the district's few bars. He had come to realize that many of these stragglers who, for whatever reason, hadn't been called back to their home kingdoms during the recall of troops were frustrated with their assignments here. They saw no need perishing within the Archaic Kingdom alongside its dying economy, and a lot of them were questioning their loyalties ... a disastrous recipe for the foreign royal heads.

This unrest was evident in the conversations that buzzed through the district and further fueled by the instigation of Chief Officer Wert Lamay. He'd hold rallies on a bi-daily basis, spewing indirect questions intended for the royal heads about why they would desert so many of their soldiers. But with them not around to answer, the soldiers had to fill in the blanks. And with what they had experienced over the past year, those answers weren't exactly peaceful in nature. It was a tactic used by the most radical politicians—the ones who led with hatred and fear.

Fane stared into the bottom of his empty glass. He was old enough to remember a man like King Dolomarpos, or at least to have heard the stories that had traveled across the realm—even if he had only been a teenager at the time. Dolomarpos had ruled through fear, but his method was blunt and easily discernable. Toth and Wert were more subtle and intricate in style, which was far scarier to Fane. They didn't bully the masses into submission; they manipulated them.

The barmaid approached and poured the assassin another round of scotch. "You're a man with a lot weighing you down," she said.

For the first time all night his eyes met hers, despite having had sat there for a couple hours—proof that her observation was correct. He took a sip of his drink, and smacked his lips. "Life," he said.

"Roll with the punches," she replied, placing both hands on the counter and leaning against it.

"I don't roll."

She smirked and stared at him before filling his glass to the rim. Such a generous portion was excessive even for a man like Fane. "You drown," she said, winking as she walked away.

Fane shook his head and stared at the decadent amber liquid. While he might have been friends of the Vevlu family, he definitely wasn't one of them. He knew how to control his liquor intake.

Stirrings outside caused him to turn on his stool and look out the window. Soldiers jogged down the street. A few of the off-duty men and women in the bar got up, opened the door and stared in the direction to where everyone was running.

"Chief Officer Wert is here!" a man yelled back into the bar before joining the flow of the crowd.

Fane followed everyone outside, perplexed by the timing of Wert's appearance. He had shown himself yesterday, which meant today should have been his day to ignore District Four if he was following his normal routine. It was also well into evening hours … another first.

Soldiers congregated, the gravel street crunching underneath their heavy boots. Wert stood waiting atop a platform, his massive chest puffed out and hands held behind his back. While he had served as a member of the Archaic Kingdom's Amendment Order for two years, he had yet to ditch the sky-blue uniform that distinguished himself as the Spirit Major—even if he had relinquished that position in favor of Chief Officer.

Next to him was a new face to these meetings, but one Fane instantly recognized from years of studying intelligence gathered by the spies of the Passion Kingdom. The other giveaway was the glowing orange orb atop the staff in his hand. This man was Elyol Brekton, son of Inias Brekton—a former powerhouse general who had been murdered during the Light Realm's last Generals' Battle.

Wert cleared his throat, much the way he did at the start of any speech. "There comes a time when a road splits into two directions," he announced. "When you're forced to make a decision that you can't turn back from." He paused and scanned the crowd. "This is that time."

Understanding what this signaled, Fane began searching for escape routes so he could get to Himitsu and alert him. He backtracked through the crowd while Wert continued: "Tomorrow afternoon marks a new beginning. For those of you who side with Chief Merchant Toth Brench, Archaic Prince Sigmund, and myself, I want you to gather behind the platform."

Fane made it to an alleyway and glanced back to see a disheartening yet unsurprising sea of people pressing forward and rounding the platform to stand on the other side. Maybe twenty percent of them stayed where they were. Wert seemed unperturbed, and it quickly became evident why. Throughout the street, hands of magma rose from the ground and grabbed hold of the defiant soldiers. Howls echoed into the night sky as their bodies were slowly torched against the white hot sludge. Elyol was killing them all.

Fane fled through the alley, but slowed near the exit at the opposite end. He peeked around a building toward District Four's boundary at the end of the street. Three blocks down, ten soldiers stood guard. He dipped his head back and gazed at the sky. Luck was on his side, for the stars couldn't break through the clouds. The two moons slipped in and out of hiding, but with the angle of their position in respect to the surrounding buildings, it could be handled.

He weaved a trail of black fire atop the barrack's roof across the street. They reached just high enough to block the moon's light, casting a shadow over him and the street. He then took care of the torches, swallowing the bright orange flames with his black ones. The glow tried fighting its way through, but with little success. Darkness swallowed everything.

He slipped into the street, still conjuring flames on the ground as an extra precaution. He wasn't naïve enough to think that the soldiers were imbeciles. While they couldn't spot Fane, they definitely saw the inexplicable black mass that had appeared halfway down the street. He needed to remedy this.

He dimmed the entire street by smothering every torch with assassin's flame. He used this opportunity to scale a nearby wall, clinging onto gutters and reaching for rails. This movement was typically carried out by the younger assassins, but he figured he still had it in him. Once on the shingles of the roof, he leapt between several more until escaping District Four and sprinting to the inn where Himitsu was waiting.

* * *

Himitsu lay on his bedroom floor, tossing his balled-up socks into the air when he heard his door unlock. He didn't bother looking when his guest entered. "Strange time for a visit."

"Better get in the right mindset," Fane said. "It begins tomorrow."

The socks hit the floor as Himitsu stared at the ceiling. "Are you serious?"

"Yes. We'll hover outside of District Four tomorrow at noon until we see action begin. Then we'll take advantage of the chaos and set our plan into motion."

Himitsu sat up with his forearms lying across his knees. "Do you think we can do it?"

"Death is far more likely than success in this scenario," Fane said as he rummaged through a drawer. "But that's the life of an assassin."

"And a Jestivan," Himitsu mumbled.

* * *

With one more chamber to visit, Chief Toth hurried through the dungeons after his conversation with Storshae. Midnight was approaching, and he needed sleep in order to be well rested for tomorrow. He knocked on the door as a warning to the guest inside. He then untied the chain that served as a lock. He opened the door and smiled at the round woman, her silver necklace squeezing the air from her throat. "Good to see you, Vliyan," Toth said.

"Good evening, Chief."

He didn't bother making himself comfortable, for this would be a quick visit. "I apologize for the less-than-flattering living arrangements over the past week."

"I understand the necessity of it."

"I appreciate your understanding," he said with a grin. "Storshae arrived tonight, so we're all ready for tomorrow. How is Prince Sigmund's hair working out?"

"I can feel his energy and have a good grasp of it," she said. "I'll be able to fulfill my duty tomorrow."

"Good." Toth grabbed onto the door, preparing to leave. "Remember to observe. Only act if necessary."

Vliyan gave a raspy chuckle that made Toth cringe. "Don't worry about me."

*   *   *

The following day Himitsu and Fane lingered throughout Crow Street for hours. They had arrived before noon … it was now approaching evening. Himitsu peered through a window and into a parlor, where he spotted a clock. "Almost four o'clock. What if it's already started?"

"We'll know when it starts … trust me," Fane said, a brown cloak concealing his face. A lot of soldiers chose to follow Chief Wert last night, but I assure you once they find out the specifics of what such a pledge means, a lot of them will resist. Then there are the hundreds of soldiers on palace grounds and inside the building who will also fight back. Your mother labeled it an 'uprising' for a reason." He paused and muttered, "It will be raucous and epic in scale."

"Which benefits us," Himitsu said. "Chaos conceals finesse."

Fane slapped his partner's back. "Quoting your father; I like it." A few moments later he said, "Guards should be switching out here soon."

He was right. Down the road, a new set of four soldiers approached their post from the opposite side, relieving the original four. The new guards' wardrobe puzzled Himitsu. "They're wearing … green and orange? I've never seen such a color combination. It's not a kingdom's colors."

"Not yet, at least," Fane grumbled. Three of the four guards being relieved suddenly removed their uniform's jackets and flipped them inside-out to reveal the same green and orange pattern. "Interesting," said Fane. "Seems one of them isn't part of the ruse."

This left one soldier—a shorter man with gray hair—as the oddball. He turned and balked at their uniforms, perplexed by what was happening until a blade slashed his throat. Himitsu released a cathartic breath as the man collapsed to his knees, clutching at his sputtering neck.

"And there's our cue," Fane mumbled. "It begins."

Something caught their attention in the sky on the eastern side of the palace, above the main barracks. A wave of lava ascended from somewhere within the city, reaching high enough to match Phelos Palace's tallest tower. It curled at its crest, readying to crash upon the unsuspecting soldiers in the barracks.

As the air rippled and temperatures soared, Himitsu declared, "I hate the human race."

37
The Uprising

The seven soldiers at District Four's entryway abandoned their post to turn back toward the district as other troops exited buildings. Some glanced in every direction, unsure of what was happening, while others preemptively took action. It didn't take long for those who were momentarily stunned to notice that anyone dressed in green and orange was an enemy.

Frenzies materialized within the streets. Fire, electricity, and wind collided. Adrenians initiated swordfights, their limbs blurring as they danced with each other. Bodies fell by the handful—men and women from all kingdoms.

Unfortunate citizens who resided in the buildings directly next to District Four fled for the city's outskirts. Parents carried babies and dragged the children who were capable of walking. The elderly limped away from danger, supported by canes or the little bit of strength they had left. For a split second Himitsu was conflicted. He wanted to help them to safety as the battles began to spread out across the district.

Fane must have noticed the struggle on his face. "It's pointless. The public needs to get back into the buildings; it's the only way they'll stay safe. If they don't obstruct Wert's path, he won't harm them."

Himitsu looked back as the fleeing civilians began to scream, splitting apart to the sides of the street. He widened his eyes in disbelief, as a swarm of soldiers in green uniforms charged down the street toward District Four. Himitsu thought, *so this is what war looks like*. His heartbeat might have killed him before an enemy.

"I'd say this is about what it looks like on every other street too," Fane said. "Wert had an entire army waiting outside the capital for a year. Now they charge the palace, and this little skirmish we're seeing in front of us will be won by Wert's men."

"When are we going to move?!" Himitsu shouted.

Fane tugged at the young assassin's sleeve, pulling him into the crowd. "Blend in with the civilians against the walls."

They watched as soldiers stormed past, the ground rumbling beneath their feet. "Kill as many as you can," Fane said.

Black flames sprouted randomly amidst the stampede, catching soldiers and spitting them back out covered in fire. They howled in agony for a few seconds before falling to the ground. Most continued to run, but some stopped to comb the area. Himitsu torched one man who had sniffed entirely too close to the two assassins.

"There!" screamed a woman, sending all eyes toward Himitsu and Fane.

Panicked civilians scattered. Himitsu drew his spunka sword and coated it in flame. He went on the offensive, stepping forward and wending between soldiers, slicing them open with ease. Fane hopped left as a combination of electricity and wind whizzed past. He countered with a blazing blast from his palms, consuming two women.

Once they cleared the area of those who had elected to stay behind, they took uniforms from two carcasses and put them on. They then entered District Four, pushing onward through scattered battles with the palace walls as their destination.

*   *   *

Dev King Storshae swept through Phelos Palace with war's cacophony reaching him from the grounds. He didn't bother hiding who he was, his gold-embroidered burgundy robes billowing behind him. Unlike past missions, such as the Generals' Battle and invasion of Phesaw, there wasn't much he felt he needed to worry about. All threats were far away from Phelos.

Officers stationed in the palace ran past in the opposite direction, heading for the staircases to help combat the revolt below. A few balked, noticing the presence of Dev royalty. Storshae didn't think much of it, but he'd lend a helping hand here or there by releasing a blast of Dev Energy into a pack, knocking them off their feet and through the air. It was nice not having to worry about a potential run-in with people like Poicus or Ataway.

The Dev King was here simply as a presence. When staff saw him, they backed into rooms like pups faced with the bottom of a shoe. He was an emergency reinforcement just in case someone formidable stepped forward during the uprising. Hopefully, such a problem wouldn't present itself, and the transition into tomorrow would run smoothly.

* * *

Archaic Prince Sigmund was seated at the foot of a long dining table, closest to the mahogany double doors. Chief Senator Rosel Sania and Chief Arbitrator Grandarion Senten sat near the head, with a grand fireplace as their backdrop. The three of them were awaiting their early dinner. They had fallen into this routine ever since Rhyparia's execution. Despite Sigmund's decision to side with Chiefs Toth and Wert a while back, he still had to attend these meals as a charade.

As a pair of waiters wheeled carts into the hall, Rosel asked, "Do you fear the contraction of a disease, Prince Sigmund?"

The young man shook his head. He refused to open his mouth, fearing that vomit would take the place of his words.

"Then why are you way down there?"

Grandarion chuckled as he tucked a napkin into his collar. "Don't fret, Sigmund. Obesity isn't contagious."

Rosel shot a glance toward the mountain of food that was placed in front of Grandarion. She looked back at Sigmund. "What's wrong?"

"Nothing," he croaked.

"You'll need to become a better liar if you expect to operate as king."

The prince's eyes fell to his plate of lamb and bowl of couscous salad with cucumbers, red onions, and herbs. On a normal day he'd be salivating, but today an appetite was a foreign concept. Rosel, once again, took notice. "The food won't bite you."

The hall darkened, as the dying orange rays of dusk disappeared, bringing their attention to the tall, narrow windows that lined the side wall. Glass tableware clattered as forks fell out of their hands, their mouths dropping in awe. They didn't need to approach the windows for a closer look, for what approached was clear as day. A molten tidal wave curtained the sky and cityscape, bearing down on the palace and threatening to swallow it whole.

Rosel and Grandarion shot out of their chairs and ran toward the windows. They gazed below to the barracks, where soldiers wearing different kingdoms' colors began to clash. It was impossible to make sense of who was on which side. In the distance, toward the south end of the wall, the gates opened. A horde of cavalry and infantry in green cloaks swarmed through, spilling across the grounds as they were confronted by soldiers who had escaped the barracks or exited the palace. Arrows rained down from above Rosel and Grandarion—someplace higher in the palace—hitting friendlies and enemies alike in the riots below.

"It's Chief Wert!" Grandarion declared, raising his voice in an uncharacteristic manner. "No other explanation!"

"Prince Sigmund, we need to take action," Rosel said. She turned to see Sigmund standing in front of the doors. She looked confused as she marched toward him. "We can't just stand around."

He didn't budge. She reached over his shoulder and tried to push the door open, but it was locked.

"What are you doing?" she asked, fear setting in. Grandarion, too, turned with a flare in his eyes.

Sigmund's gaze held firm with hers. "Rescuing this kingdom from the shackles of two saboteurs."

She paused, fumbling over words before saying, "You're falling victim to their foolery! Prince Sigmund, don't do this!"

"You've never wanted my kingdom to succeed, Rosel." Sigmund looked past her, toward Grandarion. "And especially you, an Intelian man who had worked directly under Vitio for years. Everything both of you have done has been an act of sabotage against the Archaic Kingdom, steadily weakening its economy and the spirit of the people."

Rosel tried to retort, but Sigmund's rant was unyielding. "You've always warned me of businessmen like Toth Brench, but I never stopped to think that you're the worst of them all—" he paused, his gaze burning holes into her soul— "a *politician*. And you worked alongside a woman like Ophala Vevlu—a master spy—whose job is to infiltrate, deceive, and collect only to betray. A clever ruse the three of you had going the past two years, but today it ends."

Rosel lowered her voice and gently grabbed Sigmund's shoulders. "Listen to me. This is a grave mistake. You don't know the inner workings of Toth Brench. He's connected to bad people. You think this is all for only your kingdom? What falsehoods has he promised you?"

"*Quiet*," Sigmund spat, swatting her arms away. "I wouldn't be doing this if they hadn't informed me of the support I'd have. I know I'll have to answer to Vitio, Apsa, Supido, and whoever's in charge of the Passion Kingdom. But I can do that in confidence, knowing that I have the Dev, Power, Cyn, and Still Kingdoms on my side."

Rosel backed away as snow flurries began to swirl throughout the room. The temperature plummeted as the Archaic Prince put his ancient to use—the scarf rustling around his neck. "Right now Dev Prince Storshae is somewhere in the palace. Other forces in the kingdom are Toono, Yama, former Still General Garlo, and Dev Warden Gala—and that's only a few of the names."

A bolt of electricity came from Grandarion, but Sigmund blocked it, summoning a wall of packed snow from the floor. Despite Rosel's ability of fire, she wasn't talented enough to counter a royal first-born's snowstorm. Neither of the two chiefs was formidable enough of a fighter or weaver, for their brains and experience had given them power. But even their intelligence didn't fare well when against the likes of Toono and Storshae.

Snow piled atop the floor, swallowing the legs of the two chiefs. Shivers morphed into convulsions as they collapsed into the white fluff. Then, at the verge of complete submersion, Sigmund's assault relented.

Second thoughts had seeped in, and the flurries dissipated momentarily as he stared at the two bodies. He gazed toward the windows from his spot in front of the twin doors just as the wave of lava crashed into the barracks below. With one single attack, hundreds of people were wiped from existence. He placed his face in his quivering hands and clutched at his forehead, his breaths growing heavy beneath the mounting guilt.

Then something took over him. Despite the anxiety, energy began to flow through his canals, adamant and fast. He lost control of his clout as the flurries returned, intensifying exponentially by the second. Before long, a blizzard had consumed the dining hall. Even Sigmund himself fought to stay above the snow—a mighty struggle with his energy withering away.

Then it stopped. Sigmund's upper torso was exposed, the rest of him buried. And as for Rosel and Grandarion, they lay in a grave of snow.

* * *

Himitsu ran through the palace grounds with the main entrance as his goal. He fought for every step he took, as soldiers veered from prior engagements to unknowingly take a stab at the Jestivan. It ended poorly for all of them.

As he entered the main foyer, he had flashbacks of his arrival here over a year ago in preparation for Rhyparia's second trial. This time, however, the warm smile of his mother wasn't here to greet him. He rushed up a set of steps, using the spine of his sword to strike anyone who confronted him. He didn't look at them as his enemies, but since he was dressed in green and orange, they saw him as one. Thus he had to defend himself, but did so without lethal force. He also refrained from using flames; otherwise it'd give away his ability. For now, he wanted to be viewed as an Adrenian.

As he traversed the ancient castle, he was surprised to find it deserted. Most of his progress thus far had been unimpeded, with the battles occurring mostly on the lower floors and outside. He only hoped the same rang true for Fane.

Himitsu peeked around a corner down a sunlit hall. Six officers in green uniforms were stationed outside the door he was trying to reach. Behind that door was the same chamber that had imprisoned Itta while he was still alive. And according to Fane, Ophala had been certain in her letter that Horos now occupied it.

Himitsu waited for the cue. If Fane had successfully completed his journey through the palace, then theoretically he should have been on the opposite end of the hall, past the officers, and hiding around a corner just like Himitsu.

As he stood with his back against the stone wall, he heard the guards shout, "Passion Assassin!"

Himitsu peered around the corner once more. Every window from the hall's midpoint where the door sat to the opposite end was sealed by black flame, swallowing half the hall in shadows. The fire didn't fully block the sunlight, but it dimmed it enough. As expected, the guards turned to face the wall of the abyss in a ready stance, backing away slowly. It was a display of the age-old debate between a spy and an assassin—one his father and mother constantly argued about.

Was it easier to hide in the shadows or in plain sight? The instinctive threat was darkness because it represented both the unknown and unpredictability. On the flipside, this only made it more difficult for an assassin to hide in it since attention would be drawn toward them, making them prepared for a strike.

Himitsu was to put this debate to rest. He stepped around the corner, clearly evident in his half of the hall's radiant sunlight. He should have been easy to locate, but with their minds consumed by the darkness in front of them, they had lost all awareness of anything behind them.

Himitsu stepped off, his sword readied on his shoulder. These officers had pledged their loyalties to evil men, so they had made their beds. His movement was smooth, and his footsteps were light enough to stay silent even in the Void. He decapitated two guards with one swing before impaling another through her spleen from behind. The other three turned. Himitsu whirled the woman around, ramming the end of the blade through another guard while the woman was still skewered.

He tried to rip the sword free from both of them, but was forced to barrel roll to the side as the remaining two guards pursued him. *Where was Fane?!*

One guard shot a gale through the hall, dispersing the flames in the windows and filling the space with light. And in that moment a ball of fire erupted from the end of the hall. Himitsu ducked as it flew over him and through the Spiritian traitor, igniting him in flames. The final man tried to run, but Himitsu chased him down, thrust his foot into his back, grabbed the back of his head, and slammed his face into the floor.

Fane stepped over a body. "Well, we managed to only kill five of the six."

"Not exactly humane," Himitsu said as he went back to retrieve his sword. He placed the sole of his shoe against the woman's back and yanked at the handle. It took a few tugs before it slid free.

"This is war, Himitsu. There is no humane. They'd kill us without thinking." As Fane checked the bodies for a set of keys, he said, "Jilly told me about a time when you and some of your fellow Jestivan entered the Dev Kingdom to rescue Olivia from Dev King Storshae … She said you arrived first, and when they came later, you were seated in the grass with roughly twenty dead soldiers scattered around you in the field."

Himitsu sighed. "I forgot about that."

Fane slowly shook his head. "Suppressed, not forgotten … remember that." After searching every carcass, only to come up empty, he said, "Was worth a try."

They gazed at the steel door, questioning the amount of flame it would take to melt it.

"Impossible," Himitsu said.

"What about your sword?" Fane asked.

"Do I look like Yama? I can't cut through steel as thick as Vuilni's arms."

They both turned as footsteps rounded the corner at the end of the hall. There stood Toth Brench in a gray plaid suit, his eyes widening at the disaster he had walked into. Quickly, he pivoted and ran the other way.

The two assassins pursued him, but Himitsu feared they wouldn't catch him since he was an Adrenian. His speed percentage had to be quite high.

Fortunately, it was an incorrect assumption. Himitsu tackled the man and pressed his face to the floor as he searched his pockets. All the stories Toshik had told about his father's inability to fight had been true. He had no physical talent whatsoever. Himitsu felt he might crush him as he dug his knee into his back.

"Who are you?" Toth asked, his voice muffled by the floor.

Himitsu didn't answer. Fane leaned against the wall behind them, occasionally glancing down the hallway littered with dead officers as a lookout. Himitsu turned Toth over and dug into his inner chest pocket. *Why was he dressed in a damned suit?*

He pulled out a ring of keys and tossed them back to Fane, who then disappeared to unlock the door. Himitsu stared into Toth's eyes and reached down for his blade. A part of him wanted to kill the man, but this wasn't just some man—this was Toshik's father. He gritted his teeth as he struggled with the decision, his fingers thrumming against his sword's handle.

He unsheathed it slightly, and Toth caught sight of the small exposed section of blade. His eyes grew wide. "Who are you?" he asked again. "That is the finest of blades my company makes. How did you get it?"

Himitsu drew it fully; blood coated its spunka spine. "A gift from Toshik," he said as he pressed the blade against the chief's neck. He pulled back his hood; the shadows cast by its deep hem disappeared to reveal his face.

Fear etched its way onto Toth's face as his mouth opened, babbling incoherently. "Himitsu …" he finally croaked.

The Jestivan took the sword away and stood, sheathing it at his hip. He couldn't kill Toshik's father, for Toshik had already lost a mother and sister. A sudden blast lifted Himitsu off his feet. He slid across the floor, wondering what had collided into his chest with such power. He had seen nothing.

He looked up to see a dark-skinned woman with deep blue hair and eyebrows. She stepped past Toth and casually strolled toward Himitsu. An invisible force tugged his arm forward, dragging him across the stone toward the mystery woman. These were techniques of a highly talented

Devish. She wasn't telekinetically manipulating simple objects; she was taking control of Himitsu's body.

He wisely conjured flames throughout the entirety of both halls, completely blocking the windows and creating darkness. He was surprised by the density of the black—he had expected a dimming effect like Fane's earlier flames. Something seemed off about it, but there was no time to ponder. The moment the grip on his arm released, he got up and ran toward the steel door only to be caught by someone's hand and yanked to the other end of the hall. They rounded the far corner and burst free of the shadows into another hall—this one, thankfully, empty.

Himitsu finally realized who had grabbed him—even through the untamed facial hair of black and gray. He threw his arms around the man and patted his back. "Good to see you, Dad."

* * *

Toth hurried down a spiraling staircase with Tazama on his heels. He was not only flustered, but embarrassed. "Bested by Ophala's son," Toth said. "I remember him from Rhyparia's litigation."

"Which is why he took your keys," Tazama said. "To rescue his parents."

"Get word to Wert. He's closest to the dungeons. I need him to get to Ophala's cell before the assassins."

"And what should I ask of him when he gets there?" Tazama asked, her eyes glowing burgundy.

"Kill her … and to do it quickly."

* * *

As the sun disappeared behind the horizon, Storshae explored the palace in search of Archaic Prince Sigmund. He knew which floor to search, but he wasn't sure of which door. Thus, he opened every single one he passed. The revolt had not only penetrated the walls of the palace, but had reached higher floors as the Lamaylian soldiers continued to prevail. Within the next few hours, Toth, Wert, and Sigmund would have control over Phelos, their hodgepodge army stationed throughout the capital.

A strange feathery sensation enveloped Storshae's insides as he reached a pair of mahogany doors. Water dripped from the keyholes. He placed a finger under a droplet and felt the liquid's cold bite. He had found the prince. He pulled the doors open, and a mountain of snow and slush spilled into the lobby. He stepped backward, but he stumbled as he spotted a woman with short jet-black hair and a blood-red cloak kneeling next to an immobile Sigmund. She glanced toward the Dev King and quickly morphed into a cluster of white lights that eventually fizzled out.

There was the answer to the question Storshae and Toono had always wondered. Archaic Prince Sigmund had an active Branian, and now they knew what they'd be up against if they ever had to dispose of the young man. It also meant Toth's efforts over the past year to solidify Sigmund's loyalty had been even more crucial than previously thought. If they had to battle a Branian during the uprising, the probability of success would have plummeted.

Storshae stepped through the slush and pulled the prince out of the room. He sat on the floor of the grand hall with Sigmund's head resting on his thigh. The prince was barely breathing, and it was likely he had his Branian to thank.

38
Without a Trace

Intel King Vitio and General Lars occupied the war room, brainstorming methods of taking out the *Whale Lord* as it arrived in the Gulf of Sodai. He had told Apsa during their broadcast that he and the Adren King had no choice but to accept her decision, but he'd be damned if that had actually been the truth. There would be repercussions.

"Well, the whole issue is her army of blue whales, sir," Lars said as he stared at the map of the gulf on the wall.

Vitio scratched at his face. "What about from land? Do we have any weapons or talented weavers capable of reaching it from the gulf's beaches? Or can we siege the fortress in the back of DaiSo and fire at it from high ground?"

"I see what you're getting at, milord. Whales can't attack any forces on land, but it isn't practical for us. Unless we can march a unit of soldiers into DaiSo, we're not going to reach any beaches or fortresses."

Vitio grumbled, "Queen Apsa will make sure that never happens."

"Exactly."

"So we must plan strictly for an encounter on water."

The room went silent as they perused their options. "Ah," Vitio said, his fingers sliding from his temple to his chin. "Why not make use of our energy? We are Intelians after all, which means we have an immense number of seashockers in our navy. Other kingdoms can't counter a fleet of whales because they only have one or two seashockers onboard to electrocute the water, whereas *we* have the personnel to completely staff a ship of nothing but seashockers if we wanted."

Lars nodded. "Very true, milord. We have hundreds of seashockers. If we were to put as many as we could on a ship, no whale would be able to surface and attack … they'd die before coming within a thousand meters."

There was a frantic pounding on the door. "Milord, milord!" someone shouted from outside. It sounded like Vistas, but the urgency in his normally placid voice was jarring.

Lars hurried across the room and opened the door. "What is it?"

The Dev servant barged through. He was clearly unnerved; his long black hair was matted to his forehead with sweat. He gazed at his king. "It's Phelos, milord. There's a massive revolution happening. The Amendment Order is being toppled and the palace has been swarmed. There are battles happening in the city streets—innocents and soldiers dying alike. Lava blankets the entire eastern grounds of the palace."

"Where'd you get this news from?!" Vitio shouted.

"Anonymous transmission from a fellow Dev servant in Phelos."

Vitio balked, hesitating as he leaned against his desk and stared at its parchment-strewn surface. "Dammit!" he barked. He glanced at Lars. "Gather your finest soldiers and head to the teleplatforms now! I want you arriving in the Archaic Kingdom within the hour!"

Lars sprinted out of the room, not even bothering with a response. And Vitio had come to realize that everything Queen Apsa had warned was true.

*   *   *

Chief Officer Wert Lamay tripped as he descended into the dungeons. He was unfamiliar with this area, as he tended to avoid it. Nothing sickened him more than coming down here and seeing that woman's face, knowing he couldn't kill her. Toth was always so mentally weak. But tonight proved to be a special occasion in more ways than just the uprising, for he had been given permission to cut the spy's throat.

A part of him admired Ophala for the simple fact that she had preserved her sanity in such a place as this. It was pitch black, not a single torch or candle to be seen. There was a bevy of guards stationed at the dungeon's two opposite entrances at all times, but once inside, the only life was Ophala.

Wert moved carefully, holding a torch in front of him, as he wended between dozens of empty cells. There were no walls—only a maze of steel bars. If there had been sufficient light, he'd have been able to spot Ophala from across the dungeon. He turned down a pathway, paused, and stared into its depths. As he extended his arm farther, someone's whistling carried from the end of the path. It resembled bird calls more so than a song. He pushed onward, following the fluttering sounds.

As he approached a cell at the dead end of a corridor, the whistling stopped. Ophala stood with her back against the stone wall, a foot kicked back against it. She had been playing with her nails when she gazed up to see her visitor.

"No Toth?" she asked with a frown.

"I'm sure you wished it to be him," Wert replied. "He's the only one who grants you mercy. You know if I'm here, then it means one thing."

"Not exactly why I'm bothered, but I guess I must make do."

Wert unlocked the gate and laughed. "The satisfaction this will bring me ... You remind me too much of that Tazama witch."

He drew a sword, approaching her with a menacing delight in his eyes. Ophala stood and closed her eyes, her aura radiating acceptance, as if she had prepared for this moment.

"That way!" someone yelled from across the dungeons, likely spotting the ember of Wert's torch in the distance.

Ophala's eyes opened. Wert made the decision to kill her swiftly, assuming that the strangers in the dark were the Passion Assassins Tazama had warned him about. As he thrust the sword toward her neck, his flame disappeared.

*　　*　　*

Himitsu, Fane, and Horos rushed through the dungeon. Wert's roars and ragged breaths guided them, but on too many occasions they'd collide with a steel bar in the dark. The three assassins split along the way, each trying to carve out the correct path to Ophala's cell.

Panic had set into Himitsu. With his father having had sucked the light from Wert's torch, they were relying on Ophala's ability to use the darkness to her advantage. She wasn't a fighter; she was a spy. If she could just do her best to evade Wert's blind blows and stall him, either Himitsu, Fane, or Horos could reach her.

Ophala's scream pierced through the dungeon.

"*Mom!*" Himitsu shouted, continuing to wend through pathways. He slammed into bars and literally tried prying them apart. All rationality had escaped him, and with it his composure. He sobbed as he felt his way down a path using the steel beams as a guide. He couldn't lose her—not his mother.

Flame ignited the dungeons nearby. He looked to his left to see his father holding a torch in Ophala's cell. He must have retrieved it from Wert.

Himitsu and Fane ran toward a motionless Horos. They flanked him and gazed toward the cell's back wall. A body lay on the cusp of death, slumped against the stone, minus a hand. Chief Officer Wert Lamay was bleeding out fast from his stump, his typical fiery red face as pale as ever.

Himitsu ran back out of the cell and glanced both ways down the path. "Where's Mom?" he asked.

"She likely escaped through the west entrance."

"Well, let's get out of here, then!" Himitsu yelled. "He's useless to us."

"You and Fane go," Horos said.

"Come on, Dad! Let him die!"

Horos paused as he knelt on one knee. "I want to make sure he does. Get out of here now!"

Himitsu and Fane bolted out of the cell, leaving Horos behind.

*　　*　　*

Intel General Lars arrived at the Intel Kingdom's teleplatforms several miles outside of Dunami with a squadron of steel-clad soldiers. They boarded a special teleplatform designed specifically for a purpose such as this—transportation of a large militarized unit.

A hundred men and women situated themselves on the teleplatform in a specific formation—a strategy practiced twice a week ever since Mendac built the Light Realm's teleplatforms decades ago. A string of archers wrapped around the platform's circular edge, standing close enough together to block sight of the platform's center. Behind this ring were three other circles of weavers and close-combat fighters, all of whom were crouched low to the ground. And the final ring wrapping around General Lars at the platform's center consisted of more archers, but with their bows pointed toward the sky.

General Lars signaled for the teleplatform to be activated. The military conductor flipped the lever, kicking the contraption into gear. Unlike the civilian platforms, this one didn't need to slowly build up its speed. It accelerated with enough torque to throw out someone's spine if they had not braced for it.

"Keep a proper grasp of the supports!" Lars shouted.

Just as he reminded them, an archer at the outer edge lost grip of his beam and jerked forward during the moment of teleportation. His top half didn't teleport with his legs. Blood sprayed across a dozen people positioned nearby, and as the teleplatform came to a stop in the Archaic Kingdom, his legs—severed at the waist—toppled off the stage and into the dirt.

But there wasn't time to absorb the unsightliness of it. A pillar of ice shot up and through the teleplatform, cracking the surface and impaling an archer. Then another perforated across its width, skewering two more.

A battalion of soldiers in green vests surrounded the teleplatform. Four individuals—presumably the leaders—stood at the front, each one occupying a point around the circle. A blond-haired man had been the culprit of the ice attacks. The other three were women, and their uniforms didn't coordinate with the soldiers they led. They wore burgundy. The oldest of the three ladies wore an immense cloak with holographic symbols revolving around it. A Stillian and three Devish were heading a mishmash army of Light Realm soldiers …

Lars hesitated from the absurdity of it all, but swiftly recovered. His squadron couldn't sit back in a group like this. "*CHARGE!*"

The archers on the platform's edge shot a flurry of arrows into the green-cloaked battalion. The intrinsic infantry charged with swords drawn while the weavers—the specialty infantry—stepped forward and began lighting the night with voltaic surges. Then the innermost circle of archers shot arrows into the sky from their crouched positions.

As opposing sides clashed, Lars ran off the platform. He noticed the Devish lady with the holographic cloak eyeing him down, but not bothering to pursue him. The arrows that had been directed into the sky rained down upon the field. Some struck true, but most had been felled by skyward blasts of fire from Passionians cloaked in green.

Lars squeezed a button on his leather wristband, and a blade dropped into his grasp from his forearm. He planted his foot, stopping on a dime, as a swordsman whiffed past him on a swing and lurched forward. Lars shoved the man farther off balance with his boot, but then continued sprinting through the battle without a second thought. He needed to get back to the Intel Kingdom.

As he approached the control panel, he faltered as he directed his attention toward the wall of the nearby terminal. Hanging from the building's rafters was Grand Director Poicus, his eyes a translucent white under the moonlight. He had been sacrificed—likely a long while ago. And now he served as a threat of what was to come.

Lars had led his soldiers into a trap. When he had situated them into formation before departing, it was less of a strategy and more of him simply going through the motions. It never crossed his mind that they'd be met with opposition upon arriving. Vistas had only mentioned Phelos, and Lars hadn't imagined the supposed revolution stretching this far across the kingdom. He had understood the severity of the situation, but underestimated the scope.

With the pillar of ice that had penetrated the teleplatform they had arrived on, it was now out of commission. Thus Lars pulled the lever for one of the smaller civilian transports. He then quickly rounded the battle, taking a seldom pause to electrocute a green-vested soldier. He was surprised by the lack of attention he received. As he leapt onto the slowly spinning platform, he shouted back for others to join him. Instead, they continued to fight valiantly and die at the hands of traitors they had once called allies. Meanwhile their general fled, unscathed with his tail tucked between his legs.

The Devish woman observed him from a distance. She hadn't moved from her spot. She held up a sheet of parchment and released it. It flew through the air as if caught by wind before smacking Lars in the face. He pulled it off just as the platform hit its moment of teleportation.

As he returned to the Intel Kingdom, officers who had stayed behind turned to see the Intel General slumped against a support beam—bloodied, exhausted, and terrified. These officers had witnessed him leave just ten minutes ago, but he'd had a squadron with him then. Clearly, they had been bested.

He gazed down at the parchment. It was addressed to four kingdoms: Intel, Passion, Spirit, and Adren. The very first line read: "A message from King Toth Brench and Prince Storshae Dev."

39
The New King

King Vitio and Queen Delilah each occupied an armchair in the parlor, sipping from glasses of chardonnay as they awaited more news on Phelos's current condition. Vitio couldn't sleep with such uncertainty swirling through his mind, so Delilah stayed by his side as a comforting presence.

"The last time I saw you this distraught were the weeks prior to Mendac's death," Delilah said.

He finished off his drink and stared blankly at the fireplace. "Is that so?"

"Not even the Generals' Battle had you rattled to a point of silence."

"Words fail me as of right now, love," he mumbled. "All I'm seeing in my head is one of the Light Realm's grand cities up in flame."

"You should have listened—"

"To Apsa." He sighed. "Yes, I know."

A long stretch of silence passed before Vitio said, "Toth and Wert wouldn't be doing this unless they had support. Otherwise, they know the rest of the Light Realm would simply barge in and take the land back." He paused and shook his head. "He must have King Storshae on his side … maybe a couple other kingdoms too."

"Dev, Power, and Still?" Delilah asked.

"Most likely. Prim has always been neutral, and the Cyn Kingdom is impossible to even communicate with, let alone coordinate."

Three knocks came through the parlor door. Vitio turned in his seat. "Come in." His face fell as Vistas stepped inside. "Well, this can't be good. You're nothing but a harbinger of bad news, lately."

"Milord, General Lars has returned to the palace."

"Already? It's only been an hour tops. Where are they?"

"It's just him, milord. He's in the war corridor declining medical attention."

Vitio shot out of his seat and gave Delilah a kiss on her forehead before storming out of the parlor.

He arrived at the war corridor to find Lars slowly circling a massive three-dimensional replica of Kuki Sphaira at the center. Hanging from the ceiling and constructed of real gold wiring, it was far bigger than any person.

"What happened?" the king asked.

Lars stopped pacing, his somber gaze falling on Vitio. He spoke softly. "They were waiting for us."

"Who?"

"An entire battalion of soldiers from different kingdoms, including a man using Still Energy and three women in the unmistakable burgundy of the Dev Kingdom."

Vitio's eyes narrowed as he stepped closer to his general. "And where are your men now?"

Lars's eyes fell to the floor. "Still back there," he murmured.

"*And likely slaughtered!*" Vitio bellowed loud enough to be heard all the way in Ferrous. "You abandoned your unit?!"

"I had to—"

"*Ludicrous!*"

Lars's back collided with the module as Vitio pressed forward. He tried to argue his case: "If I didn't return, you wouldn't have known what happened. Either I return and inform you immediately or I stay and die, leaving you in the dark for who knows how long while you idly sit here waiting for news. It would have been the fiasco of Passion King Damian's disappearance all over again, milord."

Vitio backed away. "And how did you escape?"

"They allowed me to. There was a woman in a strange cloak with holographic symbols that spun around her."

"If you recall our interrogations of Vuilni Gesluimant a year ago, you'll remember that she described such a woman to be the Dev Warden of Ipsas. She was at Phesaw during the invasion! You're a general; you should be able to recall important information!"

Lars pulled the parchment from his cloak. "Well, she telekinetically flung this at me right before I was transported back here—a message I guess she wanted delivered."

King Vitio snatched it and read the first line. He crumpled it and tossed it across the room. "You think I'm naïve, General?"

"Excuse me, milord?"

"You didn't run away to inform me of anything." Vitio's anger grew with more intensity as he continued his rant. "Clearly they had every intention of telling us if they had this written out beforehand, and they would've done so with or without your skills as a messenger." Vitio struck the module's wiring with his fist, sending it rocking back and forth and spinning on its axis. "You ran because you were scared … you're a *coward*."

* * *

Vitio leaned against a table in the war corridor's far corner. It was a space much bigger than the war room, but reserved for worldwide wars. It had been centuries since it had been put to use.

Lars had already left, granting the king a moment to himself before his other guest arrived. Vitio was mulling over a specific piece of information in the note he had just received. There was a kingdom listed in the newly formed enemy alliance—now called SCAPD—that he had never expected to see … the Cyn Kingdom.

Since the beginning of Known History, the Void has distanced itself from the rest of Kuki Sphaira—socially and politically speaking. It almost seemed like its own planet. None of the royal heads—dark or light—could ever succeed in garnering a response from the Cynnish royal head when coerced, nor did they really know the right way to try to get a message to him in the first place. And nobody bothered venturing too deep into the kingdom in fear of what they'd experience. The Linsani, for one, were notorious monsters with countless legends, each more dreadful than the last. It was one of the reasons why Vitio had been irate with Poicus when he had sent Lilu all the way to Spachny two years ago.

A familiar knocking pattern thrummed through the door. "Come in."

Vistas entered with a bow. "Milord."

Vitio nodded in response, pushing himself off the table and clearing his throat. "I need you to get in touch with your fellow Devish in the Passion, Spirit, and Adren Kingdoms. A summit needs to be scheduled between the royal heads. But we must first convene through broadcast to make arrangements such as location and a date."

"I'll get right on it, sir," Vistas replied. "Seems like you and Spirit Queen Apsa are on the same page, for Joy's already contacted me with a similar request."

The king's head rolled back as he sighed. "She's on top of everything, isn't she?"

Vistas was on his way out when he turned around and asked, "Is it wise for Queen Apsa and Adren King Supido to meet in person, milord? King Supido threatened her during the last broadcast."

The Intel King strolled toward the module of Kuki Sphaira hanging at the room's center. He gazed at it for a moment. "With what we're up against now, they have no choice but to swallow their pride."

*   *   *

Himitsu and Fane scurried around the palace's carcass-littered first floor, desperately hunting for Ophala. With each empty room they entered, however, the more Himitsu's frustration mounted. "Where would she have gone?"

"She may have fled already," Fane said, opening up another door only to close it immediately.

An enemy charged Himitsu from an attached hall. Himitsu dodged left and slashed the woman's hamstring as she ran past. She crashed awkwardly into a dead comrade and released an agonizing groan. Himitsu silenced her by thrusting his blade into the back of her neck.

"She wouldn't have left without us," Himitsu said.

The pair regrouped at the foyer's center and looked around. They could hear fights carrying on from the floors above. "Her letter said that she had a plan of her own once she escaped." Uncertainty flashed across Fane's face as he said, "Maybe she meant immediately after?"

Himitsu scowled, displeased if that was the case. She could have at least said something to her only child.

Horos sprinted into the foyer. "We have to get out of here now, while the uprising is still ongoing."

"Where's Mom?!" Himitsu shouted back.

"Don't worry about her. She's fine." Horos combed their surroundings. "If we're still in Phelos by the time Toth and his crew gain control, they'll sniff us out when they begin searching every building in the capital. Let's go!"

Horos ran past, and Fane joined. Himitsu paused, as he fought the urge to search the palace in its entirety. Eventually he chased after his dad and Fane. While the three assassins burst into the night, conjuring black flames to mask their presence, Himitsu dwelled on the image of his mother. He hadn't seen her in forever. Tonight was supposed to be the night she became more than a mere presence in his dreams.

* * *

Toth Brench swept through the dungeons with a lantern in hand. He had traveled down here too often to become lost. As he approached the final cell and saw whom it occupied, he broke into a sprint. He knelt down, placing the lantern on the floor, and examined Wert. His breathing was shallow, his eyes closed.

Toth slapped the golden scruff on his cheeks. "Get up, Wert."

The man grumbled, and his eyes peeled open. His gaze flickered to Toth, unable to tilt his head. "She's gone. Others interfered."

"I figured." Toth glanced at Wert's nub of a wrist. "Who wrapped you up?"

"I'm not sure," Wert said through a wheeze. "I blacked out earlier … was pretty sure I'd bleed out and die."

"Well, you have someone to thank. Let me go get you help."

* * *

The dark blue of night turned into the gray of early dawn, as the halls of Phelos finally fell quiet. The only soldiers who remained alive were those dressed in green—the colors of Wert Lamay's newly established military. Dev King Storshae stood in the throne room with Kadlest, Toth, and Tazama. All four of them gazed at the city below as the sun's light stretched above the horizon.

"How did those two assassins have everything planned so meticulously?" Storshae asked. "They were prepared. They weren't simply here by luck."

"My intuition tells me Ophala," Tazama said.

"From the confines of prison?"

His question was met with silence.

Groups of soldiers traversed the city streets below. Some were cleaning the streets of corpses while others knocked on doors, entering civilian homes and establishments to search every inch of space. It was a one-time measure that needed to be taken to root out any remaining threats to the capital. Hopefully they'd find Himitsu and the older man he was with—along with Ophala and Horos.

Storshae pulled at his collar. "With Wert currently out of commission as he's being tended to by doctors, someone needs to tell Elyol to rescind the lake of lava. This kingdom is already insufferably hot as it is."

Kadlest immediately headed for the double doors. "If it means not being near you."

Storshae stared at the back of Toth, who was leaning against the window frame a few paces ahead of him. "A new king," Storshae said.

"What's a king without his heir?"

"Ah." This brought Storshae's attention beyond the capital. The tips of Bliss Peaks were visible in one direction, but the Archaic Mountains were far out of sight despite their size. "Fair point."

Toth whirled and glared at Storshae. "Wert and I did all of this for our children. The plan was to take over this kingdom and rule it well. Then we'd turn our children into a matrimonial powerhouse. All of these other kingdoms … the royal head is dominant and powerful, but they squander all potential by marrying someone weak. That isn't to be the same here. People will respect the names Toshik and Jilly Brench."

Storshae noticed Toth's gaze occasionally flutter toward Tazama in the background. He turned and smirked at the Dev servant. "Are you looking at her for consoling?" He glanced back. "Interesting dynamic."

Toth ignored the tease. "You believe Toono will be able to retrieve my son and future daughter-in-law safely? If not, I'm sending people to Rim."

Storshae paused without breaking eye contact. "I do," he lied.

40
War's Haste

Toono followed a stream in the greenest section of mountains they'd found yet. Yama walked purposefully out ahead—a woman on a mission with no signs of slowing down. Illipsia, meanwhile, lollygagged behind, chucking sticks into the water and skimming pebbles across the surface.

"Hey, you're supposed to be keeping track," Toono said, turning to face her as he walked backward.

She frowned. "It's useless. I don't sense anything."

"Stop whining and do your job!" Yama shrieked from a few dozen yards ahead.

"I'd like it if we avoided an unhappy Yama for at least one day," Toono said.

Illipsia sighed. "She's a bully."

Slowing down, he laughed and pulled her against his hip. "I knew bullies when I was younger. Even though I could handle them, I tried my best to refrain from fighting back then." He pointed to Yama in the distance. "She was the one who'd make sure they regretted it."

After a pause, Illipsia said, "Five minutes."

They both stopped while Yama continued following the stream. Toono waited while Illipsia closed her eyes. Her grasp of Dev weaving's technical aspects was marvelous. She wasn't particularly talented when it came to clout or thrust, but if it involved a creative algorithm of EC clusters, she could crack it. It was why she had been able to avoid the eyes of Olivia over the course of an entire school year—she had tracked the Jestivan's location at all times. Clairvoyance occupied the highest tier of difficulty for abilities that a Devish intelligence officer could have in their arsenal. Like truth extracting, the number of people capable of such skills could be counted on one hand. But *they* were all full-fledged adults … Illipsia had just turned thirteen.

She opened her eyes and shook her head. "Nothing."

Toono patted her shoulder. "That's fine. Let's keep moving."

After some time, Illipsia asked, "Yama is chasing down this man all because of jealousy and spite?"

"Partially. The two of them never really got along throughout their lives."

"How long have they known each other?"

"Years," Toono said, recalling the one time Yama had told him a story about herself. "She and Toshik attended the Adren Assistance Academy, which is an academy made for Adrenian boys and girls aged three to ten. She told me that they were always at odds."

"Is that like Phesaw?"

"Not really. Phesaw's mostly a boarding school. The AAA only held classes on certain days and kept the focus on speed training and sword fighting, which involved balance, agility, and reflexes. The academy also instilled values such as responsibility, perseverance, and self-motivation into the children. But most importantly, they turned them into protectors. And when they graduated, they were assigned a charge whom they vowed to protect for life."

"And you—an orphan—were given a protector?" Illipsia asked.

Toono's eyes dulled. "Yes, even an orphan." They split away from the stream to follow Yama around the base of a mountain. He lowered his voice. "Yama guards her past with aggression, so what I'm about to say is in confidence, and you will keep it to yourself. And I'm only telling you this so that you realize there is more depth to her than you think."

The girl nodded.

"The AAA had a special division of students who dedicated themselves to protecting the underprivileged. The Adrenian children who volunteered to be a part of such a division forsook higher pay and benefits down the road. There is a wide array of circumstances that label someone as 'underprivileged' and thus a benefactor of the program. I, being an orphan, was such an example. That's how I became Yama's charge."

As Illipsia dragged a stick along the ground, she said, "That surprises me. She doesn't strike me as selfless—especially *that* selfless."

"Her reserved psyche presents that image," Toono said. "But something about Yama that nobody knows is that she too was an orphan—or at least that's what she told me long ago. And that's why she joined the program … She wanted to protect someone, as a parent would have for her." He went quiet, then added, "Don't get me wrong. She does have dark tendencies."

"So now she's your protector again?"

Toono laughed, watching as Yama split a boulder in two with her sword instead of walking around it. "She has her own goals in life that require unbelievable preparation—goals I don't know much about, if I'm being honest. And now she follows me for the time being, knowing that she wouldn't receive better battle simulations than the ones I'd present to her."

Night came, and the three travelers took residence amongst a group of black ash trees. Toono sat against a tree's base while Yama and Illipsia slept on layers of cloaks, frequently stirring in their sleep from the discomfort of the forest floor. He debated on how long he'd allow this hunt to continue. The uprising had been days ago, yet there had been no word from Storshae. He was beginning to question its outcome and hated the fact that he had abandoned it to commit to this foolish quest.

Illipsia woke up, yawned, and rubbed her eyes. The moment she took her hands away from her face, a holographic display lit up the night with Dev King Storshae's face. "Hello, Toono."

"What's the verdict?" Toono asked, leaning forward and placing an arm across his knee.

"Success. Toth Brench is king, and I'm presently in a carriage in the Dev Kingdom on my way to Cosmos, where I'll be waiting for you."

"Was it a smooth transition?"

"About as smooth as you'd expect from a revolution … so no, not really."

Toono gave him an exasperated look. "You know what I mean. Any surprises?"

"One of the Jestivan made an appearance—Ophala and Horos's boy."

"Himitsu …" Toono mumbled.

"Yes, him," Storshae said, snapping his finger. "He, along with a fellow unknown Passion Assassin, managed to free Ophala and Horos."

Toono plopped the back of his head against the tree. This wouldn't have happened had he been in Phelos as planned. Storshae could have stopped it, but he was probably enamored by the enemy's destruction amidst his own triumph. "Well, that makes future endeavors difficult," Toono said.

"The woman doesn't have her ancient, so she's useless. Toth found it still in his office."

"You're smarter than that," Toono said—although it was a lie. "She doesn't need to see through a bird's eyes to be a threat. A spy doesn't become a spy because of their ancient. It's their mind. They're cunning. You should know about this since you're Devish—a race of people prided on their deception."

Storshae's pleasurable smirk turned sour, as was often the case when the two men held discussions. "The Amendment Order has been overthrown, and that's what matters." The Dev King paused. "Try not to die out there."

The display disappeared. Toono had grown tired of Storshae's reckless disregard of the details, the subtleties that happen within the larger picture. He was nothing like the tales of his father, Dev King Rehn. And because of this, Toono would have to keep an even tighter lid on his objectives and missions in the future. An imprisoned Ophala was already a nuisance, but now that she was freed, he couldn't risk anyone else outside of his closest circle knowing his plans.

As Toono lay on his side, struggling to rid his mind of the stress, he failed to notice a shadow stir in the distant trees. It was a pudgy man, with a vest too small to button at the front—the same one who had retrieved Rhyparia NuForce from the mountains a year ago. Quickly, the man vanished, sprinting wildly to the north.

* * *

Intel King Vitio stood on a circular stage as he was lifted into Shelly's bedroom in the sky tower. He hadn't visited her room in months; his focus was on respecting his daughter's privacy. But the princess had spent the past couple months cooped up in her room, hiding from every person in the palace—including him. The only person allowed to visit had been Vistas, which Vitio found disheartening, as her father. So he'd decided enough was enough.

"Good evening, Father," Shelly said from a twisted bundle of blankets on the sofa. She seemed unsurprised by his intrusion.

Vitio inhaled deeply as he gazed up through the ceiling of glass. "Cherish this place so far from the rest of the world. All that exists are the clouds beneath and the sky above you."

"Melodrama does not suit you," Shelly said. "Leave that to Mother and Lilu."

"I miss Lilu," he mused.

"You're the one who sent her away."

Vitio's gaze fell to the princess before taking a seat in a recliner. "How's Bryson doing at home?"

Shelly paused. "Fantastic. He and Thusia are really hitting it off."

"Would he mind returning to the palace? It still needs to be scheduled, but I'll be leaving for a summit within the month. I'd like to have the both of you in the palace while I'm gone." His gaze fell to the side. "I don't have much faith in Lars at this point." He became quiet as he swam through his jumbled thoughts. He eventually snapped out of it. "Because of this," he said, "I want Bryson and the rest of the Jestivan to play a role in the war. I'm sure he'd want to hear that after being restrained for nearly a year."

Shelly picked up a file and began smoothing her fingernails. "Some of them are already doing that without your permission. Even so, times must be desperate if you've come to this."

"They are."

"Well, Father, I can't."

"And why not?"

Shelly looked up from her nails. "Bryson isn't home. He's in the Archaic Mountains with Vuilni, searching for Olivia."

Another prolonged silence followed. "What did you do?" he asked, his voice trembling.

"I snuck into your office, wrote up an entry document using your mock-ups as references, forged your signature, and sealed it to make it official," she explained, an unbearable lightness to her tone.

"The Archaic Kingdom is overrun by Toth and Wert now!" Vitio said. "Bryson is behind enemy lines and doesn't even know it! Do you even care about the boy?"

The stillness wiped itself clean from Shelly's face, her eyes narrowing at the fiercest of angles. "He is no boy," she stated. "I sent him there well before any of us knew about what was going to happen in Phelos. And don't speak all high and mighty, Father; you sent Olivia in there first."

Their eyes locked for what felt like minutes before Vitio finally muttered, "I had to. It was expected of me."

"And you made the wrong decision." Shelly gazed down at her blankets, her voice weakening with her next words: "I might have done the same."

*　　*　　*

King Vitio sat at his desk in his office while Vistas began a broadcast connecting him with Adren King Supido, Spirit Queen Apsa, and Passion Director Venustas. As each member appeared, they exchanged brief greetings. The lone exception was between Supido and Apsa, who were still not on speaking terms ever since receiving the news of the *Whale Lord* wiping out Supido's twenty Adrenian navy ships.

"You must see now why it had to happen," Apsa said a few minutes into the meeting. "The last thing I wanted was for hundreds of innocent soldiers to die, but the two of you wouldn't listen to me. Could you imagine if Toth obtained all of that wealth in addition to the land? Catastrophic for us."

Supido stayed mum, so Vitio said, "You were right, Apsa. But we must move on and focus on what's happening now."

A small, forced laugh escaped her lips. "That proves difficult if Supido doesn't escape this grudge of his."

"The two of you will have to work on that another time. For now we need to schedule an on-site summit between the four of us. We must establish short and long-term goals, with the ultimate objective being to end this war as soon as possible."

"You end wars before they start," Apsa said. "That opportunity was missed."

"Seems like you, too, hold a grudge," Supido said.

Vitio exhaled and rubbed his eyes before switching topics. "Venustas, would you happen to know where any of the Jestivan are?"

"Himitsu Vevlu arrived to Fiamma in the early morning hours today along with Horos and Fane. And I actually sent Toshik Brench and Jilly Lamay into the Archaic Mountains a while back."

"Why do we keep sending people into the mountains?" Vitio asked, clearly annoyed.

"To retrieve a citizen of the Passion Kingdom whom you unlawfully passed sentence. You do not hold authority over Olivia, for she committed no crime within your kingdom." Every other word of Venustas's statement was dripping with venom.

He paused, biting his tongue. This was not the time for petty quibbles. "Well, all of this complicates matters. I don't think Himitsu can do it alone, but you did say Horos was around. He escaped prison?"

"Himitsu and Fane freed both him and Ophala, but the spy pilot is missing," Venustas said. "I'm told she knows what she's doing, though."

"Would the three assassins be willing to reenter the Archaic Kingdom and head for Rim?"

The director smirked. "You must know the answer to that question. Himitsu is a Jestivan. If it's for his friends, then yes."

* * *

Himitsu, Horos, and Fane entered Nature's Heart, the rotunda in Fiamma Palace where they had last convened with Toshik and Jilly before departing on their separate quests. Himitsu was staring into the green leaves of the oak tree when he spotted the face of Passion Director Venustas leaning over the balcony's rail of the second floor. Passion Queen Fiona appeared next to her.

Venustas leapt over the banister and landed on the rotunda's main floor, while Fiona descended a ladder against the wall. "I hate to ask this of you, Himitsu," the director said, "but can you head back to the Archaic Kingdom?"

Horos stepped forward. "For what?"

"Bryson, Olivia, Toshik, Jilly, and Vuilni are still in the Archaic Mountains. I don't want you to enter them, but I ask that you wait for their exit in Rim. The bounty on Rhyparia's head disappears in two weeks. Olivia's punishment will have ended by then, which means the rest of the Jestivan will exit to see if she did—if they haven't already found her, that is. Everyone would reconvene in Rim and head back to the teleplatforms together, where I'm sure your combined forces could handle any threat. Bryson does have Thusia, after all. But as an added precaution, Intel King Vitio has volunteered Vistas to travel with you. He will aid greatly in the escape when that time comes."

"Sounds easy enough," Himitsu said. "I've infiltrated an enemy kingdom by myself before—and that was when I was a novice."

Horos grasped his son's shoulder. "Looks like I'm tagging along."

Fane smirked. "We enter the belly of the beast again … one mission after another." He glanced at Horos. "Looks like we're back to our old ways, partner."

41
A Pool of Crimson

With the bounty on Rhyparia's head ending within the week, Toshik and Jilly were retreating from the depths of the mountain range. It felt hopeless at this point since they still hadn't found Olivia. She was either already on her way out of the mountains or dead. Toshik retrieved a compass from his pocket and adjusted his path south. He scanned their surroundings, a gray sea of lowlands swallowed by a cluster of mountains. They had traveled the opposite way through here a month back, which meant they were nearing civilization.

"When we get out of here, Olivia will be safe," Jilly proclaimed while she skipped between broken stones, despite the heavy travel sack on her back.

Toshik wasn't as optimistic, but he kept that to himself. "Yes, she will," he said.

They traveled for another hour or so before Toshik heard what sounded like a sword being unsheathed to his right. He glanced that way only to immediately step back with one foot, draw his own sword, and deflect an unexpected blade.

Jilly whirled as the attacker planted her foot in the gravel to stop her momentum. "Yama!" Jilly said.

The violet-haired swordswoman didn't respond. Instead she stepped off, reaching Toshik in a split-second. He sloppily parried her swing, stumbling backward from her velocity. Just like when they were children at the Adren Assistance Academy or during their teenage years at Phesaw, her speed percentage was still considerably higher than his. If someone was fast enough to appear as though they were teleporting even to a trained eye like Toshik's, then that person was more than just formidable … they were unstoppable.

"Yama! Stop it!" Jilly screamed, all childlike innocence in her tone eradicated.

Yama's speed was at an all-time high, but she had no control of her cadence. Her badly timed maneuvers allowed Toshik to block her bombardment. He could tell by the fury etched into her face that her disdain for him was affecting her discipline. And he knew his relationship with Jilly wasn't the only source; this was years of his actions toward her coming to fruition.

Screaming steel pierced the air as Toshik fended off blow after blow. His moves were equally as reckless. He only wished that he had the excuse of his emotions like Yama—not his utter lack of skill.

Wind gusts materialized, slowly dragging the two Adrenians through the gravel. Toshik gazed past Yama as he blocked another attack. "Jilly!" he screamed. "Stop interfering and get out!"

Yama came to a rest a safe distance from Toshik. "Listen to him, Jilly. He won't be around much longer, anyway."

"Stop this," Jilly said, her brows furrowed with frustration and anger. Jilly always smiled. While she had serious moments, sorrow was typically the cause. This rage, however, was forlorn.

Toshik noticed another presence off to the side, seated on a stone amongst a cluster of boulders. It was a young man with bandages circling the top of his head. He watched the three Jestivan in a calm manner—one leg dangling from the rock, the other bent with his forearm resting across it.

A staff with three loops at the end was tied to his back. That had to be Toono.

A young girl popped her head out from behind a boulder and lay across it on her stomach, her raven hair hanging down the side before curling in the dirt. Were Toshik's eyes deceiving him? Why was a little girl in these mountains? And he could have sworn he recognized her from somewhere.

"Eyes over here," Yama said.

Toshik turned forward. "You have no interest in Jilly, I'm assuming."

"You're my only concern."

Yama disappeared. Toshik braced his sword for impact, but nothing came. He realized Yama wasn't on the ground anymore. Pebbles hovered in the air at various heights, and she was rebounding between them. Eventually she plummeted toward him from above. He did a back handspring, her sword skimming the toe of his shoes. He landed on his feet and leaned backward, parallel to the ground while Yama's sword glided over him. He knocked it away with a swipe of his own blade. As his body recoiled back to its upright position, he grabbed her wrist and flung her behind him. He tried ramming his sword into her back as she stumbled forward, but Yama's quickness was overwhelming.

She twirled and parried, blades scraping against each other, becoming the aggressor once again. This time she was merciless. She screamed with each mighty swing. And now Toshik didn't only have to worry about avoiding her sword, but avoiding the entire path in which she swung. Razor-like gusts of wind cut through the air from the speed of her blade—effectively extending her sword's reach by hundreds of feet. With one hack, she blasted a crater into the base of a nearby mountainside.

As chunks of mountain rained down behind Toshik, the gravel rattled beneath their feet. Yama took to the sky again, but she was slung sideways midair as a twister formed. The winds ripped against their eardrums as rocks were swept from the ground and consumed by the torqueing gales. Toshik threw his arms in front of his face as rubble pelted him. Jilly might have been causing him more damage than Yama had. He'd suffer through it, though, knowing that Yama was also overwhelmed as she tried to gain control of her flailing body, which she couldn't do without solid ground beneath her feet.

It was nearly impossible to see anything outside of the tornado, but within it Toshik noticed slabs of stone coming to a complete stop despite the winds. And now he understood the hovering rocks from earlier. There was a Devish somewhere around here. Was it the little girl accompanying Toono off to the side?

Yama's feet managed to make contact with a frozen rock. She then pushed off and reached the ground. Her feet dug into the gravel as she pushed against the tornado's torque. What had been a struggle to simply walk became a jog, which led to running, and then a sprint. She was trying to reach a speed percentage that could counter and negate the winds. And Toshik's jaw nearly dropped at the sight.

But it proved pointless, as the winds dissipated on their own. Jilly was now contained within what appeared to be a glass dome. She pounded against it with no luck—not even blasts of wind did the trick.

Toshik had only glanced at her for a split second when something slashed open his shoulder. He screamed, spinning around as Yama had blown past him. But he was too slow. She'd already vanished again, and this time it was the tendons in the back of his ankles that were obliterated. He fell to his knees and grabbed his shoulder as warm blood spilled between his fingers … all the while he could hear Jilly's muffled wails from within the strange bubble.

Yama sped past and ripped open his back with another laceration, causing a pitiful groan to morph into a roar. His face smacked into the gravel. He reached back only to feel more blood dampening his shirt. His body was draining itself, yet all he could think about was Jilly's safety. At least he knew Yama wouldn't let anything happen to her.

Then the air grew heavy—unbearably heavy out of nowhere, and it only intensified with each passing second. It was a familiar sensation for Toshik, and he knew only one person who could create it. They'd entered these mountains to find Olivia, but they may have stumbled upon a different Jestivan—likely the most dangerous of them all. Panic blanketed Yama's face—something Toshik hadn't siphoned out of her even once.

The land roared while entire mountainsides collapsed, a new landscape being molded right before their very eyes. The crust beneath them sunk. First, a few feet, but then far enough to feel like the ground had been ripped from beneath them. The bubble entrapping Jilly began to crack. Even Toono stood, gazing around in astonishment as he witnessed power the likes none of them had ever experienced before. It looked as if the mountains around them were being swallowed by the kingdom.

Meanwhile, they all thought the same thing: Would they die here?

Yama pressed forward, resisting the pressure to keel over. As she stood above Toshik, she lifted her sword against the gravity, her face red with unimaginable effort. She screamed and slashed downward with as much strength as she ever had in her life, the increased gravity aiding the effort—a finishing blow. What happened next was instantaneous.

A dress fluttered in front of Toshik, long blonde hair and a sunhat hanging down its back. The sword slashed across her chest instead of his …

And Jilly fell to the ground, a pool of crimson flooding beneath her.

42
Suffering

Bryson and Vuilni traveled south to return to the entrance of the Archaic Mountains. All they could do was hope that Olivia had made it out alive. He expected promising news, considering not only her talents, but the number of skilled bounty hunters she'd traveled with.

As he limped through the tangled underbrush of a forest—his shin tightly wrapped against the wound he had suffered from his fall against Warden Feissam—the ground shook underneath him. Leaves fell from rustling trees. The two friends stopped, inspecting the farthest reaches of the forest around them. Even Feissam wasn't capable of such tremors.

"What is that?" Vuilni asked while it continued.

"Feels like twenty earthquakes at once," Bryson replied. The sky grumbled, and he added, "And sounds like twenty avalanches."

"This isn't right. This doesn't feel or sound like nature's destruction."

"You can't be suggesting it's human."

"It's something," she muttered.

He gazed west, down the slanted forest floor. After a ponderous moment, he headed toward the noise.

"Are you out of your mind?" Vuilni said. "We're not following it!"

"Olivia might be that way!" he hollered back. "If you're coming with, let's go. I'm picking up the pace."

* * *

Time seemed to have paused as Toshik gaped at the dying image of the love of his life. The color in Jilly's face drained as fast as the blood from her chest. He crawled toward her, his feet limp behind him. Yama dropped to her knees, eyes bubbling from the realization of what she'd just committed.

Gravity had returned to normal, and the two rivals were frozen in shock as they watched Jilly's eyelids close over her cerulean eyes. The warm smile she had displayed throughout her life was gone; she was too weak to express anything—or even speak a word for that matter.

Even though Toshik knew it was hopeless, he still tried to stop the bleeding with his hands. The laceration across her chest was deep enough to have split ribs. Yama had likely struck internal organs, and considering the location—directly over Jilly's heart—there was no coming back.

"Talk to me, Jilly," he begged as he began to suck in air, heaving uncontrollably. "Hang on, love." Images of his sister and mother invaded. Once again he was going to lose a woman close to him without even hearing her voice.

Yama sat on her knees, staring blankly at the girl once filled with a spirit unrivaled. Her anger toward Toshik had taken a backseat to the overwhelming remorse over what she'd just done.

Toono joined them, his eyes on Yama rather than Jilly. He retrieved a knife from his waist. "This wasn't how this was planned," he whispered. "I'm sorry, Yama." He thrust the knife into Jilly's throat, causing Toshik's eyes to close as the Spirit Jestivan's gags rattled through the air.

Toshik fell upon her, his own body succumbing to its wounds. As the side of his face lay against her stomach, the blurry image of Toono stood above him. The Rogue Demon knelt next to him. "It was supposed to be only you. I'll make it quick." He paused for a moment. "I met a man in the Void once. His words ring true in this instance ... *Death heals anguish.*"

Toshik was thankful to feel fingers grasp his hair and lift his head, exposing his neck. He wanted this. Nothing sounded sweeter than death, for he had nobody to live for anymore. Every single woman he'd loved had been taken from him—each instance having been the fault of his own.

Toono was ready to slash Toshik's neck when Yama screamed, "Watch out!" and rammed into Toono, throwing up her sword and fending off the blade of an unexpected guest.

*   *   *

Toono's shoulder slid through the gravel. As he came to a stop, he gazed back to see Yama fighting a ... *what is that?* He sat up and squinted, not believing his eyes. He'd never seen a more peculiar creature, an entity that made Gale Thrasher seem commonplace.

A red-furred fox on its hind legs, like a human, had Yama on the defensive, forcing her to retreat as she tried to shed off a barrage of swords. It might have been close to Yama's speed, which Toono couldn't fathom. And what's more, it wielded three swords, one to each hand and a third grasped by the end of its tail. This made Yama's attempts to switch angles pointless. The fox didn't bother turning around; his tail protected his blindside as it thrashed across his back.

Toono pushed himself off the ground. He needed to kill Toshik with his own hands if he wanted the death to count as a valid sacrifice. As of right now, Yama had dealt the potentially fatal blows. He glanced toward the Adrenian crumpled over Jilly's body to see two other beings like the fox. A wolf sat in front of the two Jestivan, an aura of boredom clouding its face as it kept an eye on Toono. Behind it was a long-eared rabbit, pulling Toshik away from Jilly before dropping a bag and retrieving materials from within. Bandages and purses of crushed herb spilled out.

What were these creatures? Toono had read many books in his life, yet not a single one mentioned beings such as this. He and the wolf stared each other down. Despite the disinterest in the wolf's eyes, Toono decided not to test it. Instead he fled. He couldn't risk an altercation, especially if there were others in the vicinity. But perhaps what scared him most was the gravitational fluctuation from before. If Rhyparia was around, he didn't want to linger and find out. That'd be suicide.

Toono retreated up the newly formed crater's side. He climbed a pile of stone to find Illipsia hiding in fetal position with her hands over her head. He gently took her by the wrist, blew into his ancient, and encased both of them in an elastic bubble. They ran through the valley's outskirts in hopes to intercept Yama as the fox forced her farther away from Toshik and Jilly.

Eventually the fox dug its feet into the gravel, ending its assault. "It'd be wise to run," it said, baring its pointed teeth. "This fight would end in deaths on both sides."

Toono was glad to see Yama accept the surrender. Normally she would have continued without hesitation, but in her current mental state, she was rattled.

"Yama!" Toono shouted, now behind her. After a brief pause, during which Yama gazed past the fox toward the motionless lump of sky blue at the crater's center, she disappeared. She, Toono, and Illipsia fled the mountains.

* * *

Toshik stared at the clear blue sky while lying on his back, a pair of long pink and white ears curling above him. A rabbit hopped around him, applying pressure to different wounds. It opened his mouth and stuffed something grassy inside—a papery texture with a taste of mint and coconut. Then it began mixing something in a mason jar, the rattling of which disrupted the silence that had finally befallen the valley.

"My name is Therapif," the rabbit announced, as tears slid down Toshik's cheeks. "Despite the severity of your wounds, I think you're going to survive."

"I don't want to survive; my spirit is gone."

The rattling stopped, but then continued again. "I'm making a paste that I'll smear across your lacerations. Be wary of the sensation you'll experience upon its application. I doubt you've experienced frostbite, but that's the best equivalent I can conjure up … except this will be felt not only on your skin, but throughout the entirety of the gouge—muscles, bones, and all."

Toshik ignored the warning. Nothing compared to the pain of watching Jilly die. His gaze remained empty as the cream was applied to his shoulder. His head rolled sideways to see the fox and wolf seated next to each other. The fox was upright with its legs crossed while the wolf leaned back, using its arm as a brace, one knee up and the other arm dangling across it.

"Why'd you guys intervene?" was all he could manage to whisper.

"It's been centuries since our kind has entered the mountains, but we braved it at someone's request," Therapif said.

Before Toshik could ask another question, a woman seemingly fell from the sky and landed quietly at his feet. She held an open umbrella in her hand and looked every bit like Rhyparia, but taller and matured. The baby fat in her face was gone, replaced by a soft, slanted jawline and high cheekbones. Instead of her burgundy bandana covering her hair, it was tied around her neck. And her bangs no longer swept in front of her eyes, but were pulled back behind her ears. Was his mind playing tricks on him? This lady looked like Rhyparia's proper mother.

The woman gazed at Jilly, crouching low and pulling her eyelids closed. She then shifted her focus to Toshik, her eyes glazed and red. "Annick will show you out of the mountains. Please don't tell anyone you saw me." She paused and mumbled, "I'm sorry, Toshik."

And with that, she leapt and soared through the sky, disappearing into the distance. The fox and wolf stood and walked away without a word. Therapif, the only creature that had offered a name, rolled Toshik over on his side and smeared paste across the slash in his back and cuts in the back of his ankles. Quickly, the bunny wrapped him in bandages. "The ointment should heal you quickly, but that left ankle will take some time. I'd say a week before you can walk again … and gingerly at that. Thankfully, your other one was only nicked."

Before Therapif hopped away with his bag of supplies, he stuffed one final clump of herbs in the Adrenian's mouth.

Toshik struggled to sit up, cursing at the pain. He crawled toward Jilly, ignoring his injuries. Hopefully this treatment would fail, for nothing sounded more appealing than the numbness of death. He slumped next to

Jilly and stared at her, swirling in memories that'd haunt him for the rest of his life.

43
Toshy

A ten-year-old Toshik lay in his canopy bed, twisted in his blankets with the magnolia white curtains closed around him. He held a stuffed pig named Oinky in his arms. Torn at the seams and splotched with juice stains, it represented everything that the young boy missed dearly—his mother and younger sister, Alina.

This pig had once belonged to Alina, a gift from their mother. Now it served as a memento to both of them. Toshik used to catch his sister's scent whenever he'd snuggle with it at night, but as the months had passed, that faded too. The only comfort he gained from Oinky was the memories. For whatever reason, it had the ability to rid the haunting images of that fateful day—the day both his mother and sister died because of him—replacing them with more innocent visions: playing tag and running the peg course with Alina or reading his mother's diary, which documented all of her run-ins with extraordinary creatures.

He spent every day in his room, only leaving to relieve himself. Even meals were delivered to his door. He quit going to Adren Assistance Academy for several reasons, one of those being that he felt he no longer belonged. At first his father had scolded him for being a coward. But over time he must have realized that Toshik's hiding meant he didn't have to see the little boy's face. In a way, Toshik felt like he was doing both himself and his dad a favor.

Someone knocked on his door as he squeezed the cotton out of the pig. He stayed quiet as per his routine. It seemed like a peculiar time of day for a meal to be delivered. Then the knock turned into banging.

"Open up, Toshik!"

It was his father's voice. He scooted across his bed and placed his feet into a pair of slippers. He reached the handle just as the door was nearly knocked off its hinges. He looked up at his dad's clean-shaven face.

"Come downstairs," he said. "We have company."

"I don't—"

"*Downstairs*," he repeated with even more conviction.

Toshik followed his father through the estate, halls floored with polished hardwood, stark white drywall paneled with a matching maple. "It's time you climb out of this psychological gorge."

"What?"

"Failure," his dad mumbled to himself. He took a deep breath, repeating in plainer terms, "It's time for you to move on."

Toshik stared at the floor. "How do you stay so happy, sir?"

"Happy isn't the word; it's a state of acceptance. Of course, it's made easier by letting the business consume me."

They crossed into a separate wing until they reached a door to one of the many rooms of leisure throughout the sprawling estate. The door almost looked a part of the wall. His dad slid it open. Inside were a man in a sky blue uniform and a young girl around Toshik's age, a sunhat entirely too big for her head sitting atop it. He was surprised that his father hadn't scolded her for wearing a hat inside—even if she was a guest.

"Toshik, this is Spirit Corporal Wert Lamay and his daughter, Jilly."

Toshik shook their hands before being told to sit down. His interest piqued as he looked across at Jilly. He'd known her for ten seconds, yet something about her personality sparkled. Whether it was the cheek-breaking smile, the gleeful blue eyes, or just her general aura, he was not sure. One thing was certain, she was pretty.

The four of them settled in, Toshik and his dad each to an armchair, Jilly and her dad together on the sofa.

"What's your speed percentage, my boy?" Wert asked with a stern face.

Toshik twiddled his fingers and replied, "It's been a while, but last time I checked it was twenty-one percent."

"Not terrible," he said. "I could find better."

"For what, sir?" Toshik asked.

Wert opened his mouth to respond, but fumbled over air. He looked toward Toth and asked, "He's coming into this blind?"

Toth gave a nervous smile. "It was the only way he'd come down." He then leaned toward Toshik and muttered, "You're being interviewed to be Jilly's protector. I forked over a lot of money to land this, so don't mess it up." Toth relaxed and refocused on Wert. "My apologies, Major."

"If the boy doesn't even want my daughter as his charge, why would I choose him over more suitable candidates? Not graduating AAA is one thing, but failing to do so because of a lack of commitment is unacceptable. That is the exact opposite of what Adrenians pride themselves on."

While Toth proceeded to argue his case, Jilly stared at Toshik with a thoughtful gaze. She had an uncanny knack to appear as if she was smiling even when her lips were flat—a credit to her eyes. He made it a point to look away, instead pretending to take interest in the potted bamboo plant in the room's corner.

Toshik had zoned out by the time Wert rose from his seat. "Well, I see no point in being here," he said. "The boy isn't even paying attention. Let's go, Jilly."

Toth glared at his son, but his eyes softened unexpectedly. He sighed, "Listen. The truth of the matter is that my wife and daughter were killed during a hunting accident six months ago." As Wert fell back onto the couch, Toth explained, "Since then, my son and I have been coping in our own ways. I've buried myself in work; he's become despondent. I felt this was a way to get him back on his feet and out of the bedroom—proving that he's not a label of his past mistakes."

The major's eyes narrowed. "Past mistakes?"

"The hunting accident was a result of him. He brought his little sister into the forest. His mom rushed in after them a short while later. Sometime during that excursion—and I'll spare you the details—they were slain by a mother spunka."

Wert's gaze flickered between the two Brench men. "You tell me that story, expecting it to help your argument?" He looked at Toshik. "The boy's crying now."

"Daddy, please," Jilly said sweetly. "I'm the reason why Mommy died."

"No, you're not!" he shouted.

Toth quietly leaned forward, elbows on his knees, hands entwined. "How about a bit of negotiating? Typically it's the parents of the charge paying the protector, but let's flip that practice on its head. I can personally offer you ten thousand granules. And not only that, but I will help the Spirit Kingdom by cutting prices of the entire Brench Crafts' inventory by fifty percent for a year. No other kingdom—including the Intel Kingdom—will get such a deal.

"And during that year, Jilly will be Toshik's charge. We'll treat it as a trial run. If you're not happy by this time next year with my son's services, you'll have the right to walk away since you won't be legally bound by any charge-protector contracts. But I can guarantee you that because of Toshik's past, he'd never let anything happen to that girl. He will forever be cautious."

Wert scratched at his scruff. "And the repercussions if I were to walk away? Would you suddenly inflate your trade prices with the Spirit Kingdom to compensate for what you sacrificed?"

"I'm an entrepreneur with a good understanding of business ethics. I do not trifle with agreements—contractual or of good faith. That's a bad look for me, and would hurt my image. Besides, the absence of a charge-protector contract does not imply an absence of commerce contracts. We can discuss those tonight."

Wert grinned. "You're a smooth talker, but I'm sure you've been told this many times."

Toshik glanced at his father just in time to see his expression briefly falter. Jun had always complimented his conversational abilities. In her gross words: *It's the sexiest thing about you.* Toshik gagged at the thought of it, but then he smiled, realizing how much he'd suffer through it if it meant she was alive again.

"What do you think, Jilly?" Wert asked as he turned toward her, placing his giant hand on her knee.

She smiled. "I like him, Daddy!"

Wert got up and extended a hand. "You've got yourself a deal."

* * *

Outside the Brench Crafts' estate, Toshik sat in the grass while Jilly rolled down the gentle hill, screaming and giggling each time she did. He was infuriated. He had no desire to protect a charge. He didn't deserve the opportunity, nor did she deserve such a fate. The whole reason he had dropped out of AAA was because he couldn't protect anyone. If this girl hovered around him any longer, she'd end up dead too.

All he wanted was for the two men to end their little meeting inside, that way Jilly could go home. He wouldn't have to see her again until next week, when their arrangement would officially begin. At least then he'd have a few days to mentally prepare for this nuisance.

After her hundredth trip down the slope, Jilly ran back up and plopped down in the grass next to Toshik. "I believe in you, Toshy."

"That's not my name."

She frowned. "I like it better. Toshik has *ick* at the end of it, which sounds like *icky*." She proceeded to repeatedly say *ick*, further exaggerating its intensity each time.

"Ok, whatever," he droned. "As long as it shuts you up."

"You're lucky I know why you're so mean. Or else I'd run far away from you. I don't like bullies."

"If I told you my mom and sister are alive, and I'm like this because this is who I am, would you keep that promise and run away?" he asked.

"No, but it would make you a liar, which is just as bad as being a bully."

He looked at her. "Do you get bullied a lot?"

"Kind of," she muttered, digging her toes into the sod.

"Why do you get bullied?"

"They call me weird and say I smile too much. They call me Silly Jilly."

Toshik sighed. His mom was silly, the kind of woman who'd laugh at things nobody else in the room found funny. But her laughter alone would cause the room to roar with more of it.

Toshik turned at the sounds of the conversation his father and the Spirit Major were having. The joy in their tone was an obvious sign that a deal had been struck. Toshik fell back into the grass and closed his eyes. "Great," he said, "you can go away now."

"Jilly, we'll be staying here for the weekend since traveling all the way home and back in four days isn't practical," Wert said, jarring open Toshik's eyes. "On Monday I'll head back home and you'll stay here with the Brench family while my unit is deployed to Windwynder."

Toshik pushed himself off the ground and walked back toward the estate in an irritated silence. He'd be scolded for this disrespectful act later, but for now he'd get away with it because of the company present. His father wasn't one for public humiliation.

* * *

Toshik lay in bed with Oinky in his arms when the curtains parted, revealing his father. He took a seat at the edge of the mattress.

"I thought I couldn't have a charge without graduating," Toshik said.

"I pulled some strings."

"Why would you put that girl in danger?"

"She's not," his dad replied. "She has you."

"And look where that landed Alina."

After a pause, Toth leaned over and pulled the stuffed pig from Toshik's grasp.

"Give it back!" the boy demanded, rolling over and slapping the sheets.

"You're obsessive, Toshik. It's unhealthy. You'll never break free of the guilt if you continue clutching onto it."

"It gives me happy memories," he cried.

"Which lead to sad ones. Stop crying."

Toshik sucked up snot and wiped his eyes. "Yes, sir."

"Have you ever seen me cry?"

"No, sir."

"You're a ten-year-old Adrenian," he said. "Act like it. You've been given a job; do your job."

"Yes, sir."

Toth sighed and placed his hand on his son's head, rubbing his thumb against his temple before leaning in to kiss it. "Find a different way to cope, son. Pitying yourself isn't the answer."

* * *

In the hundred-acre backyard of the Brench Estate, Toshik was in the midst of sword-fighting his personal trainer, a retired Adren Corporal by the name of Kuiku Fito. Despite being retired, he was still young—in his mid-thirties. He had left his position as corporal when offered his current job by Toshik's father for a large sum of money. And this was done during the same time Major Sinno had been promoted to general, making Kuiku eligible to have filled the newly vacated position of Adren Major. The fact that he'd passed up such an opportunity said a lot about the sway held by the Brench family.

Under the unforgiving summer sun, sweat lathered Toshik's face as he was forced on his heels. He flicked his wrist, his sword extended in front of him as he blocked repeated swings from Kuiku.

"Why aren't you countering?" Kuiku calmly asked as he bore down on him.

Toshik couldn't muster up words through his heavy breathing, so he decided to just go for it. He parried by sidestepping, flipping his wrist, and hacking at Kuiku's hamstring. But the retired corporal was too quick, pivoting his grounded foot and lifting his leg to drop an axe kick onto Toshik's back. The boy hit the ground with a thud.

"What did you do wrong?" Kuiku asked as he sheathed his sword.

Toshik squirmed, squeezing his head as pain jolted up his spine. "I woke up today."

Kuiku stood there for a moment, as a gentle smirk set in. "Shades of Jun." As Toshik sat up, Kuiku jumped into a sparring stance with his hands up. "You see what I'm doing here?" he asked. "I'm on my toes, lightly bouncing. This allows me to switch to a right-side or left-side stance in a fluid motion."

"That's what I was doing," Toshik said.

"And it was wrong," he replied. "This isn't kickboxing, Toshik. You're sword-fighting, but you're doing it entirely on the balls of your feet. Honestly, my kick was unnecessary. All it would have taken was a slight shove, and you would have toppled over … heck, a breeze could have sent you flying like a feather."

Kuiku took a knee in front of the boy. "This is why peg courses can pose both positives and negatives as a training method. You may have heard of Ataway Kawi, the Third of Five. He was a staunch opponent of the belief that children should be on peg courses as three-year-olds, and for good reason. They may teach you balance, agility, and light feet, but those are skills applied in more advanced battle scenarios … such as fights that occur over a wide space between two extremely fast Adrenians. In those situations the individual swordfights are nothing but components of a larger game of cat and mouse—a game that requires skills learned on the peg course.

"But this, between you and me—" he wagged his finger back and forth between the two of them— "isn't tag. We're working the most basic of fundamentals. You don't bounce and skip on your toes; you keep the soles of your feet planted, and when you move, your feet shuffle. If I shove your shoulder in the future, you'd better not fall over." He paused and asked, "You got it?"

"Yes, sir."

Kuiku smiled. "Superb." He then gazed toward a blonde girl with a sunhat resting down her back, as she shoved her face into a pond, sending bubbles to the surface. "That girl's been waiting for you for quite some time now, so I think I'll call it a day."

"Please don't," Toshik said, reaching out and grabbing his trainer's sleeve.

Kuiku turned back, his expression one of pity. "You must face your demons, Toshik." He then continued toward the guest wing.

Toshik watched Jilly entertain herself with the bubbles. She'd been here for a week tops, yet it had only taken two days for Toshik to realize the simplicity of her essence. She was gleeful, stupid, and loving at all times. He found it to be annoying—borderline obnoxious, truth be told.

As he approached the pond, a head full of sopping wet hair resurfaced. She leapt and shouted, "Toshy! You're done!"

She ran at him, then proceeded to run around him in circles like a dog chasing its tail. He took a deep breath and released it slowly. This would prove to be a long year.

* * *

Another week passed, and another twenty headaches were added to Toshik's tally. The only silver lining was his successful mission into the forest with Jilly. His father had forced it upon him. He was to join one of the hunting units on an expedition into the forest's depths as they tracked down spunka. His one and only job had been to get Jilly back alive.

"I don't think I've ever seen something so scary in my life," Jilly said while picking flowers in the garden.

Toshik—who was practicing his footwork as he hacked at air—replied, "Those were just babies."

"Where were their parents?"

"Not around," he said, electing to spare her the gruesome details of a spunka family's functionality. While he was mostly a jerk to her, there were certain lines he didn't cross—her innocence being one of them. He cherished it, for it reminded him of Alina.

A long stretch of silence passed, which was rare considering his company was Jilly. He didn't think much of it, however, continuing to shuffle forward and backward with his sword in ready position. Suddenly he toppled into a flower patch; someone had shoved him from behind. He quickly leapt back onto his feet, glowering at Jilly as she gave an exaggerated frown.

"Kuiku said you need better balance," she said. "That wasn't good."

"Do you know how much trouble I'm going to get in with Unry when she finds her flowers like this?" he hissed.

"Who?"

"The gardener!"

"I'll plant new ones for her before we leave."

Toshik paused, his eyes narrowing. "Before we leave where?"

"Next Monday is the first day of school." Noticing Toshik's confusion, she said, "Phesaw, you know … the Light Realm's central school."

"And when you say 'we,' you mean you and some friend, right?"

Her mouth dropped. "You just said you're my friend!"

He shook his head. "Wait … what? No. I didn't think it was me …" He trailed off. "It can't be me. I don't go to Phesaw."

Jilly watched while Toshik struggled with the news. Adrenians didn't go to Phesaw—or at least not the skilled ones. Enrollment would have been social suicide back at AAA … not that he'd ever step foot in that place ever again, anyway. He stormed off to find his father, who was likely in his office. As much as he dreaded it, he needed to speak with him.

*   *   *

As Toshik stepped into his father's office and slid the door shut, his dad gazed up with a hint of surprise. He placed his quill into its holder and leaned back in his chair, fingers connected atop his gray vest. "When's the last time you visited this neck of the woods?" he asked.

Toshik took a seat across the desk. "Can't remember, sir."

"What can I do for you, son?"

"Jilly mentioned that I'd be going to Phesaw this year." He fidgeted in his seat. "That's a lie, isn't it?"

Toth held Toshik's gaze. He tapped a finger against his stomach. "Regardless of the fact that you must go there because Jilly will be there," he said, "I feel as if this is a good opportunity for you in more ways than just one."

"And which ways are those, sir?"

"The most important benefit is that it would get you away from here—far away from this demonic abysm."

Toshik didn't know what that meant, but he could gather from the context that it related to Mom and Alina.

"Secondly, you'd have the ability to broaden your intellectual scope. You can work on your speed and swordsmanship all you want, but that alone won't mean much if you want to amount to anything of monetary worth in this world."

"I don't follow, sir," Toshik said.

Toth paused, his face fighting back some kind of expression. "Case in point," Toth said. "Perhaps you'll expand your vocabulary a bit." He leaned forward and placed his forearms on the desk. "Everything is prepared. I enrolled you and even created your course schedule for the year. Hopefully you find there is a fair balance of subject matter."

Toshik stood up and forced himself to say, "Thank you, sir."

As he walked out the door, his dad said, "I think you'll love campus life, son. Break free of that scabbed shell."

* * *

Toshik looked on in awe as he descended the towering steps of one of Telejunction's platforms. Phesaw was beautiful, a lolling campus that stretched as far the eye could see—the most striking visual being the vivid pink canopies of Phesaw Park's cherry blossoms. A pool of students crowded Telejunction's landing stage, but it was dwarfed by the sea that spilled down the hill toward the main campus.

"Let's go, Toshy," Jilly said, tugging at his sleeve.

Jilly grabbed Toshik's hand once they reached the stage, pulling him through the tangled crowd. If she hadn't done this, they would have lost each other in the swarm. Students rammed into his chest, and he was a little perplexed by the lack of order. Were there not staff or teachers assigned to this place? Seemed like not only a safety hazard, but a lack of discipline. This would have never happened back at the academy.

They finally made it to the edge of the stage, stepping into the grass as they followed the current. At AAA, Toshik had been taller than most others, but here—a school with such a broad age range—he felt like a dwarf. He looked up to see some students with full beards.

As they finally reached the bottom of the hill, the masses dispersed somewhat. The amount of kids who stopped to say hi to Jilly surprised Toshik. From her comments about bullies, he had expected gestures not as flattering. But on the other hand, he couldn't fathom the idea of someone bullying a girl like her.

Apart from the spectacles of the painted ceiling in the lobby that circled the auditorium and the grand entrance of the Energy Directors during the opening ceremony, the first couple of hours were boring.

When Jilly brought him to a group of tables in the lobby where he'd grab his course schedule, she said, "We probably won't see much of each other during the day. Our classes are in different areas of the building, and I think your dad put you in courses I would never dream of taking."

"How do you know what he put me in?"

"Well, I'm the one who showed him the school's brochure. He sat down with me and looked through it. I saw him circling a bunch of courses, but there were way too many for a single year of school. I don't know what he narrowed it down to."

Toshik's right eyebrow arched. "You hang out with my father?"

"Yes!" she screamed unexpectedly, sending stares their way. "You guys have the most amazing baker, and he always brings me cupcakes during our meetings."

Toshik laughed and shook his head. "Luring you in with sweets."

"I like sweets because it's nice to be sweet."

Deciding not to highlight the nonsensical logic in her statement, he went silent. They reached a table, where Toshik gave his name and waited patiently for the student-worker to find his papers within a filer. "Here you go."

Jilly gave thanks for Toshik as he turned away and began scanning his schedule. He nearly ripped it into pieces, noticing it was comprised mostly of business and managerial courses. Perhaps his father thought the single speed percentage class was a generous gesture, but he likely only did that because of the deal he had made with the Spirit Corporal.

"Don't like it?" Jilly asked.

Toshik stormed off. "I'll see you after school."

"Meet me in front of the Warpfinate!" she shouted.

* * *

Toshik stepped outside of the school building later that afternoon, thrilled to escape its confines. A bag hung from his shoulder and knocked into him with each step, an anvil of textbooks bruising his thigh. He met Jilly in front of a blockish brick building that his map had marked as the Warpfinate. She smiled upon his approach. Once he was close enough, she squeezed the air out of him with the most generous hug he had ever received since Alina had been alive. Toshik's response was less than ideal, shoving her away with more force than intended.

For the first time since meeting Jilly a month ago during that hellish interview, he'd done something that not only made her smile disappear, but cast silence upon her. He tried to right his wrong by smiling himself, but such an expression felt forlorn. He doubted he was doing it right. "What do we do now that classes are over?"

"Well, we were going to study in the Warpfinate," she muttered. "But I think I'll go play in the park with the few friends I have here." She walked past, heading toward the cherry blossoms.

"I'll come too."

"Don't follow me, please," she said. "Your dorm is in Lilac Suites. Your stuff should already be in there."

Toshik watched hopelessly as she disappeared around the pathway's bend and behind the cherry blossoms. He was frustrated with himself. He thought he'd gotten over the hunting accident, but apparently he was wrong. There was something about intimate contact—familial or romantic—that unnerved him, forcing tragic pasts to resurface.

*　　*　　*

A week went by without conversation between protector and charge, but that didn't mean he had allowed his duties to fall by the wayside. Toshik kept a keen eye on Jilly from afar whenever he wasn't in class. While she was sifting through the chocolates of Tabby's Gift Shop, he was outside, watching her through the glass. When she went on her daily strolls through Phesaw Park, he trailed her.

He was doing everything AAA had advised against. He was overbearing to the point of what some might have called "passive harassment." The only privacy he allotted to her was when she was in class or her dorm. And one day she made a point of expressing her discomfort over breakfast at Dinny's Diner.

"I'm not a toddler, Toshy," she said as she picked up her chocolate chip waffle with her fingers, tearing a chunk out of it with her teeth. She then slurped her syrup from the plate with her lips. The irony wasn't lost on Toshik.

"I'm doing my job," he said.

"Do it less," she said. "I've noticed you've become popular around here. I see the girls walk past you, giggling and blushing."

"So what? They know me because of my last name and my family's wealth."

"I'll start talking to you again when you stop following me everywhere. My friends think it's weird."

"You know what happened to my mom and sister," he said. "I just don't want it to happen to you too."

She smiled, bearing teeth of all different sizes. "I'm okay. My spirit protects me."

* * *

Fall semester, winter vacation, and half of spring semester went by before Toshik finally gave Jilly the space she had asked for. It had involved a gradual transition, for he couldn't just turn a blind eye at once.

Appreciating the progress he'd made, Jilly returned to her normal self around him. She pestered him by running in circles, jumping on his back, and stealing his sword from its scabbard. She even visited his dorm in Lilac Suites.

"I can't believe you don't live here," Toshik said as he opened the door to his room. "You're a corporal's daughter."

She immediately ran toward his bed, climbed atop it, and began jumping up and down. "We can't afford this place," she said. "Your bed is so much bigger than mine!"

Toshik smirked and reached under the bed frame. "I got you something."

She leapt off the bed, landing on the floor with her butt as cushion. Chuckling, he shook his head and pulled out a stuffed eagle.

Her eyes enlarged as she gasped. "Thank you!"

"I always saw you playing in the plush barrels at the gift shop. I figured you'd like to actually own one." He gave a guilty smirk and rubbed the back of his neck. "Your spirit is like an eagle—it flies really high."

Jilly paused. She'd been pretending the plush animal was flying around the room while making *swoosh* noises with her mouth. She blinked a few times before smiling and crawling toward him for a hug.

Toshik flinched, causing Jilly to stop before committing. Instead, she said, "Thank you so much, Toshy."

* * *

It was the last week of school. Toshik waited in front of the Warpfinate for Jilly, who was running unusually late. After a while, he left to venture into Phesaw Park. There was a spot near the lake where Jilly and her friends liked to play. Luckily he found one of her friends. When he asked for Jilly's whereabouts, she'd told him that she had to go to the medical center earlier in the day.

He rushed through the park, the inexplicable image of her corpse flashing through his mind as he headed for the clinic. He was afforded a sigh of relief when he saw Jilly walking out of the building by her own free will, unharmed from the looks of things.

"What happened?" he asked.

"I cut myself falling down," she replied, holding up her right forearm and left elbow, both of which were completely bandaged.

He sucked air through his teeth, glancing up at her after inspecting the wrappings. "Are you lying? All of this from a fall?"

Her eyes sparkled as she grinned. "I'm fine, Toshy."

* * *

Suffice to say, Toshik returned to old habits during the remaining days of the school year. This time, however, he tried being less overt. He had the faintest suspicion that a bully had finally struck.

During the second-to-last-day of the school year, Toshik sat in the branches of a cherry blossom in Phesaw Park, not too far from the grassy clearing near the lake where Jilly and her friends mingled after school. Not much happened out of the ordinary—not when dealing with eleven-year-old girls at least. There was a moment when they had a screaming contest … obnoxious, but expected from Jilly. Toshik shook his head and plugged his ears.

Then a boy broke free from the trees on their right. He was tall and beefy, but likely only a few years older than Toshik and Jilly. Toshik readjusted himself, squatting low and curling the toes of his running flats around the branch.

The girls continued to scream as the boy reached them. He shoved Jilly in her back, hard enough for her to slide through the grass. Several months ago, Toshik would have already charged and retaliated on her behalf. But he wanted to give her a chance, for she always preached that she could handle herself.

The girls split apart as the bully stepped toward Jilly. She rolled over on her back with a smile. "Hey, Geno."

The bully towered over her and replied, "Do you ever shut up, Silly Jilly?"

"I got you your necklace back," she said, reaching up with a gold chain in her grasp. "The one you said belonged to your granddad, the one you had to sell."

"And how'd you pay for it?"

"I saved up the entire year!" she proclaimed with joy.

He snatched it from her grasp and inspected it before flinging it into the lake. "I don't like how you rub your happiness into everyone's face. You literally scream it at the top of your lungs."

As she gazed toward the lake, she said weakly, "You can be happy too, Geno. Just hang …"

Jilly trailed off as Geno threw a punch, and Toshik considered that his cue. He'd waited long enough for her to defend herself. He accelerated out of the tree, appearing between Geno's fist and Jilly. He caught it, and then swung his elbow into the bully's jaw.

Geno stumbled, baffled by the interference. "Where'd you come from? I thought you stopped following her around."

"Go away before I gut you."

Geno stood there speechless for a few moments, cupping his hand underneath his bleeding nose. He grumbled incoherently and fled.

Toshik whirled toward Jilly. "Why didn't you kick his butt? I know you could have."

"I wanted to try using my words and a gift."

"And you saw how he treated that gift, right?" Jilly pouted at the ground, so Toshik offered his hand. "Sometimes you don't have any other choice, Jills."

* * *

Toshik, Jilly, and their fathers were seated outside on a limestone patio behind the estate. The two children were silent for the most part, poking at their food, while Wert and Toth discussed matters of the past year. Wert spoke of his boring year-long stay in Windwynder while Toth mentioned the addition of two new merchant vessels to his fleet. Eventually the two men acknowledged their children's presence.

Wert looked over at his daughter and asked, "How was your school year, Jilly?"

"It was fun. Made some new friends and learned a lot."

Wert glanced at Toshik before refocusing on his daughter. "And what about the bullying?"

"Toshy made sure nothing happened to me."

"Well, that's what I like to hear," Wert said with a rare smile. "Looks like your boy proved me wrong, Toth."

"So how about we make this arrangement permanent?" Toth said. "Now, of course, the trade deal I had in place with the Spirit Kingdom will end—that was a one-year thing."

Wert wiped his mouth with the back of his hand. "I understand. I suppose we should begin drafting the charge-protector contract."

"Let's head to my office." Before the two men departed, Toth placed his hand against Toshik's back. "I'm proud of you," he said.

"Are you sure you can put up with me for so long?" Jilly asked after their fathers disappeared inside.

Toshik smirked. "I'd be lying if I said I didn't have my doubts."

* * *

Three years passed without incident. Toshik and Jilly were both fourteen, an age when romance began to blossom in the lives of most teens. While Jilly proved to be an exception to this trope, Toshik exemplified it. Not that his pursuits were that of romance; they were purely lust.

Toshik moved from girl to girl by the week, developing himself a bit of a reputation around the school. With these habits, he drifted away from Jilly, socially speaking. He still made sure to know where she was at all times and demanded meetings at the end of the night to discuss her day, but he no longer walked side by side with her throughout the campus.

Neither of them thought much of it until winter break when they returned to Brench Estates. They were confronted—not so subtly—by their fathers about their relationship. The two men were under the impression that their children were closer than ever before … that they might have been in love. Honestly, such a perspective wasn't unexpected. When Jilly and Toshik were at the estate, they never left each other's side. But that was only because there weren't any distractions to pull their attention elsewhere.

Toth and Wert hinted at dating and the concept of love. They discussed the exploration of the opposite sex, which was a rather uncomfortable experience for both Toshik and Jilly. For Toshik, he didn't want to alarm his father of his already lecherous deeds. And for someone like Jilly, she just didn't care about the subject.

This led to awkwardness between the two friends. Their fathers never explicitly stated it, but it sounded like an arranged marriage was in their future. Assuming these intentions, Toshik forced Jilly further away, fearing that he'd do exactly what his father had hoped he'd do … fall in love with the girl.

They became distant—even during breaks at the estate—until the fateful day of the rebirth of the Jestivan. Then, when they were forced to be on the same team with Bryson as a captain, Toshik realized he couldn't push Jilly away any longer.

At first, Toshik was thankful for Yama's budding relationship with Jilly. It gave Jilly a distraction and allowed him room to breathe. But over time something changed. Perhaps it was the mission in the Dev Kingdom, when they chased down King Storshae to free Olivia. There was something about that morning in Necrosis Valley when they fought by each other's side. The ember that had always burned in his chest for Jilly had grown into an inferno.

They spent the summer after their first year as Jestivan in Phelos to relax and recuperate following the Rolling Oaks mission. Usually they'd have gone to the estate, but their fathers were being inducted into the Amendment Order as chiefs.

"Do Jilly and I have to be here, sir?" Toshik asked while his father unpacked his most treasured rewards and trophies into his new office.

"Yes, son," he said, placing a model ship onto his desk. "We're sculpting something beautiful and powerful here. A family of two Jestivan and two chiefs—one is the former Spirit Major and the other the owner of Brench Crafts." He looked at Toshik and smiled. "We're capable of great things."

"We already have more money than we need, sir."

Toth visually perused his son's wardrobe. "And clearly you take advantage of that money. You dress like a businessman, yet refuse to act the part for some reason." As Toshik glanced down at his own attire, Toth said, "Anyway, remember that it's imperative you and Jilly be seen together as much as possible this summer. You two will become the most influential duo Kuki Sphaira has ever seen."

*   *   *

"I'm so excited to head back to Phesaw," Jilly said, crumpling her clothes in balls and throwing them into her suitcase.

Toshik took a gentler approach to his packing. He folded his assortment of dress clothes and placed them into his luggage, separating vests, pants, ties, and pocket squares to individual compartments. "It was nice being somewhere other than Phesaw or my estate," he said.

"Let's go somewhere else next summer!" Jilly yelled. "Like Sodai or Fiamma!"

"I'd like that." He went quiet, then said, "I'll also miss the privacy we had. Bryson, Rhyparia, and the others will be hounding us when we get back to school."

"I know. I can't wait to see them again!" She noticed Toshik's spirits dampen upon hearing this, so she said, "But I'll miss this too, Toshy."

Toshik flopped back into his bed and stared at the ceiling. "You've filled a void, Jills. It's still too hard for me to say what I want to say to you, but I want you to know you've healed me."

An empty silence wafted over them. It felt like an eternity passed before Jilly said, "You'll say it when you're ready."

*   *   *

The protector and charge returned to Phelos for winter break. It was the turn of a new year, as 1500 K.H. approached. They stood at the top of a gentle hill near the edge of the palace grounds—one that was reminiscent of the soft rolling hills that Toshik's estate rested upon.

Jilly had just finished making a beautiful statement about Toshik and his mother, Jun, when the crowd behind them began chanting the countdown to the new year. She tackled him, their legs and arms tangling as they tumbled down the slope. By the time they reached the bottom, she sat on top of him, ready to usher in the new year with their first kiss.

*   *   *

It was the end of March, and Phesaw's school year had come to an abrupt and violent end. Jilly sat at Toshik's bedside in Phesaw's medical building. Intelights dimly illuminated the entire floor, where most of the Jestivan were being nursed for injuries following a day full of chaos and heartbreak. The school had been invaded by the likes of Dev King

Storshae, Rogue Demon Toono, Apoleia Still, and many others. And it had been robbed of Yama and Grand Director Poicus.

As Toshik lay in bed, wrapped in bandages, he looked over at Jilly, whose eyes were bloodshot. She couldn't come to grips with the thought of Yama abandoning the Jestivan. And now she was blaming herself. He reassured her that Yama had made that choice on her own.

Jilly replied, "If only I had loved her more."

The comment stabbed at Toshik because she shouldn't have thought that way. For her to exude more love than she already did was ludicrous. Nobody showed more love than Jilly did … *nobody*. But for some reason the first question that fell out of Toshik's mouth was: "Do you love her more than me?"

She paused, eyes sinking to the floor as she said, "I don't know."

Toshik reached out his hand from under the sheets and grasped onto Jilly's. He guided her out of her seat and pulled her close. She nestled her head onto his chest, tears spilling onto his night gown. That's when he decided to say it, for it was time for her to hear it from someone—and most importantly, from him. He pressed his lips into her hair.

"I love you."

44
The Escape

A hand was placed against Toshik's back, startling him out of his dreams. He pushed his face off of Jilly's stomach and looked up as daylight died around him. His back was stiff from being curled in a ball and the strange paste healing his wounds. A heavyset gentleman wearing a brown vest too small for his body gazed down at him. "We must be leaving," the man said.

"Are you Annick?"

He frowned. "That girl gave you my name." His forehead crumpled. "Well, I suppose she's no girl any longer."

Toshik glanced back at Jilly. He tried standing but to no avail. "I brought you a crutch," Annick said, standing it in the gravel next to Toshik. "Therapif said you have one good ankle, for it was only nicked. The other, however, is inoperable."

Annick helped the young man to his feet. Toshik leaned against the crutch and reached down to pick up Jilly, but with no success. Her body had stiffened.

"Rigor mortis," Annick said. "We'll have to leave her here."

"That's not happening!" Toshik snapped, glaring back with livid eyes.

Annick's lips pursed before saying, "I don't know how it's feasible to carry her out of the mountains."

"You can help."

* * *

Bryson and Vuilni traversed the footholds between two mountains, following a path of destruction as it became more pronounced with each step around the mountainside's bend. As the crevice opened into a vast valley of rock, Bryson spotted humanistic shapes in the darkness.

He broke into a run, hampered slightly by his injured leg. As he got closer, he slowed down, realizing what he was looking at.

"Oh no …" Vuilni muttered.

Toshik turned as they approached, but instead of acknowledging them, he hung his head. Bryson gazed down at Jilly, tears forming in his eyes. "How did this happen?"

"Yama," Toshik croaked.

"Yama?" Bryson repeated, glancing at Toshik in disbelief.

"She was with Toono—"

"What?! Where'd they go?"

"They're long gone," a mystery man nearby said. Bryson had largely ignored him.

"Who are you?"

"Name's Annick."

Bryson knelt next to Jilly, as did Vuilni. He studied the slash wound to her chest, the paleness of her face, and puddle of blood underneath. A somber fury ignited within him.

"We really should leave," said Annick, carefully picking his moments to speak.

Bryson glanced up at Toshik, saw his wounds, and instead turned to Vuilni. "You get under her arms, I'll get her legs."

Vuilni nodded. The stiffness of her body made it an awkward job.

Toshik's eyes were still on Jilly's face. He inhaled deeply, wiped his eye on his shoulder, and then placed her sunhat over her face. To see Jilly appear so expressionless, so lifeless … it was like the spirit had been sucked out of the world.

* * *

Bryson, Toshik, and Vuilni exited the Archaic Mountains a couple days later. Annick, their guide, had already broken off and returned to wherever it was he had came from. The guards who were stationed at the mountains' footholds for the past year were gone now that the timeframe to receive Rhyparia's bounty had ended. It was well past midnight when they arrived in Rim. Bryson carried Jilly over his shoulder. Her body had relaxed, the rigor mortis having left it after a couple days.

They entered an old, unnamed tavern on the southern side of town that had been reserved for bounty hunters traveling to and from the mountains. Carefully, they walked across the small foyer and approached the host's desk. They didn't want to wake anyone and risk drawing attention to themselves. Thankfully, Rim was a dead town at this hour.

Toshik grabbed a quill from a holder and dipped it into a bottle. He then flipped a few pages in the book until he found what he was looking for. He signed his initials across from his name under the column labeled *Returned*.

Bryson scanned the long list of names on the parchment. The *Returned* column was depressingly empty. But he sighed when he saw *OS* initialed next to *Olivia Still*.

Toshik struggled, his quill hovering over Jilly's name. There was a third column on the sheet labeled *Confirmed Death*. Vuilni took the quill from his hand and initialed *JL* underneath it for him. She and Bryson then signed the book before grabbing keys from the wall.

"Wonder if Olivia's still here," Bryson whispered, readjusting Jilly on his shoulder as they headed up the stairs.

"We'll have to wait 'til morning to find out," Vuilni said.

This building was full of locked, vacant rooms since most hunters either hadn't returned from the mountains or had already left the town. They reached Bryson and Vuilni's room first. Vuilni unlocked the door and pushed it open. Bryson used his free hand to weave several Intelights that hovered throughout the room, illuminating a face in the far corner.

"Himitsu …" Bryson muttered. His eyes narrowed. "With a buzz cut …"

Himitsu skipped any greetings and lifted himself out of the chair, hurrying forward as Bryson gently laid Jilly across a bed. "She's just unconscious, right?" he asked.

Bryson fell to the hardwood floor with his back against the foot of the bed, hands covering his face. "She's dead."

"How did this happen?" he asked, his breathing quickly becoming unsteady. He placed his hands on her chest laceration, her dress stiff with dry blood. He then touched her cheek.

"I'm not entirely sure," Bryson replied. "I know Yama did it … on accident apparently."

Himitsu peeled back her eyelids. "But her eyes are milky white. It had to be Toono."

"He was responsible for the finishing blow, yes. But according to Toshik, she was going to die anyway."

"Where is Toshik?" the assassin asked after a quick glance around.

Vuilni stepped into the hall and glanced both ways. "I guess he went to his own room."

The room fell silent, accompanying the rest of Rim's ambience. The town slept, but for the Jestivan—despite their exhaustion—they had another restless night ahead of them. Himitsu sat on the bed next to Jilly's corpse while Vuilni leaned against the wall, her hood over her head and braids hanging down the sides of her face. Bryson blankly stared at the wardrobe handles across the room, lost in the memories of his time with Jilly.

"Perhaps we should check on Toshik," Vuilni suggested.

"He's fine," Himitsu mumbled. "My dad and Fane waited in his room just in case any unwanted guests arrived beforehand."

Vuilni lifted her head a bit. "Your dad was freed?"

"Fane and I broke him out ... along with my mother, but I don't know where she is now."

"How'd you do that?"

Himitsu huffed. "Never mind that." He held Jilly's hand. "This hurts to say, but we have to leave within the hour."

Bryson snapped out of his trance. "Why? We finally made it back to safety, and you want us to move again?"

"You're out of the loop, Bryson. This isn't safety—quite the opposite, in fact."

Bryson twisted his body to look at his friend. "Well, fill me in."

Himitsu went on to explain the uprising in Phelos, the induction of a new Archaic King, and the formation of a new enemy alliance called SCAPD, comprised of the Still, Cyn, Archaic, Power, and Dev Kingdoms.

"So we're in the depths of enemy territory," Bryson concluded with a groan. "And Toshik and Jilly's fathers are completely evil, allying with Dev King Storshae and Toono."

"That's the gist of it," Himitsu said. "And we need to get out before someone comes to find us. I'm assuming orders have been given to keep an eye out for any Jestivan returning from the mountains. And even if they haven't already spotted you, they'll see your initials in the log book."

Toshik entered the room with two seasoned men behind him. Bryson recognized one as Fane, the assassin who aided the Jestivan in the Rolling Oaks mission two years ago. The other man Bryson assumed to be Himitsu's dad. Scars ran down his cheek, disappearing underneath his chin.

"Let's go boys and girls," Horos said. "Vistas, Olivia, and her friend are waiting in the lobby."

Bryson jumped to his feet at that news. Olivia was safe. That had to count for something.

As they gathered their belongings, Fane became fixated on the corpse. He was a man that had probably seen enough death in his lifetime to have grown numb to it, but his reaction said otherwise. His expression softened; his eyes dulled.

"She was too kind for this world," Fane said while Bryson scooped up Jilly.

Bryson stepped past and echoed his sentiment: "Her kindness gave us light in our life, but closed the curtains on her own."

"And so it goes, the path of the selfless."

* * *

Their immediate goal was to get out of Rim's eyesight before daybreak. They escaped the town unopposed, with much help coming from Horos, Himitsu, and Fane. Their black flames allowed the group to move inconspicuously through the night, which was vital considering Toshik's injuries and the dead body hanging over Bryson's shoulder hampering their movement.

By the time dawn came, they were already rounding the eastern shore of the lake, bypassing the bridge that crossed the western river in fear of it possibly being a choke point. They then continued southwest toward the Archaic Desert, where Horos and Fane's waterskins proved important. Of course, they had had the option to circle the desert and pass Bliss Peaks as a more comfortable route, but comfort was a privilege they couldn't afford. It was all about time management. The maxim of their journey? *Follow the hypotenuse.*

It was a long road. If it hadn't been for his stint in the Archaic Mountains, this would have felt like the longest escapade Bryson had ever taken. At least he had energy when he had chased down Storshae in the Dev Kingdom all those years ago.

Jilly's body was decomposing, and the desert heat was both quickening and intensifying the process. The smell was putrid, and it became hard to even look at her. Eventually they all decided to take any spare cloaks or tunics from their bags and use them to wrap the body as best they could. While it didn't do much to mask the scent, at least she was covered.

Sleep deprivation ate at Bryson. They'd stop for a few hours in efforts to steal some rest, but even then, they had to rotate shifts to stand watch. And when he was able to drift into slumber, his dreams of Jilly yanked him awake in disappointment. What unnerved him more than anything was the group's silence. They had traveled together for days, yet nothing had been said outside of a few dozen sentences. Even Bryson and Olivia were mum.

It was when they entered the central grasslands when Vuilni said, "Rhyparia told me this was where she trained two summers ago with Archaic Director Senex. His wife lives here."

Bryson looked around to see tall prairie grass in every direction. Behind him were the desert dunes, growing smaller as they continued south.

"Awfully lonely place to live," Horos said.

"She said there was a tiny village of farm houses."

Rhyparia was another sour topic for Bryson. He was forced to believe that she, too, was dead. The probability that she was alive and wandering the mountains for this long were slim—especially on her own. And whenever Bryson had asked the Annick guy about her, he said he had never seen her before.

It was smooth sailing—or as smooth as could be expected—until they reached the desert's southern border. From here all they had to do was travel roughly six hours before hitting the teleplatforms. They'd be heavily manned according to the Passion Assassins, but luckily Vistas was here.

"How was it getting into the kingdom?" Bryson asked one night while he and Himitsu kept watch. The rest of the crew lay sleeping amongst scattered trees.

"Simple," he replied. "We even managed to not kill anyone. It's amazing what can be accomplished when three assassins work in tandem. But if I'm honest, we mostly ran away as fast as possible under the cover of our flames."

"So it was the complete opposite of your grand entrance in the Dev Kingdom way back when."

Himitsu smirked. "Definitely. I was reckless."

"We still are. The difference is that now we have the skill to compensate for it."

"We're as good as those old men back there," Himitsu said, tilting his head.

"Probably better," Bryson said. He then glanced at the one person who was still awake. He was upright, a cane lying at his side. "Well, I don't know much about that guy—" He paused, trying to remember his name. "Yvole?"

Himitsu shook his head. "What a stupid name. Imagine Jilly trying to pronounce it."

Bryson burst into a fit of laughter, which he quickly muffled as his companions stirred in their sleep. He lowered his voice: "She couldn't butcher it like she did 'Diatia.' Remember that …? *Diarrhea*?"

They both giggled until it went quiet again. Himitsu sighed, "And so it goes …"

Bryson nodded, another tear running down his face. "… the path of the selfless."

The group made sure to wait for nightfall before getting anywhere near the teleplatforms. They weren't too worried by what might have been waiting for them. Their group was formidable. Unless it was Storshae, Toono, or Sigmund, there wouldn't be a struggle.

When night did fall, they split apart while approaching the teleplatforms. Each group or pair contained at least one assassin. Bryson's group was comprised of himself, Himitsu, Vistas, and Yvole. Jilly's body was with Vuilni because it made the most sense. During battle, her strength made her best suited to fight while carrying a corpse.

The closer they got, the trees became sparser. Before they reached a final band of trees, Himitsu turned and nodded at Vistas, alerting him to inform Intel King Vitio and Spirit Queen Apsa of their arrival. The royal heads would relay news to their generals, who would then give the order to a couple units of soldiers to use the teleplatforms into the Archaic Kingdom. This transfer of information would take only a couple of minutes since everyone should have been where they needed to be already.

As the group waited, Himitsu looked at Bryson and asked, "Are you ready?"

"Of course."

"Vistas, stay close to us," Himitsu said.

They pushed forward to the final layer of trees as a couple of the larger teleplatforms kicked into gear. They weren't communal platforms, but military, which should have alerted the guards stationed outside and within the terminal.

They spilled out of the building in droves, shouting orders and circling the teleplatforms. Within seconds, dozens of men and women materialized on the stages. A battle ensued, and if Bryson and others hadn't been ready to ambush the enemies from behind, this would have been a slaughter—the good guys being on the losing end.

Bryson, Himitsu, Olivia, Toshik, Vuilni, Horos, Fane, and Yvole stormed the mob from various angles, while Vistas stayed glued to Bryson's hip. White electricity surged from the hands of Bryson and Yvole, scattered flames of black masking their positions. Olivia and Vuilni bulldozed their way through the thick of the fray while landing powerful blows on unsuspecting victims. Even with Jilly draped over her, Vuilni was unstoppable.

It took some time to fight their way through, but eventually they boarded the teleplatform with the goal of escape. Combat was the last thing they were concerned with. The group pulled as many friendlies as they could back onto the platform—anyone dressed in the Intel's yellows or Spirit's blues. He managed to drag four soldiers to safety before Horos shouted for Vistas to activate the platform.

The Dev servant telekinetically flipped the control board's lever, jerking the stage into motion. As they spun, the image of dying soldiers smeared around them before disappearing completely.

They arrived back in the Intel Kingdom, many of them leaning weakly against their support beams while some tumbled off the crowded stage from fatigue. Bryson wanted to breathe a sigh of relief, but instead his eyes closed shut.

45
Together Again

Lilu, Gracie, and Frederick left IWA and headed for Weavineering Tower. It was midday, and they were in good spirits. Over the past few months, their weaponry had advanced considerably; Lilu's weavineering had improved, and Gracie had begun to treat her work as a passion rather than a chore. And it wasn't a coincidence that the team's mood had lifted the moment Professor Jugtah had dismissed Arrogo.

For Lilu, what freed her conscious more than anything else was the absence of Mendac's statue at the city's first intersection. No longer did she have to walk within the shadow of such an eyesore.

And, as it turned out, the group's act of vandalism had had a beneficial byproduct. Brilliance had always suffered from a congestion problem. Horses and buggies would crowd the paved streets nose to rear, and foot traffic was equally as dismal—the wide sidewalks slammed with pedestrians hurrying between locations. Mendac's old intersection had been the worst example of this travesty. Whoever's bright idea it had been to place a towering monument in the center of it was hopefully fired a long time ago. Now traffic was more fluid with the extra space to maneuver.

A slab of stone that hadn't been destroyed from the blasts of Lilu's volters still remained. It was a section of the prior monument's base, perfectly rectangular in form and tall enough to require a ladder to stand on top of it. The city claimed to have had left it because of its significance. They called it a placeholder until a new statue could be built … but Lilu saw through their smoke and mirrors. Such a perfect geometric shape wouldn't remain from an explosion—it was unnatural.

And Lilu believed that the reason why the city was standing guard of the residual structure was part of the reason why Lilu had torn it down in the first place. Yes, she had wanted to get rid of a statue that glorified a rapist, but she had also acted on another hunch.

When Lilu spoke to Professor Jugtah about the Theory of Connectivity many months ago, he had made a peculiar statement in response: *Mendac still stands guard.* Since Mendac was dead, she knew he had been referring to the statue.

They entered Weavineering Tower's lobby and were nearly into the back halls when they spotted Professor Jugtah speaking with a secretary.

"Uncle Nyemas!" Gracie shouted.

The man turned, his beady eyes dull behind his gold glasses. He approached the group of young weavineers with folded parchment in his hand, sealed with the royal insignia of the Intel Kingdom—a brain coated in electricity. He handed it to Lilu. "We'll be heading back to Dunami tonight. Unexpected circumstances have arisen."

Lilu broke open the seal,

"Is she coming back?" Frederick asked.

"If she chooses."

They were silent while Lilu read through the letter written together by Bryson and Himitsu. Tears trickled down her face. One hand covered her mouth; the other was failing to hold the parchment steady as it shook uncontrollably. A sob escaped.

"I have to go," she said, heading toward the lobby's exit with Jugtah close behind.

*   *   *

Agnos and Tashami leaned against the *Whale Lord*'s rails as DaiSo's harbor peeked over the horizon. Smiles plastered their faces, unable to contain the excitement of reaching land. While the sea was a marvel worthy of endless intrigue, even Agnos thought he'd benefit from a mental break. Besides, the ship's supplies were nearly gone, forcing the size of portions to diminish. The entire crew was ready for some much needed rest and relaxation.

"What do you think waits our arrival?" Tashami asked, clearly referring to the certain backlash for destroying Adrenian naval vessels.

"Gray said all shall be well," Agnos replied. "She has things covered. The aristocrats on the *Brench Hilt* will be brought to Sodai Mansion, where they will be interrogated in front of the royal heads. If they refuse to answer, their lives will be threatened."

Tashami smirked. "Thankfully aristocrats aren't soldiers. They're not willing to sacrifice their lives for the sake of loyalty."

"Exactly. Then, of course, there's the matter of the slave hold. That will not sit well with the royal heads. It'll be the straw that broke the camel's back, officially cutting any ties between the Archaic Kingdom and the rest of the realm."

"That's if crap hasn't already gone down while we've been traveling back," Tashami said.

"True. It's possible that a rift has already formed." Agnos placed his chin in his hand. "Makes me kind of fearful of what we're returning to."

"What a year it's been, Agnos."

Agnos shook his head. "More like three years. When we were made Jestivan, for whatever reason, I never actually thought it'd be as catastrophic as it's turned out. We've been through just as much as our predecessors."

They pulled into the harbor and dropped anchor with plenty of daylight to spare. They had made it without opposition. Pirates aboard other ships and longboats gazed wide-eyed back in the direction of the *Whale Lord*. But their attention was on the ship behind the behemoth—the *Brench Hilt*—as it turned, veering off toward Sodai across the gulf to return the kingdoms' deposits. The Brench Hilt's emblem had been patched over with black cloth by Barloe and the crewmates who had volunteered to travel with him. Such a haul had never been seen. The Brench Hilt had gone decades without being captured.

Tashami and fellow squallblaster, Crole, rowed a longboat that also carried Agnos, Eet, and Osh to shore. A few pirates yelled greetings to Eet and Osh, for the two cabin kids of the *Whale Lord* were popular in DaiSo. Almost all of its inhabitants knew of them since they could be seen playing through the streets from dawn until dusk.

When they arrived on the beach, Crole pointed Agnos and Tashami in the direction of a homey restaurant known as Jostle and Juggle. They'd complained about the lack of quiet places to eat, for obnoxious loudmouths ran rampant in nearly every tavern. This building, however, was quaint and absent of a crowd. Most people who ate here seemed to be alone, hunched over their food and lost in thought.

The two Jestivan spent most of their first days on land sleeping. On the fourth night, Agnos and Tashami lingered in the Whale House's recreational room, where crewmates played a game of spades. An unexpected guest stepped into the room, summoning silence along with her.

Gray Whale stood just inside the doorway, her face grave. While it was rare for her to leave the Grand Cabin of her ship during a voyage, this was even more out of place. According to Barloe, the captain had never stepped foot inside the Whale House. The crew would have been lucky just to see their captain's face once in the span of a year. She motioned for Agnos and Tashami to follow her outside onto the torch-lit street.

"How'd the meeting with Queen Apsa go?" Agnos said.

"I told her about the two of you being a part of the voyage. After that, she gave me some information to relay to both of you." Gray's eyes remained stern, handing over a folded parchment. "I hope that you both return, but I'll understand if you choose not to."

As Gray walked down the street, Agnos broke the Spirit Kingdom's royal seal. He and Tashami read it while the noises from within the Whale House carried outside. For the two Jestivan, it was hard to imagine anyone in such high spirits after learning of Jilly's death. She was the soul of Kuki Sphaira, after all.

*   *   *

Bryson pried his eyes open to blinding white. Slowly, shapes came into focus as he groaned and rubbed his temple. He was in Dunami Hospital. The machinery and strange noises were déjà vu of his short stay here during the weekend of the Generals' Battle years ago. The only difference was that Himitsu didn't occupy a bed next to him; he was alone.

He sat up and called out, "Hello?"

Not receiving an answer, he kicked his legs over the side of the bed and placed his feet on the cold floor. He despised this place. As he crept out of the room, a passing nurse immediately ushered him back inside.

"You must lie down and wait for your visitor," she said.

"Who is it?" he asked as he begrudgingly returned to his bed.

She fixed his covers and said, "The king. He's never been here before, so I think he might be lost."

A deep voice carried into the room from the main floor: "Where is the boy?"

"Room eleven, milord!" someone replied.

"Well, I'll be going," the nurse said, patting Bryson's leg and walking out. She bowed as she crossed paths with Intel King Vitio at the door. Bryson awaited the scolding for entering the Archaic Mountains.

"Bryson, my boy," the king said, struggling to sit in the tiny bedside chair.

"How are all the others?" Bryson asked.

Vitio smiled. "Everyone is okay. Minor cuts and bruises for the most part. Toshik sustained serious injuries that should've killed him, but a foreign substance was used on his wounds to help them heal faster—something the doctors claim to have never seen before."

"And Jilly … what's going to happen with her body?"

"She'll be taken to Phesaw, where she will be laid to rest with Thusia. There will be an open casket memorial service in the auditorium for all student and staff to attend if they so choose."

Bryson's gaze dulled. "Half the Jestivan will miss it."

"I think you'll be surprised."

Bryson looked out the window to see Dunami Palace on the opposite side of the city. "How has Shelly been?"

Vitio scratched his beard and sighed. "Distraught is probably the best word. She's been hiding in her room for months." He paused and smiled. "But you're back now, so hopefully she'll relax."

There was another long moment of silence. "What's on your mind?" the king asked.

"I didn't do anything this past year," Bryson murmured. "I was irrelevant. Ever since I became a Jestivan, I've played the waiting game—sitting back until someone makes a move against me or my friends, then retaliate. I'm never the initiator."

Vitio nodded. "I agree, but you're not the only one at fault. King Supido and I both had a chance to stop this war before it began. If we had listened to Queen Apsa, we wouldn't be in this predicament."

"Well, I want to start taking action. I'm tired of being on the defensive. Let's put Storshae and Toono on their heels."

Vitio agreed. "And that's what I wanted to talk to you about. You are more talented than anyone in my military. I want as many of the Jestivan active in this war as possible—whether that's by a physical or mental means. You could be asked to infiltrate and scout an area or lead a unit of soldiers into battle. It all will depend on what the situation asks of you."

Bryson raised an eyebrow at his king. "No more holding me back?"

"I promise."

46
Life's Circle

It was the beginning of July, and Phesaw's Telejunction was active for the first time in fourteen months—ever since Dev King Storshae's invasion. While hundreds of students dressed in black descended the stairs of the elevated teleplatforms and spilled down the hill, there were a few people who stood out, donning sky blue. Bryson, Olivia, Himitsu, Vuilni, and Toshik lingered under the lone dead tree that sat a few yards away from the stage.

Toshik had on an ironed blue suit with a floral tie and white pocket square. Bryson and Himitsu also had on matching blue suits, but with less pizzazz. Olivia and Vuilni wore blue dresses, their hair tied back with chopsticks used as pins. Toshik had showed them how to stylize their hair in such a way. He had said Jilly used to force him to do her hair in the same style when they were younger.

They didn't speak much as they awaited the arrival of three others. Eventually they spotted two more blue suits in the crowd departing from the Spirit Kingdom's teleplatform—Agnos and Tashami.

"Is it just me, or do they look different?" Himitsu asked.

"They both look a little scruffier," Vuilni replied.

As the two Jestivan stepped off Telejunction's stage, Himitsu noted, "Tashami has a white five-o'clock shadow."

They said their hellos, but there wasn't much beyond that. Nobody cared to catch up on things—not today, at least.

The last to arrive was Lilu Intel. Her hair was done exactly like Vuilni and Olivia—even absent of her typical flower—and her dress was surprisingly plain for a royal woman. Her gaze lingered as she made eye contact with Bryson before nodding and saying hello.

It took about an hour for students and staff to file into the auditorium, including Vuilni. Only the Jestivan waited in the lobby that wrapped around it. Their numbers had dwindled to seven since a year ago. Yama was no longer one of them, Rhyparia was gone, and Jilly was dead.

Toshik pulled out a pocket watch. "It's time," he said.

He opened the door, allowing everyone to step through before he followed. The murmurs extinguished upon their entrance, basking the auditorium in an eerie quiet. But that wasn't what the Jestivan paid attention to as they descended the steps … No, it was the cerulean casket that sat open at center stage underneath the lone glass window in the ceiling. And for Bryson, it was the grand piano that sat near the edge.

They reached the main floor and noticed Spirit Director Neaneuma, Passion Director Venustas, Adren Director Buredo, and Intel Director Jugtah standing around the stage. Venustas nodded for them to proceed.

Walking onto this stage felt strange. The last time they had stepped onto it was when they first became Jestivan and were taken beneath the building. That had been a new beginning. But now, in this moment, it was to signify an end. And yes, while she'd live on in their memories, that still didn't account for the void that would be felt in their physical presence.

They gathered around the casket, each expressing melancholy in their own way. Bryson did well in fighting back tears, but others such as Himitsu, Toshik, Tashami, and Lilu struggled. As he reminisced on his time spent with Jilly, he could only smile. He didn't have a single bad memory with her.

Each of them approached the casket individually and said a few words. Toshik was last to pay his respects—he didn't disappoint:

"In the cruel reality that is life, death is inevitable," he said, fixated on Jilly's make-up covered face. "And that reality is made even crueler with a death like this. Fate shows no mercy … pulls no punches. It doesn't care about the overabundance of love you've exuded or the infectious spirit that radiates from your pores. And seeing you like this is proof. Your very essence was enough to inspire the Bozani themselves, yet you were still stolen from us at the age of twenty-one.

"Jilly and I grew up together. At first, I cursed our arrangement … charge and protector. But over time I realized she was a gift. Jilly helped me in ways that most cannot." Toshik paused and pursed his lips, trying to combat the quivering. "When people speak of healers, they think of doctors—professionals who can treat the body and heal wounds. Jilly was a healer of the soul and heart. And it was something she did unintentionally, for it was her natural self.

"The Jestivan wear blue today … Odd, I know. You wear black on a day of mourning. But Jilly wouldn't be happy if she knew we were treating it that way. She spoke of death with me one time—the night following Director Debo's memorial service years ago. She complained about the black. She said that whenever her funeral happened, she'd want the colors to be bright because it should be a day of celebration.

"So that's what we're doing," Toshik said through heavy tears. "We celebrate her life and all of the intangibles she provided to the souls that surrounded her throughout it." He paused and placed his hands on the lip of the casket, his head bowing over her body. "But don't get me wrong … I'm hurting like I never have before. She was my charge, yet she died to protect me."

The auditorium fell silent as Toshik sobbed with his hand over his eyes. The rest of the Jestivan stood behind him, granting him space and time to recuperate.

Once Toshik returned to their side, Bryson turned and addressed the audience. "During Director Debo's funeral, Jilly had sung a beautiful song in his honor. She claimed that it should be recited after any death that was a result of murder. There was a message in it that we shouldn't forget. So let's both honor her and remind ourselves by singing it today."

Bryson walked across the stage to the opposite edge and sat at the piano. He eyed the keys and took a deep breath before glancing at his fellow Jestivan and nodding his head. As he played a few notes, they began to sing. The directors then partook on the next cycle, followed by the entire auditorium the third time through.

Now Bryson couldn't fight the tears any longer. He closed his eyes and visualized the energetic young woman bouncing around Lilac Suites at seven o'clock in the morning, bashing on Toshik's door in a desperate attempt to wake him for school; stuffed animals flying everywhere as she dug through the barrels in Tabby's Gift Shop; and her obsession with Bobuel the pony. All while the music flowed through him.

He stopped playing after the tune's fifth cycle, as planned. That should have been the end of it, but then the students and staff continued to sing without the piano. Bryson opened his eyes and watched in awe as the audience was standing on their feet. The rest of the Jestivan, who had also stopped singing, had the same reaction. It was a deafening rally cry that reverberated throughout the enclosure, likely heard across the campus. Bryson had never heard anything like it.

It was the ultimate tribute to Jilly Lamay. Even in death, she had the capability of motivating a community.

Evil Bleeds,
Including its leader,
We fight for good,
So we will not fail,
And even though
Our hearts are aching,
For you, we will prevail.

As the tune swallowed the universe, Toshik collapsed to his knees. He keeled over, clutching at his face as he wept for his best friend … his *love.*

*   *   *

Bryson and Olivia decided to spend a night at Debo's house before heading to Dunami Palace. Bryson was long overdue for a visit to see the princess. While Olivia began cooking something for herself in the kitchen, Bryson kicked off his shoes in the living room and summoned Thusia.

"How're you feeling?" Thusia asked.

"Strange."

She studied him briefly before gazing over at Olivia. "And you?"

"I'm sad," she replied.

"What's going to happen now?" Bryson asked. "When you died, the original Jestivan perished."

She sat down at the coffee table across from him. "While the symmetry between the two ordeals is uncanny, it's still not quite the same," she said. "When I died, the Jestivan was together—physically. And I was that glue. I think the fact that this Jestivan had been separated already for a year eases the impact. You've already shown you can be thousands of miles away from each other and still operate smoothly."

"True …" Bryson mumbled. "We've grown distant."

"It's truly amazing to see," she replied.

"How so?"

"Well, each of you has proven you can stay motivated and chase your own goals. You don't need nine other people to hold your hand … or the directors."

Bryson shook his head. "I did nothing. Agnos, Tashami, and Lilu are doing things."

"Yeah, and what were they doing while you were in the Dev Kingdom chasing down Storshae and his Bewahr?"

Bryson hadn't thought about it that way. Although it was years ago now, he had led that charge.

"You each have played roles," Thusia said, grabbing a glass of water Olivia handed her. "They may come at different times and in different ways, but they're all for a collective purpose. And to me … well, that's the most impressive trait about this Jestivan that makes it better than the original. Here you all are, in separate areas of the realm, yet you're still managing to execute as one.

"Thank you for the water by the way," she said to Olivia, raising the glass to her lips. After a quick swig, she said, "Agnos and Tashami took down a ship of money that would have greatly aided Toth, Toono, and Storshae's efforts. Himitsu infiltrated Phelos Palace and retrieved two very important pieces to our side. Lilu is in Brilliance working on weaponry. And now the rest of you will join their efforts and put your stamp on this war."

Bryson shook his head, his eyes on the carpet. "Can we even beat this Toono guy?"

"The fact that you recognize it's Toono you must worry about, and not any of the others, is a start." Thusia smirked. "There's that Intelian mind you show so little of."

Olivia slurped a trail of noodles and said, "Toono is definitely both the brains and the might. But there are others who've hidden themselves well within—names that none of us probably know of. They couldn't have done all of this without at least a dozen key contributors."

While Thusia nodded in agreement, Bryson asked, "Can't the goddess—assuming it's a *she* like the priests said centuries ago—see everything and inform you … then you can tell us everything?"

A bewildered smile slipped onto Thusia's face, one eye bigger than the other. "When was the last time a chapel was even in operation …? Eleven hundred years ago?"

He shrugged. "There are still some priests who roam the streets."

"Those people are kind of insane," Olivia said.

Thusia's face fell. "I can't speak much of the subject. Divine law is divine law. But 'the goddess'—as you call her—can't see everything; she can see certain things. I'm not saying anything else beyond that."

Bryson sighed. "It'd just be nice if the Bozani helped."

"Be careful what you wish for."

*　　*　　*

Bryson and Olivia stepped through the innermost gate to Dunami Palace's main grounds the following morning. They had already eaten breakfast in one of Dunami's diners. Olivia told Bryson all about her adventures in the mountains—both good and bad. This included the story of one man's death at the hands of hunters who'd for some reason attacked them. But the most entertaining stories came after Bryson watched her place a pipe in her mouth.

"What are you doing?" Bryson asked, turning up his nose in disgust.

"Blame Yvole," she said, taking a puff.

"You're an eighteen-year-old woman, not an old man," he replied.

"Almost nineteen," she said matter-of-factly. "And besides, what does gender or age have to do with it?"

As the two siblings rounded the fountain and approached the main steps, they both stopped as King Vitio and Princess Shelly stepped outside. Vitio donned the grandest smile Bryson had ever seen from him—which said a lot. And Shelly …

Bryson's jaw fell open. Even Olivia had to grab hold of her pipe to keep it from falling out of her mouth.

Shelly smiled like her father, minus the tears. She placed her hand on her rounded belly and said, "Aunt Olivia has returned."

THE ERAFEEN SERIES
BY DAVID F. FARRIS

THE JESTIVAN
THE UNTENABLE
THE UPRISING
THE CHRONICLE

GET MORE

Fantasy is our specialty.

Join Sphaira Publishing's email notification list and you'll receive word whenever a new book releases. Other benefits include exclusive updates and offers, including behind-the-scenes work.

You'll also receive a deleted chapter from *The Jestivan*.

Do we have your attention?
http://subscribe.erafeen.com/

Printed in Great Britain
by Amazon

76454262R00251